The Shadow in the Water

The Shadow in the Water

Inger Frimansson

Translated by
Laura A. Wideburg

The Shadow in the Water

By Inger Frimansson
Translated from the Swedish by Laura Wideburg

Copyright © Inger Frimansson 2008

Frimansson, Inger
The Shadow in the Water/Inger Frimansson
ISBN 9781929355440
First U.S. printing

Design and composition by Susan Ramundo
Cover by Laura Tolkow

Library of Congress Control Number: 2007940801

A Caravel Book

Published by agreement with Grand Agency, Stockholm, Sweden.

Published by Pleasure Boat Studio: A Literary Press
201 West 89th Street
New York, NY 10024
Tel/Fax: 888-810-5308
e-mail: *pleasboat@nyc.rr.com*
URL: *www.pleasureboatstudio.com*

Then a spirit passed before my face, the hair of my flesh stood up: it stood still, but I could not discern the form thereof: an image was before mine eyes, there was silence, and I heard a voice.

Job 4:15-16

part I

A THIN, ICILY SHINING FOUNTAIN of spray right on the horizon. Jill saw it at the same time she heard the shout: "On the port side! Yessss! We have him!"

She'd been ready. She'd stayed out on the deck for the past four hours of the boat trip, sitting wrapped in a blanket and keeping watch over the water, her eyes stinging. Now she got up stiffly, shrugged off the blanket and crept up to the railing on her knees. The wind had increased, approaching gale force. Waves pounded the hull and tossed the boat up and down. Splashing salt water hit the deck and soaked her jogging shoes. The deck was slippery. She held tightly to the pole of the railing, her fingers sore from the cold.

A crewman already stood there. Maybe he was the one who'd shouted. He had a round, sun-burned face; his wet bangs clung to his forehead. He grabbed her elbow and pointed.

"You see him? There!"

She leaned forward and glimpsed a large, shiny, gray body, which threw itself up and out of the water's surface, barely twenty meters from the vessel. It was so close that she caught her breath. It glistened from salt and water, and as the sun broke through for just a moment, she could make out a long head.

"Yes!" the man yelled hoarsely. "He's a sperm whale!"

Tears burned Jill's eyes.

"Oh God, yes," she whispered. "I see him!"

She turned to yell for Tor, but didn't see him. When she turned back to the water, the whale heaved to the side, swung its enormous tail fin and dove. The waves rolled over and all trace of it was gone, swallowed by the sea.

The crew stared at the waterline.

"He's said good-bye for now. But he'll be back, I promise." The crewman spoke a Norwegian that attempted to be pan-Scandinavian. This reminded her that she was the only Swedish woman on the ship and that she'd come with that thin fellow who looked ill even before he stepped on board.

AFTERWARDS TOR REGRETTED that he hadn't had the strength to join her outside. She was so enthusiastic, her eyes had an entirely new light in them when, wind-blown and wet, she came into the cabin, up to him.

"Hi, Tor," she said, as she wiped the water from her face. "I wish you had been able to see that."

He smiled weakly.

One hour before they had climbed aboard, they'd each swallowed a dose of medicine against sea sickness. Nonetheless, the waves of nausea overcame him after a mere half hour and he sat in the stern, unable to move.

"You'll feel better soon," Jill said, trying to comfort him. "It usually passes more quickly if you stay outside."

He wasn't the only seasick passenger. A group of Russians was also on the boat. At first they disturbed everyone with their loud voices while they pulled on their bright yellow rain gear; one woman complained about its color and minced a few exaggerated catwalk steps. She tied a shawl around her head and pulled out a pocket mirror. They were still on the dock then. The wind was blowing strongly. A man on a bicycle was forced to dismount and made to walk the rest of the way to the boat on foot. Tor noticed the crewmen standing and talking to the captain. They seemed to have some kind of disagreement. Maybe the approaching storm, he thought. Too risky. He looked at Jill and she smiled encouragingly at him.

Finally, the rope across the gangway was lifted and they were allowed to walk on board. The Russians were first; they streamed onto the boat and marked their places with handbags and bundles. Typical, Tor thought, no matter where you go, there's always people around to irritate you.

Jill took the lead.

"We'll sit over here," she said and pointed to a handful of plastic chairs. "We'll be able to enjoy the fresh air." She got down some blankets so they could wrap themselves up. "Is that all right with you?"

The Russians came outside, too. One of them had a small silver hip-flask which passed from mouth to mouth. Jill dug out two miniature packets of raisins.

"It's probably a good idea to eat something," she said. "And, of course, to stay on deck."

For the first half hour, as they headed out through the islands, Jill sat next to him. The seagulls followed the boat, circling, watching them silently with cold stares. The mainland was silhouetted far away, massive mountains of dark shadows. They drew farther and farther away from it.

He noticed a rising fogginess in his brain.

Jill, he thought. Then she told him she was going to get up and move around a little.

The Russians were still standing there, but he noticed how they were starting to quiet down, their whoops and hollers overwhelmed by the throb of the diesel engine. The woman he'd noticed previously had pulled off her scarf, and her face was limp and white. The wind lifted her red hair in tufts, and during one strong puff, revealed the gray hair at the roots. She didn't seem to care.

Dizziness swept over him. Tor pressed his shoulders against the wall, glad that he was near the railing in case he quickly needed to lean over the edge. And then suddenly—Good Lord—the cramps grew in his midsection and he had to heave. How he had to heave! Again and again, combined with the sound of his wailing. Color leached from his face and he was shaking. *I am going to die.* How long was this trip supposed to take? The whole day, that's right. This hell had barely started.

In spite of what Jill told him about staying outdoors, the cold forced him inside. He struggled to his feet and, crouching, managed to stagger into the cabin. He was tossed about; the waves were higher now and he had no control over his body. He found a bench and fell into a heap, with his head on the table. The stench here was abominable, but he felt more secure. He was freezing; he felt he would shake to pieces from the cold.

"Do you need anything?" It was Jill. "Can I get you something?"

She lowered the hood of her jacket, pulled out a paper tissue and blew her nose loudly.

Oh, no, he didn't want anything. Just the mere thought of her bringing him something to eat, whether a sandwich, an apple or a glass of oily water, made his stomach turn. He had probably already vomited the pill against sea sickness. Jill appeared completely at ease with the rolling sea. She was used to being on vessels, guiding them through the locks. She worked with piloting vessels through the Södertälje canal. Although she seemed a bit tired, she appeared content.

She went back outside. Tor saw how the boat's lurching tossed her around on the deck without hurting her. One of the crewmen reached out an arm to her, and his jacket obscured her from view for a moment. Her white teeth, her laughter.

JILL WAS ON A MISSION to bring Tor back out into the land of the living. Jill Kylén, his wife Berit's best friend since childhood. She'd been at it for some time now. He wondered how long she would be able to hold up. After Berit disappeared without a trace more than six years ago, his entire world fell apart. He had turned into a zombie, a broken human being who no longer was able to control his life. He didn't even recognize himself; he was such a changed man. He also knew that the police had stopped searching by now.

At first, he'd been a maniac, rushing everywhere, searching, reconstructing. The weekend it had happened, he was away at their cabin on Vätö. Berit did not want to come with him, and he couldn't count how many times he'd condemned himself for not staying home or else convincing her to come along. She was going through a tough time, and as her husband he was supposed to support her, not desert her. He should have stayed at the house and kept watch over her. At least, that's what he thought now. He tried to defend himself by thinking that their marriage had become stagnant, rolling along without any effort on their part. Completely normal, as far as that goes. Only now did he realize how serious the situation had been.

He had made some feeble attempts to get closer to Berit again. Sometimes at night, he heard the sound of her crying. He would put his arm over the blanket around her body. She became silent immediately.

"What's going on?" he whispered. "Are you feeling all right?" She pretended to sleep; he heard how she fought to make her breathing sound normal.

"I know that you're awake and now I demand that you tell me what's wrong!" No, he did not really say that. He'd kept his head in the sand. Afraid of conflict. He'd always been like that, as if he would not be able to deal with her answer, no matter what the problem was. In sickness and in health. Bearing each other's burdens.

February, six and a half years ago. He'd driven out to the cabin, sat there in the bitter cold and felt sorry for himself. When he'd come home that Sunday evening, the house was empty.

Berit had told him one thing, though. She'd planned to take the subway out to Hässelby that day and talk to a former classmate who still lived out there. Justine Dalvik, the daughter of the Sandy Concern magnate. The Sandy Concern was a multinational family business which made candy and throat lozenges. Berit had mentioned something about bullying. She appeared to be struck with regret by the fact that she hadn't been the kindest of children when she was small. All children are cruel, he tried to reassure her. It's just the way children are; it's their nature. She shook that off; she didn't want to hear it.

He had gone to that woman's house later. It was an unpleasant meeting. There was something threatening in that house, something that made him aggressive.

"I want to know what you were doing," he demanded. "Everything, every detail."

The whole situation was surreal. A large wild bird flew about the rooms. The place smelled like feathers and feces.

That strange woman had trouble walking. He noticed it while they headed upstairs to the second floor. She limped. She was wearing a cardigan and a badly fitted skirt. Her eyes were heavily made up. He thought that she had to be rich; her father had probably left her a fortune. She should be able to afford better clothes. He couldn't make sense of her sloppiness. The room was filled with books, some in the shelves, some in heaps on the floor. The bird climbed around the furniture near them, making shrill sounds. That bird could attack at any time. Tor raised his arms as protection.

"How the hell can you have a pet like that?"

She didn't answer, but stood and pulled at her sweater. There were scratches and sores on her hands. Animals of prey, he thought. Animals of prey in a normal house.

He pointed.

"Were you sitting there?"

"Yes."

He stared at the two armchairs, then sank down into one of them, sank into the last trace of the woman who had been sitting here. The air was heavy with the scent of old tobacco smoke. He noticed the rings from wine glasses on the table.

"What did she say? What did you talk about?"

She shrugged.

"Typical woman stuff, the usual things women talk about, what women do."

"That's not an answer."

"She came here; she came looking for me."

"Well?"

"We knew each other once long ago. We were in the same class. Isn't there some kind of bond between people who have been in the same class?"

"Were you friends?"

"Not really," she said stiffly.

"That's what I got from Berit. You were bullied, weren't you? By her? Really bullied, right?"

She limped around the room, arranging the books. Putting them in the shelves, side to side. She was too jittery to sit down and answer him. It provoked him. Still, he tried to meet her halfway.

"Children can be cruel," he said.

She wouldn't let herself be led down that path.

"You know, it was a long time ago. And I probably wasn't much of an angel myself."

He had found Berit's passport in her desk at home and now he pulled it out of his pocket.

"For a moment there I thought maybe she took a trip somewhere. But look at this: she hasn't. She's still in the country, at any rate."

It seemed to him that he had to bring her into his search, this remote woman. She gave him a quick, shy glance.

"Have you ever thought that she just might need to be left alone for a bit?"

"What do you mean, left alone?"

"Well, she told me a little about . . . how things were, between you."

Immediately, he went on alert.

"She was crying a lot. Yes, she sat right here and cried her eyes out. It appears that the two of you didn't have much in common any longer. 'What do I have left?' she said. 'Neither job nor love.' Something like that."

His stomach cramped. *What do I have left?*

What about the boys, our boys? he thought.

He realized then that he would be forced to tell them that something dreaadful had occurred.

HANS PETER BERGMAN WAS STANDING IN THE SHOWER when the telephone rang. He heard the ring through the sound of the water and almost slipped in the soap foam.

"Justine!" he yelled, but then remembered that she wasn't home. She had taken the boat out again. She'd probably managed to row out quite far by now. Of course he could simply refuse to answer, but then again, he was afraid that it might be important. His mother had already had her second heart attack, and had just come home from the hospital. He swiftly turned off the water, wrapped a bath towel around himself, and walked with wet feet out into the hallway.

It was his boss, Ulf.

"Am I bothering you?"

"No, not at all."

"Hans Peter, I have to talk to you about something."

"Okay. Right now?"

"I'd prefer not to tell you on the phone. I thought maybe you could come in early today."

"Sure, I could do that. What's the situation?"

"Some problems."

"Anything serious?"

"I really don't want to talk about it on the phone," said his boss again.

"All right, I'll be there as soon as I can."

Hans Peter held a job as the night clerk at the Three Roses Hotel, *Tre Rosor*, located on Drottninggatan in central

Stockholm. It was a small, personal hotel with old-fashioned service, including the fact that the guests could have their shoes shined if they placed them outside the door the night before. Ulf owned three hotels in Stockholm, all in the same style. Simple rooms which nevertheless had a great deal of comfort. Hans Peter had been working for Ulf for a long time now, except for a short break while the Three Roses was being renovated. The rooms were modernized and bathrooms were added to them, amenities which previously had existed only at the end of the hallways.

When he moved in with Justine, she suggested he quit working.

"I have enough so we can live all right," she said, smiling her strange, internally directed smile. "My pappa left enough to cover both of us."

Hans Peter took her face between his hands.

"Do you really think that would be good in the long run? If I live like a parasite on your money?"

She didn't turn away.

"You wouldn't be a parasite. But you could be able to be with me all the time."

He experienced a burst of emotion.

"I'm still with you," he said. "Of course I'll come right back here to you every day as soon as my job is over."

He returned to the shower. While he got dressed, he looked outside at the garden. The bird was out. He had built a chicken-wire aviary for the bird around a cherry tree. He'd built a little house for him, too, so that the bird could sit and huddle there if he wanted. He was an indoor bird, after all. For half the year, from April to October, the bird now lived outdoors. Hans Peter found it a great relief. It wasn't normal to have such a large wild bird inside a normal residence. And not only that, the bird made a real mess with its shit. Justine usually spread out newspapers around the house, but it didn't help. Hans Peter once read that a bird shits every fifteen minutes, and that certainly seemed to be the case here. Hans Peter was not afraid of the bird; the bird had never threatened him, even if he sometimes spread his wings and flapped them so that sticky clumps of down loosened and floated over every piece of furniture as well as all over the floor. The bird would open his beak and let loose a muted, horn-like chirp, but according to Justine, that's because he was feeling happy; that's what birds did when they are content. The bird preferred Justine but didn't seem to mind Hans Peter moving in under the same roof. From time to time, he even let Hans Peter stroke his back. Hans Peter marveled at how hard and warm it was.

Justine had taken over the bird from a divorcing couple in Saltsjöbaden. When it was a chick, it had fallen from its nest and a cat had almost eaten it. The man and wife had rescued the chick, and it became so imprinted by humans that it could no longer survive in the wild. Justine had read the advertisement: "Bird for sale due to changing family circumstances." On impulse, she drove there right away.

"I'd always wanted a pet," she told Hans Peter, one of the first times they'd met, "but I'd never had one."

Later on, he was told more. Her step-mother, Flora, could not tolerate animals. She was afraid of them, found them disgusting and felt nothing good about them whatsoever.

"If only you knew how much I longed to take care of another living thing, something that depended on me and me alone, that was all for me. But she wouldn't agree to that."

"What about your father?" asked Hans Peter. "Couldn't he have convinced her?"

She grinned crookedly and spitefully.

"No," she said.

She'd also gotten a hamster once Flora had to go to hospice care for good. It was a long brown thing which looked like a rat, so she called her Rattie. Rattie hadn't lived all that long and was now buried under the lilac bushes in the garden. Flora also was no longer alive.

"The pet store was going to turn Rattie into snake food," said Justine. "Nobody wanted to buy her, and the pet store was going to change focus anyway, get rid of small animals and specialize in reptiles. I believe they felt sorry for her so they gave her to me as a present."

A frosty look crossed her face.

"I took Rattie over to Flora once," Justine said, and a nerve twitched under her eye. "She was sitting in her wheelchair. Rattie pooped on her lap. I think the little creature was nervous. Everyone got nervous around Flora."

Justine laughed shrilly, her laugh ringing out.

"That's the way it was," she said.

"It's different now," Hans Peter whispered. "Now it's just you and me. You can forget all the bad things that happened to you. I'm going to help you do it, too, I promise."

Hans Peter looked at the clock. A little over two in the afternoon. He usually started his shift at six. He'd have to leave right away. He pulled on a pair of jeans and a short-sleeved cotton shirt. It was nearing the end of summer, and a heat wave had followed several weeks of rain. All the water had made the greenery explode. Neither he nor Justine cared much for gardening. The yard sloped toward Lake Mälaren, protected from view, so they didn't have to exert themselves too much in the yard. Whenever it got to be too much, they requested the help of an old master gardener from Hässelby Gardens. He was a small, sinewy man with obvious alcohol problems. Hans Peter had looked for him a few times this summer, but he was probably under the influence. "Out on a bender," as his mother used to say about a neighbor who also was a periodic drinker. "There goes Lindman again, how awful."

The lawn needed to be mowed, Hans Peter noticed. I might as well do it myself. Tomorrow.

He was standing in the upper hallway, which also served as a library. He gazed out over the water with its rippled, changing currents, gazed past the empty dock.

Justine, he thought, and a touch of worry stirred. Then he saw her, a small point out there, leaning crazily over the oars.

JUSTINE SAW THE VISION in the mornings, at the hour when dawn was shifting to the light. She would lie on her back in bed, fragile and awake, and the contours would form slowly on the ceiling. She wanted to close her eyes, but she didn't dare, wanted to turn onto her side and pull the blanket over her body, cover herself, but her head was heavy and stiff, her neck curved back, so weighty that she could not shut her eyes. She felt how she broke into sweat under her breasts, and how her hands were lead.

A damaged face, an empty socket where an eye had been, as if it had been clipped from paper, wrinkled. She saw a half-open mouth, from which water strained and ran. Fish bites could be seen where the nose had been, but the other eye was unharmed, which was the most difficult sight for Justine to endure. This eye watched her, incessantly, completely still, while the rest of the face swayed in motion.

I'm asleep, she'd admonish herself. I'm sleeping and this is nothing but a dream. Still, when people sleep, their eyes are closed, and hers were open. She was on her back, staring into the darkness. She was awake and her head was clear. Now as the light seeped in, the face was forming again, just as it usually did, just as she usually saw it form.

Her tongue became thick and stuck, like a swollen animal.

"Hans Peter," she whispered, softly, so he wouldn't hear her.

T HE RAIN WOKE JILL. The vessel's rolling was still a part of her; she felt as if she were swaying. She was lying straight and still; the room was light and although she had slept fitfully during the night, she still felt rested. They had checked into a recently constructed hotel which had small, bright rooms. The bathroom had floor heating; she liked to linger inside whenever they returned from their day trips.

They had booked a double room for the entire week, but they related to each other as if they were brother and sister. It was out of the question to do anything else. Tor had been married to her best friend, who had disappeared; and she had known him for a quarter of a century.

Tor was still sleeping, dead tired after yesterday's whale-watching excursion. A prick of bad conscience touched her. He was lying on his side with his thin back turned toward her. He snored and a few times she had been forced to poke him with her foot.

It had taken her a long time to persuade him to leave his house and come on a trip with her. He needed to get away. After Berit had disappeared, he had stopped working and, even though many years had passed, he was still on leave from work by his doctor's orders. If he hadn't inherited money from his parents, who knows how he would have managed.

He had something manic, something despairing about him. He never gave up, never accepted what happened. Many times Jill thought it would have been easier for him if Berit had died in a traffic accident or if a serious illness had taken her. At least there would have been a body to which one could say goodbye and a grief which would have had an end.

Jill had longed to experience Lofoten Island in Northern Norway. Even better would have been Svalbard, but that was a much more expensive trip. And because of the polar bears, it could be more dangerous, too. All visitors had to carry weapons, which didn't suit her personality. She thought all beings deserved to live, and the animals had been there longer than the people.

One of the guys at work, Dag, used to tell stories about his days as a field inspector on Svalbard Island. During eight summer weeks, he had to inspect the papers of the leisure boats passing by, as well as count the birds and the polar bears. One morning, an old man appeared at the station; he'd been awakened by a crash and when he leapt out of bed, there was a polar bear in the middle of the room. The man's rifle hung on a wall, but behind the bear, so that he didn't have a chance to get it. Instinctively, he fell to the floor and played dead. He could have tried waving and yelling in order to scare the bear, but that might have had the opposite effect. The bear could have felt provoked and attacked. Beside himself from fear, the man lay on the floor and listened to the bear's whistling breath; he felt its rough nose as it sniffed around his body. Hungry polar bears could kill you; that he knew well enough.

Dag usually paused at this part of the story, and it was obvious he enjoyed people's reactions.

"Finally the bear lumbered away. The old guy came to us right away, and we followed him back to his cabin. It looked awful in there. The bear had turned over a barrel of bacon and had covered everything with bacon grease. The bear had also wrecked the tiny bath house outside. He was jittery, that old fellow, really jittery, though he was not exactly born yesterday."

Jill had to pee. She quietly tiptoed to the bathroom. It was six o'clock in the morning. She flushed and crept back to the window.

Tor was still sleeping. Trying not to wake him, she opened the curtain slightly and looked out at the chilly morning. A young sea gull sat alone with its wings drawn tightly in; it looked like it was freezing. During the night, she had heard its shrill, insistent shrieking. It was shrieking now, too, sound bursting from its entire body, turning its head and searching for its mother, not realizing that she'd done her job and it now would have to fend for itself.

Tor moved under the sheets and opened his eyes, looking toward the window as if he was expecting someone to be standing there, someone who was not her.

"Good morning," she said quietly.

He nodded and pulled up the blanket, creeping inside like a snail into its shell.

"What time is it?"

"You can go back to sleep for a while."

"No, it's all right."

"How are you feeling?"

"Well, I guess I'm fine."

"Not seasick any more?"

He shook his head.

"What about you?"

"I'm just sitting here looking at the little seagull we saw yesterday. He's still looking for his mother."

"Hmmm."

"Hope he'll be all right."

Tor didn't answer. She wasn't used to his silence, his way of disappearing deep within himself. After a moment, he coughed.

"I dreamed about her last night again."

"You mean Berit?"

"Yes."

"Was it a good dream?"

"She was living in an apartment. I was so happy that I found her. I went and rang the doorbell and she opened the door. She was smooth and round, not exactly fat but she was kind of varnished. *Is it you*, she said, but she didn't seem surprised. Her face was like porcelain."

"Porcelain?"

"Yes, finely painted, like she used to do her make up." He interrupted himself. "Like she *does* her make up!" he said with a voice filled with tension.

"Yes, like she does," Jill repeated. Tor lay quietly for a moment, then looked for his pack of cigarettes, took one, and turned it back and forth in his hand.

"She was standing in the doorway and she smiled such a welcoming smile with those lips I remember, red and shiny, but when she opened her mouth to speak, I saw that she was under the influence."

"What do you mean by 'under the influence'?"

"She was soused, completely soused, but not in a troublesome way . . . and it seemed as if that same tipsiness went into me as well, I got high just standing in the doorway and looking at her."

"Hmmm. Can you interpret this at all?"

"Not in the least."

Jill herself had tended to dream about Berit, evil, sick dreams, but it happened less and less. It was such a long time since Berit disappeared. Deep within herself, she knew that all hope of seeing her alive again was gone.

She could never forget that first conversation with Tor after it happened. The call came early on a Monday morning, the day after Berit disappeared. Jill had worked that night and had just gotten home; her car hadn't started so she had been forced to walk the entire way in the dark. The sidewalks were icy, and a few times she had been close to falling. Her brain ached from exhaustion. While she was still in the yard, she heard the phone ringing.

It was Tor. His voice was wild and nearly weeping.

"You must, you *must* know where she is!"

Must! It was an incantation.

She hadn't seen Berit for a week, had just talked on the phone in between. They'd been chatting about going out to the movies together. Jill had just moved to Södertälje and if she had a late evening in Stockholm, she usually slept over at Berit and Tor's place, their house in Norra Ängby.

Tor had come to her place late Monday night, his back bent and slumped in a way she had never seen before. She brewed some strong coffee, which neither of them drank. Jill had just finished her three o'clock shift; for the past 48 hours, she'd only slept four. She felt hollow from exhaustion and thought Tor was exaggerating. He gripped her arm and held tight.

"Did she say anything to you, anything at all?"

"Tor!"

"I mean, anything about me, about us?"

How honest should she be?

"She hinted a little," she said, grumbling. At that moment, worry hit her, made her warm, so that she had to get up and open the window. The raw February wind swept through the kitchen.

Tor was pressing his fingertips to his forehead. His face had paled with streaks of gray along his cheeks; they appeared to be pressed directly into his skin.

"Here I am, her husband for good or ill, and I'm not allowed to know!"

"What are you talking about?"

"I went to talk to that Dalvik woman, the one in Hässelby, that nutcase, the one from the Sandy Concern. You were classmates."

"Justine?" Jill asked lamely.

"Justine, that's it, what a hellish name. My wife went there to ease her conscience a little. That strange woman was the one who told me that Berit wasn't happy with our life together."

Without asking Jill's permission, Tor lit a cigarette.

"The risk is great that the greater Stockholm area is aware of the Assarson's most intimate secrets," he snorted and blew out smoke. He was still at the stage where he was more angry than afraid.

"But it's not like that at all," Jill protested.

"What do you know about it, then? What has she told you? Or rather, 'hinted,' as you said?" He imitated her voice, as he got up and began pacing between the table and the kitchen counter.

His pant legs were just a bit too short.

"She just said something . . . about the same old routine."

He whirled around; the edges of his eyes were red.

She hurried to add, "That happens to the best of us sooner or later. More the rule than the exception, really."

He turned on the water in the sink, one violent jerk, and put out the butt, his voice clear as glass:

"Do you think she's gone somewhere? Maybe she left in order to scare me?"

"Why would she do something like that? Why would she want to scare you?"

"Maybe not scare me, maybe just get me to wake up. If she thinks I'm sleeping." He laughed dryly, amused at the image in spite of the seriousness of the situation.

"But why in the world would she have gone to Hässelby?" asked Jill and the moment she spoke the name Hässelby, a shaking worry went through her entire abdomen. Although it all had happened so long ago.

THE TEMPERATURE was above eighty degrees when Hans Peter arrived at the hotel. It had been unbearably hot on the subway; he'd grabbed a free newspaper and used it to fan himself. The more he thought about his conversation with Ulf, the more he fretted. Ulf said there was a 'problem,' something he needed to say face-to-face.

A hot wind swirled down the street, whirling paper and dirt. Mixed aromas of food drifted by from the outdoor seating, and Hans Peter's stomach growled with hunger. He hadn't eaten before he headed out. A woman with an umbrella stroller was walking in front of him. The child's white sun hat blew off and spun by just as he was opening the door. Almost reflexively, he whipped over his hand and was able to catch the hat against the wall. The young woman stormed over and grabbed the hat away immediately. The hat had gotten some dirt from the wall. She rubbed the spot against her linen shirt, an angry wrinkle crossing her forehead. Her sun-tanned breasts heaved up from her low-cut shirt.

"There you go," said Hans Peter. "That hat was almost gone with the wind, so to speak."

She jerked her head.

"What are you talking about?"

Anger cut right through him, right between the shoulder blades of his life just like a fist. He had the urge to tell her off, say something hard and hurtful. But he didn't since he was not the type of man who blew up. He hardly ever got into a conflict with anyone. Even his divorce from Liv many years ago had taken place in a fairly well-disciplined manner. Liv was his boss Ulf's sister. Liv had left him for a man named Bernt and moved into Bernt's townhouse in Norra Hässelby. They now had quite a few children, and he had run into them once in Åkermyntan shopping center. The whole family.

"We can keep in touch," she whispered, placing her small, soft hand on his arm. Bernt, with his huge beer belly, stood next to them.

"Of course, of course, come on by for a drink or a cup of coffee. We're almost always home."

Of course, of course . . . nothing came of that.

And then he'd met Justine.

Just as he pushed down the door handle, the door opened from the inside. Ariadne, the woman who cleaned for the hotel, was on her way out with a plastic bag hanging from her arm.

"Whoopsie-daisy," said Hans Peter.

She was snuffling.

"You sure are in a hurry," he continued.

She mumbled something incomprehensible and turned her gaze to the floor, but he had already seen what she was hiding. He took her shoulders and led her into the foyer with him.

"Ariadne," he said.

She pressed her lips together; it seemed that it hurt her. Her lips were swollen and discolored.

"What the heck happened to you?"

She grimaced.

"I fell down the stairs at home."

"You fell?"

"Yes, on the outside stairs. I was in a hurry."

"I see."

"I'm glad that it wasn't worse."

"It looks pretty bad as it is."

She turned away from him and began to shuffle together some tourist brochures which were lying on the counter. She care-

fully placed them into an old shoebox which she had once decorated with flowery paper just for this purpose. Now he noticed
how the box was starting to look shabby.

"You'll have to make a new box soon," he said. "This one has
done its job."

"If it's worth the bother."

"What do you mean?"

"Dunno, just a feeling."

"Has Ulf told you anything?"

"No. Not told me."

Ariadne came from Greece. She had lived in Sweden for
more than fifteen years, but still spoke with a strong Greek accent.
Hans Peter usually tried to correct her mistakes. Otherwise, she
didn't put much effort into learning Swedish.

"My husband likes when I talk this way," she would say. "He
thinks it is exotic."

She was married to a policeman, named Tommy.

Earlier, she would bring her small daughter Christa with her
when she was cleaning, when Christa was small. Christa was born
blind, as blind as a newborn kitten, and was never going to be able
to see.

"What do you mean?" he asked. "What do you mean 'not told
me'?"

She cleared her throat.

"Dunno. Something in the air. Today doesn't feel so good. I'm
sad."

She could certainly be cryptic. And of course, she couldn't feel
good, looking the way she did.

"Maybe there'll be a thunderstorm," he said, changing the
subject.

Andriane wrinkled her forehead.

"Dunno."

"Are you going out?" Hans Peter motioned toward the plastic
bag hanging from her arm. She straightened her T-shirt which
was hanging over her increasing girth and rump. Her jeans were
tight; she seemed to love to wear tight, light-colored pants, which

made her appear even fatter than she was. Her hair was shaggy, her black curly locks, and she tucked them behind her ears and tried to smile. Her battered lips trembled.

"Have to get some more cleaner," she muttered. "It's all out, you know, gone."

"Of course, I understand."

"Can't clean. I have to clean."

"All right, I won't keep you."

Ariadne started to go, but then turned.

"You here early today," she said, as if she just noticed he had arrived hours before his normal shift started in the evening.

"*You're.* You're here," he corrected.

She smiled uncertainly. Her nostrils jerked.

"Yes, *you're. You're.*"

"Ulf wanted to speak to me. Have you seen him?"

"Up there." Adriane pointed.

"All right, I'll go find him."

She was on her way out the door, but stopped again. Shook her head, sorrowfully.

"What is it?"

"No, no, nothing. I be back soon."

THE HEAT CAME the same week that Jill and Tor were going to leave Sweden. A sultry, suffocating heat which forced people to drop their hectic pace and relax, even though it was past the season when relaxing was encouraged. Vacation was over for nearly everyone, and almost the entire summer had floated by in rain.

"Perfect planning," laughed Jill's work colleagues in the observation tower. "Now that it's turned so nice here in town, you head off."

Jill had finished her shift and was heading into nine days of vacation. It had been a number of years since she last took a typical Swedish sun-and-beach vacation. Instead, she took off with Tor to one of those places on the planet where low pressure was born.

Was it the right thing to do to Tor? She wondered about it as the plane started its descent through the clouds over Tromsø. Maybe he would have preferred a sangria in the heat of the sun in some small alleyway where clotheslines hung between the buildings and dogs listlessly slept.

It was hard to read him, hard to know what he wanted.

"Do you want to drive?" she asked, handing him the keys to the rental car. He nodded. As soon as he got into the driver's seat, he turned the heat up to high.

From the passenger seat she could observe him without him turning shy. He had always been thin, with the marks of a smoker on his face, those sharp lines like sorrowful parentheses from his nose on down; and his lips were narrow and etched with fine surface lines. He was now fifty-four years old, just a few years older than she was. His eyebrows had become coarser and bushier. His hair had gotten too long; it crept down his neck, sparse hairs. He sat with hunched shoulders, leaning slightly forward, tense. She watched his hands on the wheel and overcame the impulse to touch them.

"It's amazingly green here," she pointed out. "So fertile. I didn't expect it."

Red clover and bluebells. Lush waving grass. Large purple fields of flowers. She broke one off when they took a break at the edge of the road.

"You can't pluck those and put them in water," said Tor.

"Why ever not?"

"They're typical wildflowers. They wither right away if you put them in a vase."

He took the plant from her and pointed to its top with its bunch of closed buds.

"Do you know that you can read the passing of summer in these?"

"Huh? Really? How?"

"The flowers begin to bloom on the bottom. They follow a certain order, with the lowest bud opening first while the upper buds wait their turn." He held the stem so she could see for herself.

"Look at this. When they've finished and withered, the next level takes over. And once these on the top bloom, then you know that summer is over."

"Oh, that sounds like fate."

He smiled a bit.

"How do you know all this?" she asked, since this interest in flowers didn't seem like him.

"My grandmother told me. My grandmother from Burträsk."

"Oh, you had a grandmother, of course; I should have thought of it."

"She's been dead for quite a number of years now. I used to

live with her at times. Especially when things were difficult between my folks."

"Difficult? What do you mean?"

"Like things can get. Even in the best of families."

Jill realized he wanted to change the subject. She looked out at the reddish-purple sea of flowers.

"Was she good with plants? I can imagine her as a little old lady in her blooming herb garden."

"That's a good picture of her. She turned into a little old lady in the end, but she didn't spend time in an herb garden. You don't find much of those in hospice care."

Jill leaned forward and inhaled the air around the flowers in bloom. They didn't have any fragrance.

"It looks like we might get a little bit of summer after all," she said. "Imagine that nature has arranged its own calendar."

He laughed. She had managed to make him laugh.

By using the Internet, they had booked a room right outside of Vesterålen. The pictures had showed a pleasant, well-kept place, situated beautifully near the sea. They hadn't received a confirmation and Jill had tried to call a few times without result.

It'll all work out, she thought.

The evening was still light.

Now they were approaching the hotel, but they could already tell from far away that something was amiss. The buildings were there, looking just like they did in the pictures, and they saw the word *Hotel* in large letters on one of the gables. However, the entrance was barred. Tor drove into the yard which was cluttered with toys, bicycles, and rusted bed springs. A dark-skinned man looked out from one of the windows on the second floor. As they looked at him, he quickly pulled the curtain shut.

They locked the car and went in. Empty hallways, worn and decrepit. Finally they found the reception desk and stood there not knowing what to do. From far away came the sound of a television, a sit-com with canned laughter. Through the noise, an infant screamed shrilly and inconsolably. Tor pushed open a door and they caught a glimpse of a pool table and an abandoned bar. "Let's go," said Tor. "Something's not right here."

"All right," she whispered.

When they turned around, there was a woman standing in the door frame. She appeared to be Asian; she was short and wearing a polo shirt and long pants. Her eyes were wide open and she stared at them with a look so full of fear that they were frozen in place. For a long while, they all stood there as if paralyzed.

Tor was the first one to react. He took a step toward the woman. "Excuse me, but is this supposed to be a hotel?"

The woman lifted her hands and clasped them under her chin. She did not answer.

"The sign said 'hotel,'" he continued. "We thought that . . ."

Then the woman began to shake her head, slowly at first and then more quickly. The entire time she looked at Jill, pleading through a mute and suffocating horror. Jill had seen that kind of look before; she recognized that wild fear. She'd seen it on the faces of pigs on the way to the slaughterhouse, and she'd seen it on Panda, her favorite horse at riding school, the day Panda stood with a broken leg in the meadow. She had seen it on Justine as well, that time when they all were small and she and Berit forced Justine into the rain barrel by the church in Hässelby. *You're a fish, Justine. And what do fish eat? Worms!* Now she saw that look on the woman in the bare room.

Vaguely, she felt Tor take hold of her arm.

"Let's go. There must be some kind of mistake."

She lifted her foot to overcome her paralysis. At that moment, the woman opened her mouth as if to scream. But no scream came out, just a shrieking howl so that they could look right down her throat, seeing her tongue and short teeth. And her eyes shone like white, scared lizards.

Once they were back sitting in the car, they saw the sign which they'd missed before. *Statens asylförläggning för flykningar.* The State Asylum Refugee Camp.

"How the hell can they put people from such distant countries up here so far north? No wonder they get so strange!" Tor said as he started the car, his hands shaking. Jill was shaking all over, too. A rising tide of worry began to fill her and dampened all her happy, expectant feelings.

MICKE USUALLY PARKED the car on one of the side streets in the neighborhood filled with stately houses, and then he'd proceed on foot. He really did not know what he wanted there. Maybe just to see her. Maybe that would be enough.

It was so sleepily still and quiet, all these blind house façades. Summer was lingering on, but nothing moved among the trees, no voices, no laughter. Shouldn't these people be happy, these people with their flashy mansions? Fine cars they had, too, better than his old rust bucket.

His father, Nathan, had despised them.

"What happens in a Swedish community on a Sunday afternoon? As silent as a graveyard. Where are all the people, you wonder. Well, they sit in their bunkers and stare at television or whatever else. We'll never be like that, Micke. Promise me that. Never be like them."

He had been so strong and so real. No death in that body.

"I'm going to take you to real living, my boy, to a village in Zanzibar, where it seethes with life. You're going to come with me, Micke, just as soon as you're done with school. We'll have the world's toughest travel bureau. Nothing for weaklings, believe me! Micke, you'll be my partner."

That woman's house was built in stone and was situated off to the side down by Lake Mälaren. He had seen her working on the grass in the lawn with a scissors in her hand. When he sneaked closer, he saw what she was up to. She was snipping brown slugs right in the middle. He observed her face when their guts spilled out over the sides of the scissors. Not a single grimace, not the slightest tremble.

He'd been there many times. It had become a need inside him, an urge. He had to see her. He lay there, pressed against the half-wild bushes. She was not going to discover him until he wanted to be discovered.

Once a long time ago, he'd been inside the house. That was shortly after she had returned from that fateful journey. Alone. Micke's father no longer with her. She had left him alone in the middle of the jungle and gone home.

That's what he was forced to hear that time. He was forced to hear it all straight from her. She had to say it right out loud with her false female mouth.

"I was forced to leave him because we never were able to find him. What was I supposed to do? I had no choice."

He was sixteen years old when she left his father in the jungle. *You're still too young, Micke. You're too young to come with us; you have to finish school first.*

Nathan had taken that woman instead. That new woman with that strange name. Justine. She was the one that he had taken to the deep green jungle; he had watched out for her and protected her, just as he always did for the people he loved. So therefore she should have stayed there when Nathan disappeared. She never should have returned. It was the greatest betrayal on earth.

"I've never loved anyone the way I loved your father."

She had used those exact words and he remembered how she looked when she spoke them. Her eyes, which filled and ran with tears. How she held him close and hugged him, the smell of her sour sweat.

Never loved anyone as much. It sure sounded great and beautiful. Just like a song. He would have been content with that, gotten on with his life. He could have grieved and missed his father along with her.

But now another man had moved into her house. The woman in the stone mansion had betrayed Nathan, not just once but many times over.

ARIADNE'S CLEANING CART was pushed against the wall, loaded with small soaps, shampoo packets, toilet paper rolls, cleaning spray, scouring powder and heaps of clean, folded linen. Hans Peter nearly tripped over a pile of dirty sheets on the floor and growled with irritation. Of course, there were not that many guests so early in the afternoon, but she really ought to have stowed the linen before she left. Should he point this out to her when she returned? How would she take it, considering how emotionally unstable she appeared? The thought hit him that although they had been work colleagues for many years, he didn't know her.

Earlier, when she brought her daughter with her, he was often annoyed. The girl would lie on a cot in the porter's room and gulp down candy so that there would be sticky marks everywhere, even on his books. He never said anything. He understood that it could be difficult to find babysitters. But the mere fact she had assumed she could take her child to work annoyed him no end. She should have asked first.

He had tried to talk to the girl at times, tried to get closer to her. He didn't know much about children. She would turn her empty eyes toward him but she rarely replied. Her thick, messy hair everywhere on the pillow. Her name was Christa. How old would she be now? Beginning puberty?

All the hotel rooms were occupied one floor up. They were in rows, smokers in rooms facing the inner courtyard garden and non-smokers facing Drottninggatan. Between them was the long, windowless hallway, which, for now, was painted a soft apricot. Halfway up the walls, there was a pattern of antique amphora. Ariadne's face lit up when she first caught sight of the motif, and her expression turned soft and far-away. The pattern reappeared on the doors, where a centered, light gray urn surrounded the room's number, painted in olive green.

Hans Peter pushed the dirty linen under the cleaning cart with his foot. The door to Room 5 was half open, and loud dance music pulsed inside. Ariadne often turned on the radio when she was cleaning and many days she would sing along with the refrain. She had a strong and full-bodied alto voice. But today was not one of those days, he thought, not a day for singing.

He pushed open the door and looked in. The light was on in the bathroom; puddles on the floor indicated that the guest hadn't pulled the shower curtain shut when he or she had showered.

"Ulf," he called, even though he knew that the room was empty.

No one answered.

He turned around and began to walk along the hallway over the thick, chalk-white carpet. It hadn't been vacuumed that morning, which was quite apparent. Yet again he cursed himself that they hadn't chosen a different kind. Both he and Ulf had been duped at the Rug Center in Barkaby. The salesman had told them that this carpet was made for public areas.

"You don't see trash; it melts into the carpet's pile, but at the same time it is really easy to vacuum up with a good vacuum cleaner. And look at the shine! A really exclusive carpet for your guests to set foot upon. Why don't you get it right now, since you're already investing so much in refurbishing?"

Ariadne usually grumbled as she ran the vacuum cleaner over the carpet over and over again.

"Look! All threads! They go to carpet like electricity!" What she meant was that the static electricity in the carpet would pull the trash right to it. Hans Peter had seen her crawling around the floor like a big baby, picking up hair strands by hand.

Right outside Room 8, a guest had spilled red wine onto the brand new carpet, and although they had made many attempts with salt and methylated spirits, the stain was impossible to remove. Hans Peter noticed it now, right where he stood, and he was overcome by a feeling of exhaustion.

He called out, louder this time: "Ulf, where the hell are you?"

The sound of an unlocking door came from farther down the hall. One of the doors opened, Room 10, one of the non-smoking rooms. Hans Peter's boss peeked out with a bath towel around his middle. His wet hair stood up in tufts from his head. Hans Peter had never seen him dressed in anything but a fine suit or a well-tailored blazer and pants. He felt himself staring.

"I just took a shower," Ulf said, and there was an unusual touchiness in his voice. "I swear, it's like having a fever, enduring this heat."

He made a sweeping gesture. There was something new and unprotected in him, which made Hans Peter even more nervous. Ulf's hairless chest looked so pitiful, with its well-marked ribs. His arms were flabby as if they had no muscles at all and the skin was so tight and yellowish over his shoulders he resembled a concentration camp prisoner.

"How are things going?" Hans Peter asked lamely.

Ulf smacked his tongue, but didn't answer. His fingers picked at the bath towel aimlessly.

Excluding the rooms themselves and the small room behind the front desk, the hotel didn't have any place where you could be undisturbed. Not even the little breakfast nook in the lobby, which used to be part of the hallway. Here the windows faced the street, so guests from the countryside could sit and observe the crowds of stressed Stockholm inhabitants on the way to work. Ulf had placed a few tables and chairs and a counter where breakfast could be set out. It was a simple breakfast, no excess like at some of the finer competition. Just the usual *filmjölk*, breakfast cereal, two kinds of bread, home-made orange marmalade, *medvurst* and cheese as well as thermoses with tea and coffee. Ulf's elderly mother had taken over the breakfast duties. She was over eighty, but still energetic and active. Whenever Ariadne was ill, she even took over the cleaning.

Room 10 still hadn't been cleaned. Ulf straightened the bedcovers and motioned for Hans Peter to sit down. The sheets were blue-and-white checked, creating the illusion of a luxury bed. Ulf's clothes hung over the armchair, black pants with the crease visible and a white shirt. Linen jacket and tie. Ulf turned away and slipped into a pair of patterned boxer shorts. When the bath towel fell, Hans Peter caught a glimpse of Ulf's thin hams. Hans Peter swallowed with embarrassment, drew his legs up, and leaned his shoulders against the wall. He had a bit of back trouble, which would come on at times when he couldn't relax.

"Damned hot," Ulf muttered again.

"Yes, you're right there. But it's supposed to turn soon; at least that's what the weatherman said yesterday."

Ulf laughed. He took his clothes and disappeared into the bathroom, leaving the door open behind him.

"The weatherman's always wrong."

"That's the truth. This summer they kept promising highs with good weather, and instead it just kept raining and raining."

"You said it. By the way, great that you could come in early."

"No problem."

He could hear the soft rustling of clothes from the bathroom.

"I just ran into Ariadne," Hans Peter said.

"And?"

"Did you see her?"

"Yes, what's up?"

"She doesn't look too good. She said she'd taken a fall."

Ulf came out again, stuffing his shirt into his pants and pulling his belt together.

"Uh-huh."

"So she said. Some stairway at home."

"Maybe so." Ulf appeared uninterested.

Hans Peter changed his tactics.

"It's not the first time, is it?"

"No, but she says she's clumsy; she even jokes about it."

"I wonder how things are going with her at home."

Ulf shrugged.

"Who knows?"

"Have you met her guy?"

"Must have seen him some time or another."

"He's a policeman, right?"

"Something like that. It must not be easy with the kind of kid they've got. Lots of extra work, I can imagine."

"You're right there."

Ulf was ready now. He sat in the armchair and placed one leg over the other. He wore soft leather loafers and black socks. From outside came the sounds of sirens, shrill and in a rush. The window was cracked open. The sirens died away; now there was just the usual murmur from the street, the clack of heels, laughter. Hans Peter let his gaze wander beyond the curtain. A dove flapped past and disappeared toward the roof of the house across the street. Ulf sat quietly, glowering at his thumbs. He rolled them back and forth in jerky circles.

"You mentioned something along the lines of a problem," Hans Peter said carefully.

"That's right."

"Does it have anything to do with Ariadne?"

"Ariadne? No, no, it has to do with me."

Hans Peter's stomach turned icy.

"And?"

"Yes, well, in the long term it will affect her as well. And you. All of you who work here at the hotel, I have to say."

Ulf lifted his face and looked straight at Hans Peter.

"The thing is, I just found out that I am seriously ill."

"What?"

"That's what's going on. They've found a tumor where it's not good to have tumors. Not good at all, when you get right down to it."

"What are you talking about? A tumor? Where?"

His boss pointed toward his own head.

"You mean . . . your brain?"

"Yep."

"Oh, damn."

"That's the way it is."

"What are you . . . I mean, don't you . . ."

"Operate, you mean?"

"Well?"

"Sure. But they say, those idiot doctors . . ." Ulf's voice broke and he seemed to shrink into his arm chair, then he fell over forward, stiffly, but managed to come to himself again and stayed on his knees on the floor.

Hans Peter stood there, dumbly, his arms outstretched.

"Ulf?"

Ulf swallowed; the sinews on his throat were visible.

"It's all right," he said gruffly. A moment later, he added, "They say it's inoperable." He said every syllable distinctly: "IN-OP-ER-ABLE."

"That's how it is?" Hans Peter whispered.

Ulf clapped his hands so loudly that the room echoed and he got to his feet.

"But we haven't seen the end of it. They don't know who they're dealing with."

The bell tinkled from the downstairs entryway. Right after that, they could hear Ariadne's heavy puffing on the stairway. Ulf stepped out into the hall as mechanically as a doll.

"You can come here, too!" he called.

Her face was shiny with sweat. Her rose T-shirt had sweat spots.

"Well?" she said tonelessly.

Ulf picked up the bath towel which was lying right inside the doorway. He stood turning it, wringing it, round, round, round, in his long, pale hands.

"I'm going to sell this damned hotel," he burst out. "I'm sick, you see, sick here, in the brain. A little animal is eating away at it; cancer is its name. It's nibbling away my brain substance. But I'll show them! I'll show them all! There are experts in the United States, there are professionals there who know how to do things, not like here in Sweden, and they can help me. I'll pay them and they'll help me and I'll be healthy again."

ULF HAD LEFT by now. Ulf Santesson, her boss. Neither of them dared to stop him, or even open their mouths to ask all the questions welling up inside them. He went down the hallway, down the stairs, through the door and he disappeared. The tiny bell tinkled wildly when the door shut behind him.

Ariadne went to the window, or rather, her legs went of their own accord, her swollen, fluid-filled legs and her heels with their cracks. These days she was ashamed of her body. That that had not always been the case.

She leaned out the window, but she didn't call out, didn't speak, just watched how her boss with short, quick steps forced his way through the crowd, how he zigzagged through without flinching. From up here, his neck seemed too thin and rickety for his round head, as if his head had grown, as if his tumor was in the process of widening it. He had thrown his jacket over his shoulder. She thought, think about your wallet; watch out so you don't lose it!

She felt overcome with swelling; her aching lips burned and were so stiff all of a sudden, so impossible to form the words.

From far away, she heard Hans Peter's voice. It came to her like a hiss.

"What are we going to do now?" he was saying. "What are we going to do?"

She turned to him with difficulty.

"Is he going to die?" she whispered. "Hans Peter, is Ulf going to die?"

And in the middle of uttering that short, threatening word, she began to cry.

He was a nice guy, Hans Peter. She'd always thought so. He helped her to finish cleaning the rooms and he vacuumed the hallway carpet, a thing she hated to do. She remembered how happy they were when that carpet was first rolled out in the hallway. If she had come along to the store, she would have refused to buy it at once. First and foremost because of the color. It was crazy to have a light-colored carpet where people tramped through straight from outside. Men just didn't get things like that. Men just aren't practical.

She brewed coffee and made some sandwiches from the bread left over from breakfast. Britta was bringing new bread tomorrow. Or would she? How would things go from now on? Was she, Ariadne, going to lose her job and have to stand in line in the unemployment office? This was the only thing she knew. She felt at home here at the hotel, it wasn't too big; it was just enough for her to manage. And of course, Christa could come with her if she needed to; she had in the past. It was a kind of security to know she could.

"It'll work out," said Hans Peter, comforting her. It was as if he were reading her thoughts. He took a bite of his sandwich and chewed greedily. She was struck by how similar they were, Ulf and Hans Peter. About the same height, skinny, sharp corners. But Hans Peter had dark hair and brown eyes, brown like her own. She brought her cup to her lips and drank carefully. At once she noticed that Hans Peter had changed. He didn't have brown hair any longer; his hair had turned gray. It must have happened a little bit at a time, and she hadn't noticed it before since she saw him every day. His hair was thinning on top; he was becoming bald, just like Ulf. Like most men when they got older. Not Tommy however. His hair was still thick, in a crew cut, and it showed no signs of thinning.

"He's going to the States. They'll be able to help him there," Hans Peter said. "Those doctors over there are really competent;

they're further ahead in things like oncology. I've read it and seen it on TV."

"Oncology," she repeated. That was a word that she knew.

"They will cure him, believe me!"

"Yes, but it costs money; he must have money. In the United States, you have to pay doctors."

Then she remembered what Ulf had said about selling.

"The hotel," she said. "That's how he gets the money."

"Let's wait and see how things play themselves out."

"What about us? Will he sell us with the hotel?"

"Now, let's not rush to conclusions. Things will work out. Things always work out."

He poured more coffee for them. It was four-thirty in the afternoon. She really would have to get going. She tried to get up but wasn't able to rise. Hans Peter smiled at her.

"Please don't worry, Ariadne," he said quietly.

She drew a deep breath.

"I won't."

"Promise me. Nothing improves by worrying."

She sniffed. Damned tears. If she only wouldn't start crying at the least little thing. She swallowed thickly and noticed that Hans Peter was changing the subject.

"How are things going with your daughter? It's been a while since I've seen her."

"Christa? Oh, she's fine."

"She's getting to be a young lady by now, right?"

"Sixteen."

"That big already? A teenager?"

"Yes, indeed. She started *gymnasiet*. She has a student assistant, a person who helps her with her studies."

The moment she thought about her daughter, a sudden sense of hurry came over her. She had to go home right now, had to hurry as fast as she could; she had to catch the subway to Brommaplan and then the bus to Ekerö. It was a difficult trip; she was tired. Still, she stayed where she was.

"There's many ways to help the kids nowadays, don't you think?" said Hans Peter.

She nodded. She wanted to talk about the different things that could be used to help blind people these days, but not now; there was no place for it inside her now.

"His mother, Britta," she said. "Do you think Britta knows?"

"Maybe."

"A mother knows," she said solemnly. "A mother always knows."

She brushed a few crumbs into her hand and dusted them into her half-finished coffee cup.

"A mother has . . . how should I say . . . like a radar for her child. And Ulf is a child, for his mother."

She imagined Britta standing before her, her wrinkled plump arms, her energy-filled, happy small eyes. She saw how tears came to those eyes, and, again, she began to cry.

THE STREET was crowded outside the building where he lived with Nettan. Nettan, his mother. Nettan in her ragged punk hair cut. Nettan with a dragon on her stomach. Its tattooed head stuck up over her panties.

This morning she was at it again. She was standing underneath the stove fan, smoking.

"How old are you, Micke!"

As if she didn't know. She was the one who had birthed him. It took forty-nine hours and she couldn't go to the bathroom for an entire month afterwards and certainly couldn't have sex, but she didn't want it then, either. He knew the story down to the last single detail.

"What do you want?" he asked angrily.

"Damn it all, Micke, you're twenty-two years old now. You can't go on like this. It's time for you to move out on your own."

He could be so pissed off when she said things like that. In its own way, it was a kind of betrayal, too, her nagging.

Earlier, the cars had been lined up next to the sidewalk and there wasn't the slightest gap. He cruised around awhile and searched, although he knew from the first that it was pointless. Finally he gave up and parked the Chevy as far away as Kvarnbäcksgatan, even though he wouldn't be able to keep an eye on it; anyone could come by and mess with it. It had happened before. Some damned idiot had broken a mirror and sprayed *fuck* on the hood. Even though he'd painted over it, you could still see the word. He wondered who it was, and whether it was the same gang who usually sprayed graffiti on the stucco façades on Drottningholmsvägen. As soon as graffiti was cleaned off, new graffiti was back. He thought someone should lie in wait and rush out and grab them the minute they showed up. That's what the people should do, the ones who owned the buildings.

When he'd wandered back, he saw Nettan coming from the subway. She was wearing her black Capri pants and a pair of high-heels which made it difficult for her to walk. She had two plastic grocery bags in her hands. He realized at once how hungry he was.

They reached the entry almost at the same time. He opened the door for her, and she clipped out a short "thank you." It was a quarter to seven, and Nettan was coming home from work. She had started a second-hand boutique with another woman which they called *Clothes and Small Pink Things*. The tiny objects they had for sale were not necessarily pink, but it seems that they had a much broader view of what colors they offered. For example, in the display window, they had a grouping of butt-ugly poisonous green porcelain cats. He had been on her case about that. "Are you and Katrin color-blind or what? It's called *Pink*, so you should keep to pink stuff." That was during one time when he'd stopped by the shop. He knew that Nettan liked to have him drop by; she liked to show off her son and fight with him a bit. Katrin, the other young salesgirl, had no kids.

Right now she was not in the mood for banter.

"And what have you been up to the whole day long?" she snapped, her hot temper showing as she began to unpack the grocery bags. "You get a job, by chance?"

His palms were prickling, as if they were falling asleep. He picked up one of the milk cartons to put it in the refrigerator, but she grabbed it away from him.

"Huh?" she said, and now her voice was the usual nasal and nagging way it could be whenever she was in a really bad mood.

He let his arms hang, and went to stand by the window. He nipped a leaf from one of the potted plants on the sill, and pinched it so that the juice flowed.

"Don't be such a nag," he said. "I've told you that I'm working on it."

She clanged a frying pan onto the stove and squirted a bit of oil into it. After a moment, it began to hiss and sputter. He listened to the sound of the knife on the cutting board.

"Working on it *how*?"

"Interview with Pressbyrån."

"Pressbyrån?"

"My interview is next week."

"Hmm." She didn't sound convinced. She stood there and jerked the frying pan around with quick angry movements. His father Nathan had gotten tired of her, and Micke could understand why. Nathan and Nettan. The names sounded good together, like a nursery rhyme. But of course, it hadn't worked out.

Their wedding photo was in one of the cubbyholes of the roll-top desk, under a heap of papers. Every once in a while, he would pull it out and take a look at it. Nettan wearing a low-cut dress and with small flower buds in her hair. She looked so young in the picture; she looked like a child with her round cheeks. Nathan was wearing a white suit and the shirt was unbuttoned at the top. Unshaven, like men in cigarette ads. He was holding her, his hands wide and blunt. Hands just like his own.

Right after the wedding, Micke's twin sisters had been born, Jasmine and Josephine. They were grown now and had moved out a long time ago. He rarely saw them, but didn't miss them all that much. Truth to tell, not at all.

Right after dinner he filled the sink with water and did the dishes. She usually would calm down then, not keep on haranguing him. His strong fingers held the brush and scrubbed. Nettan was standing next to the sink, leaning on the counter.

"I don't intend to throw you out," she said pleadingly, as if it hurt to say the words. "But at least if you would get a job, Micke, that would be something. When I was your age, I'd already been working for years. First at Gulins and then at H & M. I worked until the girls came, right up until the delivery, in fact. I took a taxi from work directly to the maternity ward."

I know, he thought. And two years later, you had me.

Out loud he said, "I'm going to, I said."

Twenty-three, one year older than he was. That was her age when she was in the delivery room and felt split right up to the dragon's fire-breathing tattooed mouth. Well, maybe that was a little bit of an exaggeration. But still. Micke had never asked to be born, and yet she acted as if it were his fault that she'd had to suffer so much. Well, then, she should have just had a Caesarian!

When Karla Faye Tucker was twenty-three years old, she killed two people with a pick-ax. He had looked up *pick-ax* in the dictionary, and it was some kind of American ax. She got what was coming to her, though. First a hell of a lot of years on Death Row. And then early one morning in February, a completely normal Tuesday morning, they tied her down on the white sheets of her execution table and cut her curly hair. There she lay and her eyes rolled wildly, her heart banged, until the man, the one with the needle, came in.

At that time, he was sixteen years old, and that was the year that Nathan disappeared.

He remembered the discussion at school the day after the execution, some for and some against the death penalty. Their teacher, Eva Hultman, had taken some newspapers to school and the whole class got caught up in the discussion. Eye for an eye, tooth for a tooth. Should a person who has taken someone's life be allowed to keep his own?

But hey, she showed remorse. She had even gotten herself saved. She got married to the prison pastor; she had turned both saved and good-looking to boot.

Just because she was a woman, and white, and really lovely to look at doesn't mean that she should be judged any differently than a man. Otherwise, what is equality?

It was true, Karla Faye Tucker was beautiful. Eva Hultman handed out copies of the article with her portrait. Rich, curly hair.

He thought how death flowed into her veins and a strange excite-ment filled him. How she lay there with her arms outstretched, bound like someone crucified. Lay there waiting for the end of her life.

Even the Pope had pled for clemency.

The shine on Eva Hultman's glasses flashed.

"And now you have to hear this! There was one single person who could have saved her from execution. Does anyone know who that would be?"

Hands in the air, even Micke's.

"The governor of Texas, that Bush."

"Right. And do you know what he said, Mr. George W. Bush? In spite of the fact that even the Pope had tried to change his mind?"

"He said, '*Nope.*'"

"Correct. He said, '*Nope.*' And not just that. He amused him-self by doodling a little sketch making fun of Karla begging for her life. He made her voice into a nagging little girl's. *Please don't kill me, pleeeeeease don't kill me.*"

At that moment, Madeleine Hellsing burst into tears. She leaned over her desk and howled.

"I was thinking about her all night," she sniveled. "How she laid on her mattress in the cell, do you think she wore a night-gown, could she sleep? Can you imagine knowing a thing like that, knowing that it's the last time you're going to go to bed at night . . . and when the door to the cell opens, everything is going to be over, all over, forever?"

He liked thinking about it. Even now, when over six years had passed. He would lock himself in his room and curl up on his bedcovers. Take out the picture of the doomed to death. Continue the story from the point where Madeleine Hellsing broke down.

Karla Faye Tucker sitting on her cot. Dawn. Her clothes next to her, which someone has laid out for her; you have to be well-dressed for death. How her hands tremble and shake. How she doesn't quite manage it, so someone has to help. They put on her clothes as if she were a child. White blouse and pants, white sneakers. She bends down, tries to tie them. Clothed in white like a saint and beaten down. Maybe she turns and vomits. Maybe a lock of hair falls into her mouth to take in her muddy breath, the oily warm aliveness which still leaks out from inside her. The guard is standing at the ready. Touches her shoulder almost shyly. All right, she has murdered people; she's hacked at least one innocent person to pieces, but in the early morning hours he can show a glimpse of humanity.

The time is quarter past five. Is she weeping? Does anyone hear any clear words from her? *I am ready to meet Jesus and I am going to meet him now. I will wait for you with Him.*

Then the path to the room of death. How she must have been supported, how she constantly had to stop and brace herself with her cold fingertips. Again and again, slow down until the guard had to look at his watch.

Please come now, Mrs. Tucker. Everyone is waiting.

She pulls herself together and does what is asked. But at the last stretch, they still have to pick her up and carry her. Finally she is inside the room with the tiled walls, the one she had feared for so long, and it looks just as she had imagined it. The floor cold and shining. One single piece of furniture, right in the middle of the room, a kind of bier. She sees it at once and makes a sorrowful attempt to turn around.

Dignity, Mrs. Tucker. Dignity.

A sound from one of the guards, the younger one. But Karla Faye Tucker has ceased to resist now and walks the last steps toward the bier on her own.

Then come the straps on her midsection and limbs.

Micke usually fantasized that he was sitting in one of the audience chambers outside, the ones that had those large, glass windows. That he was one of the reporters who had received permission to watch the proceedings in order to write it up for his newspaper. He sat as far front as he could, so close that he could see the drops of sweat on her brow and how she jumped like a fish stranded on a bridge when the man in the doctor's coat stepped inside.

Did he say anything?

Good morning, Karla. Now the time has come. You have been waiting for fourteen years, and the hour is at hand. If you look slightly to the left, you will see the relatives of the victims. You can ask them for forgiveness, and you may even receive their grace, but that is not enough. They will not be at peace until your punishment is finished.

Then he leans over her, and then the injections, three in number.

Number One makes her unconscious.

Number Two paralyzes her.

Number Three causes her heart's sluggish beats to stop.

J ILL AND TOR HAD ARRIVED at such a strange small town. Strange because the entire place was blue. Factories and houses, even the street lights along the dock, now wet with rain: all were painted blue. Later, they got the explanation from the girl at the hotel reception desk. The entire town was supposed to be turned into a work of art. The idea was the brainstorm of a local artist. It was the time right before the Millennium, when everything was gray.

"It's not for me to say," the girl said when Jill asked her about the change. "But I would want to decide for myself."

"You're not able to decide?"

"There's been a number of controversies."

As it turned out, the girl's father belonged to the more militant wing which refused to paint their houses. He wouldn't do it even if he got the paint for free, and he bombarded the local paper, *Lofotposten*, with angry letters to the editor. In the same newspaper, the artist was presented and given space to explain his vision. The town's own son. He had studied in Krakow, and he'd been almost broken by the depressing, gray environment, he told the journalist. And then he got the idea for what could be done.

"He must have thought it was just as ugly here as in Krakow," the young woman exclaimed, still filled with indignation. "How could he? He has his roots here just as we do!"

"Well, what do you think of the result?" Jill asked stubbornly.

"He started out with such a big mouth, saying that everything would be done by last year. Ha! It's never going to be done! There will always be people who refuse to live in an artificial Blue Hell."

Jill, on the other hand, was impressed. She wandered through all the blue, taking photographs and trying to catch nuances and changes. She imagined her own home town of Södertälje. Just think! What would happen if they did the same experiment there? Scania and Astra. The hospital. Saint Ragnhild's Church. The concrete foundation of the Mälar Bridge. The station house . . . maybe even Hall Prison, situated just outside town. That would be a day-brightener, that would!

To her great delight, she found that a number of the buildings were decorated with literary texts, hand-painted directly on the walls. On the shabby back patio of a harbor shop she found a haiku by Lars Saabye Christensen.

LYSPUNKT I.

Gartneren skjelver
gartnerens fingrer skjelver
over rosens vekt.

POINT OF LIGHT I.

The gardener shakes
the gardener's fingers shake
from the rose's breath.

While she was reading, a woman came out carrying the garbage. She stared at Jill suspiciously.

"I'm just standing here reading," Jill hurried to explain.

"Huh?"

"Well, look here for yourself. Tears are coming to my eyes. What a wonderful way to bring poetry to the streets so that everyone has the chance to see it."

The woman shrugged her shoulders. Even though she worked in the building and went to the garbage cans every day, she had probably never noticed the poem. She smiled crookedly. "No, I've only noticed that," she said, pointing to some graffiti painted close by. *Fucking cunt.* It wasn't hard to understand the meaning behind that.

Almost against her will, the woman walked up and read the poem, standing next to Jill as her eyes took in the carefully printed text.

"Well, well," she said, and her smile became narrow and embarrassed. "You know how it is, things to do, not enough time."

"Gartnerens fingrer skjelver over rosens vekt." Jill tried to memorize the verse. She would go back to their blue hotel and tell the whole story to Tor. This morning he was silent and unreachable. She wasn't able to touch him.

Lyspunkt. Point of light. Is there ever any point of light for someone who has lost his life's partner in such an unsettled way as Tor had? Jill was going by the bookstore. It was not very large and mostly had stationery and postcards. In the window, a book was open with beautiful pictures of nature on display. Silhouettes of mountain ranges. She decided to go inside and buy it and ask them to wrap it as a present. When she stepped back out onto the street, it had begun to rain again. Her nose and fingertips were freezing.

She reached the hotel and took the elevator up, looking at the edges of her face in the reflection of the panels.

Fifty-something. Me, Jill Viktoria Kylén, a fifty-something woman.

She grimaced and rubbed a corner of her sleeve over her teeth. It wasn't possible to turn them back to white these days, no matter how long she brushed them or cleaned them with salt, which she'd heard was an effective method. Her eyes were blue, but without the same deep blue shade she'd had when younger. They'd washed out, just like her hair. Thin and rat-colored, sometimes she'd dye it, use that menopausal henna in the bathroom. At the moment it hung shapelessly and striped, with split ends.

Perhaps she ought to cut it? Maybe she was just too old for this hairstyle?

He was standing by the half-open window and smoking when she arrived.

"You should knock, you know! You scared me half to death!"

"Tor," she said quickly, before she would be able to think. "If you saw me now for the first time ever, if you'd never seen me before . . ."

"Well?"

"What would you . . . how do you think you . . ."

To her great surprise, he threw the cigarette out and closed the window. Then he strode across the carpet and took her into his arms.

THE BIRD HAD STARTED to act strangely, as if something was bothering him. He sat with his wings down and screeched, screeched so that it hurt her ears.

"What's the matter?" Justine whispered.

She had been standing in the upper room, staring down into the compact greenery. Evening was coming, but the heat was still smothering. She imagined hearing the call of apes, or fragments of saw-like sounds from very small insects. That was the way things had sounded at night, all the jungles' screeches and sounds, while she lay awake at night while the others were sleeping. She shivered, all of a sudden freezing in the heat.

"I'm coming," she called and hurried down the stairs.

The cage was built in a wide circle around a tree, which was meant for the bird to hop from branch to branch or even fly for a stretch if he wanted. Usually he would come right over to her and press out his black beak while he gave out friendly clucks. Now he was limp and silent. She pressed her face against the net, felt his breath as light, tiny puffs on her upper lip.

"I'll get an egg for you," she said quietly. "An egg with a dab of butter and some meat. You shouldn't be sad. You shouldn't be sad and afraid."

Hans Peter had built the cage, an aviary of chicken wire and wood. She never would have imagined that he was so handy.

"The bird has to get outside," he said. "He needs the ultraviolet light."

Of course, he was right. Breathing indoor air exclusively was bad for living creatures.

"Sun and wind in his feathers, that's what this little guy needs."

From the very first day, the bird had felt at home there in the garden. Fluffed himself up, sat and enjoyed himself. She had been worried about cats and other birds who might stress him by their mere presence. After the rain, it so happened that *björktrastar* hopped about in the grass near the cage, but they seemed to ignore him, and he them.

She took a deep breath, got ready to begin comforting him again. *I'm here now, little friend. I'm here.* The bird fluttered his wings and flew to the other wall of the cage. He ruffled his feathers, which seemed less glossy. Justine twisted and turned around. Something must have scared him.

Everything appeared normal. The abundant, suffocating greenery, the water like an oily floor. She saw her car parked farther away, close to the driveway's exit. She thought that if Hans Peter had decided to drive, he would be back much sooner. Sometimes she would drive in and meet him at work. Sometimes it had happened that she'd come into the hotel and spent the dark hours of the night on his cot in the night clerk's room.

"What is it?" she said softly. "If you could only tell me what's going on."

The bird had his beak wide open. Maybe he was thirsty? Justine opened the chicken wire gate and stepped inside the aviary. She saw at once that there was water in his bowl.

"What is it then?" she whispered. "Is there something here that you are afraid of?"

The sound of wings beating in the air, and then the claws on her arm. She held it straight out so that there would be a good place to sit. The bird's feet were cold. He held tightly to her and he screeched. She stroked him over his back, but that did not seem to help.

WHEN BERIT DISAPPEARED, Jill's immediate reaction was that there must have been some kind of misunderstanding. A healthy, middle-aged Swedish woman just doesn't fall off the face of the earth like that. Much later she understood that she had had a shock reaction. Denial.

A few days later, the evening newspapers began to write about Berit, her best friend since childhood. *The Berit Case*, they called it, with a banner headline over her friend's well-known face. Against her will, she began to realize that something inconceivable had happened. The reaction phase hit her so strongly she felt dizzy.

She went out to search many times, confused and without any real plan. Judarnskogen and Grimsta, the exercise path near Åkeshov, all the small lanes and forest groves of Hässelby. She began to use more and more of her free time searching, even though she realized that there was no real use. All possible places had already been gone over. She also knew that Tor had been to Justine's house, and that Berit had apparently met Justine right before her disappearance.

She even visited the publishing house where Berit worked: Lüdings. She had visited the editorial offices once before, to pick up Berit to see a play at the City Theatre, although she no longer remembered which play it had been. Annie Berg was coming along, too. Annie was Berit's closest colleague. Berit was in a good mood that afternoon. She brought out a bottle of sherry which she kept hidden behind some books in the bookshelf. She giggled rebelliously.

"I offer Sonja Karlberg this whenever she's signing a contract. She demands it. But now it's our turn to take a sip of this good medicine."

Jill knew about the problems that Berit had with a famous author. You had to treat her well because her books were high on the best-seller lists, but she was temperamental and demanding and needed to be flattered.

The mood at the publishing house was completely different when Jill returned. Everywhere she could see obvious signs of departure. She ran into Berit's boss, publisher Curt Lüding, almost immediately. He was standing right inside the door, unfolding moving boxes. He opened the door when she rang the bell. His shirt-sleeves were rolled up and he had dust in his hair.

"Who are you looking for?" he asked.

"Berit," she said before she could stop herself. "I mean, sorry . . . I'm a friend of Berit's."

He let go of the carton and studied her, a sad look in his eyes. "Yes. Berit," he said. "Have you heard anything? Anything good? Tell me you have some good news!"

"Sorry, no."

"If I could only understand what she was up to. Do you think she's doing this to punish me?"

Jill looked puzzled.

"You see, we're right in the middle of leaving; the whole business is going up to Luleå. I can well imagine that it came as a surprise for some of the people working here. Berit got angry when I told everyone, actually. Really blew her stack." He rubbed his forefinger under his nose. Wrinkled his brow. Jill noticed that his glasses needed cleaning.

"I'm just going around and checking things out," she said lamely. "Maybe I'll find out something; maybe someone will say something that gives me a hint."

"You have no ideas?"

"No, but I hate just sitting around not knowing."

"You're righ;, this is a real trial. But all I know is that she intended to go out to Hässelby on Sunday to care for her parents' grave."

"I've heard that, too."

"What happened then? What about that woman Justine Dalvik? Why did she go visit her?"

"No clue," Jill said, and felt her stomach clench. "I haven't the vaguest idea."

"I've come to suspect that she went out there to initiate a book project."

"What do you mean?"

"Berit was always interested in the fate of women, and Dalvik's story is absolutely fascinating. She's the daughter of the Sandy Concern magnate, just for starters. And she took part in that catastrophic jungle excursion. Didn't two people die in terrible ways during that trip? That girl, what was her name again, Martina, I think. She was the daughter of the famous concert pianist, Mats H. Anderson. And then the group leader, Nathan something or other. He just disappeared. A terrible story. There's been quite a bit about that in the papers; you've undoubtedly seen it yourself. Maybe Berit thought that she could create a book about that Dalvik woman. She's like that sometimes. She digs around for a project without letting anyone know about it. Keeps it secret. And then, *bang!* There's a book. She would sulk a bit if you didn't match her enthusiasm right away."

Annie came out of her office. She was wearing a white, unfashionable skirt and a flowery apron. She was carrying a pile of books in her arms.

"What do you want me to do with these?" she asked, sounding slightly tired and bored, holding out the books toward Curt Lüding.

"Annie, I . . ." He made a dismissive gesture. "Oh, just throw that crap out. They had their day a long time ago. Or maybe we should give them away, to a hospital maybe? No, wait, they've gotten rid of hospital libraries a long time ago. You know, just do what you want with them."

At that moment, Annie became aware of Jill's presence. Her face changed color.

"Hi," she said. "Long time, no see. You don't have any . . ."

"No, I don't."

"Well, no news is good news, I suppose. I was afraid you had something awful to tell us."

"Actually, I would like to talk to you for a bit. If you have time. I'm just going round and round, searching for a hint. I feel terrible about this."

They went to sit in Annie's messy office.

"You can see that this place is going to hell," Annie said without much emotion. "We're barely able to publish the books we're committed to before we move."

"Are you moving already? I thought that Berit said something about the end of summer."

"He wants us to clean out the place," she said, nodding toward the door. "I think he wants to leave as soon as he can. The rest of us have to get up there once we've arranged a place to live in that northern Hell-hole. *If* we move. It's so damned difficult. No one wants to move. We all have our lives here; we're all established. But we might have to do it. You know, the publishing world is a bit different. There's hardly any openings. Certainly an employer's market, this one."

She bit her lip. The skin under her chin was loose and baggy; she seemed to have gotten older.

"Do you know what you're going to do yet?" Jill asked carefully.

"No, I haven't made up my mind. I have two kids, too, two boys. They're in school. I have to support them and me. But to pull them out of their comfortable environment with all their friends and everything . . ."

Annie fell silent. A telephone rang somewhere.

"As far as Berit goes . . . ," Jill began.

"Yes?"

"Do you have any idea where she could have gone?"

"It's hard to comprehend. Just vanished, one day to the next. I'm really worried about her."

"Do you think . . . it might be something with her job? Lüding was hinting along those lines. That she was keeping herself away as a matter of choice."

Annie met her look directly and seriously.

"No. I don't think so at all. I'm afraid, Jill. I'm afraid that something bad has happened to her."

A few days later, the police contacted Jill. They phoned her at her workplace; she'd just been employed by Sjöfartsverket, the Government Shipping Office, and she became nervous when Fred handed her the phone.

"May we meet you? We just need to talk to you." It wasn't really a question; it was an order.

She had moved to Södertälje recently. She'd found an apartment in one of the red apartment buildings down by Bergvik. It was on the bottom floor, so she had no real view of the canal entrance, but that really didn't matter; she certainly had more than enough water views from her work place in the tower over the locks. On the other hand, she often lay awake at night and listened to the large freighters as they passed through on their way out to the Baltic Sea or in to Lake Mälaren. She would try to guess which one it was. She recognized many of them by the sound of their motors. *Marine* from Kingstown was the loudest one. It vibrated the glass in her windows.

She had just broken up with Pelle, with whom she'd had a shaky relationship for the past nine years. They'd never lived together, which was just as well, or they might have killed each other. At least that's what she liked to think. They each had their own apartment, hers in Råksta and his in Alvik. They worked at the same place, Haglund's Rör, a typical male milieu where she was the only woman. She was the one sitting in the office, answering the phones, writing the invoices and paying the checks for the dozen or so employees; she was the one making coffee and taking care of them all until one day she had had it. So, for better or worse, she quit and chose an entirely different career. Guard at the Locks, or Vessel Traffic Service Operator, VTS, which was the official name. That was her new domain.

By now, she was used to living alone. She'd seen up close what marriage could do to people. Berit and Tor. Her best friends of all. Or rather, she was aware of what people could do to each other within a marriage.

In the beginning of the investigation, Tor led the list of suspects. Jill knew the statistics. Whenever someone is a victim of violence, a close relative is usually behind it. So she was on her guard when the police called her in for a hearing. Still, she had to tell what was really going on. Berit and Tor had grown apart.

"You've known them for a long time, haven't you?" It was a policewoman who was asking the questions. She had braids, light freckles on her nose, and was quite young.

"I've known Berit since we were small. We were in the same class all the way through school."

"At that time you were living in Hässelby?"

"Yes."

"And her husband Tor?"

"He came into the picture much later."

"I see. Do you know how they met?"

"He had a boat, a sailboat with a motor. Berit had a summer job working as a waitress and he came and ate there a few times, so that's how they met, in the summertime."

"What did she do after graduating? Did she go on to college?"

"Yes, she studied languages."

"And?"

"She didn't know what she wanted to do. But languages can always come in handy."

"Of course. And then she met Tor and they became a couple."

"Yes."

"How long were they married?"

Jill thought a moment.

"Since 1975. They took off for Copenhagen and got married there. At Gustaf Church. I was one of the witnesses, and so was another friend."

"OK. How would you describe their marriage?"

Jill was unsure of what to say.

"The usual. An ordinary marriage."

"How do you see an ordinary marriage?"

"I really can't put my finger on it."

"Many arguments?"

"Actually, no, no more than average. But I know that it was difficult in the beginning. They lived in such a small place when the kids were born. There's just a few years between the boys. They lived in Tor's one-room apartment. I thought they should have waited to have kids until they'd found a bigger place to live. Now they have their own house, and it's just the two of them. It should have been the reverse." She laughed nervously.

"Yes, you could say that."

"I think their marriage was just all right."

"Just all right?"

"You know, people grow apart, not much to talk about anymore once the kids have left the nest, if I can put it that way. And there you are, and suddenly it's: Ah! Here we are."

"That's what you believe?"

"Yes, it's calm and somewhat dull. The risk is obvious."

"Are you married?"

"Of course not! And that's why!" Jill made an attempt at a joke, but the policewoman didn't change her expression.

"Okay," the policewoman said. "What about their alcohol use?"

"Huh? What do you mean?"

"Tor and Berit's alcohol habits."

"Very moderate. At the most a bottle of wine on Saturday evening, hardly much more than that."

"You're sure about this?"

"Of course. Has someone said otherwise?"

"Not at all. But we have to ask."

"Right, of course."

"Have you ever had reason to believe that Berit felt threatened by her husband?"

"By Tor? No, no, absolutely not."

"You sure?"

"Tor is not that kind of guy. He's kind and somewhat of a softie. He'd never do anything like that!"

"I hear what you're saying. Do they still have the boat, by the way?"

"No, they sold it and bought a summer house on Vätö. But you probably know that already. I don't think that Berit was so fond of sailing, actually."

"No?"

"First the boys came. Jörgen and Jens. It's not easy to have small kids on a boat. And later, well, she felt . . . she didn't know enough about it. She felt she was the underdog. And she wasn't fond of that position."

"All right. Just a couple more questions. How would you characterize Berit Assarson? You're a person who has known her all her life."

Jill thought deeply about this for a moment.

"Good-looking, self-confident, hard-working," she said at last. "A typical leader type. She knows what she wants and doesn't let anyone put her down. Thoughtful. Sweet to her friends and family. Always sending cards and small presents when you have a birthday. Amusing books . . ."

The policewoman took notes.

"Have you noticed any change in her behavior lately?"

"She seemed a little bit down, when I think about it. Worried about her job. The publishing house was going to move up to Norrland and she didn't want to go. She was actually a bit depressed. She could get really down at times, but it had to do with her menstrual cycle. Life's ups and downs. That's how it is."

"Does she have any enemies that you know of? People who didn't like her?"

"She might, but I've never heard about any. She would have told me if that were the case, I'm convinced of that."

"Did you get together often?"

"If we don't get together in person, we always keep in touch. We call each other up, you know, things like that. I've just moved to Södertälje, so it's harder, geographically speaking. But that doesn't mean much when you're good friends."

The policewoman fingered her braids.

"This may seem like a strange question, but can you describe how close you were to each other?"

"We're like sisters, really, sisters. You see, we were both only children, and we found each other on the first day of school, and we've kept close ever since."

T OR STOOD FOR A MOMENT, holding her. She was almost as tall as he was, but she felt much different than Berit. She was more robust, like a tree-trunk. Straight and hard. Her hair and her face were wet.

"If I saw you now for the first time?" he repeated.

She stood with her head turned away.

"It's raining," she said roughly and moved away slightly.

He nodded. Her hair was soft.

"Well, here we are at the birthplace of low pressure zones."

They were standing so still that he could feel how a weak, almost unnoticeable trembling went through her body.

"You're freezing," he said and it seemed that with those words he grew; strength was drawn into him, deep down in the crevices and empty places where sorrow had chafed. Slowly he took off her jacket, went to his knees and took off her shoes. Her feet were long and slim, without flaw. They felt like clumps of ice. He took her hand and led her to the bathroom. The warmth from the floor streamed into them both, through the soles of their feet and up their legs. He held her hands in his, rubbing them. She had round fingernails, clipped short, no polish. So different from Berit, so totally different.

"What was that you asked me when you came in?" he said. "What were you thinking?"

"I don't know. Sometimes I feel so . . ."

"So . . . ?"

"So invisible."

Later they sat in the car and it had stopped raining. The wind had died down but it was cold, sharper than yesterday.

"Where do you want to go today, my beautiful maiden?"

There was something new and secretive in the fact that she kept quiet. Finally he clapped his hands loudly.

"I know! We'll just drive around! Drive west as far as we can go. We don't have to watch the time; we have no set plans. We can just do exactly what we want."

A shy, content smile.

The landscape was constantly changing. Dramatic mountains and cliffs were interspersed with meadows where sheep grazed, and then there would be sandy inlets, now deserted with not a single person in sight. The short summer tourist season was over. They passed through villages but also single houses, where the red paint was giving way to the original gray of the wood. Many of the farms had been abandoned, shining windows with no life. The road was dry and it had been freshly redone, mile after mile of pure black asphalt. After a number of hours, it ended, rather abruptly, without any warning signs.

"Well, now we've come as far as we can!" Tor declared. "East of the sun and west of the moon!" The fairy-tale phrase had leapt into his mind, an expression from a time long ago. He saw his sons before him, two sets of blond bangs, sucking binkies, drooling saliva. How easy it was to influence them those days. They reacted to the slightest shift in his voice. *Pappa, you're not angry, are you?*

They got out of the car and locked it. Walked on large tufts of moss and heather and finally reached the water. Even there, they could hear the distant clang of a bell around the neck of a sheep. The sun broke through and lit up the sea to a field streaked copper.

"I'd go crazy if I were forced to wear that bell," Jill said, and now she was herself again. "Never to be able to get away from that sound. Well, just think about it, won't you? It's like an external tinnitus that some mean person has forced on you. The question is whether or not you could classify this as animal torture."

"They probably don't react the same way we would," Tor said. "There must be a reason for the word *fårskalle*, as dumb as a sheep."

"Hmm." She stood there, peeling a banana, bit it and chewed. Among the stones near to the water, a flock of *sädesärlor* were practicing their flying. She watched them.

"It's turning into fall," she said at last. "Then it's going to be dark and lonely. Would you like to live here the whole long winter?"

"Hell, no. Would you?"

She laughed.

"No. You'd have to be a strong person deep inside and one with nature to live out here year 'round. And I'm not that type. And you're probably not either, Tor."

"You can say that again."

"What do you think about the future?" she asked suddenly, and in the wind she looked serious, her eyes teary, her chin jutted out.

He did not want to talk about that; he usually didn't want to hear of it. People kept telling him constantly that he had to accept things. They wanted to make him say, "Yes, I'll sell the house and pull myself together, start anew."

He had his odd jobs, but he hadn't wanted to take any work for a long time. The money he had inherited from his parents lasted the first few years, and then he sold the summer house. He lived in a miserly fashion; his only weakness was his cigarettes.

Even the boys were starting to make comments. Jörgen, the oldest, had gone even further. He'd made such a dramatic scene that even the famous Lars Norén couldn't have done it better!

"Can't you open your eyes to the facts? Mamma is never coming back! It's awful and sad and horrible, but look, you've got to let her go and free yourself. You're going to fall apart otherwise,

Dad, I promise you! If you can't do it on your own, then maybe you should see a therapist. You probably should have done that long ago. Should have learned how to talk, Dad. Your whole generation . . ."

He looked just like his mother as he stood there: wide shoulders, well-trained muscles, her eyes, her mouth. He wasn't their little boy any longer, their first-born son, Jens' big brother. No, he'd grown up to be a cynical stranger.

"What are you talking about?" Tor burst out, shaken by the sudden attack. He was used to being handled with kid gloves. No one harangued a man who had been left behind in such a traumatic way. People were careful with him. They didn't argue; they didn't openly criticize.

Jörgen swallowed, his lips making a dry smacking sound.

"We never saw you," he said, and his tone of voice was still rising, there was a great deal bothering him; that much was clear. "We never saw you. You were never there. Have we ever *talked* to each other, you and me? I mean, really talked. Were you ever interested in us? We were mostly in the way, weren't we, Jens and me. Did you really want to have children? No way. Mamma, she was the one behind it, wasn't she, but you could have said no. It would have been more honest toward her and toward us."

"What the hell are you talking about? You don't know one damn thing about it!" He reacted to his own choice of words, but he felt forced, forced into a corner by his own son.

Jörgen continued, raising his eyebrows, his bangs curved into his eyes.

"Or were you so horny you couldn't stop? Ha! I'd have a tough time believing that! Did you and Mamma even like each other? There's only one thing I remember about our childhood. You know what it is? Silence! How things were at the dinner table. You never touched each other, never hugged, never gave each other a gentle touch. You should have separated a long time ago; it would have been best for everyone concerned. I tell you, it wouldn't have hurt us one bit. It would have been a thousand times better for the two of us if we could have grown up with divorced parents than to have the two of you as role models for us. You've damaged us. You could have made Jens and me just like you, but thank God, we're stronger than you were. We've been able to free ourselves and turn out to be normal human beings."

Jörgen fell silent but was far from finished. All this had happened on one spring day when the nightingale was singing from the lilac bush. It seemed as if the nightingale was not able to get enough air.

Tor got ready to answer but a searing pain hit him right across the heart. He still remembered what he thought that moment: This is just great, you damn kid. You've given me a heart attack!

ARIADNE went grocery shopping at the Konsum grocery co-operative on Brommaplan. Skim milk, a can of ham, vegetables. She plucked a few candies from the candy bins and put them into a bag, thought of her girl, and at that moment, her headache hit her like electric jolts behind her eyes. The cashier, who always wore flowery clothes, was sitting at the till as usual. Ariadne usually thought of her as "the flowery one." Probably around fifty-five, flaming red on her neck and cheeks. She'd been sitting there for as long as Ariadne could remember. Still, they didn't know each other. They greeted each other with the distance of strangers, as if each time they saw each other was the first.

"That'll be 173 crowns," the flowery one said, and while Ariadne took out her wallet, she thought she saw a glimpse of disgust in the cashier's eyes. Ariadne leaned forward, her chin lowered toward her chest, but knew that it wouldn't help. The cashier must have already observed her swollen and abused lips. The impulse to say something, give an explanation, came over her. *I tripped over the stairs at home. Lucky I didn't break my neck.* But she said nothing. Her hand was a bowl, receiving her change in coins and cash.

She had to wait for quite a while for Bus 305. She usually had to wait. The line behind her became longer and longer. She was one of the first and the grocery bags in her hands felt heavier and heavier. It was past six o'clock already. She should have gotten here earlier. She managed to find a seat and kept her head turned away, watched trees and meadows whisk past, a few horses with tan manes. Christa had begun to nag her about taking riding lessons. Ariadne was against the idea. Large animals made her afraid, those enormous and crafty beasts, and she realized that she would have to be the one to take Christa, be the one to go to the stall and help out.

"You have to realize that you can't do everything," she had tried to make clear to her daughter without mentioning her handicap; it was there anyway, always there no matter what. Christa stumbled toward the wall, tossing her head so her hair flew and letting her snot run down her face.

Last fall Tommy had taken them to the stables where the police horses were kept, protectively laying his arm around his daughter's shoulders and leading her to Mara, an old, bony mare who would soon be ready for the slaughterhouse. With her heart in her throat, Ariadne watched her daughter's hand, how the gray workhorse carefully searched for something to eat. Ariadne had peeled some carrots, She gave them to Christa and listened to the powerful chewing from those large, flat animal teeth.

"Mamma, I really want to," her daughter had kept saying the entire ride home. Tears glistened on her apple-round cheeks. Tommy sat quietly with both hands on the steering wheel. Ariadne knew what he was thinking.

A half an hour later, the bus pulled into the stop which had been named Lindkvist's Corner. It was almost seven in the evening. Ariadne's light pants were twisted; they were cutting into her stomach. She felt that she had to pull them into place, but was too embarrassed to do it while others watched. When she stepped down onto the gravel, she felt dizzy for a moment. She saw a woman running across the field with two dogs. She was afraid of dogs, too, and she saw how one of the dogs was off the leash, the bigger one. She closed her eyes. Her head hurt, ached. She took a better grip on her bags and began to walk.

Their house was close to the road, but not so close that it was bothersome. There wasn't much traffic here anyway, mostly the neighbors, and there weren't many of them. To their left, close to the entrance to their road, a recently widowed woman lived, and to the right, past the empty lot, was a quiet family with two children. An ill-kept summer house had been on the now-empty lot, but it had been torn down once the owner had died, and there'd been no activity there since. Rumor had it that the grown children could not agree on what to do with the property.

On the other side of the road was a field where deer, hares and pheasants crossed. Early one morning, Ariadne had also seen a moose. It marched through the grass on its long legs. She'd called to Tommy, but the moose was gone by the time he got there.

"Once people start developing the property around here, that'll be the end of our peace and quiet," Tommy often said, and he always raised his voice as he described how rows of townhouses would rise up right outside their kitchen window and how their own breathing space would disappear.

"The day that happens, well, it'll be a real hell! Once they get started, they say they'll begin right here with the field!" Tommy's jaw muscles hardened and Ariadne would think of Christa's rubber balls which she used to throw around the room when she was younger. She had trouble locating them and would angrily feel her way along the walls, tearing apart everything that stood in her way.

Their house was yellow, made of wood. Ariadne had been content the first time she saw it. Wood, such a strange but friendly material, not cool stone like at home in Greece. You didn't need the cooling property of stone in a winter land like Sweden. They were recent newlyweds, she and Tommy, the day they moved in. He picked her up on the steps and carried her over the threshold—she remembered that—his arms underneath her body. She'd held one arm around his neck, screamed from both laughter and fear. He was certainly strong, but she was big and yet fragile, a child already on the way.

Even before she got to their house, she saw that the doors were closed, and the windows, too. A chill went down her back. She had to stop, rub her forehead, clear her throat loudly and close her eyes. Then she took a deep breath and began to walk again.

The car was in the carport, so he was home. His green BMW, with a crack in the taillight from when he had backed into a stone last weekend. He had gunned it. *I'm really angry now, and you're gonna feel it!* The sun glowed like fire on the façade. She stepped up onto the outside terrace, noticed that the flowers in the pots looked like they were dying. She stuck her finger in the earth. It was still damp, so it wasn't that they were too dry, but they had red spider mites, which came from nowhere and were impossible to get rid of. This often happened, and she didn't know why.

The outer door was locked. On the tall brown door was a bronze door-knocker, a lion with exposed teeth, which Tommy had received when he turned forty; his co-workers had gone in on it. After a few years, it had gotten ugly and the color had turned, and it didn't help that she time and again went over it with her cleaning rags. Blood pulsed in her lips while she bent and looked for her keys. Her hand was shaking so hard it was difficult to find them, but finally she did and was able to push open the door.

The air in the hall felt suffocating. Why did he close all the windows? Behind her she heard a bird singing, one of those black ones with yellow beaks; it liked to sit and sing high in the birch tree and in the winter it made footprints in the snow underneath the automatic bird feeder. Tommy was against the fact that she liked to feed the birds. He said that it lured rats. Up to now, she'd still been able to keep at it. *Is it normal for a living creature to be outside in that kind of cold?* Whenever she said things like that, he'd laugh, and a spark of the old Tommy could come back. Between his eyelashes, the gleam in his eyes was mild.

"Hello," she called out, but her voice was dampened and dull. She didn't want it to sound like that, so she called out again: "I'm home now. Hello!"

Christa was lying with her eyes closed on her bed in her room, wearing just her underwear. Her doughy stomach bulged out, her bra dirty and burled. She had put one leg up on her bent knee, flapping her foot.

"Christa?" Ariadne said. "Mamma's home now. I was a little late."

Her daughter didn't react. When Ariadne bent over her, she saw the CD-player. She lay a hand on Christa's foot. The girl jumped and pulled out her ear plugs.

"Mamma?"

"Yes, sweetheart, it's Mamma. I'm home now."

"Are we going to eat?"

"All I have to do is boil the potatoes and then we'll be able to have dinner."

With surprising agility, the girl leapt to her feet. Ariadne handed her a T-shirt which was lying on the floor, but when Ariadne bent down to get it, her head seemed to want to explode.

"It's so hot," Ariadne said with difficulty. "Even though it's already evening, it's still hot. What we really should do is go to the dock and take a dip in the water."

The swimming beach was only five minutes away on foot, but it had been a long time since they'd been there. When she was little, Christa would splash at the edge of the water, but she didn't like it much, all that wetness which she couldn't catch and couldn't see. When a five-year-old boy ran past and splashed her, she'd gotten an attack of something resembling asthma. Tommy had been with them that time, and he ran after the boy, caught his shoulder and shook him so hard that his head whipped back and forth. It had looked grotesque, Ariadne had thought, like whiplash.

Ariadne peeled a few potatoes and filled a pot with water. She opened the can of ham and cut herself on the lid. One drop of blood fell onto the ham and was sucked in, leaving a dark mark.

"Iron," she mumbled in Greek and heard her own laughter, "just a little extra iron."

Her daughter was sitting at the table now, with a heavy and pained expression; she raised her upper lip so that her teeth showed. On her chin, a pimple was getting ready to burst.

"He went out," she said.

Ariadne jumped.

"What?"

"He was home but then he went out."

"Pappa, you mean?"

"Uh-huh."

"I'm making dinner now, and it's going to be done soon. Are you hungry, sweetheart? We'll eat in just a minute."

The pot hissed as it came onto the burner, a fleeting smell of things burning. She took a cloth and began to clean off the counters, clean off the stove, clean off the lamp hanging over the table. A sticky layer of grease, how could she have missed it? She rinsed it quickly with water, wrung out the cloth, looked at her hands and their knuckles, how they whitened and pinched, and then the door opened and he was home.

HANS PETER LIKED TO READ when things were quiet at the hotel, once the guests had gone to sleep in their rooms. He had a large heap of books on the shelf in his porter's room and nowadays they were left alone, no more sticky children's fingerprints. A blind child's fingerprints. One who had to find her way by using her fingers as eyes. Hans Peter stretched out on his cot, and turned the table fan so it blew right at his shirt collar. Oh, how wonderful!

At the moment, he was in the middle of an old French classic, *Letters from My Windmill*, by Alphonse Daudet. He had barely gotten through the first few chapters, but he was already enjoying Daudet's descriptions of the landscape in Provence. An idea was forming in his head: We'll go there. I'll take Justine on a weekend trip.

He had tried to convince her before, but she had resisted. The terrible things she'd experienced during that horrible trip to Malaysia had turned her against the whole idea of airplanes and travel.

It took almost an entire year before she was able to tell him about what had happened there, and then, just a bit at a time, often broken with crying jags. She'd been with a man there, Nathan, who had taken her to the jungle.

"We were the first group; he had such big plans. He wanted to create adventure vacations, where people, you know, go out into the jungle and spend the nights there, living there, eating, I don't know, leaves and roots. And monkeys, one of the men who belonged to the Orang Asli tribe shot a monkey.

She hiccoughed and her words broke apart.

"I never ever ever . . . they had small bodies and sucked right into your skin . . . never again . . . leeches, do you hear me!"

Nathan had been her lover. He had taken her into the jungle to test her courage. One morning they woke up to find him gone. They looked for him for hours, for days. They never found him. Finally they had to make the unpleasant decision to leave. Justine would get stiff and her eyes would get empty as she said: *We had to leave him there and go.*

After enormous difficulties, they finally arrived at a civilized area, and then another tragedy occurred. In order that Justine not be left alone, they put her up with a young Swedish artist who had also been on the trip. Her name was Martina and she was, as it happened, the daughter of a famous concert pianist, Mats H. Andersson. Nathan had hired her to make a brochure for his business. The very first day in the hotel, a thief broke into their room and murdered Martina with a knife.

"It was my knife, my *parang*," Justine whispered as she buried her face in Hans Peter's sweater. "He took my *parang* and he stabbed her. Was it my fault that he did it? Should I have gotten rid of that knife? Yes, I ought to have gotten rid of it. I was never going back to the jungle, what need would I have for a jungle knife like that? I knew it . . . the whole time. Nathan had given it to me, and I know that I thought giving something sharp brings bad luck."

She cried and wailed, turned white; her fingertips became ice-cold. He sat there and held her, rocking her in his embrace.

"Of course it wasn't your fault. You must understand. It doesn't do any good to torture yourself with these thoughts."

She had been in the shower during the murder. Afterwards, she became paralyzed with shock. Hans Peter understood that they hadn't treated her well after the murder. The local police department had grilled her in a room behind bars, led by a hard-eyed man with bad skin.

Hans Peter became upset when he heard about all the bad things that she had experienced. What she needed was a support group, friendly ears and soft voices, to be able to talk through her traumatic experiences. Of course they wouldn't have anything like that in Malaysia.

The trauma had made her sick and emotionally unstable. And although so many years had gone by, she still could have nightmares.

Alphonse Daudet. Hans Peter lifted up his book and glanced over the text on the back flap, where the author was introduced. He usually did that in order to find out what he could about the classical authors, how they were as people, how they dealt with their lives. Daudet seemed to be a successful kind of guy. His books were printed in large editions. He was happily married and with time became fairly well off. But his former sins lay in wait for him. While he was young, he'd lived the high life and managed to get a latent form of syphilis, which flared up and condemned him to a wheelchair. It finally took his life and he died, at fifty-seven, right in the middle of dinner.

Just a few years older than me, Hans Peter thought.

He didn't feel like reading this evening. Too many things whirled through his thoughts. Worry about Ulf and their future. Ariadne. Justine.

Right at the moment he thought of her, Justine called. Her voice seemed raspy and estranged. As if it were split.

"You just disappeared," she said.

He remembered that he'd forgotten to leave a note saying that he had to leave for work early that day.

"I'm sorry. I had to go and I was in a hurry."

"Why?"

"Things have happened at work. I'll tell you more about it when I get home."

"But Hans Peter, if it was so urgent, why didn't you take the car?"

"I should have, you're right. But I didn't."

She was silent for a moment.

Finally she said, "When are you coming home?"

"Tomorrow morning, as soon as everyone's checked out. Like normal, you know that."

He heard how she breathed into the mouthpiece.

"I love you," he said.

She didn't answer.

"Justine!"

"I'm afraid." Her voice came like a gasp.

"Listen to me, Justine, there's no reason to be afraid. All of that old stuff, that's over!"

"Right."

"Well, then. You have to leave it behind you. We've talked about this lots of times. You're strong, a grown person; nothing can scare you."

"But it's the bird."

"What about the bird?"

"He's acting so strangely. I don't know what's going on with him."

"What do you mean, he's acting strangely?"

"He's flapping his wings about and won't settle down."

"Do you think he could be sick? Maybe he ate something that didn't agree with him?"

"No . . . he looks afraid. As if . . . there's something out there . . ."

"Why don't you lie down and go to sleep? It's late. I'll come as soon as I can."

She fell silent. He heard her swallow.

"Do you want to come over here?" he asked. "Jump in the car and drive over and you can share my cot!"

"No, Hans Peter. The bird . . . I don't dare leave him."

SOME MEMORIES NEVER FADE. The rain barrel by the cemetery in Hässelby, for instance. The rain barrel stood by the wall next to the little white building they used to call "the house of the dead."

The game wasn't Jill's idea; her imagination wasn't as fertile as Berit's. No, she was more like the wagging tail. But maybe she had been the one to suggest that they go to the cemetery that afternoon. Although she defended herself against the idea, the memory returned, flickering back to her. She remembered that it had been a way to get out of that house, the Dalvik house.

Let's go look at your mother's grave.

They'd first been at Justine's house, that tall, stone house down by the lake. Jill didn't want to go and neither did Berit. Not really. There was something threatening about that house, something that made them shiver all the way down their backs. They did not want to go in; it was as if they risked getting caught inside and becoming part of terrible things that happened there.

Justine's mother had died in that house. Just fell down on the floor and died. A vein had burst in her brain. The blood had filled her cranium, coming out through her eyes and nose, ears and mouth. That's what Jill imagined when she thought about it, and the sight came to her at night, gave her nightmares and she woke up screaming with fear. She would creep next to her mother's sweaty nightgown, and all of that was Justine's fault. She could have left them alone, not forced them to come inside.

She bought us. That was how we became the underdogs. Berit and I were in the same class. We found each other the way small children do: we'd grown into each other, had become one and the same person. Justine was the wedge which constantly tried to come between us. This is how I remember it now as a grown person. No one wanted to be with Justine. From the very first day, she was the one who was different. There's always someone like that in any group, small or large, kids or grown-ups. Every group needs its scapegoat.

But what was it about Justine that made her into the scapegoat? It was hard to find an answer to this. Maybe her name? It sounded so unusual, so foreign, so strange. But there were other children in the class with uncommon names, even though there were not many immigrants in that part of town. There was a Hungarian girl named Kinga. They accepted her without difficulty. And in the other class in their grade, there were the Finnish twins Jussi and Kari. Even though they had a slight accent, they became the class leaders.

Maybe it had to do with what happened to her mother? That should have made her into someone who needed protection. A poor, motherless friend, like Snow White or Cinderella. No, children don't think like you'd expect them to. She had a new mother, too, who was very pretty. And her father was rich as Midas. He owned the Sandy Concern and all the candy factories, not just in Sweden but also abroad. Justine had filled her backpack full of Sandy candy. *You can have some if you play with me.* Direct, without any flourishes. She tried to buy friendship. She would fling out her hand and let the candy fall where it would, and sometimes she would hide the pieces, make us crawl on all fours and look for them, humiliate ourselves.

Otherwise, she looked like we did. Just thinner. So thin that you felt you would prick yourself if you touched her. But no one liked to touch her, at least, not nicely.

The rain barrel . . . I remember that day now. I suddenly see it clearly in front of me. It was fall and we'd been going to school for a few weeks. Justine had invited us home to her place. We'd said no so often. We'd hit her in the stomach and in the face and we'd yelled out: *Leave us alone!* It was as if she didn't feel it. Finally we gave in and came with her. And we were greedy for candy, that's true. Can you blame young children for that? First we had to lie on our stomachs and hide behind the bushes. She wanted to make sure that her mother wasn't home. Flora was her name, and finally she *did* come, wearing a dress and shiny new nylon stockings. We thought that she was beautiful. You could see pictures of women like her in *Damernas Värld* magazine. She stepped into a car that was waiting for her. The air smelled like exhaust and perfume. Once the car had left, Justine got up and opened the door to the house.

"Come on!" she said, and at once she was the strong one, the leader.

I was afraid the entire time we went up the stairs to the upper floor. *It* had happened there. She showed us the floor where her mother had lain, dying. Justine was four, and she'd been right there. The sun glowed on the parquet floor. It was hard to imagine that the mother had been there with her empty, busted-open eyes and all that blood, but those details didn't come to me until later that night, when I was home, trying to fall asleep. Then they kept coming, for months.

I stood in the sunshine; it was warm in that room. Still, I felt like I was freezing.

"Let's go," I whispered, or maybe even whined in a defenseless little voice. "Come on, Berit, I want to go home. I have to go. We're going to have dinner soon."

Berit wasn't listening. She crept along like a soft, clever animal. She began to glide over the rugs. Sniffing. *Where is the candy? You promised us candy. Where is it?*

I had to get out. Panic grew inside me, but Justine held us in place.

"Here," she said, and we were in her room now, and under the bed was a box filled with candy. We could take as much as we wanted. I think I took honey- and fruit-flavored ones. Those were the ones I liked the best.

"We're going now. I have to get home. My mamma will get worried otherwise."

No, she pulled at us, held on to Berit's jacket, held on tight. I remember that her fingernails were bitten down; the skin next to them had sores.

"First I have to show you something in the cellar!"

We walked down the narrow stairway. At any rate, this was closer to the exit. In one of the cellar rooms, there was a large laundry tub, an old-fashioned one for soaking laundry; that's what people used to do in the olden days. And there, right before our eyes, Justine began to tell us how Flora punished her when she misbehaved. She almost seemed proud of it when she told us, her chin high in the air, boasting.

"She puts me in there, right in the water. She says she's going to boil away my stubbornness."

We stared at her.

"Nooo!" Berit said.

"Yes, indeed, she does!"

"We don't believe you!"

"She still does it, anyway."

"What about your pappa? What does he say?"

She turned away from us then and refused to answer.

Torture. Of course she was exaggerating. She was making it all up in order to impress us. If it were true, it would have come out by now. People would have called the police. Of course she was lying; that was obvious. Wouldn't we have seen something otherwise? Wouldn't her body be covered in burn marks? Wouldn't our teacher—what was her name again? something with M—wouldn't she have raised the alarm when she saw it? And she would have seen it, wouldn't she? Teachers are supposed to see things like that.

That was what was wrong with Justine. How she lied and boasted. That she never refused to use any means to get us to feel sorry for her. To force us to let her be one of us.

"Let's go to the cemetery and see the grave!" Yes, yes, it was me who made the suggestion, but it was in order to get out of there. We were like prisoners in that house, and at any minute Flora could come back, beautiful Flora with her straight nose and her hard fingernails. They were red like rose hips. Made for pinching right into your skin.

We ran to get Flora once, but that was much later. That time when Justine fell down the mountain. We ran the entire way to the house and Flora opened the door, wearing curlers.

Justine is lying on the mountain. Please, Mrs. Dalvik, please come.

She got angry then, as if she didn't want anyone to see her. She tied a cloth around her hair curlers so that her head looked grotesque and lumpy; she ran in her boots after us. She was angry through and through and she yelled at us the entire time: *I've told you again and again not to play on the cliffs.*

Justine was still lying where we left her, but she'd managed to pull most of her clothes back on. One of her legs lay at a strange, nauseating angle. We helped carry her home and she didn't say a word.

After that, she never returned to school.

I notice I want to avoid this. I don't want to think about this. Because we did go to the cemetery; it wasn't true that I had to go home. I just said it, made it up. There was an old man seeing to the graves. We looked at the grave belonging to Justine's mother; she'd found the way directly. She leaned against the gravestone.

"My mamma is here, in the earth underneath us."

It was a bright sunny day, so none of us became frightened, but I couldn't help thinking that Justine's mother's hands would suddenly start digging up through the surface of the earth and grab our wrists. Perhaps draw us down to her. Punish us because we did not play with her child.

It was a silly song we sang. Children are good at thinking up these kinds of rhymes. We went over to the low, white house where the dead were kept, the ones who hadn't been stuffed into their graves yet. The door was locked. I remember that Berit checked it. She looked through the keyhole and hissed that she saw a coffin in there. *It's brown and the lid is open. I see that there's someone inside.*

"Let me look!" I exclaimed and at that very moment I wanted to experience the exact same thing that Berit was experiencing. I wanted to see a dead person for real. I pushed her away and put my eye to the keyhole. To my disappointment, everything was dark.

I was just going to say something about this, a simple accusation actually, but right at that moment, we heard footsteps in the gravel. It was the old man we'd seen before. We hid until he disappeared.

"Are we going to play?" Justine asked. At least, I believe she was the one who said it.

The rain barrel caught our eye just then. It stood beneath the downspout. Probably there to catch rainwater for watering the flowers. Berit said, "I know! Let's play fish! Justine, you'll be our little fish."

Justine didn't protest. She agreed to everything, because those were the rules.

"Do I have to take off my clothes?"

The answer was yes. Who ever heard of a fish with clothes?

To this day I still can see her shrunken little slit between her very thin legs, looking nothing like mine, which was round and like a roll, and so was Berit's, for that matter; I'd seen it when we'd gone swimming, so we knew how it was supposed to look. She gave us her clothes, one by one, and we laid them out on the gravel in front of us.

She couldn't get in on her own; it was much too high. We grabbed her bony body and flung her inside. The water splashed everywhere; there was something green on the edges. She gasped as the cold water hit her skin, and for a moment I thought it sounded like she was crying. But she wasn't. She was laughing, shrilly and cockily: "Now I'm your fish!"

She began to splash around and water flew everywhere, even on us.

"Cut it out," said Berit, and she slapped Justine.

But Justine didn't stop.

We kept an eye out for the old guy. We were afraid that he could hear us.

"The old man's coming," I whispered, and Justine finally got still in the water. We saw that she was freezing. Berit said something about digging up worms to feed our fish, and Justine got completely crazy and tried to climb out of the rain barrel.

"I'm not that kind of a fish," she said. "I only eat leaves."

We hit her again. I remember that now, although that wasn't what we'd planned; we just wanted her to keep quiet. Fish don't say anything; they are completely silent, and we were playing now and our game was that she was a fish. We found some long sticks and pretended they were fishing poles, but then we began to hit her with them, and she just stood there with her fingers clinging to the edge of the barrel, and she didn't cry. She just took it.

Berit and Jill had never spoken to each other about that incident once they were adults. Not of that, but they did talk about Justine, just as they did about anyone who had once been in the class picture. Happy comments, happy memories. Justine was the one on the far left. Her hair was parted and some was behind a barrette. No one else in our class wore their hair like that. We had bangs or curls. Mrs. M, whatever her name was, stood with a pleated skirt and low shoes. Right in front, standing on the classroom floor, were those twin ponies, Berit and Jill.

When Jill turned thirty, Berit had made a blow-up of that part of the picture, the two best friends, and framed it. "To my best friend in the world." Jill still had that picture; she had hung it above her bed. Two rosy-cheeked nine-year-olds with knee socks and sandals.

Berit had given a speech.

"This is Jill as I've always known her, the one I grew up with. We had the good luck to be raised in secure, stable homes without divorce and arguments, and without the mental poverty which you can find in many places. The warmth of our childhood formed us and made us into the good and wise human beings that we are today." She interrupted herself with a giggling fit, so typical for her, and everyone laughed.

"Jill and I have never argued," she continued. "We're blood sisters and we're going to keep going and live until we're ninety! Then we'll jump off the cliff, hand in hand with our bent old-lady fingers!"

I T WAS DARK NOW, a dark and cloudy summer night with a hint of rain. Oh, how wonderful it would be to have a refreshing, cool rainstorm to drive away all that suffocating heat. Justine had just called the Three Roses Hotel and talked to Hans Peter. For a time things felt better, but now her fear was slinking back. Her hands trembled, her lips were becoming dry, her mouth as well; she began to have short coughing fits. She thought she ought to go take a shower, that everything would feel different once she was clean and scoured.

The day had been hot, and she'd sweated a lot. She turned off the lights and went into the bathroom, took off her clothes and was about to turn the faucet on, when she heard a sound on the staircase, a sound which did not belong there. Nervously, she stood still, listening, finally opening the door extremely slowly. Everything was silent now. Fumbling, listening all the while, she managed to get her clothes back on. Was she going to be caught like a naked animal in the middle of her own bathroom? No, never! She remembered the movie *Psycho*, the way the music built, the water which turned red.

Justine stood in the library, and outside it was dark. The bird. He should be used to the night by now, should have it in his genes that night was part of the twenty-four-hour cycle, part of life itself. He had been living with her for so long now he had lost some of his natural instincts. But not the one about night and day, the mild light of dawn made him cluck with anticipation. He would fly to her and land on her shoulder with great skill. His wings had never flown great distances, just intermittent circles through the house. Of course the house was tall and had many floors, but the bird never had the opportunity to become really tired.

Justine made out the aviary now. Her eyes had gotten used to the dark; she looked through the tree. The bird was in there. He had probably flown to his sleeping branch or gone inside his little house. What was making him so nervous? Was someone out there, someone who wanted to do her harm?

"Of course not!" she said, but her voice broke. She wasn't able to be strong.

During her trip to Malaysia, she had left the bird to fend for himself. It had been the only solution. He had been locked in the attic, and she had put out a great store of water and food. She remembered how things were once she returned home. The stifling smell of bird droppings, how he came flying to her and hit her on the face with his wing feathers.

Those days afterwards: she was on her knees and scrubbing. The bird sat on her back. Walls and floors, up and down, the entire house. Like a ritual, a way to return to how things had been.

To the time before Nathan.

ON THE OTHER SIDE OF HEMSLÖJDVÄGEN, there was an area with *kolonistugor*, tiny gardening huts, for community gardens. Micke liked to jog there, to run along the idyllic gravel paths, around Little Lake and finally return home. He took good care of his body, made sure he stayed in shape. Nathan would have approved; he was Nathan's son and could endure hardship. For long periods at a time, he would run every day whether the weather was stormy or burning hot.

But at other times, his strength would disappear. He never knew why. One morning he would wake up extremely tired, exhausted in both body and soul. Sometimes it would be related to something Nettan had spit from her mouth. She could be so damned insensitive. She could fling open his door and howl like a crazy person:

"The hell with it all! I can't take it anymore! I just can't take it!"

As if everything were Micke's fault. Everything in her sad, boring life. *Isn't everyone responsible for his own life?* Didn't she usually say that herself about him?

"No one can do everything for you. You don't get anything for free in this life. You've got to learn this. You have to get things going yourself if you want to be successful. Never give up, Micke. Keep fighting no matter how meaningless things appear."

She could go on and on like a revival preacher.

He wanted to move out. As soon as he managed to get his life in order, he was going to move, not live there one day longer than necessary. But first he had to find a job that he really liked. Not just any old crappy job. He didn't know what exactly that would be. But it would come to him if he only had some peace and quiet. Then she'd be rid of him and he'd be rid of her. Then he'd get his own place.

It was during one of his jogging rounds that he met Henry and Märta. They were old, certainly over eighty, but he'd never asked. People didn't do that; even he knew better.

Henry and Märta lived in one of the *kolonistugor*. They used to move there in the spring the minute the water was turned on, and then they'd stay until the beginning of September, when they returned to their small apartment in Bandhagen.

One evening, Micke was jogging and suddenly Märta was in his way. She had pushed her walker through the gate. She was clinging to it, pale, almost see-through even though it was the middle of the summer. A pair of ill-fitting brown pants covered her stomach and was held in place right underneath her breasts by a shoelace. Her sweater was crooked; Micke could see a wrinkled shoulder and the strap of her bra.

"Please, please, do you have a minute?"

"What's up?" he asked nervously.

"Well, you see, it's our cat."

"Huh?"

"He's fat and brown, well, more reddish. I guess you'd have to say he's red."

Micke stood there, bent over and panting. He had lost his pace anyway, so there was no point in stressing.

"What's happened to him?"

"He's disappeared."

The old woman's chin began to tremble, as if she were going to cry any second.

"And?" He shrugged; sweat was making him itch. He was wearing shorts and a boxer's shirt. He'd have to take a shower the minute he got home. He felt an unusual shyness.

"You see, we've noticed you, kid. You're often out and about in the neighborhood. I was thinking you might see him because you're moving around here so much. We call him Raven. Even though he's a cat."

He nodded briskly.

"Got it. Raven. I promise I'll keep an eye out for him."

She gripped her walker tightly.

"You're a good kid, I can tell. And if you find our Raven, we promise we'll . . ."

"Hey, no problem. Really," he said. "It's okay.

Strangely enough, he was the one who found the scraggly cat. It was not until the next day, though, when he was out jogging. He was already on the way home, heard a sound. He'd needed to take a pee so he'd gone into the bushes. Then he saw it, an old-style beer crate turned upside-down with two stones on top holding it in place. Inside was the cat.

Raven was unharmed but exhausted. Who would have done such an unnecessarily cruel thing?

He squatted and called to the cat.

"Raven . . . kitty, kitty. Is that you, Raven?"

His throat felt hot; he was not used to animals.

He lifted away the stones and turned the beer crate over, slowly and carefully. He stuck his hand inside and petted the cat's fur. He thought the cat would hiss, maybe stick out his claws and take a swipe. He was already expecting to see blood on his hand. Then he'd get pretty damned angry, all right! His muscles tensed.

Instead, the cat crept up to him and began to purr. The cat's fur was soft and cool. It was unbelievable. That damned cat seemed to like him!

He finished turning over the crate and lifted up the cat, holding it next to his chest. He couldn't run now, but he took giant strides. The cat made no attempt to free itself. Rather, it lay against Micke's sweater as if drugged. Later he would have to pluck a number of reddish hairs from his clothes. But that wouldn't help much because Nettan would still find some and laugh her spiteful laugh.

"Devil take me, have you finally found a girlfriend, Micke?"

Not until he reached the tiny house did the cat try to get

down. He held it with one arm and opened the gate with the other.

"Hello!" he called out.

The house was old and looked ready to fall apart. The veranda had to be painted; a number of roof tiles had fallen off. The door was slightly open, so he called out again: "Hello! I have your cat here!"

The old man came out. He was just as sickly white as his wife. Maybe that's just the way things are when you get old; maybe skin lost its ability to take on color from the sun. He had long, thin hands with blue veins running like spider webs over the back of his hands.

"Raven!" he said, with a choked-up voice, and the cat reacted; it opened its paws and jumped down, running into the house like a bad-tempered red streak. From inside, Micke could hear first a slight scream and then laughter and whooping.

"Henry, Henry, do you see who's come home!"

They wanted to invite him to coffee right then and there. He said he didn't want any; he didn't drink coffee. Maybe a beer, then?

Micke finally had to give in. It was a misty day, some rain in the air. He had to bend his head to get through the doorway. The woman was in the kitchen and poured cream into a bowl. There was no real stove there, just two hot plates on the counter. The counter was covered with greasy shelf paper. The cat sat on the rag rug.

The living room was minimal. Right in the middle of the floor were two falling-apart arm chairs and a pine-wood table, which looked much too oversized for that narrow space. Against the wall was a rib-backed settee, and, on a pedestal by the window, the television. Cobwebs covered with sawdust hung from the ceiling. It smelled sour and musty, maybe mold, mildew, and old cups. Behind a curtain with sunflowers on it, the old folks had their bed. Everything was so crowded and drab that he felt uncomfortable.

Micke sat down on the lumpy sofa cushions and he was

starting to freeze, which always happened if he wasn't able to take a shower right after exercising. The old man opened a can of "people's beer," the kind with next-to-no alcohol. He placed two glasses in front of him and poured.

"You found our kitty; you saved his life."

Of course, he had to tell them how he found the cat.

"Who could have done such a thing? How can there be such evil in the world?" The old lady wailed, rocking back and forth. White hair grew from her chin and upper lip. Her husband stroked her on her cheek. It looked nice, somehow, even though they were so old.

"What can we give you? How can we thank you?"

He pulled out his wallet, took out a hundred crown bill.

"No, really, you don't have to do anything."

"Of course I do! That little cat, he gives our lives meaning, you see. We have no children and no relatives, well, at least none that we especially like, hee, hee, hee. We don't have anyone but our Raven."

The cat lay in the woman's lap and watched him constantly.

"We want to give you something, do the right thing by you," the old lady said.

Finally, he had to take the folded bill.

When he was about to leave, he noticed the wall over the window by the door. A rifle hung there. The old man noticed where he was looking.

"I've had it plugged," he said quickly.

"Huh?"

"The rifle. You can't use it any more."

"You can't?"

"I inherited it from my brother. He was a hunter. But I've never . . . ." He lowered his voice. "Märta's against that kind of thing. And me, too, for that matter."

"All right."

"A thing like that only has its uses when uninvited guests drop by. Drunken thieves can't notice whether you can shoot it or not. At least, that's what I'd like to think."

"Well, I gotta go." Micke stepped out onto the front-door

landing. He felt the old man's hand on his arm.

"Hey, just one thing. You're not supposed to have guns hanging there out in the open like that. These days, there's some kind of law that you have to keep them in a safe-box. Or chain them. Or something. I don't really give a damn. Things you don't know can't hurt you, right?"

"Right."

"So don't go broadcasting the fact."

"Of course not."

"You know how folks are. Always gossiping."

So it happened that he started to visit them now and again. The next time he went past, he saw a ladder leaning on one of the walls, reaching to the roof. The old man was climbing up on his shaky old legs. Micke had to open the gate and go in.

"Excuse me, but what are you up to?"

Henry hadn't gotten past the first rung, so he stepped right back on the grass. Held on tightly to the ladder and shut his eyes.

"Thought I'd fix the roof."

Micke saw the roof tiles in a pile on the ground.

"Lost a lot of them," Henry muttered. "Though that was a ways back. Not those ones. The others were useless, gave them to the wife for her potted plants. But I found these new ones in the attic. Well, you can't really call them new. They were leftovers from the first time the roof was fixed, though that was before my time."

"It looks a little unstable," Micke said.

The old man grunted.

"It's higher than you'd think."

"And you just have to put them up there?"

"Yep, just slip them in."

"OK, let me climb up and fix them."

"Naahh, you don't have to."

"I'll do it."

"Yes, but you're on the way somewhere, doing your exercise."

"I'll do it later. Now I'm fixing your roof tiles."

Henry took a few steps back.

"You really want to? You're sure?"

"No problem."

"I was just a bit dizzy, you see; it came over me all at once."

"Really, it's no problem. I'll take care of it." He put his hand on the old man's shoulder. He was amazed at how feeble it felt. Almost sharp. As brittle as a chicken bone.

Later on he did other things. Helped them cut the grass, repainted the house where the paint was falling off in strips.

"It's almost like having a grandchild," Märta said, and her light-blue, almost colorless eyes watered.

"Ah, don't worry about it," Micke said. "Glad to help."

He had never been so close to elderly folks. His own maternal grandmother had remarried and moved to Alicante, in Spain. She wasn't all that old, either, come to think of it. She'd been pretty young when she had Nettan. And Nathan's parents were already dead; he'd never met them. Now Henry and Märta, they were cool. He didn't mention them to Nettan. She'd just ruin everything.

They'd bought the place sometime in the Seventies.

"Long before you were born," Henry chuckled. "We were young then, well, relatively young. Have you ever thought about that, how long you're young? When does old age begin?" Sometimes he could start philosophical speculation and become practically chatty.

The house was built in 1909. So, almost a hundred years old. It had been built by Carl-Gustaf Lindstedt's parents, Märta told Micke with pride in her voice.

"Do you know who he was? Maybe you're too young to know?" She wrinkled her bushy gray eyebrows and peered at him. "One of the greatest Shakespeare actors of our time. And I'll never forget his role as Primus Svensson in *Babels Hus*. It was on TV. When was that, Henry? The beginning of the Eighties, wasn't it? But you weren't even a sparkle in your father's eye then, kid."

"Yes, I was."

"Well, then, at least you weren't allowed to watch grown-up

programs. But that series was great; it was all about a *koloniom-råde*, a communal garden with houses, just like this place. But not this one, no, that one was in Enskededalen. He lived there, Primus Svensson. But they tore the whole place down to build a large hospital. Do you remember, Henry? All the bulldozers . . . and all those fine little garden patches, all plowed under. It was theft; it was . . . theft." She quieted down and sniffed up her nose. The cat rubbed against her legs. She petted it, her thoughts somewhere else.

"And there was the Tre Knas. But that was long before your time. Gösta Bernhard and Gunnar Knas Lindqvist and Carl-Gustaf Lindstedt. They called themselves Tre Knas." She giggled at the memory.

Just like an old lady, he thought. A real old lady, for sure.

But he didn't show it. Instead he asked: "Aha! Is that where the word *knasigt* comes from?"

"Hmm. You may be right there. Probably. You're not so dumb, are you?"

One day when he'd just finished cutting the grass, he was given a copy of the key for the tiny house.

"We want you to have it." Henry looked serious. "In case something happens to us. You never know in this world. The Grim Reaper can come any day. And sometimes he doesn't strike hard enough, and you're stuck lying there like a damned trussed-up chicken. You never know, like I said. Märta and I have discussed the situation. It's always good to have a key in reserve. We could have given it to a neighbor, but, honestly, we don't trust the ones around here. Or how should I put it? We don't want them coming around and snooping. This is our place. I mean, there's probably nothing wrong with the neighbors. But then you keep getting into long discussions. How's it going? How's it going with you? You understand what I'm getting at?"

Micke nodded. The key lay in his hand. There was a small, plastic tag on it. Green and white with polka dots.

"You live so close, maybe you can stop by now and then to see if everything's all right. I mean, during the winter half of the year. Because we won't be here then. At least not so often. Public transportation can be a real hell then. And by the way . . . what are we supposed to do here in the winter? No, we really don't want to come out here, then."

Micke nodded again.

"Glad to do it," he answered.

"YOU"RE LATE," HE SAID, in a friendly manner. "Christa and I have been waiting for you. Waiting for our little mamma to come home."

She stood with her back to him. Her throat seemed constricted when she swallowed. She lifted the lid for the potatoes and pricked one with a fork although she knew that there was ten minutes left.

"We've been waiting," he repeated, louder this time, and she heard how he walked over the floor. "Right, Christa? We've been waiting awhile."

"Yes, Pappa." The girl's thin, concurring voice.

"The food's almost ready," she mumbled. She burned herself on the lid, jumped and dropped it. It clanged against the stove's enamel.

He was close to her now, right next to her; she could sense his restrained breathing.

"Where've you been?" His arm around her waist, binding, pressing.

"Work . . . of course."

"So you were at work?"

"Yes."

"This long?"

"The bus didn't come. I had to wait . . . I'd gone shopping and there was a line at Konsum, and I missed the bus because there was a line, you know, at the cashier's. So I had to wait . . . the bus doesn't come all that often. You know that."

He forced her around, his eyes narrow and ice-cold. To think she had once loved those eyes and his wild, blond strength, that she once . . .

"There was a line at the cashier's," he said, and again, imitating her voice. *"Was there a line at the cashier's?* You must have bought a hell of a lot of stuff."

She fell silent, felt her heart pumping.

"Don't you finish work at 3:00 p.m.? Three in the afternoon? Isn't that right?"

"Of course," she whispered.

"It doesn't take this long to come home. Not even if there's a line at the cashier's."

"There was something extra at work."

"A little extra, you say?"

"Yes."

"Well, what was it? Extra guests?"

"We talked for a while. Something important came up."

"You talked?" He let go of the tight grip around her waist and lifted his hand, touching her face with his fingertips. They burned like fire.

"That's right."

From far away she heard how Christa began to make noise with her eating utensils.

"So who did you talk to instead of coming home and taking care of your family?"

"Hans Peter talked. To me."

"Hans Peter?"

"Yes."

"And what was so important that you had to talk about it today? So important that other things had to take the back seat. Other things!" He yelled the last few words; she saw saliva flying from his lower lip. At that moment, the telephone rang. He pushed her away so violently that she banged against the kitchen counter. It hurt her hip. He went out into the hall with long strides. She looked at Christa. The girl sat banging a fork against her drinking glass, rapidly and mechanically. It clinked.

"Please be quiet," Ariadne whispered. "Please, Christa, put down the fork."

He was out in the hall. He was talking on the phone. At times, he was laughing. She wondered who it was. Probably a co-worker. She placed the plate of ham on the table and garnished it with tomato slices and parsley, poured the sauce over it and sprinkled garlic salt on it.

"Soon it's done," she said.

Her daughter sat there with her face turned up. Her pupils traveled in her eyes. They had tried to teach her how to keep her eyes still, at least while she was not alone. She never remembered.

"Just the potatoes left," she said.

They ate dinner. Ariadne cut the food for her daughter, just as she always had done. He sat watching her. Ariadne had lost her appetite.

"Little Chrysalis, be careful," her mother had warned her. Her parents had called her by that name, as if they were waiting for her to break her shell and spread her enchanting wings. "I can understand very well what you see in that blond stranger. But my dear little girl, I see more than you do because I am not in love."

What does a mother know?

He had almost finished his studies at the police academy. He'd come to their island with some friends. She stood and watched him walk to the newly installed pool, take position on the edge, ready to hop in. He was wearing a tight bathing suit and, in the light, the hair on his body resembled a golden sky.

Ariadne's parents ran the hotel. That he chose just this hotel must have been a sign. At times, Ariadne sat at the reception desk. The evening he arrived by boat, she was there, and she was the one who wrote his name into the register. Tommy Jaglander.

"Do you speak English?" he had asked, even though she had just greeted him in that language.

"Yes, sir."

"Good."

"Yes?" she whispered, on her guard as to what might be coming next, not really confident in the language. It had to do with food, however. He was allergic to millet. So allergic that he always had to carry medicine and an injection. *Millet?* What was that? She had no idea.

"I have to be sure that you're not using millet in your food preparation," he said. "But if you do, please let me know so that I can avoid it. Otherwise you might have a dead tourist on your hands."

She went to get a dictionary to make sure she understood what he was talking about. Then she said, "I thought millet was bird food. Like you give to parakeets."

He laughed so loudly that she could see the gold in his molars.

The minute he had gotten his key and gone to his room, she took a peek at his passport. He was five years older than she and had been born in December. A Sagittarius. Living in Stockholm, Sweden.

During the night, she dreamed of a being that was half-human, half-horse. He jumped over the sand with a bow in his hand and aimed right for her. He came so close that she could feel the sand spray into her face. She trembled softly all the way down her back, and she woke at that moment with a feeling of warm, spilled milk between her legs.

He left and then he returned. During the course of a year, he came to their hotel no less than three times. By now she had managed to learn a few phrases in Swedish. And he could say a bit more than *kalimera.*

Although he was a foreigner, he managed to impress her parents. He made them weak. He duped them, she now thought, after the fact, although she did not know exactly how. All he had to do was show his one side, the pleasant, charming side. He was polite, bronzed from the sun, happy.

Slowly but surely, they began to loosen ancient rules regarding honor and morality. They gave her time off, set her free from reception work.

"Little Chrysalis, you need some time off. Take our Swedish guest and show him around our beautiful island."

So when he finally, formally, asked for their daughter's hand, they took him to their hearts as a beloved new family member. They thought they knew him. He had told them so much through gestures and simple words. About himself. How it was going to be in Sweden. He was so convincing that even her mother finally capitulated.

A few days before the wedding, the unbelievable happened. Ariadne's father had a heart attack. It happened early one morning as he got up to go to the bathroom. His wife woke from the strange sounds and threw herself across their double bed in order to catch him before he fell. They both tumbled to the ground, her body taking the brunt, her embrace holding him. But it didn't help. He died on the stone floor, in his wife's arms.

So instead of a wedding, they had a funeral. Ariadne had to hang up her beautiful white wedding dress and put on black. During this time, Tommy was a great help to them. He held her hand during the entire funeral service, let her cry and cry. He embraced her mother and offered to let her live with them in Sweden. Whenever she wanted. Even in a month or so, once everything had been arranged.

A week later, he and Ariadne stepped onboard a flight which would take them to Arlanda Airport. During a hastily performed ceremony at Stockholm's City Hall, the innocent Greek girl became Mrs. Tommy Jaglander. On her finger, she wore two simple gold bands. After the wedding, they had lunch at Stallmästaregården together with Tommy's colleagues, who had worn their police uniforms to the ceremony. They were witnesses.

Ariadne had imagined something different. She had thought there would be happiness, celebration, music and dancing till dawn. But it was what it was. And since all her relatives were in mourning, this was a more suitable solution. Even she agreed on that.

"Your mother can come later," Tommy comforted her. "She can live with us in the new house; she can help us watch all our children."

As it happened, it didn't turn out that way. During the entire seventeen years that she and Tommy had been married, her mother visited only four times. Partially, Ariadne herself discouraged the visits. She couldn't stand seeing in her mother's eyes the fact that she knew and that her original worries had been well-founded.

During the months after their daughter had been born, Tommy began to change. He let her see glimpses of his dark side, the complete opposite of the side she had fallen in love with. They had been called to the doctor's office for a conference. Something was wrong with their child's eyes. Christa sat in her baby car seat and slept. She had been screaming all night, and now she was worn-out and silent.

The doctor was named Nowakowska, and her Eastern European origin showed in her accent as well as in her last name. Tommy criticized this later on, saying they should have seen a Swedish expert. Their child was certainly worth more than that! Why did they have to suffer Eastern European garbage!

Doctor Ewa Nowakowska had cold fingers. She smiled toward the car seat.

"You have a sweet little girl there. Very cute and pretty with those long black lashes."

She lifted a handful of papers and shuffled them in silence for a moment. On the windowsill was a plastic stork with a bundle in its beak. A light yellow hair tuft stuck out from the bundle.

They waited. Christa whimpered and lost her binkie. Ariadne picked it up and put it back and managed to get her daughter to fall asleep again.

Doctor Nowakowska straightened her glasses and cleared her throat.

"As you might have noticed, something has gone wrong."

Those were her exact words: *something has gone wrong.*

How could anything go wrong? The child was protected in her mother's womb. A woman's body is constructed for this, has a special little room for this. A secure, snug room where the embryo was supposed to grow into a fetus, and from a fetus to a child.

"We've examined her," continued Doctor Nowakowska. She was wearing a necklace with a cross. It dangled and swung as she moved. "Unfortunately, there is nothing that we can do. To speak clearly, your daughter will never be able to see."

Tommy had gotten so angry at her words he seemed out of his mind. He leapt out of his chair, leaned over the desk, balancing on his knuckles. They were massive; she hadn't noticed that before.

"What have you done to her!" His voice was thick and trembling, like that of an animal, coming from deep inside his voice box.

Doctor Nowakowska jumped back. Having to tell someone their child had a handicap or even had died was the most difficult thing she had to do. In medical school, they had practiced these situations, role playing one afternoon. Back then it felt like theater.

"Please listen to me. As doctors and experts we have done everything in our power. But Christa's handicap is natural. It happened while she was still in the womb."

Tommy didn't take that to heart. At first.

"My wife has gone to her pre-natal appointments. You should have noticed something was wrong! Why else do you bother with maternal care? Isn't it supposed to be making sure that everything goes all right during pregnancy, or what?"

"Of course, of course. And Sweden is more advanced than many other countries. But not everything can be detected."

"You haven't been observant enough. Tell me the truth. You've been careless!"

"Please, Tommy . . ." Ariadne reached for his wrist, but it was like granite. He whirled around and his mouth had shrunk.

"You agree with them!"

"No . . . but . . ."

He looked at her, let his gaze go right into her, into her eyes, beneath her skin.

"She can still have a good life," Doctor Nowakowska continued, deeply affected by the reaction of the new father. "This is

not a catastrophe by any means. I know of many . . . there is help
and special education . . . that is, when little Christa grows bigger.
And we can give you the telephone numbers of parents in a similar situation."

Tommy had gone to the baby carseat. He gripped the handle
and lifted it so abruptly that Christa woke up and began to
scream. He stopped in the doorway.

"I demand to speak to an expert."

The doctor laughed nervously.

"You've just done so, my friend. You have spoken to me, and
I am the kind of expert that you want to talk to."

Tommy turned to Ariadne. His eyes were sharp slits.

"Come on, we're going."

A SUDDEN WHINING NOISE made Justine jump and hold her breath. Then she looked around. The clouds were slipping in the night sky like curtains on a stage; behind them was the moon. How close it seemed. She could easily make out its lines and craters.

Now she looked at the garden with its silver leaves and shadow forms. She turned her eyes to the aviary. The bird? No, he was sitting and sleeping, probably quite high up, with his head under his wing. Should she go to bed, too? It was twenty minutes to one in the morning.

She stared at her feet, begging them to move, to walk slowly to the bedroom. She would open the sheet and climb into the empty space that was Hans Peter's side. Put her arm over that space and call forth the feel of his back, his strong back and hips.

But when she lifted her head again, she saw the water of Lake Mälaren. The surface shimmered in the light from the moon, shifted as the wind touched it.

No, it slid into her, *no*. And on her upper lip, drops of sweat broke out. She pressed her lips with the back of her hand and felt great fear and sorrow.

She had been out with the boat today, just like almost every day. She rowed out a few hundred meters; she had trouble gauging the distance these days. And in the winter, everything had been so different. Even the darkness had a different shade, more gray.

Just like all the other days, this afternoon she had gone to her knees on the bottom of the boat and peered into the clear water. Seaweed and trailing plants, a few fish. It was deep here, how deep she did not know.

Was it deep enough?

Hans Peter did not like it when she went out in the rowboat. He thought this was on the edge of madness. She told him it was important to her. She needed to collect her strength, her life. She needed to *contemplate.*

She tried highbrow arguments to convince him: "I find a certain calm out there between the heavens and the water. You must never try to take it from me or try to hinder me. You and I are not the kind of people who force each other; we will never ever do that."

"You're a bit crazy, you know." How he tried to laugh it all off. "But we all have our small idiosyncrasies."

"Don't you see how important it is for me?" She cooed, made herself tiny, crept into his forgiving embrace. "It's as important to me as your books are to you."

It had been winter on the edge of spring back then, six and a half years ago. The ice was thin and brittle. The slack female body, tied to the kick sled, was made still heavier by the stones she had tied around the dead woman's waist. She had pushed the kick sled out onto the ice, far, far out, so far that she'd almost broken through herself. One last effort, a push, her hands leaving the wooden handle, and, with a great amount of bubbling, the kick sled turned on its nose and tipped right over the edge of the ice.

THE AIRPORT WAS RIGHT in the middle of nature. In order to get there, they had to drive through winding narrow roads and finally over a pasture complete with bleating animals. The car's tires were covered with mud and cow manure. They parked outside the terminal building.

"And we've driven so carefully all week long," Jill sighed. "Now the car looks terrible. What is the rental company going to think of us?"

"Ah, they're used to it." Tor lifted their luggage out of the car and began to walk. It was time to start their journey home. Their vacation was over. He had thought he would see this as a relief or at least be indifferent. He was surprised this was not the case.

The waiting room was completely empty. Were he and Jill going to be the only passengers to Bodø? Was an entire plane going to take off just for them? They checked in and dropped the car keys into a return box on the wall. Later on, employees from the rental company would pick them up.

"Our little car," Jill said, and looked out over the almost empty parking lot. "I've actually gotten quite fond of it."

She pouted in that childishly playful way women do sometimes. Berit had done the same thing, at least in the beginning of their relationship. He'd forgotten that. Everything appeared so distant. His entire life.

They found a place to sit down to wait. Behind the cafeteria counter, a sleepy teenaged boy rattled things around. It smelled like coffee that had been left standing too long. The plane was supposed to take off in a half an hour, but there was no sign of it. A few hundred meters beyond the airport, there was a cemetery with white crosses and stones. It also looked as if it were dropped down in the middle of nature.

So different from home, he thought. We have our sheltered and well-cared-for cemeteries where we can go to remember our loved ones. Grave-tending weekends, outdoor candles, the aroma of moss and fire. Shivering people in large groups, standing close beside one another for warmth, listening to the horn music of the Salvation Army. A constant, hazy rain transforms them to shadows, wipes the expressions off their faces. Why does it always rain on All Saints Day? Maybe his grandmother was right when she said that "It's angels crying with us, the living."

He pointed toward the gravestones.

"Strange place for a cemetery, don't you think? Right next to the runway."

"Well, you see, the dead don't complain about *støj*."

"Huh? Stoy?"

She peered at him, the skin over her nose wrinkled. Then she quoted from memory in Norwegian: "Noise is the environmental issue which people living near the airport are most concerned about."

"They're most concerned about the noise?"

"*Akkurat.* When the sound becomes undesirable, it is called noise. This is why they've put the airport right here in the middle of the animals and the deceased."

He couldn't help making an expression which egged her on.

"But never fear." Jill continued to quote in Norwegian: "'The government's goal is to reduce the SPI, the Noise Index, by 25% between 1999 and 2010.'"

"Wonderful."

She fell silent, snuggled closer to him on the sofa.

"Everything feel all right?"

"Yes."

"Content with our trip?"

"Sure. Yes, I'm content."

"You don't regret me talking you into it?"

He snorted.

"Not at all."

"And yet you never got to see the whales. It was a magnificent experience."

"So I understand," he said drily.

Jill opened her shoulder bag and took out a package. She blushed.

"For you."

"For me?"

"Yes."

"Why?"

"Just a little remembrance. And as a thank you for coming with me."

"I should be the one thanking you." He heard how empty he sounded.

He turned the package over. It was rectangular and hard. Probably a book. She'd bought him a book.

"Should I open it?"

"If you want to."

It was indeed a book. A photo book. The cover was toned blue—sea, sky, mountain range. In the middle of all that blue was a Hurtig rowboat. Red, white and black, photographed from above. He paged through it.

"The pictures were so beautiful, so I thought . . . I couldn't help myself and bought it."

"Thanks, Jill."

"There's photos of whales, too. Gray whales. No one needs to know that you never saw them in real life. At least you were close by in principle, just a few meters away. You can still describe them to your pals."

My pals, he thought. *Who could that be?*

A long time ago, he and Berit had had friends. The time when they thought life would go on like this forever. They went out as a couple, invited people for dinner, celebrated Midsummer together. But he never truly felt a part of it all. It was usually people Berit knew. People from the publishing world. Her childhood friends. Jill, for example, and her guy at the time. What was his name again? Pelle? A rough, go-for-it, body-building type. They didn't really fit together, those two. Berit had talked about it with him; they agreed. He realized that he didn't know all that much about Jill, even though he'd known her for so long. She probably knew much more about him.

She had gotten up and walked over to the window. She looked like she was listening for something. She had put on her make-up before the trip, put on her official face. It was over now. Now they were going home. She was going to work; she was getting up at six o'clock the next morning. And he? Well, he'd continue waiting, of course. Searching and waiting. And see his sons now and again. Was that all there was left of that life he'd carefully built?

He hadn't seen Jörgen since the day that Jörgen had yelled at him and then he had been scared to death when Tor fell to the floor and clutched his heart. He'd called for an ambulance right away and he went with him to the hospital. Once they arrived, Tor was swept right into a treatment room and set up with IV lines and test apparatus. He wasn't even allowed to get up and go to the bathroom. Jörgen sat on a stool next to the cot, a round, perforated steel stool. It looked uncomfortable, and it hurt Tor to see it. *You should go home, now, Jörgen. It's not going to get any worse than it is now.*

No, his boy sat there stubbornly. A few hours later, Tor was released. His heart appeared healthy and whole. What had been wrong?

"Maybe a stomach ache of some kind," the doctor had said. "Sometimes it gives symptoms that resemble a heart attack. Certainly, it is much better to come in and get it checked out than . . . Well, you get my drift."

He took a taxi home that night. Jörgen went to Solna, where he lived with a girl. Were they still together? What was her name again? Helle, that flat-chested Danish girl?

When Berit was still with them, the boys would often come home spontaneously and bring their girlfriends. That didn't happen any longer. His youngest son Jens had become angry and disappointed when Tor had been forced to sell Vätö. Jens had often gone there with his girlfriend, but he seldom mentioned helping out with repairs or costs. They hardly did more than the dishes before they left.

He knew that Berit would have been deeply disappointed, too. If she ever returned. Did he sell the summer house in order to punish her? Subconscious revenge? A psychologist would probably surmise something like that. Berit had loved Vätö. He could imagine her before him, stretched out in a chaise lounge on the veranda, a book in her hand. She always had so much to read due to her job.

There were a number of books out on the island that she had worked on. *The Big Book of Mushrooms*, for example. And many of Sonja Karlberg's novels. He had noticed the titles and wondered if anyone would ever publish books like that today. *Fate's Salon* was one of them; *Before the Sun Sets* was another. The covers had been drawn during the fifties. They must be romance novels. All at once, he remembered how Berit would complain about the novelist, a lady with a short fuse. How she would run up to the editing offices with a typo she found in one of her books and how she would fly into a rage and throw the book so hard that it would fall apart.

Tor had taken almost all of the small personal things with him when he was in the process of selling Vätö, but he let the furniture be part of the sale, including Berit's books.

A loud roar shook the windows and almost knocked a plastic coffee cup off the edge of the table. The plane was coming in for a landing. Tor went to stand next to Jill. She smelled of soap or perfume. They watched the plane land together.

"There it is," said Jill, shrugging her shoulders.

A woman with wine-red tufts of hair and wearing overalls was pushing out a cart with nothing on it but their luggage. She waved in the plane with two little yellow paddles, and it came to a stop only a few inches away from her. The sound of the motor died. The woman anchored the wheels with blocks and pulled covers over two of the propeller blades. Then she coupled a gas line. She had wide hips underneath her overalls. A small shiver of desire went through Tor. He gave Jill a little tap.

"Look at that!" he said. "What women can do!"

She nodded silently. It was time to get on the plane. To his surprise, the little plane was almost completely full. He thought about saying to Jill something joking such as *Where did all these people come from?*

Then he saw her face.

She was crying.

HANS PETER HAD JUST STRETCHED OUT on the cot in the porter's room when the doorbell rang.

Damn, he thought. I thought all the guests were in for the night.

His back was aching. He hoped the slipped disk he'd had a few years ago wasn't coming back. Many times he'd tried to convince Ulf to put in a lock with a number pad so that everything would be much easier even though he realized that such modernization could put him out of a job. But Ulf refused. Ulf always wanted things done in the traditional, time-tested manner. It was part of his brand identification.

The doorbell rang again. Hans Peter slowly got to his feet and ran his hand through his hair, or at least the little bit of hair he had left. His mother usually worried about that every time they got together:

"You ought to find something against hair loss, Hans Peter. Maybe you have some kind of illness. You have to be careful with illnesses you know. If you take medicine in time, it can be completely cured."

He tried to explain to her that his hair loss had to do with aging, and that it was a normal process. She jumped as if he'd hit her.

"Age? But Hans Peter, you're not old at all! And take a look at your father! I know you've inherited his hair!"

His father would give him a wink and then run his hand through his thick white hair so that the dandruff whirled up.

"We're not old, are we, H.P.? Whaddaya say? No moss on these rolling stones!"

His mother had great difficulty accepting the fact that she did not have grandchildren and that now it looked like it was too late. She would push the thought away. Lately, she appeared to have the beginnings of dementia. Or maybe just *forgetfulness*, a much kinder word. Her two heart attacks had not improved the situation.

The doorbell rang yet again, harder and longer this time. Hans Peter opened it. A man was standing there, tall and strong but with a round, almost childlike, face. His hair was stubby and bleached by the sun. It didn't look affected by baldness. He was wearing black jeans and a tight white T-shirt that showed off his muscular, brown arms. A sweater hung over his shoulders, the arms tied over his chest. His had intense blue eyes with a bright shine, as if he were wearing colored lenses. He held out his hand.

"Good evening," he said. The man's voice was rich, but also somewhat tense. Hans Peter had an ear for that kind of nuance.

"Oh . . . good evening."

"Perhaps you might have an empty room for the night?"

"I'm sorry, afraid not, but let me check." Hans Peter had the feeling that a curt negative answer would release a violent reaction. That's stupid, he thought. Maybe he's been bitten by the same fear that haunted Justine. Hans Peter went behind the reception desk, took out the ledger and began to page through it, even though he knew full well that the hotel was completely booked. The man stepped closer, leaned over the counter. He had hair growing on his tanned fingers, peach fuzz, blond. He had a gold ring on his left ring finger.

Hans Peter cleared his throat.

"I'm afraid that it doesn't look good," he said and attempted to look sorrowful and compassionate.

The man snorted. "What do you mean? Are you upset? You ought to be happy that business is going so well."

Hans Peter realized that his face was turning red.

"It's just an expression," he mumbled.

"Aw, I'm just joking," the man said. "Forget about the room. I just wanted to come inside for a minute. Look around and talk."

"Why?"

"The fact is, I know you. Well, at least I know who you are. And you're the one I want to talk to."

Hans Peter closed and put away the ledger. His underarms pricked with an uncomfortable feeling.

"I'm afraid you must explain yourself."

"Jesus Christ, don't look like such a 'fraidy cat. You'd think you'd seen a ghost."

"Forgive me . . . but have we met? Maybe you've stayed here before? If that is the case, forgive me if I do not remember you. We have so many guests and it's impossible for me to remember all the faces."

The man stretched, his big body cracked. He puffed out his upper lip so it curved.

"Hans Peter Bergman," he said. "That's you, isn't it?"

"Yes, that's me."

"You live in Hässelby. You live together with Justine Dalvik and have been together for the past five years. Not married, just living together, take note of that."

"That's true."

"Doesn't she want to marry you? Or does she want to maintain control over her great fortune? Or is there another reason? Maybe you don't want to marry her?"

A ringing sound appeared in Hans' ears. It seemed to spread all the way through his neck, making it difficult for him to concentrate.

"Calm down," the man continued. "It's not as strange as it seems. We've had our eye on her, earlier. We knew that she was up to something. But we couldn't find anything that would stick."

"Who are you?" he managed to blurt out, as a sense of rage beginning to build inside him. "Who do you think you are, coming in here and throwing around all kinds of accusations?"

The man changed, his face broke out into a smile. His hand was offered again.

"I'm Tommy Jaglander. I'm married to your co-worker Ariadne. As she's probably mentioned, I'm a police officer."

"You are?" Hans Peter said with an empty tone.

"My wife has forgotten her key ring, I thought I'd stop by here to check since I was in the area anyway. If she left it here, that is. Have you seen any keys that you don't recognize? Perhaps?"

"No, I don't believe I have."

"She can be careless sometimes, my wife. One day she's lost her wallet and the next it's her keys. Does your woman do the same thing? I mean, isn't it a typical female thing? They're always boasting about their multi-tasking, but I sure don't know about that!" He laughed loudly, roaring. Hans Peter tried to laugh, but couldn't. Instead, his politeness took over, the good behavior that his parents had trained in him, especially his mother.

"Maybe I can offer you something? A cup of coffee, a sandwich, perhaps? Or maybe you must be going."

To his great surprise, the big man agreed to have coffee. Hans Peter poured water into the machine and measured a few scoops. While the coffee was brewing, he spread some liver pâté on two thick slices of bread and sliced up some cucumber. He set the table in the breakfast nook. The window was slightly open; he heard the sound of drunken teenagers hooting and yelling.

"Come on and sit down, why don't you," he said. "Sorry I was put off earlier, since you knew who I was and I didn't know if I ought to know you or whether I was embarrassing myself."

Tommy Jaglander stretched out his long legs. He had well-polished shoes. When he placed one leg over the other, Hans Peter noticed that there was a price tag still stuck to the bottom of one sole.

"I've come here to pick Ariadne up at times," Tommy said. "But you weren't here. I only ran into that Santesson guy."

"Yeah, he owns the place. Go ahead, have something." He pushed the plate of sandwiches. Jaglander was about to reach for one when he stopped himself.

"I've got to ask, do you know what's in the bread?"

"It's just normal rye bread. Ulf Santesson's mother bakes for us; we serve it for breakfast."

"No extra ingredients? Like millet, for example?"

"Millet? What's that?"

Jaglander gave a little speech. It was obvious he'd done this many times before.

"It's a kind of grain. It's grown in Asia and Africa, but it's sometimes grown here, too. In Europe, it's been grown since the Stone Age. It was really common here in Sweden up until the Eighteenth Century. Porridge was made from the grain, and it was even used for baking and food preparation. And if I get the littlest bit of it in me, I'll die on the spot."

"Jesus."

"So you understand that I have to ask. Of course, I always have an injection and some antidote on hand." He pointed to a small black backpack, which he'd placed on the floor by his feet. "It sometimes takes a few minutes to work. It's not a hell of a lot of fun, though, to feel how your airways are slowly closing up."

"I don't believe that Ulf's mother uses that millet stuff when she bakes. She's a bit on the conservative side, just like her son. But just in case, let me give her a call. Maybe the hotel will have other guests in the same situation."

"As far as I know, there are only two people in all of Sweden who have this allergy. Me and some woman."

"I'll give her a call anyway. Can you tell me what time it is?"

"Eleven-thirty. Hey, just don't worry about it. I'll skip the sandwich, if you don't mind. Old ladies go to bed early."

Hans Peter poured the coffee. He didn't dare have any himself; he was afraid he wouldn't be able to sleep all night. He ate one of the sandwiches and drank a glass of water.

Jaglander looked around.

"Nice hotel," he said.

"It's all right."

"*Tre Rosor*. The Three Roses. Why do you think they call it that?"

"I'm afraid I don't know the answer." Hans Peter was surprised that he'd never asked the question himself.

Jaglander blew on his coffee and then drank.

"From what I understand, you've had a great deal of work to do today."

"There's always a great deal of work at this time of year. Lots of foreign guests. People have started traveling again after September 11th."

"You mean there was a drop-off here, too?"

"As far as foreign tourists go, yes."

They were silent. There was the sound of a flushing toilet from one of the rooms above them. Tommy Jaglander cracked his knuckles. Hans Peter had always hated that sound. Jaglander seemed to notice that.

"Is she a good worker?" he said unexpectedly.

"Huh?"

"My wife. Does she do a good job?"

"Of course she does. This is a tough hotel to clean, you might have noticed. But she digs right in."

Jaglander cracked his knuckles again. He leaned forward over the table and fixed Hans Peter with his almost glowing eyes. Hans Peter reflexively leaned back. No one would want to be interrogated by that bulldozer.

"I believe I know what you're thinking now," said Jaglander, and his face was blank and unmoving.

"What . . . what are you talking about?"

"You're pouring coffee and the thing you really want to do is punch me in the face."

"Huh? . . . Why would I want to do that?" A picture of Ariadne and her broken, abused lips went through his mind.

"I can read people, you know. I see right through them. It's part of my job, and though I don't mean to boast, I'm pretty good at it."

Outside, a woman gave a heart-rending cry: "You . . . deee . . . dee . . . emon! I'm going . . . to ki . . . kill you!"

Jaglander didn't move.

The woman screamed again and began to run. They could hear her high heels. A few moments later, it was silent outside again. Hans Peter pushed the plate with the one remaining sandwich to the side.

"I'm afraid you have to make yourself clear," he said.

"Ha! You're scared again!"

Hans Peter shook himself.

"Tell me flat out what you've got to say."

"Your woman. Justine Dalvik. I know you heard what I said a few minutes ago. That we've been keeping an eye on her because she's not on the up-and-up. But you don't want to hear that. So you're trying to pretend you didn't hear it at all. It's not going to help you, Bergman. As soon as I'm gone, you're going to be turning it over in your mind, again and again."

"Not on the up-and-up?"

"One of my colleagues was the one who kept her under the shadow of his wing, so to speak. Hans Nästman. He was a fine policeman from the old school. He's dead now, unfortunately. Cancer. A hell of a sickness, cancer."

Hans Peter stared at him. His entire body felt like wet sand; arms, legs, the whole body felt forced to the ground by its weight.

"What did you think she'd done?" he asked tonelessly.

"Let me tell you, I certainly wouldn't pick someone like her for my bed partner."

You devil, he thought, confusedly. Out loud he said, "What did you suspect?"

"Do you really want to know?"

"Yes, I do!" He was practically yelling.

"Killed people."

THE MORNING WAS CHILLY with a hint of fall in the air. Jill unlocked her bicycle and brushed off the wet seat with her palm. That hardest time of the year was getting closer, the time when morning fog made vessel navigation difficult. Many captains did not even bother making an attempt to go through the canal. Instead, they chose to anchor at Bornhuvud and wait there until conditions improved. That meant that the pilot could be stuck on board for a number of hours, even though he was almost at the Locks, where he usually would disembark and go home for his nine-hour rest period before the next piloting duty. Time and again, the employees at the Locks would have to go out and get him with one of their small service boats.

Jill rolled down the hill toward the water and followed the path along the canal. It was fifteen minutes to six. Not a single person was in sight. Some mornings, she would run across some deer that enjoyed feasting on the plants in the gardens. They appeared completely fearless; they stood there calmly and watched her. Their home was the forest around Ragnhildsborg. Out here there really was wilderness, something she hadn't known when she decided to move here. A pure bonus, she thought. City and countryside in one and the same place. Just over thirty miles from Stockholm.

She passed by the small boat harbor on the right, and the long, gray boathouse made of corrugated metal. A short bit farther on was the golf course, empty and forlorn. They hadn't had many golfers this rainy summer. Right next to it was the yellow-tiled factory building, which had served as a tobacco factory and later as the offices for the local newspaper, *Länstidningen*. What was it used for now? She had no idea. But the doors to Larsson's Greengrocer's were wide open, and she saw folks milling around inside. They began their day earlier than she did, poor things, and every single day, too. There were always people who were worse off.

Her own schedule would appear tough to an outsider, but she wouldn't have it any other way. She'd had more than enough of regular office hours. Today she was going to work from six a.m. until two-thirty p.m. and then she would be free until that evening, at ten p.m. Then she had the tough night shift all the way until six a.m. Then she'd go home and sleep a few hours, returning to work at three p.m. and continuing until ten. But after that, she had three full days off, and every five weeks, she had nine days off. She'd just gotten back from vacation in one of those nine-day periods.

She pedaled her bike quickly and with determination as she made it up the hill before the bridge over Lake Mälaren. Finally, she gave up, got off and pushed the bike the rest of the way. It was true that you could get out of shape in no time. It just took a few days for her to be out of condition. Sometimes she went to the gym near the South Pool and trained. Maybe she should do more of that, increase her routine to three times a week.

I have to pull myself together, she thought. Everywhere you hear how important it is to exercise. She'd begun to put on weight around her stomach and that bothered her. She'd always been slim, but ever since she'd stopped smoking a few years back, she'd gone up twenty pounds. She doubted she'd ever lose them again.

Well, fat was probably better than lung cancer. She kept telling that to Berit, who was a chain smoker. *Was?* The word cut through her. She was gripped by a sharp longing; her middle tightened. She opened her mouth and yelled into the fresh air: "Berit! Damn it! You better come back now!"

Then she fell silent, embarrassed by her outburst and questioning her sanity. Nervously, she looked around, but no one seemed to have noticed. She felt about to cry; she cleared her throat angrily and swallowed.

"Jesus, pull yourself together, Jill!" she whispered. "Pull yourself together!"

On the right side of the bridge was the obsolete observation tower. It had been a mistake from the very beginning. Many of her colleagues had told her what it had been like to work there. Due to the traffic, the tower shook and vibrated so strongly that it was impossible to have more than a half a cup of coffee at a time, otherwise it would slosh out. And if you had to go to the bathroom, you had to walk all the way down the stairs to the basement.

She reached the top of the hill and no longer needed to pedal. She cruised down. Her eyes teared up from the wind. During the time she was away with Tor, the heat wave had broken, and her colleagues were going to tease her about that. Not a single one of them could understand why she chose to go to Norway on her vacation.

"For that kind of money, you could have gone to the South Seas!"

She had no desire at all for the South Seas.

It had been difficult to wake up that morning. She'd gotten home after midnight. Tor had offered to let her stay overnight at his place to avoid taking the commuter train so late at night. She'd said no, hoping to catch the last train of the night, which she'd done. It was late Monday night, and fairly quiet. Otherwise, she wasn't all that fond of taking a commuter train at that hour. Right before one o'clock in the morning, the train rolled into Södertälje Station. For the last miles home, she splurged on a taxi.

Jill opened the gate to the Lock area, went inside, and locked up her bike. Even though there was no vessel in the locks at the moment, she could still smell the typical mixture of diesel, grease and oil. She took the elevator to the control tower. Fred and Nisse had just arrived. She worked with the two of them most often. The night shift was on the way home. Fred gave her a welcoming hug.

"How was it? Good?"

She just nodded. Her head ached from exhaustion.

"How about you guys?"

"Fantastic. Don't you see how tanned we've become?" Fred rolled up his sleeve and showed off his arm. Nisse took hold of her shoulders and examined her. "But not you, I can tell! You're as white as asparagus! Never got a table by the window, am I right?"

She laughed.

The room where they sat was highest up in the tower with a view of the two canal approaches. Their desks stood in the middle of the room; they'd pushed them together to create one large work space. Tinted glass panes made up three of the walls. The fourth held all the screens and monitors for the various bridges. Jill put down her backpack. She went over to test the soil in the hanging flowerpots, which were themselves decorated with porcelain flowers. She'd been the one to hang them there. Good. The soil was damp. Someone had taken care of them while she was away.

For the next few shifts, she was going to be the person who sat in the so-called traffic chair. This meant that she had total responsibility for the exact location of the vessels as they passed through Södertälje's waters, both where they were presently located as well as where they were heading. Their watch included the archipelago from Landsort as well as the entire Lake Mälaren and all of Stockholm west of the Locks. She had to note everything that was on the move within the area into an electric navigational chart. She observed the vessels as green echoes on the radar screen. She could also see their names, their course, and their speed. Every vessel longer than forty-five meters had to report to VTS-Central.

At the same moment she sank down into her chair, they were called by the pilot of the *Listerland*, which had just left Köping. She recognized his voice, it was Billy Anderberg. When he heard her voice, he sounded happy. He asked to switch from the official traffic Channel 68 to Channel 11, which was the "chatting channel."

"Welcome back!" Billy hooted. "How many polar bears did you shoot?"

"Ten!" she replied swiftly. She liked Billy; he was funny and easy-going. At the same time, he had a depth which both fascinated her and made her worried. They'd gone out to eat a number of times together. She made sure that she paid her part of the bill. He was a pal, no more. Sometimes men had trouble understanding these things.

Channel 16 was the emergency channel. Someone was always listening to it on every vessel. Channel 16 was the one the large ferryboat *Estonia* used for its may-day call almost ten years ago. So much time had passed since that tragedy! She remembered Gerd, one of the girls from their gang in Hässelby when they were growing up. Gerd was a foster child at the Östman's place and one of the bullies, at least when it came to bullying Justine. Gerd was on board the *Estonia* the night it sank. It was her bachelorette party. She was getting married for the third time. She and her five friends disappeared into the deep with the ship, together with eight hundred other passengers.

Time to make her report to the automatic telephone-answering machine, a service for the pilots, which included information about the water levels and the navigable channels. She picked up the phone and began to read.

"Water level in the Baltic +20, Lake Mälaren +1, Hjulsta -1, Västerås -1, Kvicksunds Bridge +2. Channel information for Lake Mälaren: Bryggholmen, east Oknöhäll, red light on the buoy, although light has gone out; Lina Sound, mooring-post 13 is out . . ."

Nisse came clattering up the spiral staircase carrying three mugs of coffee he'd gotten in the staff room. Nisse was going to be sitting in the pilot's chair this shift while Fred sat in the channel chair. The person in charge of the channels opened the bridges and went out and moored the boats while they were in the locks. Nisse's main job was puzzling out the pilots' schedules, which could get terribly complicated. From time to time there was a lack of pilots. Maybe some were sick, or others had not yet finished their required rest period. A pilot was required to decline a job if he knew he hadn't rested up enough. Otherwise, it was too risky. The waters around Lake Mälaren demanded concentration and many years of experience due to the shallows and narrow passages. People were surprised when they heard that. Aren't the boats steered by computers nowadays? But the fact of the matter was that there were no programs sophisticated enough to leave the responsibility to a computer. Not only that, the technology was too vulnerable. A computer could be hit by an electric blackout, especially during thunderstorms. And other vessels could show up at any time.

Jill and her colleagues were encouraged to accompany a piloting tour sometimes in order to have a better understanding of the pilots' work and therefore their own. But of course they had to do this on their own time. Jill had made a number of these tours when she was still new and enthusiastic. Once she'd accompanied Billy Anderberg on a piloting run from Köping to Södertälje. During that trip, Jill realized that she actually had all of Lake Mälaren on a navigational chart in her head. The night was clear and there was a full moon. They had sat in the darkness high up on the commander's bridge.

"Know what?" he asked as he looked out over the water.

"What?" She was afraid he would say something personal, something that would make her have to hurt his feelings, but he didn't.

"*Ser du månen i det blå, allt du önskar kan du få,*" he began to sing. "If you see the moon while at sea, you'll receive everything you wish." He stopped himself and became serious. "Did you know that the moon is the sailor's best friend?"

She laughed quietly. It sounded like a line of poetry, or a line in a little gift book. She knew that he wrote; he kept a soft-covered, black book in his pocket. Once he let her read some of the things he wrote. At first she was embarrassed; who was she to judge poetry! But to her great relief, she found she enjoyed it immediately.

"You're a real poet, Billy; this is great! Send this in to a publisher!"

He gestured away.

"No, no, no, this is just for me and some of my girlfriends. Pure therapy. It can get awfully lonely at night."

She didn't give up.

"Honestly, I know of a publisher. Do you remember my best friend Berit? I must have mentioned her before. The one who disappeared. There's another woman that I met at her publishing house who now works for a place called Bladguld, and they publish poetry. I know that. I can show her what you've written if you want me to. It's worth a try."

"Bladguld? Gold pages," he said ironically.

"Well, yeah, what about it?"

"It just sounds so . . ."

"Do you remember the author Tobias Elmkvist? He was from Södertälje. His books were published at Bladguld's. I have one of his poetry collections. You can borrow it if you want to."

"Tobias Elmkvist? Wasn't he the one . . . ?"

"Yeah, he was the one who happened to kill some guy in Östergötland, but he is still an awfully good poet in spite of that."

"Just happened to kill some guy," Billy said sourly. Their conversation split off into more ethical questions of guilt and morality, and Billy's black book stayed in his pocket.

Jill looked out over the water, which was restless, shining. The morning rush hour was in full swing across the bridge. She saw a bus with schoolchildren on the way to the South Pool to go swimming with their teachers. Yuck, she thought. Just think of having that kind of responsibility for a gang of wild ten-year-olds in bathing suits. No, a teaching career had never appealed to her, even though her mother had been a teacher. Or maybe just because she'd been one. Jill dreamed of being a journalist and had even taken a few courses with Poppius. That came to a screeching halt when she never got any jobs. It just was too uncertain. For a few years, she tried free-lancing, but she had trouble selling herself.

She'd ended up at the plumbing firm completely by accident. Her parents were going to replace the faucet and toilet in the old bathroom. They hired Haglund's Plumbing and one of the guys who came to the job was Pelle Johansson. And so things took their course. They became a couple, even though they didn't live together. They never had children, either, which was a lucky break she now thought, after the fact. They would have been terrible parents. They were just much too different.

Once when she was very young, Jill had gotten pregnant. It was by accident. She didn't even know the guy; it was a party and they were both very drunk. She couldn't forget the excruciating conversation with the social worker before the abortion. They didn't give her enough pain medication before the procedure either. It was as if they wanted to punish her. As if she'd done something ugly and inappropriate and now she had to take the consequences. She'd been twenty. The child would have been almost thirty by now if she'd gone ahead and had it. Perhaps would even have become a parent, making her a grandmother. A strange and sometimes melancholy thought.

Something caught her eye. An older man with brown pants and shirt stood on the quay with his fly open, pissing right into the canal.

"Nice view," she said caustically.

"Well, don't look, then," Nisse countered.

"We won't have that later," said Fred angrily. "Once the security fence is installed. Then we'll be really isolated. That damned Bush; it's all his fault. What the hell does he have to go and invade Iraq for!"

The planned security fence was a consequence of the new safeguards against terrorists which were put in place internationally after September 11, 2001. According to those regulations, all harbor areas were to be cordoned off and protected, even smaller ones such as Södertälje's locks. It had already been done at many places. The pilots muttered against it, it was more difficult for them to get to the vessels.

The pissing man straightened up and wobbled unsteadily.

"Wonder if he'll fall in," Jill said. Things like that happened. A few years ago, one of her colleagues had witnessed a man fall in and in spite of the fact that they'd all rushed out and tried to reach him, it was too late. The man drowned right before their eyes. Afterwards they found out that it had been his birthday.

"Well, I certainly wouldn't want to take a dip in that cold water," Fred said sarcastically. "And all the crap that's in it. Of course, it was worse years ago when the sewers emptied right into the canal. Think about how close the hospital is, all the crap from there. Nice, isn't it?"

Jill grabbed the telescope. The man had zipped up and was wobbling toward the north gate of the locks where there was a bridge for pedestrians. *At your own risk* was written on a sign. With great difficulty, the man climbed down to the narrow passageway and balanced over it. She followed his steps via the telescope. Then she noticed that the ice protection was gone from the west gate of the locks.

"Look over there!" she exclaimed. "Who should we call?"

Fred swallowed a mouthful of coffee.

"Relax, sweetheart. They took it away yesterday for repairs."

"How do you know that?"

"I was working overtime."

Fred decided to go sit next to Nisse and together they went through the list of available pilots. In spite of his tan, Nisse looked worn out. Jill knew that he had problems on the home front. His wife wanted a divorce, but they were still living together in the family home in Pershagen. Sometimes they went to family therapy and on those days he'd come to work with a dogged expression and a short, curt tone in his voice. Jill looked at her two colleagues sitting side-by-side in front of the computer screen and she was filled with tenderness.

Just like a tired, old family, she thought. That's what we are. Christmas and New Year's, joy and sorrow: we experience everything together. We know each other inside and out, and we respect each other in spite of our faults.

She stood up and stretched. Nisse looked up.

"Can you check and see if the *Fagervik* is really coming to Landsort at 11:30?"

She'd intended to go to the bathroom, but she sat back down and called: "*Fagervik. Fagervik.* Södertälje VTS, Channel 16."

No answer.

"I'll call on the transmitter from Västervik, or maybe from Visby; he must be able to hear one of those."

She reached them, and confirmed that they were on schedule and their position was correct.

She began to notice her lack of sleep now. She felt empty and brittle. Her eyes burned. As if through a fog, she heard Nisse call up one of the pilots.

"Hi there, Jakobsson. I thought I'd send you to Landort and take in the *Fagervik.* OK. Sure. And, by the way, there's a lot to do here. I'm thinking of giving you a back-to-back job. Take out the *Seewaal* at 19:00. What do you say to that?"

The *Seewaal*. All at once her mind was back on board the *m/s Leonora*, the boat which had taken them out to see the whales. She thought of Tor. They had parted too abruptly last night; she'd had to run for the commuter train.

"Thanks for the company," he'd called after her. "I'll be in touch."

She got up, walked down the spiral staircase, and went into the bathroom. She stood there for a few moments, looking at her washed-out face. Her tears rose in her eyes again, balanced a second and then fell over the edges of her lids and burned their way down her cheeks, hanging on her chin for a moment, let go and were absorbed by her sweater.

"What the hell is wrong with you?" she whispered fiercely. "Is it menopause, or what's gotten into you?"

She ripped off a piece of toilet paper and blew her nose. Then she went back up to the tower.

MICKE had never had the chance to say good-bye. That still was difficult for him. Micke had stormed out of his father's apartment in anger. Nothing could be resolved now. He'd expected that Nathan would call that night; he'd waited all evening for the phone to ring. But it never did. Now, many years after the fact, Micke understood that Nathan had been busy packing. Nathan was responsible for a long and difficult trip. But still, he could have made a brief call in the middle of all that, just to check on the situation.

The day before Nathan's departure, Micke had taken the subway to Nathan's apartment, a two-room on Norrtullsgatan. Nathan's apartment was centrally located and nice as hell, not too much furniture, though that wasn't important. His two sisters were going to have the use of the apartment while Nathan was away. Nathan hadn't brought Micke into that decision. This bothered him, although he realized that his sisters were quite a few years older so it was more natural for them to live there. But it would have been great; it really would have been. Be on his own for a month. Get away from Nettan's hawk-eye.

Nathan opened the door. He was wearing khaki shorts and a T-shirt. Nathan was shorter than Micke, but he was well-built, with defined calves and biceps. There was a gym in the basement of his apartment building.

"Hi there, Micke, come on in!"

Nathan had a strange hat on his head, which looked similar to a cowboy hat.

"What do you think?" Nathan asked, as he touched the brim of his hat.

"Awful."

"You know, you have to protect yourself from the sun and all those damned mosquitoes."

"Yeah." Something thick in his throat.

"How's it going with my boy?" His father put an arm around his shoulders and led him into the living room. There was a military duffle bag, an older kind, leaning against the sofa. On the table there were plastic bags filled with T-shirts and underwear, as well as a pile of plane tickets and Nathan's passport.

"As you can see, I'm in the middle of packing. I'm only taking this backpack, nothing else. You don't need so much in the jungle. If I need anything else, I'll buy it there. *Parangs*, for example."

"What's a *parang*?"

"A knife. Very sharp, very effective. Try and smuggle that in a backpack. Security forces would jump right on you. Not so smart, right?"

"Nah."

"And they're cheaper there. In Jerantut."

"Jerantut?"

"Nowheresville with a few shops. It'll be our jumping-off point into the jungle."

"Do you have to have those knives . . . those . . . pa . . . *parangs*?"

Nathan grinned.

"The natives are dangerous! . . . No, just kidding. But it's the jungle, you see; the plants grow like crazy. And we'll be the first white folks going to that area. Just imagine! And then there are wild animals. I have no desire to stand face-to-face with a wild tiger with no means to defend myself."

"Nah."

Nathan pointed to his backpack.

"Not a luxury model, of course. But it's important to do this on the cheap. I got this at the Military Supply Store, bought a few things there. Much cheaper than the Nature Company. They make a pretty penny at that place. I did get this hat there, but that's the only thing."

Nathan lifted up a pair of green, used military pants and held them against his legs.

"Take a look. Nothing wrong with these, right?"

Micke shrugged.

"Nah," he said dully.

"It's supposed to be cheap to travel with me. That's my business idea. People should be able to afford it. I don't want rich snobs; this is a different mentality. I know those rich guys; they want you to take care of everything for them, help them carry their stuff, even wipe their asses when they get Montezuma's Revenge. No, it's going to be the kind of people who want to have an adventure, great people; those are the kind of folks I want with me. The average Svensson. People who want a challenge but aren't made of steel. I want to give them something exciting without making them go bankrupt. A memory for life. That'll be my niche, or will be if I have my way. This is going to be fantastic, all of this. Later, once you're out of school, Micke, you can be part-owner of my company."

"Uh-huh."

Nathan kept going on and on. He had a whiff of alcohol about him.

"What do you think we should call ourselves? Gendser and Son? Gendser and Son Tours? Gendser and Son Adventure Travel? How about something with Challenge? Adventure Challenge? ... What do you think?"

Micke was the one who came up with the name: "How about Cheap Trip?" He said it defensively; it just came out.

"Cheap Trip!" His father threw his hat straight up into the air. "You're a genius, kid! I've always said so! A real genius! I'm going to put you into PR; study hard now, and you'll be the PR man in our company! The minute you graduate!"

He'd hired a girl to be on this first trip; she was supposed to take photos and make up a brochure. She was part of the first group, the *experiment tour*. Nathan told Micke about her.

"Martina's her name. She's very good-looking. Check this out, but don't tell your mom."

He opened a magazine with a color picture of the girl. Yes, she was good-looking all right. She had a camera over her shoulder. It looked like an advanced model. She was wearing a jeans skirt and a linen shirt. She had one leg up on a wall of some kind. She had sleek, thin legs and she was quite tanned.

He read the headline: THE CONCERT PIANIST'S DAUGHTER SHOWS US THE WORLD. Against his will, he glanced through the caption.

"With her camera as her only company, Martina, 25, daughter of well-known pianist Mats H. Andersson, is a girl who's not afraid of the unknown. She goes to all the hidden corners of the world and shows us places that we'd never dreamed existed."

"She's a tasty one, isn't she?" Nathan crowed. His teeth shone an almost unnatural white. He lifted a glass from the windowsill and took a swallow. "We're meeting up with her in Kuala Lampur; she's coming straight from Nepal."

Micke felt jealousy stirring.

Nathan ruffled his hair, hard. Nathan's hand was on his neck, bending it down.

"What do you say, kid? She making you horny?"

Micke forced him away.

"By the way, you want something to drink? I have some sodas in the fridge."

"All right."

Micke went into the kitchen. The counter was filled with dirty dishes and used glasses. The refrigerator was almost empty. Just a few beer bottles and one bottle of soda. He opened it and drank.

"You got a girl?" Nathan asked. "You're not saying much. How's it going with the women, anyway?"

"Fine."

"Just don't let 'em catch you. Promise me that."

"Sure."

"It never works out. Just ask someone who knows. A man with experience."

His father had been married twice and lived with someone for a while. In addition to Micke and his two sisters, Nathan had three other children. Girls. Now he lived on his own. There was that woman in Hässelby, but he wasn't living with her.

His father took out a bundle of dollar bills and flipped through them. Then he stashed them into a leather pouch which he tried out, tying it around his neck and letting it fall underneath his T-shirt. It stuck out like a coffee bun. He pulled it off with a jerk.

"Fuck, that's not going to work."

Then he pulled on a pair of old well-worn sneakers, and he walked back and forth across the room with them.

"I'll throw these away later," he said. "I'll have worn them out completely."

Micke swallowed some more soda.

"When are you coming home again?" he said bullishly.

"In a month or so."

"Hmmm."

"Maybe you can work on the name while we're gone. Make a logo, too. Cheap Trip. Maybe we should add an 's.' Cheap Trips. What do you think about that? Come on, don't look so angry. This is just a test trip. I'm going there to test the waters, make a few good contacts. Afterwards we'll really swing into action with the business. After I get back. How many more years until you graduate? Two, right? Come on, *tempus fugit*, time flies, just as it said on our old grandfather clock back home. *Tempus fugit*, it's Latin, you know."

The telephone rang that moment. Nathan held it between his ear and shoulder as he went about his packing. It was obvious he was talking to a woman. Probably that new one in Hässelby, Justine something. Whatever her name was. Micke hadn't met her, but he knew she was going with them to the jungle.

No. They had never had the chance to say good-bye, and it was all that Hässelby woman's fault. He'd suddenly felt superfluous, tired of the whole thing. Waved and left. He was far down the stairs when his father opened the door and yelled.

"Micke!" His name echoed in the stairwell. He didn't answer, pretended he was already gone.

This tortured him afterwards, a knife-twist straight to the heart. That they hadn't had the chance to say good-bye.

That Martina girl didn't come back from Malaysia either. She'd been stabbed to death at the hotel, in the room she was sharing with Justine Dalvik. Damn that woman. If there had been any justice in the world, that bitch should have been the one murdered instead. She was the one who betrayed Nathan. And she wasn't all that good-looking to boot. Old and fat. She'd die soon enough anyway. How had Nathan ever fallen for someone like her?

He remembered that day he went out to her house for the first time. That stone house in Hässelby. He'd called her up and she'd promised that he would have the chance to meet her. Just what I need, he thought. You old whore.

She was strange. Seemed sick in the head. They were sitting in a completely blue room and she just got up and ran up the stairs. He waited for a long time, but she didn't come back. Finally, he went into the hallway and was attacked by black wings all around him; he'd screamed and gripped the hand-rail. He saw that woman at the top of the stairs. She called down to him again and again, but he had difficulty making out what she was saying.

"Don't be afraid; the bird is afraid. He's much more afraid of you than you are of him!"

As if she could understand anything about his fear.

Finally they were able to talk. That's what he'd come there for, anyway. He wanted to know. She talked about tigers. And elephants. That Nathan could have been trampled by a wounded or angry elephant, in spite of his knife.

No, they would have heard something if that were what had happened. Wasn't there a whole group of them? If an elephant had gotten angry and attacked someone, wouldn't they have heard the sound? The trumpeting, the screams? Death in the jungle was hardly silent.

Then she made a sentimental speech about how Nathan was a man of adventure and more drivel of that nature. That he'd died when he was happiest. Boots on, the middle of life. Nathan sure as hell wasn't wearing any boots.

How do you know whether my father was happy or not, he thought. Stupidly enough, he'd started to cry, howling, all snotty, just like a little kid. He was ashamed whenever he thought of it. He hadn't been able to stop himself. Then she came down the stairs on her butt, sliding bump for bump, until she reached him, hugged him, stroked his hair.

"I've never loved anyone as much as I loved your pappa."

Then it got really strange and weird. Sick, sick, sick. She got this horn, this old-fashioned mail horn, and she started blowing into it.

He stopped crying immediately.

How did he find out? How did he get the news that Nathan was probably not ever coming back?

Fragments of words, of phrases.

A priest. Yes, damn it all, Nettan had asked a priest over to help with all that crying. How she knew him he had no idea. He was just sitting there one day, on the leather chair, the clinking of cup and saucer. Those minimal coffee cups which were never used because they were too small—they usually drank from mugs; they had hundreds of them; they'd even imposed a ban on buying more, not even as birthday and Christmas gifts.

Micke walked over the floor, and it crackled like sugar under the soles of his feet, it was his mother's voice, shrill and demanding: *"Come and sit here a minute, we have to talk."*

Nettan had wrapped her hair into a bun on the top of her head; her ears stood out; they jingled with her long silver earrings, and she had a light-blue scarf around her neck.

"Micke!" Her voice turned clear and sharp. "Stop dragging your feet like that; come and sit down at once! This man is a priest! He is here and we are going to listen to what he has to say!"

So he couldn't get away; he was roped in like a calf who was going to be branded. The priest held out his little paw of a hand, and Micke grabbed it and shook it hard. The priest's cheeks hung like wrinkled bags.

"Your mother requested that I contact the foreign office and the embassy in Kuala Lampur," he said.

Nettan jumped out of her chair, ran into the kitchen, looked out the window.

"The girls, they ought to be here any minute. We have to wait for the girls."

"Your sisters?" the priest asked, although he must have known that. "Your twin sisters—what are their names again? She told me before, but I've forgotten, you see; as for me and names . . . of course it's a must in my line of work, but still . . ." He puffed air from his nostrils, perhaps this was supposed to be some kind of laugh, a way to step back from the difficult errand—the words which he would soon have to say and which no one wanted to hear, so that he wished he could just pick up the words and leave, let them out on the street or in the subway, that is, if he took public transportation; let them fly away as if it had all been a misunderstanding.

The twin girls arrived, Jasmine and Josefine. Identical, but with different hair styles. One had her hair cut short like a boy's; the other had wavy locks. White jeans and jacket. The smell of spray filled Nettan's living room and she went out onto the balcony to smoke. The twins followed her, then the priest, and finally he went out, too, because in the end it was important that he know. He didn't want to miss a single detail, a single syllable.

"As I mentioned before," the priest said as he plucked up a handkerchief and held it in front of his nose—he seemed to have trouble with tobacco smoke and was starting to sneeze, "I've been in contact with the embassy." The sound of wings, a dove flew past. In the corner of the balcony, the Christmas tree leaned against the wall, all the needles gone and with one piece of glitter left, near the top.

"No, no, let's go inside!" said Nettan, as if she realized that the priest could catch a cold if they stood out there in the cold and what kind of a hostess would do that! So the whole group of them turned around and went back inside and for a few seconds; there was an embarrassing crowd in the doorway. Finally, they managed a bit of order: The priest, back on the leather chair, Nettan on the sofa with her legs crossed, the girls on two different chairs which they brought from the kitchen. He stood leaning on the doorpost.

"Of course, we can't know anything for certain," the priest intoned. "But people who disappear in the jungle . . . and have been lost for as long as this . . ."

A picture in his mind, Nathan with the natives, maybe keeping him as a slave. White people had kept black people as slaves; maybe they wanted revenge.

No, Micke didn't like that picture.

Maybe Nathan became their leader; that was just as likely.

The twins closed their eyes, both exactly the same way. There were streaks of mascara on their cheeks. And Nettan's broken voice: "He'll come back. Your father is the kind who survives. Right? He's that kind."

The priest kept silent. Finally, he opened his mouth to say: "We must never give up hope."

AFTERWARDS HANS PETER WAS SURPRISED by his own reaction. And his strength! His power increased, filled him like pulsing lava. First, when he stood up, he was hot and sweaty, his shirt stuck to his back. Almost immediately, the heat fell away and he seemed to be enclosed in an armor of ice. He grabbed hold of the chair and lifted it, and for a tenth of a second he felt as if he would throw it right at Tommy Jaglander. He banged it down and pushed it under the table with a painful screech. Something closed around his chest, binding his ribs, made him huff short, sharp, hoarse breaths. His anger made his words indistinct, but not weak, not at all!

"I want you to leave!"

Jaglander slowly got to his feet. He put his hand on the table, the same spade-like fist that he probably used to bruise his wife.

"Wait a second, that's just what we thought," he said defensively as his nostrils widened. "I didn't say it happened, just what we suspected."

"I'm asking you to leave the hotel." Hans Peter heard his own voice, clear and formal, on the edge. Afterwards this would surprise him even more. Here he was, giving orders to a policeman. Interference with a police officer, or whatever they would pin on him if they really wanted to send him up the river.

Jaglander's mouth broke out in a crooked smile.

"Okay. I got the message. I'm going. Thanks for the coffee."

He picked up his sweater which he'd left on the porter's counter and tied the arms back over his chest. There was something pleading about that gesture, as if he regretted saying those words, as if he wanted to take them back.

She killed.

The door shut behind him with a metallic click from the lock. Hans Peter remained standing; he was holding his hands together so hard that his fingers had turned white. Then he was hit by a headache; it exploded in his head, whipped a band around it, a white flash in front of his eyes.

She killed.

He thought about the time he met her. Those first times after he had found her. She'd fainted in the vicinity of Tempeludden. She'd been jogging; she slipped and fell. One of her legs was stronger than the other one, the remnants of an injury she'd sustained in childhood. He helped her home and after many more visits, they realized they'd found love. Neither of them was young any longer, and to experience happiness once more at their time of life—what a gift from heaven!

She was a sweet companion and a wonderful lover. But then there were those other sides, like deep, dark holes in her psyche. Craters. She let him see them relatively early in their relationship. In order to warn him, to give him the chance to flee.

Her sobbing, her despair and feelings of guilt.

"People around me disappear. Think if it happens to you, Hans Peter! Bad luck follows me around; it would be best if we never met again." Her naked face, where blood came into her lips and made her thin skin look purplish-red. He kissed those lips, licked them. She awakened in him a desire which he'd never felt before.

"You silly little girl. A human being can't be the bearer of bad luck. You know that."

How he had to sit there for hours, stroking and petting her until she was calm again. "Justine, I am never going to let you go; from now on, it's just the two of us. Just us two. Now and forever."

He knew that those words sounded rather high-flown, but he was drawn to them, and she seemed to hear them and relax.

Nathan Gendser, the man who had disappeared in the jungle, had been her lover. Surprisingly enough, this didn't awaken any jealousy in him. The man was most likely dead. And good for him, too, even though one shouldn't think those things and certainly not say them aloud. Nathan had hurt her; they didn't belong together. He had tricked her into going on that dangerous jungle excursion to test how much she could stand. A woman of her age. Plump and tired. She hadn't seen through him. Of course, love can make you blind. Hans Peter had realized at once what was going on. The minute she had told him about it, he was able to see through to Gendser's true character. But he never told her; that would be another insult.

The papers had written a great deal about his disappearance and the murder of the girl afterwards. All that was before he'd met Justine. Still, he remembered the headlines. Once she'd shown him a photo. Nathan Gendser astride a Harley-Davidson. She'd stolen the photo since he had never wanted to give her one.

"This is him. This is what he looked like."

Looked like. She used the past tense.

He snatched the photo and gave it a good look.

"Nice. A real macho hero."

She had sniffed away some tears, but didn't burst out crying, and she suddenly took the photo and ripped it in half. They were up in the library that evening; they'd lit a fire in the fireplace. She tossed the bits of the photograph into the fire. Together they sat there and watched the flames lick up the remains of Nathan Gendser and transform him into ash.

"Stop blaming yourself!" he encouraged her. "Nathan Gendser was the one who was supposed to be the group leader, not you. You had no experience of exotic and challenging environments. The whole thing was his idea. His project. His responsibility. You had nothing to do with it."

It took time to convince her, time and effort.

Then there was the whole thing with Martina, the daughter of a celebrity no less; of course the tabloids were out in full force trying to get their fill. There were days when Justine didn't dare leave the house. They hid in the bushes, those paparazzi and hyenas. Threw themselves at her the minute she opened the door. She even felt guilty about Martina.

"We had arrived at the hotel . . . I was in the shower and I was so tired. I remember that the water turned cold and I thought there'd be no warm water left for her if she had wanted to take a shower after me; it wouldn't be enough. But it was like I couldn't move . . . and I kept the water running; it was as if I would never be really clean again. Have you ever been in those kinds of countries, Hans Peter? Have you ever had your entire body covered in bites and bruises? Have you?"

"No, sweetheart, never."

"It was a man, barely more than a boy really, and he was lying dead on the ground right in front of our hotel that very first day when we arrived from the airport. I said to Nathan, I said, Nathan, do you think he's dead? And Nathan was just yelling at the cab driver, who wanted to have more money. I don't think Nathan even saw the boy. What that country did to us . . . and the jungle . . . and the mud . . . we were never dry; our clothes started to rot right on our bodies and in the morning, when we had to put them on, they were stinking and wet. You can't get clothes dry in a climate like that. How do they manage, those people who live in the jungle? There are people who live there, short and wiry, they call themselves the Orang Asli people. How do they manage to dry their clothes?" At this point she began to cry wildly, and Hans Peter embraced her and held her tightly.

He let her talk. Thought it was good for her. He knew from experience how things could be when you didn't talk. Many years ago, his sister Margareta had crashed her car and died. Silence grew in his parents' home for many years afterwards. He'd been in the middle of his studies at the university, which he broke off so that he could be home and take care of his parents. Frozen by shock, he'd broken off his entire future.

"That must have been a nightmare of a trip," he murmured and let his fingers play with her hair; she lay there with her head in his lap, lay there with a frozen face and her eyes closed.

"They asked me if I heard a sound while I was in the shower. Can you hear anything, Hans Peter, if your ears and eyes are filled with water? Can you?"

"No, you can't," he whispered. "Absolutely not, it's not possible."

"I saw her right away when I came out. She was on the floor and a knife stuck straight up from her skinny back. It was my knife, my *parang*. I'd gotten it from Nathan."

"Yes," he murmured and felt how her body stiffened, her neck straight and tense. He gripped her fingers, ice-cold, and began to massage them, her fingertips, the soft flatness of her palms. Slowly the cramp left her tortured body.

"They caught him later; it must have been him. They let me take a look at him through a peep-hole. He was squatting in that area; it was like a hole; it must have been a cell, probably a cell. His spine stuck out like a fin. I believe it was him, but how can I be sure, how can I be, Hans Peter?"

"You were right to flee back into the bathroom when you saw the knife," he whispered; he'd heard this story now so many times that he knew each chapter, each detail. "That man was desperate, He could have killed you, too, pulled out that knife and used it on you, plunged it into your body. If someone has killed once, they'll kill again, because the barriers have broken down, the normal barriers that most of us have, most except those sickos, those crazy and desperate ones. What a loss that would have been to me, what a loss, my beloved, beloved woman."

"Do you think . . . do you think they might have condemned him to death? You know, in those countries . . ." She sat up and looked at him with eyes shining from fear. "I've forgotten how things played out . . . what happened to him. Maybe it wasn't even him. Maybe just a little starving thief looking for money. What did I say when they forced me to look at him. What did I say, Hans Peter?"

She sniffed loudly and began to hyperventilate.

"Like an . . . an animal, a thin, wretched animal, he sat on the floor, dark and naked, what did I say? Did I say to them: Yes, that's him? Did I make him a victim? Because I didn't remember?"

Hans Peter's headache showed no signs of letting up. Hans Peter went to the medicine cabinet and took out some headache medicine, poured water in a glass, and swallowed. *We're keeping an eye on her.* Jaglander's words echoed inside his brain. He remembered how disconsolate Justine had been, to feel like a suspect. She had no preparation for this kind of thing; she was weak and impressionable. That policeman, Nästman, he was the one who had boorishly blurted out his belief that Justine brought bad luck wherever she went. Can a Swedish policeman really say something like that? It was true that many tragic and inexplicable events had taken place since Justine returned home. But to give her the blame! Kicking someone already down!

Hans Peter massaged the skin around his temples. Closed his eyes, tried to relax. So he was dead, now, that Nästman. He got his punishment at last, Hans Peter thought childishly. Anger still gnawed at him. It was beginning to subside but he wasn't tired; he would be totally unable to sleep. He filled the sink and washed the dishes. Then he went around the hotel, wiping up any spills that Ariadne had missed.

Shortly after he'd met Justine, Flora Dalvik, Justine's stepmother, had died. She had lived in a nursing home in Råcksta and had been paralyzed after a stroke. Sadly, she had passed just as Justine had brought her home to visit for the first time since the stroke. Not too surprising that Justine felt guilty about that.

"It was too much for her emotionally. I should have figured that out beforehand, idiot that I am. Old, sick people are too delicate. I just wanted to make her happy for a while; all the days are the same at the nursing home. And the nurses, they all praised me when they should have warned me that it could be too much for her. They said, just think, if every one of our people had someone like you, coming for visits, taking them out on excursions. I wanted to make her happy for a little while, Hans Peter, and she just sat there and died!"

Again he would have to comfort her.

"Don't you think it might have been better for Flora anyway, to die in her own home? Surrounded by her own things, everything she was used to, secure."

"I don't know!" Justine cried.

"Well, think of the alternative. A sterile and strange hospital environment. Overworked and stressed people around her, tired and worn out. She got to be with you, instead, her closest relative. Isn't that much better?"

It took a long time before he found out the entire truth, a long time until Justine began to tell him about all the abuse her stepmother had heaped upon her while she was growing up. That old bag was some kind of sadist. That life must have influenced the child Justine in a negative way.

Inside, he determined that he was going to help her, listen to her, encourage her to leave all her terrible traumas behind her. Once long ago, he'd studied theology and philosophy. He had talents in caring for souls; people had always interested him. And now, here was the woman he loved.

Bad luck often comes in threes. A proverb that probably had a ring of truth to it. Around the same time that Flora Dalvik died, Justine's former classmate, Berit Assarsson, disappeared. A mystery written up in the papers. Unfortunately, she had visited Justine just before she vanished. This meant that the police, just as Jaglander had boasted, had kept an eye on her. As if Justine hadn't suffered enough! How much can one person take?

She was increasingly unstable right now. She'd turned inward and was afraid of something which he didn't really understand. She couldn't talk about it; she would clam up and hide inside herself whenever he asked about it. Her fear came in waves, he noticed. For long periods of time, she felt well; she was happy and full of confidence. Then she could sink into the darkness. He had tried to get her to consider visiting a doctor, but when she was most depressed, she had difficulty listening. And when she was happy and strong, there was no need to see a psychologist.

It's kind of like living with an alcoholic, he thought. And somewhere deep inside him, he felt relief that he had this job to absorb his concern, because it gave him the chance to catch his breath.

A RUSTLING MOVEMENT in the leaves. Someone. Someone.

With a creeping, slow movement, she walked out onto the balcony. Her feet were naked; she leaned over the railing, brushed her hair behind her ear. A distinct noise down there somewhere, a branch which snapped, broke. And a terrible noise from the bird. Justine had never heard him sound like this before.

She yelled right out into the darkness: "Hello! Anybody there?"

She tried to see the entire yard at the same time, and called again:

"Who are you? If you want something, come out!"

She heard the bird hiss, eject short peeps. Flapping of wings. She heard how he kept striking them against the net until they bled. Birds can panic, often in a group but also when alone. Panicking is part of their nature, just as it is with herd animals like horses or grazing antelope on the savanna. Instinct tells them to flee without thinking. She would have to try to calm him down.

"I'm coming," she called out and jumped back seeing the reflection of the moon in the water; it was as if it wanted to blind her.

She turned and went into the bedroom, pulled on long pants and a sweater, fell on her knees inside the closet pulling out everything she saw in boxes until she found the scarf, the same scarf she'd used when she brought the bird home. His former owner had suggested that she let him clip the wings before transporting him, so that the bird wouldn't get frightened and hurt himself. Justine refused. She was hit by the idea to take the scarf she was wearing around her neck and use it to wrap the bird. The soft cloth against his feathers calmed him.

She took her purse and made sure she had both wallet and keys. She turned on the lights in all the rooms before she opened the outer door. She held her umbrella with the point straight out.

The wind was still. She stepped onto the porch and listened. Even if she heard nothing now, she knew someone was out there. Her certainty made it hard for her to breathe. It seemed as if all the small hairs on her neck and back were straight up.

"I'm coming now," she called, but it sounded like she was cawing. "I'm coming to get you now!"

The grass was wet and rough. She imagined slugs, those long, brown slugs. She could step on one and the thought filled her with disgust. She usually killed them, snipped them in half, but that was in the daylight when she knew what she was doing. *Decapitate*, she thought. *Caput* is Latin for head. A wave of nausea gripped her stomach; she thought she might throw up.

Shoes, she thought, she had to protect her feet with shoes. So unprotected without shoes. With fumbling hands, she unlocked the door and there were her sandals, her safe, well-used summer sandals. She stuck her feet into them and snapped them shut. When she stepped back into the garden a second time, she sensed movement by the hill and the crunch of footsteps on gravel. Not fleeing, but determined. Someone had been waiting in her yard but had now decided to leave it.

The feeling that she was about to faint increased.

The bird flapped around in the aviary in blind, crazy fear. When he heard her coming, he fell to the ground and sat there with gaping beak. She saw his eyes roll wildly in the moonlight.

"It's just me," she murmured, and all at once she wished that the bird had a name; it would have been easier to sing his name like a lullabye and quiet him. She'd forgotten to ask his former owner and then let it be; she didn't have the ability to formulate a name to fit. Those days it was just the two of them—she and the bird. There wasn't any room for fear.

She unlatched the door to the aviary and squatted on her heels. She used her forefinger to stroke his flat head; he opened his beak wider and hissed. It looked like he needed a few moments to recognize her. Then he relaxed.

When she lifted him up, fresh guano covered her arm; his fear had made his bowels loose. She sat next to him on the grass, let him sniff the shawl which had once brought him home. His cocoon, his womb. Carefully, she wrapped him in the cloth and held him against her chest as if he were a baby. He lay with his eyes half-closed, his little heart beating fast.

"We're going now," she whispered. "We're not staying here any longer."

She held him tightly with one arm and held the umbrella out before her like a lance with the other. Behind her, the waters of Lake Mälaren glittered like small white knives; the wind was waking up, and she could smell the mire.

She walked toward the car, thought again that she could just make out someone, a form squatting by the lilac bushes, and she jumped so much she bit the inside of her cheek. The taste of iron, something syrupy thick against her tongue. Her purse slid; the straps fell off her shoulder. She had to jangle it and click it open. With the umbrella stuck under her arm, she drove her fingers into her purse. She found the car keys, her thumb on the control, *click, click*. She whipped the door open, placed the bird on the passenger seat, threw down the umbrella, and sank behind the wheel. Only when the engine started did she begin to feel strong again.

It was ten after two in the morning. Justine drove up Sandviksvägen and turned left on Lövstavägen. All the houses were dark. She turned on the high beams and increased her speed. The bird lay on his side. His beak was half open. He stared at her with one round eye, but he was quiet, back to his senses. She met a taxi or two, but it was otherwise empty on the roads. Maybe she ought to have called Hans Peter and warned him. No point in that now. She would soon be there.

She managed to find a parking spot on Tegnérgatan between a city jeep and an old VW. It was tight, but she could still squeeze her car into it. She felt calm and collected. She lifted up the bird and blew on his head, murmuring comforting words. He gave out a few small sounds but was no longer in a panic. She decided to leave her umbrella in the car.

Hans Peter opened the door immediately. He hadn't gone to sleep. His face seemed pale and worn out.

"Hi," she said. "I came after all."

He took a step backwards as if he didn't recognize her.

"Hi . . . ?"

"Hans Peter!" she said loudly.

"What's that? Did you bring the bird with you?"

"Yes . . ."

"Justine, what's going on with you?"

"Something scared him," she said. She wanted to press her body against him, breathe in his scent and warmth. "I told you. There was something in the garden. He was completely panic stricken."

Hans Peter's eyes had red edges. She stroked his chin; it seemed to her that he pulled away.

"What's going on with you?" she asked. "Has something happened?"

He straightened his back; more normal, but there was a strange tone in his voice.

"Was it really all that smart to bring the bird into the city?"

"He was so frightened; he was hysterical. You should have seen him. His fear was contagious."

She began to tremble again.

"Justine," he said, but he did not embrace her.

He went to get a coffee cup which he filled with water and gave to the bird. At first, the bird hissed, but then stuck his beak into the water and drank with a loud clucking sound. Hans Peter sighed.

"We can't have him here."

She shook her head.

"It's not dangerous."

"But think of the guests! They'll have a cow if a big wild bird starts flying over their heads. He'll scare the shit out of them. The hotel will get a bad reputation, especially nowadays with all those bird flu fears . . . people have died of that, you know."

"Maybe in Vietnam, but not here in Sweden."

She decided to sit on the cot behind the counter, the same cot where she'd slept with Hans Peter many times, her back against his chest and stomach. She gently unwrapped the scarf. The cloth was spotted with blood and guano. The bird shook himself and seemed about to fall over. He took a few careful steps over the blanket, but he didn't fly. A broken feather dangled toward the floor. She carefully touched his fluffed wings.

"He doesn't want to fly. He's in pain."

"Justine," Hans Peter said again.

She turned her face toward him, ready to cry.

"All right, all right, we'll take care of it," he said hastily. "He'll have to stay back here and we'll have to keep the door shut."

"Thanks."

He sank next to her on the cot.

"Hans Peter," she said, "you are so kind. I love you."

"What do you think was going on?"

"Someone was in the yard."

"An animal."

"No."

"Did you see anyone?"

She nodded.

"What did you see?"

"It wasn't clear . . . but I got frightened."

He put his arms around her shoulders.

"I'll make you something warm. Hot tea, maybe. Would you like that?"

He was totally back to normal. She leaned back on the pillow, drew the blanket around her body. Watched him fill the tea kettle with water.

"Hans Peter," she said.

He was standing with his back to her.

"Are you angry that we came?"

He didn't answer and she decided not to repeat the question.

DARKNESS ALL AROUND HER. With great effort, Ariadne got to her knees, searched for the switch. No. Now she remembered. Tommy had screwed out the bulb. It was the last thing he did before he shut the door to the pantry. Her fingernails searched along the smooth wall, sliding down. She reached the door handle and pushed it down. Locked.

He'd left afterwards. She'd heard the car start and she hadn't heard it return. *Christa.* The name stabbed her insides. The whole time it went on, she tried to be silent, not scream, not worry her girl. Christa probably knew what was happening anyway. She had an unusual ability to understand the atmosphere.

Ariadne had washed the dishes and cleaned up the kitchen. She dropped a glass right onto the hard stone floor. The sound was harsh. Ariadne was creeping on the floor looking for shards when Christa entered the kitchen.

"Watch out, don't walk in here; you can get glass in your foot."

"What are you doing, Mamma?"

"Don't come in here. Go to your room and wait."

But it was too late. Christa gave out a short howl, stood on one foot and there was blood on the stone floor.

"Don't you think you've damaged her enough!"

Tommy's shoe hit her in the tailbone. She turned and fell on the floor by the stove. The pain made her grimace, but she said nothing, didn't make a sound.

She kept on picking up the shards of glass and then vacuumed up the rest after she had led her girl to the bathroom and cleaned her wound. Christa kept crying out loud, making a great deal of noise blubbering through all her snot. Tommy yelled at Christa as well: "Jesus Christ, shut up."

Yes, it was that kind of a day, that kind of an evening. She knew all his lines; she'd heard them over and over and they were always the same. He could be calm for weeks, charging up while everything appeared calm and totally normal, and yet in the end the explosion would always break out. In him it was a kind of illness, a boil that burst its pus.

It was already beginning while they were eating dinner. Christa spilled peas onto her lap. She was sitting there, jabbing with her fork, twirling it, making noise. Tommy's jaw hardened.

"Can't you help her! Don't you see she's not getting a thing onto her damned fork? Can't you find easier food to serve her than peas?"

Ariadne got up and got a spoon, placed the handle into Christa's hand, led it to the plate.

"Here, the spoon will help make it easier."

Tommy's fist hit the table so hard that the plates jumped.

"Table manners!" he yelled.

Christa's arms sank into her lap.

"Sixteen years old and eating like a child! When will she be able to act like a human being?"

Ariadne made the mistake of starting to argue. She should have known better by now; she ought to know that talking back only made things worse.

"Peas are not that easy to eat," she muttered. "Christa can't help it, the peas are so small."

"Then why in the hell do you put peas on the table? Why don't you think of something else since you spend an eternity shopping?"

Ariadne sat stiffly and heavily in her chair, not daring to move, to change her position in the slightest.

"Look at her!" Tommy commanded. "Look at her! She looks like hell! Sticky as a pig around her mouth; potatoes and sauce in her hair. A sixteen-year-old girl should be one of the finest things nature created. Blooming, lively and wonderful. Do you think that's what happened here? Aren't you proud, Ariadne? Aren't you proud of the human being you've created? And Christa, do you realize that it's your dear mother's fault that you can't see? Do you realize that? Answer me! Do you realize that?"

Christa's hand searched the table, found her glass and gripped it hard. He was ready for her. She'd done it before, gripped it so tightly that it broke and milk and blood spilled out between her fingers. With a jerk, he grabbed the glass away from her and put it on the counter behind him.

"Now we're going to eat, dammit!"

She had been surprised by the initial phase of her pregnancy. Who knew that it could be so difficult? She didn't have any friends, any women her own age to talk to in this new country. And she didn't want to say anything to her mother, not yet. It was too early; there still were a number of things that could go wrong.

Tommy was gentle and full of patience. He made her toast and tea, which he brought to her and placed on the nightstand.

"It'll pass," he said. "It's difficult in the mornings, but it will pass."

He laughed and stroked her cheek. His sisters had already had a number of children.

She lay there with her neck straight and without a pillow. If she moved the smallest bit, she would vomit. The smell of the toast wafted into her nostrils, and she wanted to ask him to take away the tray, but she didn't have the energy. He was so kind and thoughtful; she didn't want to hurt his feelings, make him feel like an idiot. This would bring about a paralyzing crying bout and exaggerated sentimentality.

"It'll pass," the doctor said when she came to his office. "Do you understand my Swedish?"

He spoke slowly and carefully, and when she didn't understand him, he used pencil and paper. He took his time.

"I've been in your country," he confessed to her. "I'd like to buy a house there on an island. A little white house with warm walls. In fact, I've already picked one out."

He opened a drawer and pulled out a photograph. It was not her island, but it had a similar name. She turned her head aside and started to cry. Again the doctor told her that things will get better.

"It is completely normal to have morning sickness, but it will end. Try staying in bed for another hour if you can. Don't stress yourself; take it easy."

He put his hand on hers; just a few minutes ago he'd been looking inside her, opened her vagina with cold metal, hurt her.

"Everything looks fine," he said. "You're in the tenth week."

Ten weeks of nausea! If only it would stop! Pregnancy is not an illness. It is totally normal and a woman is made for bearing and giving birth to her child.

"Take it easy in the mornings, and before you know it, you'll be feeling good again." He repeated this as she was about to go, making sure she understood what he was saying.

Still, the nausea wasn't morning sickness; it was morning, noon and night sickness; it never let up. A corrosive scorch when she swallowed, waves of nausea at any smell. And everything had a smell: the dust on the armchairs that Tommy inherited, the cloth in their seats, the soap in the bathroom, her fingernails whenever she clipped them, and even *Dagens Nyheter*, the morning newspaper, which she stubbornly insisted on trying to read.

She tried to hold her breath, to breathe through her mouth, but fragments of smells would still reach her, turning her inside out as she bent over to vomit.

She hadn't gotten a job yet. You needed to know Swedish to get a job. She spent her days in their apartment but finally she couldn't stand being cooped up any longer; the walls were closing in on her. She filled her pockets with plastic bags and fled outside.

The wind would help. She stayed away from the outdoor hot dog stands and the entrances to the fashionable shops. She wandered along the sidewalks. The cold April daylight was painful; the days had midday thaws, but the nights were freezing. She would be washed with homesickness, longing for what had been, loss, the time when she had her entire life before her; right now she felt as if her life was starting to run out. It was the kind of situation that made her an invalid, which didn't end even as the months went by, even as anyone could see from her body what was going on with her.

It was time for her second doctor's visit, and by now she knew more Swedish. The doctor became concerned when he saw her blood values.

"Are you still nauseous? Can you really still be having morning sickness?"

As if she were lying; as if she were exaggerating.

He prescribed some small white pills and told her to be extra careful with her oral hygiene. That was it.

"The pills will make you drowsy and tired, but that probably won't matter much since it seems as if you have nothing which demands concentration. You are a housewife, aren't you?"

The miracle happened, the pills worked. They cured her, made her feel normal again. It was a blessing which even relieved Tommy. Her weakness had been getting to him. Ruined his mood.

Ariadne called her mother and told her the good news. Her mother's voice was thick with emotion.

"Is it true, my little dolly?"

"Yes, yes, it's true. And you'll have to come here soon and help us. Tommy has bought a house. We're going to move there in the summer. He says that there is room for a grandmother, too."

One evening, Tommy opened the medicine cabinet and found the pills. He came out into the kitchen with a serious look on his face.

"Ariadne, this medication has your name on it."

The floor heaved.

"Yes?"

"This is medication."

"It was for my nausea. From before."

"Can a doctor really have told you to take medicine even though you're expecting a child?"

She nodded, saying nothing.

"Doesn't he know that any medication can give the child fetal injuries?"

She looked at him with fright.

"But . . . but he just said . . ."

"There was a kid on the farm where we lived, his hands grew straight out of his body as he had no arms. His mother had taken medicine while she was pregnant. Do you think he had a happy life?"

"I didn't know," she said. "I'll throw them away."

"How long have you been taking them?"

"Ever since I started to feel better."

"How long was that? A number of weeks?"

"Yes," she said wildly. "Many weeks."

There wasn't much room in the pantry, so she barely had a place to sit. She drew up her knees and leaned against the radiator, but she was heavy and swollen; her whole body ached. He often hit her with the side of his hand on places where it couldn't be seen. Sometimes he got so angry he made mistakes. Like yesterday evening, when she'd moved away in the wrong direction so that most of the blows landed on her face. He had been extremely angry that time, so angry that he hadn't managed to regret what he'd done yet.

She sat there in the darkness and tried not to cry. Christa would never hear her give up and start crying, never hear her despair. Her girl usually disappeared into her room. Christa had only asked once: "Mamma, why did you take those pills?"

Her face was defenseless and empty. She stood holding something; yes, it was her hair tie. She'd pulled it out of her ponytail so that her hair hung freely in a wave. Ariadne prepared to answer, but Christa continued: "Is it true what Pappa says . . . that I could have . . . been able to see?"

"No," she whispered.

"But Pappa says so."

"Pappa is sad. Sadness shows many ways. Sometimes hard to understand. Pappa wanted you to have your eyes. That's why it's like this."

Her girl threw her head back so that her thick messy hair swept behind her. Her eyelashes were dark, like tight palm fronds. The whites of her eyes glimmered beneath them.

Ariadne took her arm, held her close.

"I'm sorry, too. I'm sad and sorry, despairingly sad," she said, roughly. "One thing you must know. Whatever Pappa thinks, it was not the pills."

Tommy had made a great deal of commotion, of course. Contacted the laboratory that made the drugs, threatened a lawsuit and to bring in the media. However, the only answer that they gave him was that there was no evidence that this medicine was connected to any damage to a fetus. Tommy refused to accept their declaration.

OF COURSE! The thought hit Tommy the moment he reached the roundabout at Brommaplan. Drag the lake! He had read all the files on Berit Assarsson's disappearance, but damn it all if there hadn't been a single mention of dragging the lake! Was it possible that no one thought of it at the time? Good old Nästman, he hadn't been all that with it at the last, probably because of his illness.

Tommy had met Nästman when Nästman was at Rikskrim, the national criminal investigation office. His older colleague had a sympathetic way about him: he listened to people, didn't use that tough police jargon which the older guys used with the new guys. At times, they ate lunch together. Nästman was already showing signs of his illness, but no one understood yet how serious it was. He often talked about Justine Dalvik and wanted to know what Tommy thought of the matter. This surprised Tommy and made him happy.

During Nästman's last few weeks, Tommy had often gone to visit him at the hospice in Stockholm. Nästman had a large and rather pleasant room and he had photos of his sons and their wives or girlfriends on his nightstand. Taped on the wall was a drawing of a large centipede with lanky legs. *To Grandpa,* a grown-up had written: *Get well soon and come and play with me. Love and kisses, Malin.* Tommy sat looking at the drawing, and sorrow overcame him again. His own Christa would never make a drawing; it was a part of life that she would never have, and it would not be the only one.

Hans Nästman didn't say much by then. He mostly lay on the bed with his eyes shut. Now and then, his eyelids would open and he would try to fix his gaze on the person sitting by his bedside. At times he was even able to squeeze out a smile. Tommy held his hand; there wasn't all that much to say. Sometimes a young nurse came by and made sure that everything was as it should be. Of course it was. There was nothing that cutie could do, nothing anyone could do to change the situation.

Thank God, Nästman didn't seem to have much pain; he probably got as much morphine as he needed. The most difficult thing about visiting was the smell, a smell of rotting and excrement. Tommy always had to breathe through his mouth those first minutes. He tried not to let it show. There were always flowers on the table from the colleagues at the police station, but it appeared that Tommy was the only one who came to visit. Some days he found Nästman's wife, Katarina, sitting there. She was good looking for a woman over sixty. Thin, dark hair done up, strong lipstick. Tommy remembered her face during the funeral, how she looked up at the ceiling of the chapel, her wide, empty eyes. He wondered what happened to her afterwards. Did she find a new relationship? Or did she not want anyone after her Hasse. Maybe he should give her a call and see how she was doing these days. Often it was long after the funeral that the great loneliness would occur.

It would be a feather in his cap if he would be able to solve the case and put that wealthy man's daughter behind bars. But the case was dropped, to Tommy's irritation, much too early. Now, many years later, he had gotten approval to take up the case again from the cold case department's leader. And damn it all, if that wasn't just what he was going to do.

From the files, Berit Assarsson disappeared right after she had gone to visit Justine Dalvik to talk about a bullying situation when they were children. Dalvik had said in her statement that Assarsson had stayed for about an hour, had drunk a number of glasses of wine, and then had left the house. No one had seen her after that.

It was understandable that it took a while before the police began to search in earnest. They didn't have all the resources in the world, and often people disappeared only to show up again a short while later. Tommy had gone through the files, but there were still a number of details to clear up. Were there any footprints near the edge of the water that day? Had it snowed? What about the ice? If it had been above freezing, the ice may have started to melt during the days before the police were on the job. He'd have to check with SMHI and after that get permission to drag the lake.

Nästman suspected Justine Dalvik; he'd told him that much. But there was nothing they could find to link her to a crime. What was the most likely thing to have happened? Did Dalvik just go nuts and kill her former classmate? All right. Not out of the realm of possibility. Hans Nästman had thought of that, but he didn't have the strength to keep going along those lines. On paper, he was still working full time, but he had already begun radiation therapy, was gone a lot, was not able to concentrate.

Well, who could have concentrated under those circumstances, Tommy thought. It gnawed at him; it made him uncomfortable. Tommy was afraid of becoming sick and dependant on other people. His greatest fear was finding a lump under his skin, a hard little knot that wasn't supposed to be there. Every evening he checked his body's softest spots and sometimes he found something which he insisted the doctors remove, even though they told him it was nothing more than fat deposits. Benign, no threat. But you never could know if they might turn malignant, could you? One of his uncles had gotten a tumor and one of his legs had to be amputated. It hadn't helped. The cancer spread throughout his body and he died in great pain. No one had told Tommy that cancer was an inherited disease, but he still couldn't get any guarantees that it wasn't.

He drove past the Wallenberg cemetery site on its large hill with cypress trees standing as somber bodyguards along the path to the graves. Tommy was tortured by the thought of death, or rather, thoughts about the end of life. No one sensed this about him; his colleagues thought he was a man without fear, full of fun and stubborn as sin.

Nästman had not been the only one on the Dalvik-Assarsson case. Still, it appeared that no one had really put the time and energy into the case it needed. From pure curiosity and on his free time, Tommy had been out to Hässelby and had poked around. The Dalvik place was a stone building, high and narrow, right on the waterfront. No clear place to observe it. Strange, really, that a great industrialist like her father chose such a mediocre dwelling. Sure, it was close to the water, but that house was nothing to boast about. It was isolated; in principle anything could have happened in that garden. Though it was winter when Assarsson disappeared, of course. If Dalvik murdered Assarsson, she hardly could have dug a grave. Not there and then at any rate.

What could she have done, though? The thought had been nagging him for quite a while. Could she have cut up the body and frozen it? No. Her freezer wasn't big enough for that, Nästman and his men had checked that out at the time.

Driven it away? Stuffed it in the trunk of a car and dumped it in a suitable spot? It would have been heavy, but if Dalvik had enough adrenaline at the time she probably could have managed it.

No. They would have found the body during the past six years. Somebody taking a walk with their dog.

He thought of the garbage transfer station at Lövsta, outside Hässelby. All the large heaps of slag, those large containers. A wonderful place for terminal storage. But she still would have to have cut up the body, and butchering a body into its component pieces was a difficult skill to master. And could a woman even do it? Tommy had never met Justine Dalvik; there was no direct reason for it. He knew nothing about her size, her strength, her psychology. But he was going to find out. The statute of limitations for murder was twenty-five years.

Lake Mälaren with its dark waters. More than one corpse lay rolling on the bottom. He thought he'd go to Malmgren, the leader of preliminary investigations, and suggest a dragging of the lake. Maybe someone would protest that Assarsson should have floated to the top by now, or gotten caught in an anchor or a wobbler. Talk about lack of resources. No, he'd wait for the right opportunity. And as soon as it came, the minute he got the green light, he'd blow the case wide open.

Tommy drove underneath the carport of his own home and parked the car. The windows were empty and dark. With a yawn, he got out and locked the door and stretched, drew the cool night air into his lungs. Nice that it wasn't so hot anymore, nor all that dark, though a few clouds slipped past the moon. Maybe rain was on the way. The field stretched before him with bushes as hulking shadows. A roebuck called, or maybe it was the howl of a dog?

He placed his shoes neatly side by side on the hallway floor. The heel of his foot was sore. He should have thought about putting on a moleskin as a precaution, as his shoes were practically brand new. Why do new shoes always create blisters?

He tiptoed into the kitchen. The kitchen counter gleamed; the floor was free from splinters of glass. Just to be sure, he squatted down and examined the floor in all directions. He turned his ear to the hallway. No sound. He opened the refrigerator and took out a bottle of Calvados and poured a small glass of the brownish yellow drink. Not much, just enough to have the taste on his tongue, to enjoy the aroma a short while before he went to bed.

He opened the door to Christa's room a crack and peeked into the sultry darkness. Calm, even breathing. She was sleeping. He was gripped by the thought of going into the room, bending over her pillow and burrowing his nose into her black locks, damp from sweat and sleep. *I love you, my child, I love you.* He could get so irritated by her sometimes; she was so clumsy. He really shouldn't; she couldn't help it. For a time, he tried to take her running with him. He thought if he held her hand, if they ran on wide pathways, and if she made sure to lift her legs high enough, it would work, but no. She didn't want to. She didn't refuse; she seldom did when he suggested something, but she moved so stiffly and mincingly that she looked like a marionette. The whole thing looked pathetic.

This daughter brought nothing but sorrow. And there hadn't been any more children, either. It wasn't his fault. He'd gotten Ariadne pregnant three times, but each time she'd miscarried. Her fault, her uterus was to blame with its constant, almost continuous menstruations. He hadn't imagined that marriage would turn out like this. Of course it served no purpose to think like this; no one was really to blame for how he or she was created.

She was a good woman, in spite of everything. He knew that he was often unjust. When those blinding rages came over him, he could get so upset that it seemed his heart was shaking. Ariadne was sometimes compliant and sometimes completely crazy; he saw his daughter as a copy of her mother, her large, padded body. She turned fat; it was in her genes, a result of her culture. A woman was supposed to be hefty in Greece. Ariadne's mother had been just like that, too. She probably still was fat. They hadn't seen her for a long time, and just as well. Ariadne got strange when her mother was visiting. They sat at the kitchen table, heads together, tight, identically fat; he couldn't understand what they were saying.

He sipped his drink, added a few drops to his glass. He saw the key to the pantry high up on the bookshelf. A bit of it was sticking out over the edge. A sudden anxiety made him hurry. It was so strangely silent in the house. He reached up for the key, stuck it in the lock, turned it.

When he opened the door, Ariande fell out onto the hallway floor.

THE *MAVERIK* FROM GRONINGEN was so large that it was at the limit of what could pass through the locks, measuring 135 meters from stem to stern. She was a refrigerated vessel that brought fruit from South America and cargo from Supra on her return. There was always tension in the observation tower when this enormous ship was entering.

It was just after ten o'clock at night. Jill had managed to sleep for a few hours, but still didn't feel rested. That was one of the major drawbacks of working shifts: trying to sleep during the day when the rest of the world was awake and active. Some workers in the neighboring apartment building had been busy drilling, and the sound pierced her brain. She felt dizzy and a bit unsteady as she biked to work for her night shift.

It had rained while she was sleeping, but now it had stopped. The air was clear. In spite of her helmet, her hair had turned wavy and ugly because of the humidity. She dragged a comb through her hair and searched in her purse for her mirror. The Coast Guard called. The light in Norsborg's lighthouse had gone out.

"All right, I'll check on it," she said tiredly. She checked the list of all the lighthouses and found out that that particular lighthouse was not so vital, so she didn't need to make a navigation warning. She yawned, got up, and walked to the window. The *Odin*, a Pal Line vessel with home port in Hamburg, had just entered the space between the lock gates. Down on the quay, Fred walked holding the line as if he were walking a massive dog. The pilot was waiting there, wearing his shiny yellow jacket. A pilot apprentice was waiting next to him. When the vessel was tied into place, they climbed on board and walked up the six flights to the bridge. Jill waved, but wasn't sure whether they saw her.

It looked to be a hectic night ahead. The *Maverik* had one hour until she reached the locks and was going to meet the Danish *Dura Bulk* at Sällskapsholmen. Opening the E4 bridge was planned. But now both pilots had conferred and decided to meet north of Lina instead, since it would be too difficult to wait and hold the colossal vessels still in the narrow passage. The problem, however, was that it would now take longer for the *Maverik* to reach the E4 bridge and the railroad bridge right next to it. Both bridges had to be opened at the same time. The opening times were dictated by Swedish Railways and were even published in their commuter train timetables.

The water in the canal was shiny as wax. She watched the *Odin* slide out of the locks and disappear down the canal. Fred was still on the quay; he was talking into the speaker to a pleasure boat which was waiting next to one of the gates. Probably on the way to a guest harbor.

"Come in if you want to go through the locks." Fred had to call a few times. People on pleasure boats were sometimes surprisingly confused, as if the voice coming from the speaker was part of a candid camera joke. Finally the little boat slipped inside, shyly and ashamed, like it didn't want to be discovered. The lights glowed green in the darkness. Fred leaned over and took the 140-crown fee, the cost of leaving Lake Mälaren. Shortly after that, she heard his footsteps in the stairwell. He didn't like to take the elevator since he'd once been stuck in an elevator and had to sit and wait for hours.

"I always thought I was the kind of person who could keep my cool," he told them. "But I'll be damned, you should have seen me in that steel cage; I got so goddamn panicky."

Jill thought about Fred's wife, wondered how things were going with their divorce plans. Maybe she'd ask about it later, once the rush was over. She liked Fred. He was stable and secure, never was provoked or stressed. It was like he was made for this job. It was hard to see him so unhappy. He's gotten older, she thought. He no longer had spring in his step, his shoulders drooped, and his head had sunk into his neck bones. He was old, really; he didn't have all that many years to go until retirement. But the changes seemed so obvious.

Now Fred was standing by the monitors and opened the remote-controlled Mälar Bridge so that the *Odin* could pass. On the screen, she glimpsed at the growing line of cars, knew that there was cursing and growling behind the wheels. These days people had trouble waiting even a few minutes.

When the pilot from the *Maverik* called and said that he'd arrived at Sällskapsholmen, Fred opened the Mälar bridge and then both he and Nisse went down to the quay. On the monitor, Jill observed how the vessel passed through the bridge bascules and shortly after that how it slid through the canal, silent and white as a ghost ship. The prow reflected in the water. Slowly, slowly, the *Maverik* glided, to prevent knocking against anything; there was just a few centimeters' room between the gates of the locks. Jill stood at the window and watched her colleagues, how they gestured and talked into their hand-held radio communicators. The pilot needed help to see if the vessel was completely inside.

Just then, her cell phone rang. She had the German group Rammstein's *Du hast* as a ring tone, and Tor had chided her for that: "You're not a teenager any longer, Rammstein!" Her feelings weren't hurt; she took it as a pleasant jibe, the kind of thing he needed to do; in fact, both of them needed the banter. During their entire vacation, she had hoped that someone would call her cell phone. It happened once, when they touched down in Tromsø. The Norwegian telephone company had left her a text message welcoming her to Norway. For the rest of the time, her cell phone was completely silent.

At last she managed to pull her cell phone from her purse.

"Jill Kylén," she said, using her business voice.

"Am I bothering you?" It was Tor. She felt happiness spread through her body.

"Not at all, I can talk for a few moments, but things are a bit crazy here at the moment. How are you doing? Have you recovered from the trip?"

His voice sounded both sluggish and tense.

"It was so awful . . . you see, I was dreaming."

"A dream?"

"Yes. I'd just fallen asleep. And it woke me up."

"Yes?"

"I was standing at the waterfront, and a bit out in the water; I saw something floating."

He fell silent.

"And?" she asked slowly. "What happened then?"

"I knew I had to go into the water; it was necessary, I had to see what . . . who . . . it was."

"A human being, then?"

"Yes," he said tonelessly. "It was a human being."

She waited.

"It was as if my feet sank into the sand; the sand filled my shoes, held me down. I tried to lift my feet, and now my muscles ache all along my legs. I mean, in reality. Do you understand me, Jill?" He raised his voice. "My muscles ache as if it really happened."

She swallowed.

"You must have gotten a cramp," she said. "A cramp while you were asleep."

"Maybe."

"It does happen that a person can cramp up while sleeping."

"Maybe so."

"What happened then?"

He cleared his throat and began to cough, that unpleasant smoker's cough which came right after he'd been sleeping. She waited silently. He managed to breathe and continued: "I heard a voice behind me," he said, "and when I turned around, she was there. You know, that woman."

Jill's office telephone began to ring. She took a deep breath, felt as if she couldn't get enough air.

"Who are you talking about?"

"That woman, Justine Dalvik."

Six rings, seven.

"Tor, I must . . ."

"I understand."

"I'll call you back later; are you home?"

"I'm sorry, Jill. I shouldn't have called and disturbed you at work."

"It's okay. I'll call you back," she said, but he'd already hung up.

"Damn it," she said, as she lifted the receiver of her office phone, but it was too late.

At the same time, the pilot of the *Odin* called: "We passed Fläsklösa five minutes ago."

"Roger, *Odin*," she replied, while at the same time tapping her cell phone to retrieve Tor's numbers from the list.

It took an hour and a half before she was actually able to call him. Tor didn't answer, and she guessed he'd gone back to sleep. Jill didn't dare call again; it would be too much to wake him, that is, if he were really sleeping. Things quieted down around two in the morning. She decided to lie down on the sofa in the break room, her jacket as a blanket. She was freezing and felt slightly ill.

Dawn began to break around five in the morning. By then, she was sitting in the extra chair by the window, her legs propped up on the table. The air-conditioner hummed. Nisse got up and looked out toward the pedestrian path which ran beside the canal.

"The can collectors have arrived," he announced. They both saw how an elderly man with plastic bags rummaged in the garbage cans.

"Anyone want coffee?" asked Fred.

"Thanks, sure, if you're getting it." Jill stepped out onto the little balcony and took deep breaths of the fresh, morning air. A lone car drove past on the way to the city center.

Certainty surged through her, certain knowledge.

Justine, she thought. She realized what she had to do, both for her own sake and for Tor's. She would have to go and see that woman.

AFTERWARDS, THERE WAS ALWAYS THE RECONCILIA-TION. This had its own pattern as well. But this time, Tommy had difficulty waking her. Ariadne hadn't been sleeping; sleep was impossible in that cramped pantry. The space was filled to capacity and poor in oxygen. She seemed to be in some kind of unconsciousness, where she could somehow intuit his rising anxiety. She was suspended in lethargy derived from the pain in her limbs and muscles, from sitting curled up in such an unnatural position. Her blood had flowed to her feet; parts of her body had become numb. He was touching her chin, trying to bring her back to life, turning her head back and forth.

There was something about his smell, a chemical smell of fear in the cold sweat now running from his palms. She recognized it; it was the same as last time, and the time before, the times he hit her especially hard.

But he'd never treated her as badly as he had last night.

This was what she thought as she was trapped in the pantry, stuffed with all the things that had no place in the rest of the house. There was neither attic nor basement, so boxes, Christmas decorations, the extra table and chairs, winter shoes, an old computer, as well as the dismantled crib from Christa's babyhood were crammed together here.

There was a pulsing pain in her jaw; she listened for a sound, for the car; she searched around her mouth with the tip of her tongue, and suddenly something hard fell into her hand. One of her teeth.

Then she cried for the first time that evening and fell unconscious.

He carried her to the bed, but he was no longer strong; his muscles had lost some of their power, and he took short pauses. He dropped her onto the sheets, unbent her arms and legs.

"Ariadne, answer me!"

At this point, she was the stronger one; but he didn't know it, only she did. She felt nothing of triumph or happiness.

"Do you want anything to drink? Are you thirsty? I'll get something for you."

Her mouth was closed shut and his hands wandered all over her body erratically, searching for buttonholes, unbuttoning her clothing. He kept the lamps dark. She knew that. It was always like that because he could not bear to see the black and blue marks on her body; he certainly wasn't the one who made them, not a loving husband like himself.

The mattress was so soft it kept her from moving. He took off her sweater and her bra; he left her panties on. He wrapped her in the sheets. If only he could wrap her like a corpse in a shroud, if only she no longer had to wake up, if only that day would come. His violence against her kept increasing, from a few punches and slaps to pure and simple beatings. How could he explain her death to his work colleagues? Oh, he'd certainly find a way out of it with a lie. Say that a psychopath had attacked her and he found her bleeding on the front steps. Would they then cut her up and look for old injuries? Would they interrogate Christa?

The feeling of a glass cooled her lower lip. His arm under her neck.

"Try and drink something, you'll feel better, my poor little friend; try and open your mouth now."

A strong taste against her gums and tongue, something alcoholic.

Where is Christa? Is my girl asleep? Where is she?

If she should die, if he hit her so much that she died, Christa would then be all alone with her father. No. That could not happen. She swallowed; it went down her throat. She forced herself to open her eyes. He leaned over her like a hulking shadow. She could not make out his features, but she read his body language and saw that he was tired. He was tired of being the punisher; now she would have to embrace him quickly and forgive him. He was going to take off his jeans and white T-shirt and creep into bed next to her. He would lie tightly behind her and pull her close to him; she would feel his member, weak and sleeping, but after a short, short while it would wake up in short jerks and rise against her. He would pull down her panties and take her from the side, come into her gently and carefully, not hurt her any longer or do her harm. He would press his ear tightly against her face and wait for her, and not stop until she broke out in a sniffling howl which could be either pain or desire. Only then would he roll off to his own side of the bed and fall asleep.

part II

SATURDAY. SHE WAS SUPPOSED TO WORK TODAY, and then she was off for a while, Sunday, Monday and Tuesday. The weekdays gave her a breather, until later in the afternoon, when it was time for Tommy to come home. Ariadne never knew what kind of a mood he would be in when he returned. There was no way for her to protect herself.

What if she would return home? Leave Sweden and return to Greece with Christa?

No. Not to the village with all the black-clad women. How they would look at her with their wrinkled faces. *So the goat has returned to the herd?*

She could say that he died. That she had become a widow like her mother. She could say it, and for a while they would believe it. But soon enough, Tommy would know where they'd gone and then he'd come after her. Just thinking about it made her hunch up. A rising whine in her ears, the feeling of a diarrhea attack coming on.

She was standing in front of the bathroom mirror putting on foundation and rouge. If she didn't open her mouth, no one could see that she'd lost another tooth. This was the tooth behind her left canine tooth. She'd put it in her bra, but then she realized that it was too late to go to the emergency room and have it put back. She'd heard that putting a tooth in milk or keeping it in the saliva within a cheek was the way to keep it safe until reaching the dentist's office. Then there would be a chance for it to reattach.

Tommy was busy in the kitchen. He made coffee and was pressing juice. Now he came to the bathroom door, his round cheeks slack.

"Good morning, darling."

"Morning."

"You've gotten up."

"Yeth."

"I'll drive you to the bus later on."

"Don't have to." Lisp. Difficulty forming words.

"That's okay. I'll do it anyway. Then I'll take Christa out to Adels Island. What do you say to that? Maybe we'll find some chanterelle mushrooms. Wouldn't that be nice, chanterelle mushroom sandwiches? You like mushrooms. It's been raining again, and they really take off. Or do you think that the chanterelle season is over? What do you think?"

She'd taken some pain medication.

The coffee was too hot on her lips.

"Drink some juice, then. Here's a glass."

Burning fire in all the small wounds. She drank anyway; she feared she would awaken his temper.

"We'll come and pick you up later. Christa and me. Even though it's Saturday, you still get off at three, right?"

She nodded.

"Go up Observatory Hill; we'll wait for you with the car. You know, to the left of Kungstensgatan. You can usually park there."

A pole of ice through her spine.

"You're very kind, Tommy. Thank you."

Her mother had only spoken to her about it once. She'd asked Ariadne directly: "I'm worried about you, my little dolly. Are you sure that things are all right?"

How can you answer a mother who lives in a far-off country?

"This house is so nice. He's so hard working," she answered.

Her mother's knotted fingers plucking.

"I see the house is nice. I see many rooms and many large windows, and I will tell this to everyone back home once I return. They will be jealous. But you? How are you doing? Inside?"

Her mother gestured toward her own heart. Her hair had turned white and there were glimpses of scalp underneath.

Ariadne forced herself to smile.

"Inside all is well. Don't worry, Mamma. I'm fine inside."

Ariadne's mother had not been able to create a relationship with her granddaughter. Christa became tense and reserved, and she didn't understand a word her grandmother said. From the beginning, they'd planned that Ariadne's mother would stay for a long time, but it never happened. After the first few days, her mother would ask to change her flight so she could return home.

"Why, Mamma? Why?"

"Don't you see I feel something is going on? Whenever I stay here, something is forced off-balance."

Nothing would make her change her mind.

Christa entered the kitchen wearing her pajamas, sewn with a colorful childish pattern, too childish for her age, though what did it matter?

She stopped, wrinkled her forehead.

"Mamma?"

"Good morning, Chri . . . darling." Ariadne tried not to lisp.

"What are you up to?"

"Your mother has to work today," Tommy explained as he entered from the hall, saving Ariadne from having to say anything else.

"Come in and have some breakfast. Afterwards, we're going to take a ride on a ferryboat, you and me."

"Ride the ferry?"

"Just you and me. We'll do something fun."

They dropped her off at Ekerö Center and the bus came right away. It was a cool, gray day with a hint of rain in the air. Once she sat down, she took out her sunglasses and put them on.

JUSTINE WAS AWAKENED by the bird pecking at her nose. She was on her side and the bird's warm feet pressed against her upper arm. She remembered where she was, and sat up. The round clock on the wall showed twenty-five minutes to seven. She hadn't slept many hours, but she still felt well rested. She heard Hans Peter on the other side of the door. He was talking to a female guest. There was the clanging of coins; she heard how one of them fell to the floor and rolled away. Hans Peter and the woman laughed. The smell of coffee wafted in under the door.

Again, fear had mastered them, both Justine and the bird. It was the third time in just a few weeks. She didn't dare stay at home alone in her house. Again, she'd taken the bird with her and driven to the hotel. She wasn't sure that Hans Peter cared for it.

The bird hopped onto her wrist. He loved sitting there, right at the base of her thumb. He was heavy. She stroked him over his feathers; he fluffed up and rubbed his head against her knuckles. Carefully, she opened his wings, one by one, and inspected them. There were a few scabs left from his earlier attempt to escape his terror, but his wounds were healing nicely and none seemed to be infected. She held out the cup of water to him, and he drank with quick, clunking gulps.

There wasn't a window in the sleeping area, but if she listened carefully, she could hear the steady sound of rain on the cobblestones. Hans Peter's pillow had an impression of his head. She burrowed her face into it, before she took the edge and shook it, and then she fluffed up both pillows. She combed her hair while standing in front of the minimal mirror and straightened out her clothes. Her pants were wrinkled; she should have removed them before she fell asleep. She was freezing; her arms had goose bumps.

Pictures from the night before came into her mind, but now they didn't scare her. Instead, it seemed strange that she'd gotten so frightened. She shook herself, overcome by intense rage. Who was the intruder in her garden? She should have stayed at home and taken care of that person instead of fleeing. She shouldn't let some sick nutcase drive her away from her own home. Well, she certainly hadn't been so plucky last night, but now in the light of day it appeared simpler.

The bird had landed on the back of the chair. He sat on one leg, drawing the other leg up underneath him, which showed he was feeling well.

"You'll have to stay here," she said in a low voice. "We'll be going home soon, but for now, stay here and don't make a mess. Otherwise Hans Peter will get angry with you. And you'll cause trouble for the cleaning lady."

The bird put his head to one side and looked at her. She noticed that he'd left some guano on the floor, so she found some paper towels and cleaned it up. Jokingly, she threatened the bird with her finger: "I told you not to make a mess!"

She carefully opened the door which led to the night desk. She caught a glimpse of Hans Peter's back; he was standing there shuffling some papers. There was also a couple struggling with some suitcases.

"Psst!" she whispered.

When he turned to her, she saw he looked tired. The light fell onto his face so that his wrinkles and lines stood out in clear relief. The thin skin under his eyes was shaded violet. She felt the sting of a bad conscience.

"Can I come out?" she whispered.

He nodded.

"Sure. And grab some breakfast, too. You know where it is."

"Thanks." She slid past him, giving him a small hug on the way. He nodded, but appeared distant. She went to the breakfast nook. A number of guests were already sitting at the tables; she caught fragments of conversations in English and French.

"Good morning," she said in English, and received some friendly smiles back.

Britta Santesson, old and retired, the mother of the hotel's owner, came out with a loaf of bread wrapped in a napkin. She carried it as if it were a newborn. It had a heavenly aroma. When Britta caught sight of Justine, she came over to say hi. They'd met a number of times before, and Justine had liked her from the first. This morning, however, she appeared strangely dejected.

"How is everything going?" Justine asked.

Britta Santesson's expression showed she didn't want to go into the matter.

"Here, try some bread. It's fresh from the oven."

"I know how good it is."

It was obvious the old lady did not want to talk about her troubles.

"Fall has set in for good," Britta said, changing the subject. "You know, I've always thought fall was nice. I don't like the heat, but I don't dare say anything after a summer like the one we've had. I don't understand those retirees who move to Spain."

"Maybe they only live there during the winter. In order to get away from the snow." Justine cut some slices of cheese and placed them on her bread. "Is it raining now?" she asked.

"There was a heavy shower, but it's probably over now."

Justine stroked her own arms and shivered.

"To think that the weather can change just like that. It wasn't all that long ago we had that heat wave."

"Are you here to pick up your man?" asked Britta Santesson.

"Actually, I spent the night here with him. Some nights I long for him so much I just have to jump in the car and drive over here."

Britta Santesson smiled weakly.

"Sometimes it is pleasant to have a man to sleep with."

"That's right."

"It's been a long time for me."

"I see," she said with a sympathetic voice.

"It's been nine years since Gunnar died, and ever since I've been alone in bed."

"Oh, what did he die of?"

"Old age."

"Oh."

"He was older than I was, much older. It was his time, but it doesn't matter. I still miss him no matter what."

Justine was surprised that Britta was now so talkative, and Justine had the feeling that she really wanted to say something entirely different, but couldn't manage to spit it out.

A middle-aged couple walked into the breakfast nook. They were holding hands, and they looked around the room uncertainly. Britta made a welcoming gesture toward one of the empty tables. She cleared the used plates and mugs; then she noticed the coffee was out and hurried to make some more.

Justine finished eating and went back to the room where she'd slept. The bird flew up the moment he saw her and landed on her shoulder. He burrowed his head beneath an earlobe and clucked gently. Hans Peter came in.

"Can we go home soon?" she asked. "I'm worried something has happened to the house."

"Soon," he said. "There are just a few more people who need to check out; the others are going to stay another night."

The hotel had some unique rules. A guest had to check out by nine a.m. Most of the guests knew this, and since many of them were tourists who wanted to pack in as much sightseeing as possible, this was usually not much of a problem.

Justine lowered the bird down to the back of the chair and put her arms around Hans Peter.

"You look so tired, sweetheart. I'm sorry that I came and disturbed your night's sleep."

He kissed her, but there was something stiff and absent in his manner. The bell rang on the counter. He drew himself from her embrace and went back. Justine sank onto the cot and stayed there. The door was not quite closed; she heard one of the guests trying to pay and check out. He spoke heavily accented English: "I don't understand. You say not accept credit card?"

Hans Peter's calm, soft voice; how she loved him for his patience.

"I'm sorry, sir, but I believe when you checked in we informed you we only accept cash payment at this hotel. I'm sorry."

"Is Sweden undeveloped country? Everybody take cards now. Maybe you want glass beads?"

Hans Peter laughed politely. "I am very sorry, sir. But you can see the sign yourself. No credit cards."

"Why the hell?"

"It is our niche: a small, old-fashioned hotel, with good service in a stressful time. Almost all of our guests appreciate it."

"And if I not have cash?"

"There's an ATM machine right outside. I'm very sorry if this causes you any trouble."

The man was muttering, but then Justine heard a woman's reasonable voice, and she understood the English word *charming*. Justine wondered just how long Ulf Santesson could keep going with his strict hotel rules. It made things difficult and was out of step with the times.

"Well, that's it!" Hans Peter called to her, so she knew he was ready to leave. Justine took the scarf and was just about to wrap the bird in it when she heard someone else come in. She went out to the counter to see what was happening.

She'd met Ariadne once before, a while back. But now when she saw the strong woman's face, Justine felt like fainting. Hans Peter stood by the outer door, as if to keep an unseen enemy from coming in. His whole body was tense, his mouth half-open in a silent yell.

"Hi," Ariadne mumbled. Her lips were swollen and broken, and although she'd tried to cover her injuries with make-up, it was obvious that she'd been beaten up. Her face seemed crooked, almost inside-out, and one of her eyes was completely swollen shut.

Hans Peter marched across the black-and-white tiles of the stone floor straight to Ariadne and stared her in the face. Ariadne didn't move.

"I take it you've fallen down the stairs again," he said, his voice tough and accusatory, a tone Justine had never heard him use before. Ariadne didn't answer. She looked down guiltily.

Justine came out around the counter, anger growing inside her. She took Ariadne's hands and held them securely.

"What's happened?" she asked.

"Her husband beats her up. He does it over and over and she does nothing to stop him!"

Justine turned to Hans Peter.

"But, sweetheart, what is she supposed to do?"

"She should leave him!"

"Hans Peter," Justine said pleadingly. Hans Peter went back and tested the door handle, making sure it was locked. Then he went into the breakfast nook and sat down at one of the tables. Without a word, he cleared the used dishes to one side. Justine came over, pulling Ariadne with her by her large, cold hands. Ariadne moved carefully, it was obvious she was in great pain.

"Sorry I yelled like that," Hans Peter said.

"It's all right . . ."

"I just get so angry," he continued. "If you would only stop protecting him and stop inventing stories like you fell down the stairs. I bet you don't even have stairs. It's so obvious. No man who acts like that should be protected."

Justine brought over a chair for Ariadne.

"Is it true that he beats you?"

"Yes."

"How long has it been going on?"

"Well . . ."

"A number of years?"

"Yes."

"Have you brought a complaint to the police?"

"Her husband is a policeman, Justine. That bastard is one of them."

It was quiet for a moment. Justine had taken Ariadne's hands again; she'd sat down next to her, knee to knee. Justine glanced at the ceiling a moment. The lamp was dirty; she saw a dead insect on its back in the glass. She said, "Is there anyone you can talk to?"

Ariadne shook her head.

"Not anyone?"

"He . . . he would . . . kill me."

"Let's take her to the emergency room," said Hans Peter. "They'll document her injuries. Let's do it now. Come on, let's go."

Ariadne let out a low scream.

"No, Hans Peter. Don't say that!"

"I've known you for so long; we've worked together for years. I can't stand seeing you like this. It's my duty as a fellow human being to help you. Don't you understand?"

"No," Ariadne groaned. "Please . . . you are so kind . . . but no questions more. Let me be. I start cleaning now. I have lots to do."

Justine let go of Ariadne's hands.

"Listen to me," she said. "One thing I promise you. We are on your side. We are your friends, Hans Peter and me. Do you think you could move to Hässelby and stay with us until a divorce comes through? We have enough room for you . . . and don't you have a daughter, too? You can take her with you. Come stay with us. I guarantee that he will not be able to harm you at our place."

Ariadne sniffled and rubbed her hand under her nose.

"You don't understand," she said, not very clearly. "Thank you anyway; thank you so much."

THE HOUSE WAS UNCHANGED. No one had been there while he was gone. Tor hadn't expected anyone, either. He didn't have anything that needed care, neither pets nor houseplants, and his mailbox had enough room to put in a week's worth of mail.

Still, he thought he'd walk around and look for any signs that someone had been there. Not from Berit, of course not, but maybe from the boys, Jörgen or Jens. Maybe a little note on a slip of paper: *Hi Dad. Welcome home. We stopped by to check on the place while you were gone, take care. Later.* The boys still had their keys from when they lived at home. But why would they come over to an empty house? They had never bothered when their father was home.

He poured a glass of whiskey and sat down at the kitchen table. The box of photos was still where he'd left it the night before he left with Jill. He'd taken it out. Pictures of Berit, of their life together. Everything rhapsodically documented. Their engagement. Her young, child-like face with her eyes wide open and questioning. She had her hair up in a French twist. He'd never liked it, but he never dared tell her that, either.

Their marriage in Copenhagen, simple and austere. Berit had wanted a big, fancy wedding, but he refused. The Swedish Gustaf Church in Copenhagen, the capital of Denmark, was their compromise. He remembered that Jill had been one of the people there as a witness and also caught a glimpse of her in one of the photos taken later, at the dinner held at *De styv små hem*. Berit was already expecting when they got married, but it wasn't showing yet. There was a photo of her pregnant, her large belly photographed from underneath. He remembered how he squatted down to get the proper perspective. Then Berit as a young mother and many, many photos of the boys and their mother. Not many of him. He was usually the one behind the camera.

It hurt to look at the pictures. Still, he had to do it, torture himself, punish himself, which reminded him how he had let her down. Not just once, but many times over. For instance, when the boys were being delivered, he didn't have the courage to stay with her. He despised himself because he couldn't stand the smell of blood and ether. *I'm going to step out for a moment, but I'll be right back.* He was dizzy from the sounds of instruments hitting stainless steel. *I'll come right back.* But he didn't. And that was his betrayal. Her dry lips formed his name, but he left anyway, walked along the blindingly bright corridor, where women were screaming behind closed doors. He wanted to clap his hands over his ears and run, but he marched straight ahead and out the front door.

He didn't go home, just drove around the city. He felt like a jerk, but he couldn't bring himself to return, not until the next morning. Both times. Both children had been born in the *vargtimme*, the hour of the wolf, between three and four in the morning. The first time, she'd wept when he came back, turned away from him, didn't want to look at him. The second time, she was toughened.

Forgive me, Berit. I was a real asshole. I didn't deserve to love you.

Her parents had never accepted him. He remembered the old man's mistrustful handshake the first time he was invited to their place in Hässelby.

"You work with numbers, I understand."

"That's correct. I'm a certified public accountant."

Tor could still remember the sultry, humid air. They were standing in the greenhouse. Berit's father grew cucumbers and tomatoes.

"I see." Berit's father took off his cap and ran his hand through his hair. He was old; even Berit's mother was old. They'd had her late in life. They watched over her like hawks. Their only child.

"You'll take good care of her now, won't you?" Berit's mother had said as they sat in the car, ready to drive to Copenhagen. She had leaned through the window, strict, discontent. "I'll say it again; it would have been much nicer with a real church wedding. Not running away like this, as if a wedding were something shameful."

Berit stuck her arm in front of him and touched her mother's hand.

"Mamma!" she said, pleading.

No indeed, he really hadn't had a good relationship with his in-laws.

The kind of man who adds things up on paper.

They were hoping for someone more solid, closer to the earth, someone who could take over the greenhouse business when the old man had to stop. Tor wasn't formed from that mold, and therefore he was never good enough for their daughter. Luckily, they never had to realize that he couldn't take care of her and protect her. They'd been dead for a long time.

His body was heavy with exhaustion, but at the same time he was wide awake. Norwegian jet-lag, he thought, and smiled bitterly. He poured himself another glass of whiskey. He ought to be hungry, but had no appetite. He picked at the photos awhile. Shortly after Berit's disappearance he'd collected them all from various places and put them in the box. It all started when the police asked for some recent photos. Most of them were older.

Some of the pictures had lumps of adhesive on the back. He had pulled them out of albums. Every photograph of her. Why? Was this sick? Understandable, really. Keep her collected, lid on, stay!

He was getting somewhat tipsy.

Sitting and talking to himself.

Or rather with her. No, to her. Because he got no answers. She smiled flatly from her photographs, looking past him or right through him. On some of the older pictures, the color had almost completely disappeared. She appeared pale and disillusioned.

"Well, what about the trip!" he exclaimed. "When you turned forty-five! Our around-the-world trip! You didn't expect that! Now don't come and tell me that it wasn't a surprise!"

Of course, that was a success. At least in the beginning. But on the plane to Sydney, she'd gotten acutely ill. No one knew what it was; he'd suspected malaria. But it wasn't that. Instead it was some strange virus which made her shiver with a high fever for over a week. She wasn't up to much after that.

"The hell with it, Berit; that wasn't my fault!" he exclaimed.

No, today he didn't have the power to call her forth. Sometimes he could, and she would appear, sitting in her black dress with her legs crossed, shining nylons, attractive. She'd just sit there and accuse him.

"You cheapened me, Tor. You never really took me to your heart. I can never forgive you."

Oh yes, he remembered. Other kinds of betrayal. Her clumsy attempts at seducing him. Clumsy, because he hadn't been ready for sex at that moment. When a man has no desire for sex, he's tired and unmotivated. Or worked to death at tax season. Is it a question of guilt and being in the wrong in such cases?

He picked up a photo and looked directly at her. It was a photo from when she was ready to go to work, a low-cut blue dress, their last summer together. Her arms were bare and soft; she easily got sun-burned. Her mouth was half open; he observed the space between her teeth, which had irritated her so often, but it had always been like that. No dentist in the world would have been able to fix it, even though they'd tried with both clips and metal.

He'd have to drink more whiskey, have to make himself tired. But his brain didn't shut down. The first light of dawn made the trees appear as black silhouettes. A lone bird's peeping came through the open window; soon they'd start their migration, gather in thick flocks and take off for the south.

Jill.

And suddenly he had another kind of longing.

He wasn't able to go to sleep until the late afternoon. He'd decided to lie down on the sofa; he'd taken the box of photos into the living room. He slept for a few hours and woke up screaming. A nightmare. Berit floating on the water, face down, with her limbs unformed, like those of an animal. He stood at the water's edge and knowledge filled him; a body like that, really, there was no hope. How he still wanted to jump in and save her, grab her clothes and haul her out. But his feet stuck in the sand, and he started sinking, sinking and lurching. A movement behind him. That woman who lived in the tall, white house. That woman Justine.

He didn't look at the clock, just lifted the receiver and called Jill. It was her home number; he knew it by heart. She routed it to her cell phone. She was at work, but he didn't realize that right away. He understood by her voice that he was disturbing her; even though she said he wasn't, he knew he was. But he had to get the dream out of his system. She listened to him, asked him questions. In the background, he heard the sound of a telephone ringing. Finally, she had to cut him off: "Can I call you back? Things are getting hectic here."

He felt ashamed and hung up.

Probably because he was messing around with those photographs. That's why he'd dreamed of Berit. Otherwise, he rarely dreamed of her these days. He was beginning to have difficulty remembering the details of her face; it was getting harder and harder to reconstruct them in his mind. In this dream, she was turned away from him, without a face.

He lit a cigarette and immediately started coughing. His cough was beginning to make him nervous; sometimes he coughed up gray clumps of slime; he studied them thoroughly, looking for traces of blood. As soon as he saw the slightest trace, he'd quit smoking, but not until then. This much he knew.

He was freezing. He'd gone to sleep in his clothes, his body tender and sore as if he'd been out exercising intensely, yes, aches and pains everywhere in his legs and calves. He got up and took a shower, brushed his teeth. He took his time, shaving his face carefully; then he put on corduroy pants and a clean shirt.

What time was it? Not yet midnight. He looked for his car keys and finally found them in one of the desk drawers in his home office. Once this had been the playroom for the boys, filled with their car tracks and Lego towers. He had a melancholy longing for Jill. But she had the night shift and was going to work tomorrow evening, too.

He put on his jacket and went out to his car. It was a Saab. He'd owned it for years and if he could have afforded it, he would have bought another car long ago. After a few tries, the engine turned over. He backed out of the garage and began to drive.

A RIADNE'S CLEANING CART was difficult to maneuver this particular morning, as if the wheels were locked. Hans Peter had helped her pull it out of storage and fill it with towels, bed linens, soap, toilet paper, and those small, flat packages of shampoo. But now he and Justine had left. Ariadne stood in the breakfast nook and watched them disappear up along Drottningsgatan. The wind was blowing, and Justine's hair whirled in all directions. She was carrying the bird in her arms just like Ulf's mother carried her freshly baked bread.

"Maybe you think a bird like this is unpleasant," Justine said that morning when she came out of the room with the bird. "I don't know if you like birds. But you certainly don't have to be afraid. He knows which people I like."

Ariadne did not know how to respond to that.

Justine shook her hair out of her face and pointed toward the room behind the night desk.

"Unfortunately he made a bit of a mess," she said with an embarrassed smile. Justine looked so sweet and much younger when she smiled.

"I take care of it."

"No need, I already cleaned it up. I don't think you can see anything now."

The bird was large and gray, with black feathers. He peered at her and Ariadne wondered what he was thinking. Can birds even think?

"What is his name?" she asked quietly.

Justine made a face.

"Oh . . . he's never had a name. It just happened that way. Sometimes I wish he had one, but for the most part, we're fine without one. I never managed to think up a name which would suit him. There's a risk that he'd lose his . . . I don't know . . . his dignity, especially if I started to call him something like Efriam or Putte or anything like that." She laughed. The bird gave out a low caw.

They were standing in the doorway, ready to go. Hans Peter put his arm around Justine's shoulder. Justine looked right into Ariadne's eyes. Light surrounded her. She held out a slip of paper with a telephone number.

"No one should live with what he's doing to you. It's unforgivable. You know where we live and you can call us whenever you need to. Please don't forget."

Ariadne turned red.

"It work out," she whispered.

As soon as they'd left, she began to memorize the number. It was easy, rhythmical, with many eights. It went into her brain and found a place to rest. She would not forget it. Then she ripped up the slip of paper into many bits and threw it into the garbage bag.

Ariadne was in one of the rooms and was taking the sheets off the double bed. There were hardened flecks of sperm. It nauseated her, and she'd never reacted like that before. A couple in love were here last night. Or maybe not. Sperm flecks did not necessarily indicate making love.

The radio was on, mostly out of habit so that the time would go faster with some music. But today was not a day which she wanted to go faster.

We'll pick you up later. Meet us at Observatory Hill.

He was going to be nice for a long time now, kind and friendly to the point of exaggeration. She never knew whether he was play-acting or not. His kindness could go on for a week or several months. That was what made everything more terrible:

that she never really knew. There were always signs, of course, that the period of kindness was about to end. The way he stuck out his lower lip so it hardened and turned dark red. The way he started to comment on her looks, on the things she said and did or didn't do. The way he wanted to take back on all the nice things he'd said before, that she wasn't worthy, and how could he have ever imagined that she was.

Yes, it was precisely like that. Now she had a recovery period, but just long enough so that she could endure another round of his abuse. She looked at her hands. Her pinkie finger on her left hand was swollen; she must have jammed it. Her eyelids were itching like sandpaper. Usually she washed her hair and took a shower after she returned home from work, but she hadn't had the chance yesterday. Dirty and ugly, no one was allowed to see her like that, no one other than him, and that made his contempt grow.

She wetted a washcloth and shook cleaning powder into the toilet bowl. It was obvious that the guests had used it. On the radio, there was a program with questions and music. People could call in and win a CD. Sometimes Ariadne would know the answer. It didn't happen often, but it did happen. Then she would become childishly happy and wanted to run around and tell someone, but usually she was alone in the hotel when she was cleaning.

A question came up, and even though it seemed her head was full of oatmeal, she knew the answer right away.

"What is the largest island in the Greek archipelago of the Dodecaneses?"

"Rhodos," she mumbled.

The woman in the radio hesitated.

"What did you say they were called? . . . Dodo . . . ?"

"Dodecaneses."

"Islands, islands, hmmm . . . there are so many islands, I'm not sure which one I should take."

"That's right, there are a lot of islands. I can help you a little bit. This group of islands is also known as the Twelve Islands."

"I see."

"Doesn't ring a bell? Well, give us your best answer."

"Crete." The woman was almost angry, as if she knew that it wasn't the right answer and wanted to give the program host some of the blame.

The music the woman chose was by Cornelius Vreeswijk and it had a number of singing and laughing children. Ariadne went around the room and collected wrappers from chocolate bars, banana peels, grape stems. There was garbage everywhere, on the window sills and on the nightstands. If only people would use the wastebaskets, things would be so much easier for her. She threw it all in the garbage bag, and took out some clean sheets.

Finally, she looked for a tip, which was usually left on the desk underneath the remote control. In vain. A tip was a welcome addition to her wages. Once she asked Hans Peter about it.

"How we do it, divide it in half?"

"Ah, don't worry about it," he'd answered. "You're the one doing all the hard work."

Hans Peter and his woman. Justine. What a strange name, certainly not Swedish. But she looked Swedish. Blonde, somewhat curly, medium-length hair. Greenish eyes. There was something about her gaze. As if streams of light and strength had radiated from her pupils and straight into Ariadne.

Here is some of my strength. Don't settle, strike back!

That strength. She wasn't able to receive it; it had melted to small pieces, worthless shreds.

She held on tightly to the toilet brush and scrubbed with hard bursts. Water splashed up on her arms.

You're not worth better. Others' shit.

She flushed and placed a new roll on the holder. Folded the end into a small triangle, easy for the next guest to grasp. She stepped out of the bathroom. Finally finished with the first one! She reached for the remote control in order to turn off the radio just as the program host was reading the next question.

"Who was the Greek goddess, the daughter of Okeanos and Nyx, which we usually identify with revenge?"

Ariadne heard her own voice and was surprised by how clear it sounded.

"Nemesis," said the voice. "Nemesis."

A LITTLE BIT INTO SEPTEMBER, Henry and Märta moved back to the city. Micke helped them. He packed his Chevy full of their things and drove them to their place. It took a few trips. As usual, they were humbly grateful.

"You know it feels good to know that someone's keeping an eye on the place during the winter," said Henry, as he wriggled the window closed on its hinge. "How lucky we are to have met you!"

"Hey, no problem," Micke mumbled. He was always embarrassed when they poured their gratitude over him. He'd offered to rake the leaves, too, and soon it would be time for that, because the rainy days seemed to have set in for good.

The old couple were sad and sorry to see another summer come to end, perhaps the last one in the colony garden. They thought this every year now. They were fragile and scrawny, and who knew how the winter would treat them. The cat also did not like to move back into the apartment. Somehow it knew and it had kept himself hidden all morning so that Märta was getting slightly hysterical as they brought the last cardboard boxes to the car in the misty rain.

"Micke, my dear, I know we can't keep you long, but Raven . . ."

He was standing there with his car keys in his hand; he'd backed the car up onto the grassy area which led to Hemslöjdvägen. The trunk was filled with bags and banana crates, as was half of the back seat. Märta and the cat were supposed to sit on the other half.

"There's a way," said Henry. And so he'd asked Micke to take a detour to the ICA grocery store on Abrahamsbergsvägen to buy some sardines in tomato sauce. That was the beast's favorite treat. The trick worked. Henry barely had the lid off and the can on the front steps when the cat appeared. No one could say where he'd come from; he'd probably kept hidden in a good spot and watched them the entire time, just waiting for them to leave. How did he think he was going to take care of himself? Silly, stupid beast. Raven slurped up the sardines with his triangular head at an angle, and he made loud smacking sounds. As soon as he'd finished, Henry lifted him up and placed him on Märta's knees, as she had already jammed herself into the back seat. She was holding a bouquet of marigolds in her hand, the last ones of fall. No actually, there were more flowers, orpines; she'd taken him to the flower bed and pointed them out.

"You can certainly pick some of these if you want to. Aren't they pretty? Maybe you have a girlfriend. You can make her happy with them. Or maybe your Mamma? Wouldn't that make her happy? Tell her with greetings from Henry and Märta."

Their apartment was musty and depressing; their furniture gave him an uncomfortable feeling. It reminded him of something from his earliest childhood, but he couldn't remember what. They'd lived in a rental, and their landlord wasn't exactly interested in keeping the place up. Micke used the bathroom, and the toilet didn't flush; he had to use a bucket of water and dump it in the bowl. He dribbled some water over his hands and then dried them on a stale, filthy hand towel which looked like it hadn't been changed in a hundred years. Even he could see that.

"Are you two going to be all right, now?"

"Thank you, thank you so very much." Henry fumbled after his wallet and refused to give up until he could at least reimburse Micke for the gas. As far as that went. It cost money to own a car, that's for sure.

"Come and visit us any time," said Märta as she gave him an awkward hug.

"Maybe we'll pop over there some day if we have sunny weather," said Henry. "Sometimes I really long to putter around in the garden. But don't worry, we'll get a ride in from the *färdtjänst*." The cat wove around his legs and meowed.

"But you, Raven, you'll have to stay home then," Märta clucked.

Micke wondered how they'd managed before they met him.

"Take it easy," he said, and when he got to the yard, he could see them in the window. They were waving. They held up Raven and pretended he was waving to him with one paw.

He got into the habit of stopping by their gardening hut every day. He raked leaves and put things away, and even put together a compost area where he could dump the raked leaves. Sometimes he ran into the neighbors, but he greeted them curtly. He really didn't want to have all that much to do with them. The neighbor to the left insisted on introducing herself. She was elderly, but not as old as Henry and Märta.

"I'm Inez Molin. What's your name?"

"Michael," he said tightly, and noticed he used an English pronunciation.

"*Majkel*?" she repeated.

"Yes."

"Are you related to Henry and Märta in some way?" Her face came right up to his, as if to inspect it and weigh him. It seemed as if her eyes were loose in their sockets, they were runny and red. A stained brown beret was pulled over her head.

"Cousin's kid," flew out of him.

"Yes, it appears that they weren't able to have children of their own." The old lady just wouldn't give up.

"No," he answered and made an obvious grab for the rake.

Thank God, she now dropped by less often. The weather was turning more into fall and there was a great deal of rain. The cold was raw inside the hut, but underneath the bed he found a heater dating from the Stone Age. It was green with a curled cord. It sparked when he plugged it in and gave off the smell of burnt dust. If he sat close enough to it, he would get nicely warm.

Sometimes he picked up the rifle and felt it. It weighed more than he thought. The barrels were ice cold. He held it up to his shoulder, pretended to fire.

He took with him a pad of drawing paper and some pens. He liked to sit there and draw. Nothing to show anyone else, absolutely not, but he was excited by the pictures he drew and that was worth something.

He drew women, naked women, bound women. Legs up in the air, chained in shackles. He drew round breasts which floated out like round pancakes. He thought of Karla Faye Tucker and the needles which slowly entered her body.

A few times he headed out to Hässelby, but it wasn't as easy to hide in the bushes. He saw that woman a few times; she was also raking leaves together with that new man, the one who had replaced his father Nathan. The big chicken cage around the tree looked empty. Maybe the bird died, or had flown south to warmer country.

Things at home were horrible. Nettan was in one of her nagging moods. Maybe menopause? He tried to stay away when she was home, but sometimes he had to go home and sleep. It hadn't gotten so bad yet that he wanted to spend the night in the clammy hut because then she would wonder where he'd been, nag him and ask what he was up to. The whole deal with the gardening hut in the colony garden was his and his alone. It wasn't anyone else's business.

There he would sit at the large table and sketch out his future. Or he huddled next to the heating element, wearing the thick, dark green sweater his mother had knitted for him during a phase when she was always knitting.

The thing was, he'd thought of something there in the silence of the gardening hut. The thought grew in him, a fantastic idea which made his whole body tingle. He, Mickael Gendser, twenty-two years old, and with his whole life in front of him, would begin where Nathan left off. Or hardly even begun, really. He would breathe new life into the adventure trip project. Cheap Trips. He owed it to his father to pick it up again. It was the honorable thing to do.

And there was one more thing to do with honor. That woman in Hässelby. She'd betrayed Nathan in two ways. He was going to punish her for that.

TOR DROVE WITHOUT A PLAN, following the small streets in Åkeshov and Blackeberg, and found himself in Hässelby. He couldn't feel any trace of the whiskey, though if a police car showed up and they made him blow into the test-tube, he would probably fail; he realized that. Still, he didn't really care. The purring sound of the motor made him calm and relaxed, as if he was floating on tar.

He was alone on the streets, but he wasn't the only person awake. He knew Jill was sitting in the control tower, working. He imagined her in front of him, her broad back bent over the radar screen, her fingers over the keyboard and the papers. He felt a real physical longing to embrace her, touch her skin, let his fingertips go through her hair and stroke her ears; she had funny small and well-formed ears; he'd noticed that. Her dry humor, her patience, her tender heart and her concern that things go well for him.

Six years of absence.

But I wasn't the one who left you; you were the one who left me.

He drove past the cemetery, where Berit's parents were buried. He remembered that her father had been called, as a joke, The Cucumber King. He was a respected man in gardeners' circles and he'd gotten various certificates, which Berit had hung up in the cabin on Vätö after her father had died.

A long time ago, Tor had come up with the name The Cucumber Kid for his soon-to-be wife. A whole lifetime ago, a time when nicknames appeared by themselves. He felt a cramp in his chest as he thought of it.

He slowly drove past the darkened villas and townhouses. It was dark everywhere. People were sleeping, gathering strength for the work day ahead. Honorable, solid people who did their jobs and their duties. The last time he visited his doctor, the doctor scolded him. Started going on and on about something called LOH and paid sick leave and the law and what a doctor had to write about the health of his patients. Gustav Vederöd was a real old-fashioned house doctor, a friend of the family, not some stressed clinic doctor who could only spend a few minutes before hurrying off to the next patient. Doctor Gustav, as they called him within the family, was a general practitioner and took care of the boys when they were small and suffered the usual illnesses and accidents. But this time . . . he'd pushed his glasses to the top of his head, and his voice was light and nasal.

"They're on my case at the social insurance office; they're really picky lately. They want to cut off your payments."

"Well, it's such a small amount, they can hardly count it. It's nearly negligible," he hissed back.

"This is about you as a human being."

"What about it?"

"This is your third period of *sjukskrivning*, leave for medical reasons. Right? I've given you three in a row, and, Tor, you can't go on like this, you must try and pull yourself together."

Pull yourself together. A phrase Berit used. *You've got to pull yourself together and get this done.*

"And?" he asked. "What do you mean by that?"

"You've got to understand, Tor, I can't keep signing you off for sick leave, even if I could possibly, possibly, manage to convince the social insurance office one more time. There's also your high blood pressure to consider, for instance. But honestly, I'm not doing you a favor if I write this off one more time."

"So what do you suggest? Are you going to send me to a shrink?"

The doctor pushed up the sleeves on his white coat. It seemed to have shrunk over time. He looked stressed.

"You know, you have to want to go yourself. That's the only way it works."

It was quarter after one in the morning. He turned left at the Yellow Kiosk, which was now a hot dog stand, and began to drive in a zigzag manner down to Lake Mälaren. He hadn't planned it; he just ended up there.

Another time, late winter, 1998. Why hadn't he taken the car then? Well, he wanted to take the exact route that she'd taken and in the exact same way. He knew that she had gone out to Hässelby twice in one week. He wanted to try to understand what was going through her mind, what she was feeling. It was too late to ask. The only thing he could do was to reconstruct her very last day.

He knew that Berit had taken the subway to Hässelby Strand, the last station on the route. From there, at least the first time, she'd taken a walk to her parents' graves and it had been very cold. She'd lit candles at the graves and had forgotten her gloves on the gravestone. The police had given them back to him much later. They were stiff and hard and there was nothing of her smell left in them.

From there, she'd found herself going to Justine Dalvik's house, as if something were luring her there, dragging her against her will. That *huldra*, that forest-demon woman, damn her. Berit had gone there twice. The first time she came home half-frozen and full of fear. She'd taken a bath and gone to bed early and when he wanted to comfort her, it went all wrong. She thought he wanted to have sex with her; she'd misunderstood him.

That's the way it was, he thought. We were not in tune with each other, except for in the beginning, that shimmering start of their time together.

He'd arrived at the house, that tall, white, stone house. Between the branches, he could see that there was light in the windows. He shivered. He turned off the motor and sat there.

Was Justine Dalvik awake in the middle of the night? Did she still have that bird? Having a large, wild bird like that was certainly a sign that she was not normal. He thought about what

Berit had said, that Berit and the others had bullied Justine during their school years. Some beings, animals as well as humans, draw the dislike of others. His maternal grandparents had a chicken on their farm that the other hens attacked. He was a boy; he tried to protect it, frighten away the others from the flock when they came with their hard beaks.

"Give it up, boy," his grandmother said. "She's got the mark; she won't be rid of it."

"Yes, she will!" he yelled. He was seven years old and very sensitive.

One evening at sunset, his grandmother wrung the bullied chicken's neck. The flock had pecked her black and blue and she had next to no feathers left. Grandmother had cooked the chicken and the smell lasted for a long time in the house. He refused to eat it and his grandmother said that she understood, but it was Nature's Law, eat or be eaten. Afterwards, she admitted that she wished she'd buried it anyway. Neither she nor Grandfather had ever stuck a fork into a chicken as tough as this one was.

He got out of the car and shut the door. He lit a cigarette, took a few steps forward, watched Lake Mälaren glitter in the moonlight. The wind had started to pick up. The gate was open, it was crooked and rusted and probably wasn't used any longer. He glimpsed a parked Volvo inside the yard.

What am I doing out here? he thought. What am I up to?

He crushed his cigarette with his heel. He went closer to the house, knowing full well that the person inside could not see him since the lights were all on. He looked straight into the kitchen. He saw Justine Dalvik. She faced the window and it seemed she was looking directly at him. She was fully clothed and totally pale. She looked older than he remembered from the last time he'd seen her. He didn't see the bird. She was standing at attention, listening. Not for him, he was sure of that; he'd sneaked up completely silently. But maybe the bird heard him. Maybe birds were like dogs, with a guard instinct.

Sudden sympathy. Sympathy for her, because she suffered and was tormented. She felt ill; that was obvious to him.

Justine, he thought. You are the one who last saw my Berit. You know something, you must know something, but how can I get you to speak?

She was standing as still as a wax figure. Suddenly all at once, she disappeared from view. He heard the outer door open and how she yelled right out into the darkness: "What do you want? Stop bothering us! Leave us alone!"

ARIADNE BEGAN TO CLEAN the next room. She was on hands and knees, creeping around the shower cabinet and scrubbing and scraping along the rubber seams. It was easy for red flecks of mildew to build up in damp areas. Ulf had been careful to explain this to her the day he hired her many years ago. He looked serious but at the same time a little bit embarrassed.

"You see . . . the quality of a hotel is judged by the cleanliness of its bathrooms. That is to say, if the toilets are dirty, the hotel will get a bad reputation fairly quickly. I want all of my employees to keep this in mind." He'd then opened the shower cabinet doors and pointed and demonstrated how the corners should be done.

By now, the quiz show was over, and boring dance music poured out. She thought she'd just go and turn it off when someone touched her from behind. She couldn't help screaming from fear. When she whirled around, she saw that it was Britta Santesson, Ulf's mother.

"My dear child, I've frightened you, forgive me. I didn't mean to," Britta began, and then fell silent.

Ariadne clumsily got to her feet.

"I'm fine," she mumbled.

The old lady leaned against the door post.

"You need help," she said.

"What . . . you mean?"

"I'll help you clean."

"No . . . no . . ."

"Don't be ridiculous! It's not like I don't have eyes in my head! And another time, you'll help me; it will all even out in the end. So don't even start!"

Britta did not wait for an answer, but took the vacuum and began to work immediately; by one in the afternoon, the entire hotel was clean. Britta made some coffee and took out bread and cheese.

"We'll have to recover our strength, now, won't we?"

It wasn't until then that Ariadne realized how hungry she was. But it was difficult to eat, difficult to chew. The empty hole left by the lost tooth ached and her tongue kept searching the spot while she ate. She took small bites, breaking off pieces with her fingers and putting them in from the edge of her mouth. Britta watched her thoughtfully.

"Oh, sweetie," she said, shaking her head.

Ariadne knew that within herself she had tears. Just a few hours ago, her tears overwhelmed her heart, brimming over again and again. Now that was no longer the case. Her tears seemed different, and she couldn't explain why. Now she felt as if a rod of iron had worked its way into her, bracing her upright.

"Thanks for your help," she said.

Britta nodded. After a moment of silence, she started a new topic.

"I heard that Ulf has talked to all of you."

"Yes, he did."

"He's going through a tough time right now."

"So I understood."

Britta cut a slice of cheese. She sighed.

"Life is not always a dance upon roses, and even if it were, the roses would have thorns."

"A nice picture." Ariadne looked at her.

"Hmm. Well, anyway, he is feeling a bit better today. He's contacted a clinic in the U.S. They have real experts there."

"He going there now?"

"Yes, and then we'll see what they have to say. If things don't work here, maybe they'll work somewhere else. That is, if you have faith."

"Yes," Ariadne took a deep breath.

"And the money, too. Things cost money over there."

"Mmmm."

"Ulf has sold two of his hotels. He'll probably tell you himself any day now. It was settled yesterday."

"It was?" she asked tensely.

"Yes, so now this one is the only one left."

"He told us he was going to sell every one."

"We'll have to see. Maybe it won't be necessary. We'll just have to wait and see."

Ariadne trembled from relief.

"I hope so," she said.

Britta rested her hands in her lap. Outside, the wind was banging a sign on the building across the street. Fall was certainly here now.

"They are your children no matter what. No matter how old they are. Well, you know how it is. You have a child yourself."

"Mmm," Ariadne agreed, and thought of Christa, wondered if she and Tommy had gone to Adelsö in spite of the weather.

"By the way, how are things going with your daughter?" Britta asked in a friendly way.

"Fine, thanks."

"I've been thinking . . . her blindness. Have you thought of looking in another country for help?"

"Not really . . . it's from birth. It was like that when she come out. She had no sight."

"I understand."

"They say nothing they can do."

"They often say that. But you shouldn't believe everything."

Ariadne got up and cleared off the table.

"I must go now," she said. "You are kind, Britta. Thank you very much for helping me clean."

The elderly lady watched her with a face that was light and wrinkled.

"It's fine, dear, I had nothing else to do."

"I promise I keep my fingers crossed for Ulf."

"We'll both keep our fingers crossed, dear. We'll keep our fingers crossed!"

It was two in the afternoon and she had almost an entire hour at her disposal. She said farewell to Britta, who promised to lock up. Then she left the hotel, quickly walking down the stairs and away. Outside the entrance, she put on her sunglasses. It was raining, but that was not what mattered to her.

It was Saturday, but there weren't many folks about. She decided to take a short cut through the cemetery next to Adolf Fredrik Church, and she stopped for a moment to look at Olaf Palme's grave, to bend her head, genuflect, and then hurry onwards. The rain washed over her face. Christa. Did Tommy remember to bring her raincoat if they actually decided to go to the forest? Otherwise, Christa would certainly catch a cold. She was delicate, had weak lungs. He'd made it sound like a wonderful adventure, that whole forest thing, but she knew that her daughter preferred to stay inside the house, lie in bed, and listen to her CD-player. She seldom opposed her father's suggestions, though. At times, Tommy would hit her, too; not often and not hard, but it happened. His disappointment showed itself this way. He had wanted many children. He'd told her that from the beginning, when they were newlyweds.

"Little girls who look like you. Little boys who look like me. You and I will make a whole clan, all on our own."

Yeah, right.

She arrived at Sveavägen and crossed the street, running between the cars, even though it was a red light. She slid inside the Konsum grocery store, then stuffed her sunglasses into her pocket. She must be able to see properly.

Those streams of light and strength she'd gotten from Justine's eyes, they were still inside her; she felt it. They'd shrunken and had been about to fade away, but now they were returning, stronger than ever, and she found herself growing strong as well.

She went right up to the shelf where bread was displayed. This was a store with a wide selection, but she rarely had time to make it here to Sveavägen, she always had to rush home. Hurry, hurry, her life was one of stress and fear.

She was in a hurry this time, too. Her hands fumbled as she searched among the bags of bread that were fresh and ready to go. There were a number of kinds from Bondgården's Breakfast Breads. Tommy liked their Breakfast Breads. That would put him in a good mood. And what was so amazing about a land like Sweden: they were always so careful to list the ingredients on the packaging, with clear print, as well as the nutritional value per 100 grams. Protein, carbohydrates, fat, fiber, nutrients.

She chose two loaves of bread with different ingredients. That was all she bought. Then she paid for her purchase and left the store.

She was having an incredible amount of luck today. The car hadn't come yet. She followed the path up to the astronomy building and had to catch her breath; the path was so steep. Some ducks were sitting in the grass. They looked like they were suffering. She thought that maybe their breasts were cold, that is, if ducks were made anything like humans.

Far away near the playground were benches where people could sit and admire the view of the city. Today no one was here, no one but her. Quickly she took off her jacket and held it over the two bags of bread. Hidden under the cloth, she switched the loaves from one bag to the other.

One of the packages she closed carefully and put into her bag. The other she kept in her hand as she walked back down the hill. She passed the ducks, and stopped. They quacked softly, stood and shook themselves, watched her.

"Are you hungry?" she cooed softly. "Come and get some tasty Breakfast Bread!"

The entire flock got up then, and waddled over to her. She broke the bread into bits, which she scattered around the grass. The ducks had no fear whatsoever. One of them, a brown-flecked mamma duck, came and ate the bread right out of her hand.

Ariadne kept her voice calm and low.

"What fine ducks you are. What wonderful ducks. Are you cold and hungry? Here's some food for you."

Finally there was nothing left of the bread at all. She glanced at her watch. Three minutes to three. She stuffed the empty plastic bag into one of the street corner trash containers and reached Kungstensgatan at the same moment that the car swung in.

CHEAP TRIPS. Frigging-fantastic name. Micke played with different font styles on his computer, imported pictures, even made templates for business cards, using his own name. What title should he take? Michael Gendser, Vice-President? Travel Agency Boss? Yes, it was worth a great deal of thought.

So far everything was well and good, and even stimulating. But then? Practically speaking. How do you start a project like this, weigh the pros and cons? He started to realize that he had no idea how to begin. Should he go to the patent office? Do they still have patent offices these days? He had a vague memory that Nathan had mentioned some of these things, and even that there was some government support for business initiatives. Why hadn't he listened a bit better?

For the first time in his life, he realized that there had been good reasons to finish his studies and not just drop out as he'd done after his second year. Nettan had exploded, which had just made him tired. I can go back in a few years, he'd thought. Study at Komvux, if I want to. But right then he was bored to death with everything that had to do with school and studies.

He'd needed money, of course, and Kevin, the brother of one of his former classmates, let him work in his cleaning company. For the most part, he got window cleaning, and by the end, he'd become a window-cleaning wonder. He usually worked with various guys from South America. Small, dark-eyed men who never stayed long; one day they'd just be gone. They had names like Juan and Pepe and understood next to no Swedish. On the other hand, he managed to learn quite a few Spanish words, and that could always be useful. Even with Cheap Trips.

Micke hadn't heard from Kevin for a while. He'd tried calling Kevin on his cell phone and even left a few messages. His wallet was getting empty.

While Nettan was at work, he checked on a website hosted by the employment office where you could test and see what kind of a job you'd be best at. You had to answer 120 questions about what you liked to do. His results showed that he should consider biomedical analysis, laboratory engineer, or physicist. What a joke that turned out to be!

For Nettan's birthday, he went to the gardening hut, picked a large bouquet of the dark pink orpines, and set them on the living room table. Nettan discovered the flowers the moment she came in. She looked them over with a mixture of pleasure and suspicion.

"Ah ha! What's this?"

"Happy Birthday! How old are you this year, 29 again?"

"Oh, cut it out! Where did you get these?"

"Don't worry about it."

"Did you shoplift them?"

"No!" he said angrily. "I didn't shoplift them!"

She kicked off her high-heeled ankle boots and began to massage her feet.

"Come on! Tell me!"

"You want to interrogate me because I tried to make you happy?"

"All right, all right already."

He'd won the first round.

It was Friday evening. She fried some steak fillets and opened a wine bottle. This made him nervous; wine could spin the whole evening out of control. You never knew how her body would react to the wine. It had something to do with her body chemistry. Her biology. The days right before her period she could get so enraged over the littlest thing he'd actually be afraid of her. She would attack him, punch him right in the stomach and pull his ears until he could wrench himself free. It was embarrassing and unpleasant. At other times she could start howling and crying so that the tears flew. Then he'd try to comfort her and sit next to her, pulling at her punk hair, telling her that she was still cute and sexy and not the least bit old, and any day now she'd find a guy who really loved her. He was somewhere out there, of course; he was real. She'd just have to find him.

He had no idea how this evening was going to go.

He helped her set the table, shaping the ends of two candles so that they fit into the much-too-narrow glass candlesticks she'd gotten as a birthday present from her pal Katrin. He managed to find some white linen napkins which she said were in a box.

"How nice," she stated when everything was finished. She poured some wine into their glasses. "It would have been great if Jasmine and Josefine could have been with us, too. But they were busy this evening. They're going to drop by on Sunday instead, so make sure you're at home."

"All right."

She sighed and stretched. The rain on the windows like polka-dots. It had been raining steadily for a number of days, and his shoes had gotten muddy when he was out at the gardening colony.

"TGIF," she exclaimed. "*Skål!*"

He laughed. "Thank God it's Friday!"

"Fantastic!"

"How are things at the shop?" he made conversation. "Are you selling anything?"

Her face clouded over immediately.

"It's been totally dead the past few days. God only knows why. But Christmas will be around the corner soon, and then I hope the place will really take off."

He realized that he'd skated out on thin ice and this conversation could lead back to her whining about him and that it was time to move out or get a job. He'd have to change the subject and fast.

"Cute top," he said, pointing at the black, low-cut sweater she'd put on. It appeared new. She still looked good, was petite and as thin as a teenager. Only if you got close to her face could you see that she had small lines and wrinkles. You could see it even better in the mornings, before she had time to put on her make-up.

"Thanks. Do you really think so? Is it really cute? It doesn't make me look too pale, does it?"

"No, no, absolutely not."

"I bought it as a present to Nettan from Nettan." She cut a piece of her meat and began to chew slowly. She took another sip of wine. "And let me tell you, it's not second hand, either!"

But then she started an attack anyway.

"How did your interview go with Pressbyrån? Did you get it?"

"No," he said shortly.

"So you intend to keep leeching off me, right?"

"Actually, I have completely different plans."

She stared at him. Her upper lip snarled like that of a wolf.

"Oh ho, so you do!"

"Yep!"

"May I dare ask what kind of plans you have in mind? Or is it a state secret?"

"I'll let you know. There's a few things that need to fall into place first. But then, Ma, then you'll be surprised!"

He took a large swallow of wine, choked and coughed. She began to pick her teeth with a toothpick, waiting him out.

"Actually, I want to know a few things," he spluttered. "About Nathan."

Nettan lit a cigarette and took a number of long drags.

"What about him?"

"Like what kind of education he had. Stuff like that."

"Education? He didn't have any damn education. He dropped out of school just like his son. The apple doesn't fall far from the tree, does it." She snorted and blew out smoke.

"Well, what did he do after he dropped out, then?"

"He headed out into the wide, wide world; a real globetrotter, that one. He sure could do whatever he wanted, not like some people. I had to get a job the moment I left school."

I know, he thought. First Gulins, and then Hennes & Mauritz. Out loud, he said: "How'd he get his money? He couldn't just pick up and go like that without any cash."

"Cash! He'd boast how easily he could come up with cash! "The boy with the golden britches": don't you remember he'd call himself that? And to be honest . . . I haven't the damnedest idea how he did it either, but he always had money while we were together. A job here, a job there. He was also good at computers; you know that. He did a lot of support for those big computer companies. He got a lot of money that way. People will pay anything when their computers are on the blink. And he also had stocks and stuff like that. Before the bubble burst that is. That son-of-a-bitch lured me into buying some shares in . . . well, never mind, there's nothing I regret more. At that time I was thinking that we might as well get married."

"Was he really all that awful?" he asked expectantly.

She puckered her lips, immediately looking old and ugly.

"I don't want to discuss it with a puppy like you."

"But come on! Can't you tell me anything about how you two got together? Don't I have the right to know?" He was taking a risk now. Either she was going to be mad as hell or else she would go on and on about all the good times that had existed, at least during their initial time together. The time the twins were conceived, as well as himself.

"Clean the table!" she commanded, and stubbed out her cigarette. "Then you can put some scoops of ice cream in two bowls; take the nice ones with the medals on them. And pour some Bailey's over the top, and don't be stingy about it either! After all, it is my goddamn fucking birthday!"

He had to put on some music, a CD by the singer Lena Ph. *Ont, det gör ont, det gör ont*—the right song in the right place, that one! *Pain, it hurts, it hurts.* She'd sat down, holding her feet, her toes spread open. Her malformed feet always caused her pain.

Micke waited. He'd done the dishes, dried them, cleaned the stove, put the kitchen back in order. Now they'd reached the point where they sat and drank coffee, with a great deal of Bailey's, this time in glasses.

"Please," she said, and pleadingly stretched out her feet toward him.

"All right." He moved a little closer to her, and put her foot on his lap. He began to press and massage her strangely shaped toes. The slight smell of foot odor wafted into his nostrils. Nettan closed her eyes and enjoyed the massage.

"I don't know why women wear those torture instruments," he said teasingly.

"To please the guys, of course."

"Hmmm."

"Well, just think about it. Imagine a cute girl wearing comfortable nurses' shoes! How sexy is that on a scale of one to ten?"

They both laughed.

"Okay," she said. "I'll tell you about your dad. Of course he had his good sides. He was handsome. He was the kind of man you could show off and say, this one belongs to me and no one else! You could feel proud when others looked him over, other women. And whenever I'd come into a place, he'd put his arm around me right away and kind of demonstrate it. We met at a bar on Fleminggatan, really close to Saint Erik's Hospital. I used to go out with Vilma, if you remember her. She moved to Malmö later on. She had black hair and always wore thick make-up."

"Huh?" he said uncertainly.

"Doesn't matter. Nathan also used to go there, together with some of his pals. They had a regulars' table next to the window, and one day we started a conversation and that's how it went."

"It did, eh?"

"Yes, he could be so romantic. He always brought roses whenever we went out on a date. Dark red ones, expensive ones. The kind with the long stems. I thought it was kind of unnecessary, since there was, like, no chance of putting them in any water; we were going out right away. But I certainly felt appreciated, that's for sure."

He gently placed one foot down and she placed the other one in his lap. She had a corn on her pinkie toe; it looked infected.

"At the time, he was married to that woman Ann-Marie, but marriage never stopped him from going out with other women. He was notoriously unfaithful by nature."

"Notoriously?"

"Yeah, like there was nothing anyone could do about it. He had kids with her, too, your half-sisters Ann and Marie. Cute, huh! They were five and seven when he got divorced. Well, to dump a woman, that's one thing, but to dump a woman and leave her alone with the responsibility of raising kids, that's something else . . ."

She cut herself off, yelling. He'd touched her corn.

"Don't you think you should see a foot doctor? What are they called? Podiatrist?" he asked, and tried to sound joking while he did so.

"Do you have any idea how much it costs?"

Oh boy, there he was back on the thin ice. He gently and carefully stroked her wrist. "And then after you, there was that Barbro woman? Jenny's mom?"

"Well, who the hell knows? He certainly got into the pants of a number of other women. Is that enough now? Do you know everything you need to know?"

No, he thought, but he didn't know how he should continue asking questions. He shrugged his shoulders, patted her foot a little, and set it down on the floor.

"I want to know why you don't have a girlfriend, Micke," she said slowly as she reached for her pack of cigarettes. "I mean, if I can answer your questions, you can answer mine. You're not going to get angry, are you?"

"No," he said shortly.

"The thing is, I wonder about it sometimes. Mothers do that, we can't help it. Katrin has also wondered. You're good-looking,

Micke, just like he was. You're cute, you have muscles and all the stuff that women like."

He felt his blush starting, spreading both up and down from his neck, glowing like fire on his earlobes.

"Katrin asked me right out, do you think he's *one of those*, and I said, no, not Micke. He's not like that."

Now he was starting to get angry, really angry. And he had all the right in the world. But that would not be the tactical thing at this moment. What he wanted was for her to tell him more about Nathan. Give him some tips without realizing it.

"Cut it out," he said.

"Excuse me for asking, but have you . . . have you ever slept with a girl? You have, right?"

"Couple of times, why?"

"Just wondering. I was just starting to get a little worried. Not that I would have thrown you out because of it. I mean if you came home one evening and told me you were gay, that is. Jonas Gardell is gay. And he's quite successful. Not to mention his partner, Mark Levengood. He's done well for himself, too."

"I'm not gay."

"You sure about that?"

"Damn it, Ma!"

"Well, it wouldn't have bothered me, but your father would have raised his eyebrows all right."

"Why's that?"

"His only son."

"What about it?"

"He had plans for you, you better believe it. Think for a minute, one boy and five daughters. Of course he'd have plans for you!"

He began to feel a surging pride.

"Was . . . was he happy when I was born?"

"No doubt about it. Of course he was happy. Already four girls and then this baby with this peepee. You looked so much like him, too. You should have seen some of the old photos of him when he was around three or four years old. You were the exact copy."

"I was?"

"Yep."

"Where are those photos now?"

"No idea. He took all that stuff with him when he moved in with Barbro. All his private stuff."

"But . . . why'd he leave? Did he fall in love with her while the two of you . . . ?"

She got up and took a few unsteady dance steps.

"Life is not always that easy," she said, a bit tipsy. "Your father . . . he was one of those . . . he had some good inside him, sure. But you couldn't depend on him. He was a restless soul. He was probably made to be a globetrotter from the very beginning . . . in body and soul. Psychically, too, I mean."

TOR WAS WAITING OUTSIDE of Jill's entryway at a quarter past six in the morning when she biked back from work. A great heap of cigarette stubs was on the sidewalk. Jill got off her bicycle and stared at him, completely surprised. He laughed with embarrassment. Then he stepped out into the lamplight, took hold of her handlebars, and wriggled them back and forth until she had to let go.

"Sorry," he said. "I'll go soon. I was driving by, and then I thought I'd stop here and stretch my legs."

"Huh? I've been trying to call you! Are you really on your way somewhere?"

"Well . . ."

"Come on in!" she exclaimed, taking her bicycle back and locking it underneath the bicycle shelter.

"Jill, you've been working all night. You have to sleep."

"Don't talk nonsense. Come on in, right now!"

"Okay, just for a bit."

She hadn't made the bed; she hadn't cleaned. Her suitcase still stood, partially unzipped, right in the middle of the floor.

"I'm thinking about having a cup of tea. Would you like one, too?"

"Sure, thanks."

She turned on the water and took out a tin of black currant tea.

"I can't offer you anything to eat. I don't keep anything at home."

"I'm not hungry."

She put two mugs on the table. They had a flowery design; she'd gotten them from Berit.

"Sorry I called you and disturbed you at work last night."

"You didn't disturb me."

"Sure I did, but I felt so . . . so . . ."

"Are you feeling better now?"

"Yes, I've been driving around in the car all night. Yes, now I feel better." He looked at her and smiled.

They heard the sound of a vessel's motor from the lake. Jill knew which one it was, the *Baltic Viking* on the way to Köping from Poland. It was carrying liquid ammonia. The *Baltic Viking* was a large vessel with its home port in Oslo. One time she'd been on board with Billy, the pilot. Almost the entire crew was from the Philippines. Billy had joked with them, gestured in her direction and whispered, in English, *second wife*. All of them grinned, understanding. Many foreign seamen had a wife and children in their homelands, but also a second wife in Scandinavia.

The tea was finished. She poured it and set out honey, butter, and *skorpor*—twice-baked toast—on the table. Tor sat there, warming his hands on his cup. His thin, edgy hands with broken cuticles, fingers stained with nicotine.

"Do you often dream . . . about her?" Jill asked carefully. "It happened while we were at the blue hotel."

"Not so often these days, actually. Before, just after she disappeared, I dreamed of her the minute my head hit the pillow. But I hardly ever do now. And the worst thing of all, I'm beginning to forget her face."

"Six years is a long time."

"Six years and seven months."

"Right."

"I was out driving last night for hours. I don't know why. It just happened. I landed up in Hässelby."

"You did?" Jill said, unsure.

"Lots of things have changed out there. Have you seen it? They've rebuilt the subway and . . ."

"No, I haven't been there for a long time."

"My parents-in-law, their place, it's been torn down. All the greenhouses, too, which he had, Berit's father, that is. His entire life's work gone. Now there's townhouses there instead."

His entire life's work gone, she thought. Everything important to him, including his daughter. She remembered how they used to play together under the dirt-covered workbenches, the raw smell of clay pots and earth. Once Berit had slipped and crashed through a glass pane. Her elbow was cut up and she had to go to the hospital for stitches. Her father had gotten angry: "How many times have I told you not to play in here!" It didn't help. There was something which drew them there, so they would sneak back inside, between the aromatic, well-tied plants. Sometimes Berit would pick a cucumber or a tomato. The taste was strong, different. Vegetables don't taste like that any more. Nowadays people only sold hard, imported vegetables from Holland which have no aroma.

He'd had a number of ancient grape vines, old and twisted, as well. Every fall at this time of year, they'd be weighted down with sweet grapes. She would get some to take home, and they had to eat them within a day or two or those small black fruit flies would spread throughout the house and start reproducing in the soil of her mother's potted houseplants.

"Did you take a look at their graves?" The sentence spilled out of her. "I mean, of your in-laws. Considering that Berit didn't have any brothers or sisters, that is."

"Oh, the cemetery takes care of that. You pay them a fee every year and they make sure it's all taken care of."

Jill crept into her bed, pulled her blanket over herself. She always felt a little frozen after the night shift. Tor drank his tea and watched her.

"Are you tired?"

"Not so much. I've gotten my second wind."

"You know what happened then? I was driving around Hässelby and before I knew it, I ended up at Justine Dalvik's place. It was almost as if the car were driving itself."

A chill like ice went through her.

"I see."

"It was the middle of the night, of course, and there wasn't a single soul up and about. Except for her. Her whole place was lit up. I saw her; she was in the kitchen. She appeared all shaken up about something. And right then, she tore open the outside door and screamed to someone or something to go away and leave her in peace. Honestly, it was a little creepy."

"Was she screaming at you? Did she see you, do you think?"

"Oh, no. I'm absolutely convinced she didn't see me. And I didn't see or hear anyone else in the yard. It was horrible. I think she's not right in the head."

Jill pulled the blanket over her chest.

"I wonder how much of this was our doing," she whispered. "Our fault, I mean. When we were young. I've thought about it a great deal lately. We had practically no empathy. We were truly awful to her many times. But she . . . she never cried, so we thought she sort of agreed to the whole thing. Somehow. Always bringing candy with her. Sandy Concern until we could hardly eat it any longer. You know, her father . . ."

"I know."

"And one time, we, we who were her classmates . . . once up on the hill cliffs . . . I can barely think about it. She broke her leg that time. She didn't come back to school after that, not for a long time. But she didn't tell her parents any of this. Why she broke her leg, I mean. No, she never told on us. And by the way, her mother wasn't her real mother. Her father remarried, to his secretary, I believe. Her name was Flora. The name sounded like a beautiful flower. We thought she was regal; she was nothing like our practical, hum-drum mothers. She always wore fine clothes and nail polish and lipstick."

Tor pointed at the enlargement of Jill and Berit which was hanging on the wall.

"I haven't seen that before," he said.

"Berit gave it to me awhile back. It was taken the day we started third grade."

Tor placed his tea cup on the table and moved to the bed, sitting right next to her.

"We look so innocent!" she exclaimed. "Look closely, what sweet, delightful little girls. But appearances deceive. Do you think that all children are so cruel? I've thought about this quite a bit. Do children have no sense of empathy? Maybe not. Children can be extremely concerned about injured animals. But to the children their own age? Or was it just Berit and I who were so cold and cruel, Berit and I and another girl, Gerd? And there were some others, actually a number of us. You know, I think Justine did not have a single friend. She always attached herself to us; she had no sense of pride. She was always alone. Her real mother had died right in front of her eyes in her own home, when she was just four years old. Don't you think that was enough trauma? Did we really have to lay stones on the board and squeeze the life out of her?"

Tor carefully lay his arm around her.

"I think that this happens in every generation and throughout the entire world," he said. "Things were like that in my school, too. Or schools, I should say, since sometimes I went to the school up by my grandparents."

"Jeez, how did that go?"

"I should have been teased since I didn't talk like the others. I had a Stockholm dialect, and they all spoke another dialect. And when I returned to Stockholm, I had the Burträsk dialect. But I could fight, you see. I made other kids respect me."

Jill had trouble imagining Tor using his fists.

She leaned against him and closed her eyes.

"We had a nice trip, didn't we?" Tor said somewhere above her head. She nodded.

"Jill, I have . . ."

She wound her arms around him and pulled him to her, covering them both with the blanket.

"Let's rest awhile," she whispered. "I think we could use it. Both you and me."

THEN CAME DAYS WITH STRONG WINDS and rain which made the water turn black and whipped up white froth on the waves. Justine thought that she would have to take her flat-bottomed rowboat out of the lake soon; it shouldn't stay in the water during the winter like last year. The wood had suffered.

Hans Peter seemed more and more disturbed by her rowing trips out over the water.

"Are you taking that boat out again? It's getting much too blustery."

No, I won't, just today . . . and maybe tomorrow . . . not ready yet to let go of control.

When Hans Peter was sleeping, she'd put on her life vest and row out. The water made the boat bob up and down, threw cascades of waves over the railing. She would pull hard on the oars. It was hard to steer, hard to maneuver. She thought about her father's large motorized sailboat, she'd learned how to handle it, but late one Midsummer night, it had been rammed by a speeding motorboat and now it stayed tied up to the dock. The operator had been a drunken man her own age. He had to spend a long time recovering at the hospital.

Justine didn't bother to have the boat repaired. The rowboat was enough for her.

Here, somewhere? She never knew for sure, she thought she remembered, different areas each time. She let down the anchor;

it fell in with a dull and reluctant splash. Then she brought in the oars, being very careful that they not get loose from their oarlocks and fall in. Be lost to her. Bobbing directionless out here, with risk of overturning . . . she nervously pulled at the edge of her life vest. She wondered whether the ice would set early this year. Like it did *that time.* Her life became easier when the ice closed everything off and sealed it. She was freer; she could relax in a different manner. But there were dangers there as well. On sparkling winter days, jig-fishermen could be sitting out there for hours. Then she would get restless, force herself to spy on them with the binoculars from her library, watch their every move.

For most of the time, she kept it away from her. *It.* She kept it away from her, but out of the blue questions would pop up in her mind. How long would it take for a body to decompose in fresh water? What about clothes, plastic, wood? How much time would it take before every trace had vanished? Before she could be safe? The skeleton of the kick-sled would sit there for a number of decades, until the nails rusted through and it fell apart. A kick-sled would not be much of a threat. But teeth, hair, skin.

She'd used string to fasten the body to the kick-sled. Regular string from a household roll. And then the scarf, which she'd wrapped around Berit's throat. How long could string hold a body to a kick-sled?

Sometimes it happened that she saw an eye. If she crept from her seat so that the wet, hard, bottom ribs of the boat hurt her legs and pain burned in her knees. If she let her upper body lean over the railing toward the water. Then, sometimes, she could see it. An eye in shreds quietly staring, it glowed beneath the algae and seaweed. She forced herself to return its gaze, while her stomach acids churned up into her throat.

This is where it is. How should I mark this spot?

Open water in every direction, she did not have the ability to judge distances. And the next morning, the eye may have moved. Stared greenly from the stones, looked sorrowful and empty. She would get a runny nose, and her chest hurt when she swallowed.

A flock of birds, screeching as they flew toward the boat, making her crouch and huddle down.

Hans Peter had woken up. He was off work today. He came down the stairs in his robe and noticed her sodden clothes. He was starting to get so surly and curt.

"Good morning," Justine greeted him.

"I've asked you to leave that rowboat alone."

"It's not dangerous," she said stubbornly.

"I disagree."

"Hans Peter, I grew up by this body of water; it's like a part of me."

There was no answer to that.

At that moment, the bird came swooping into the hallway, landed on the hat rack, took a few double steps. The bird had been allowed to move back inside. They noticed that he preferred being inside his safe house. He drew up one of his legs and began to clean his feathers, pulling them with neat tugs.

Justine took off her wet clothes.

"I love you," she said. "Please forgive me if I am not all that you'd hoped I would be."

"I love you, too," he said, but as he looked at her, she saw a distance in his eyes.

"Hans Peter?" she said, pleading.

He grimaced.

"I'm just a little tired. It'll pass."

LATER ON THAT DAY, they went to visit Hans Peter's parents. His mother, Birgit, had had her second heart attack. She wasn't up to doing much anymore. They were both elderly, nearing eighty, but they still lived in their family home in Stuvsta. His mother had been brusque and on her guard around Justine during their initial visits, but although they would never develop a close relationship, they'd begun to relax in each other's company. Birgit had changed even more after her last heart attack. She listened more, and was no longer as critical.

After Hans Peter's divorce, Birgit had not welcomed the new girlfriends he'd brought home for visits. Birgit Bergman was a woman of authority and principle. It was difficult for her to accept that Hans Peter and his former wife had decided to go their separate ways. It didn't help that Hans Peter told her it was a mutual decision they'd weighed for a long time.

"You haven't given each other enough chances," was her comment. "And you have to do that, you see, in any marriage. How else do you think you can make a family work?"

Hans Peter had always had trouble standing up to her. After his sister Margareta died, he'd moved back with his parents and supported them for a number of years. He'd broken off his studies; he'd been majoring in theology and philosophy at the time, and was even thinking of becoming a priest. He had told Justine how it tore him up inside, dealing with their sorrow and silence. Finally, he'd had enough of taking care of other people's souls. For a long period of time, his parents had left his sister's room undisturbed, but one day he decided to clean it out and turn it into a dining room. That was his first revolt, and it had obviously succeeded. Right now they were sitting in that very dining room. His parents had made the house more accessible; they'd taken away the raised wooden strips between the rooms, and given the toilet a raised seat. Birgit had gotten much thinner; her skin was yellow and waxy. Justine watched her from the corner of her eye. Death was drawing near, step by step, she realized. He'd already marked Birgit, but was still holding off for a short while. It wasn't yet her time. *I'll just take away a bit of your ability to move, a little bit of your hearing, your memory, and the strength in the beats of your heart.* An image of Flora formed in her mind, how her stepmother had lain in her room in Råksta as if she were a bundle among several which had to be cared for; how they'd lifted her up and tried to feed her some food. The soup, which ran down her chin and under her bib; the diapers, which always stank of urine. When Flora was at the height of her strength, she had always been meticulous about her appearance to the point of overdoing it.

The memory alone made Justine turn her face and take a few deep breaths.

Hans Peter's father had worked as a sheet metal worker; his mother had been a high school teacher. A strange combination, Justine had thought when she first met them. They were exact opposites. Kjell was a loud, boisterous, happy kind, who liked a good joke. Justine had always found such people difficult. They had a façade, and there was no possibility of sliding behind it. Which one did Hans Peter resemble most? Thank God, neither of them. Neither in looks nor behavior.

There was a dusty portrait of Margareta in the bathroom. She was blonde and laughing; you could see she had her father's chin and mouth. Hans Peter was dark-haired. Or rather, used to be dark-haired. Maybe that was from Birgit; she was white-haired now, and shrunken.

Are we going to look like that, she wondered, and she wanted to take Hans Peter's hand, but he'd just climbed up on a stool and was changing a light-bulb. Kjell was standing beside him, holding the new one.

"How's it going, Hans Peter? Do you have any manhood left? Or has she sucked it all out of you?" He gestured toward Justine and bellowed with laughter.

"The bulb's been out for a while," said Birgit. "We don't dare climb up on things any longer. We'd certainly fall and break our necks. And as far as I'm concerned, I've had enough of hospitals."

Birgit turned to Justine.

"It's not easy getting older. Keep that in mind."

"Right."

"You're still young, but you're not that young anymore. Right? How old are you, by the way? I've asked before, I'm sure, but I don't remember."

"A bit over fifty," she said, wanting to avoid it.

It seemed as if a sad veil fell over Birgit's eyes.

"Then it's too late."

"Mamma!" said Hans Peter from his spot up on the stool.

"What?" she replied angrily. "Do you think it's not too late?"

His father broke into the conversation: "You could have been a little more, hmmm, shall we say *active*? I think that's what your mother means, H.P. We could have heard the traipsing of little feet in the house. She's been missing that."

"Well, that's just the way it is!" Hans Peter said frostily.

"Stop calling him H. P.; he's not a steak sauce," said Birgit with irritation. "I've asked you a million times, Kjell, but you keep it up! Try and listen to me for once! He was christened Hans Peter; maybe you've forgotten?"

"Sure, sure, but come on, why not joke around a little? Life is more fun! But not for sourpusses, of course."

"People can disagree about what makes a good joke."

"Yes, that's what you always say."

"By the way, that's enough about me wanting grandchildren," Birgit continued. "I've lost the battle. You kids are not the only ones who are too old for it. We are, too. The tip-tapping of little feet is too hard on old ears like ours." She smiled bitterly.

Justine tried not to listen. She lifted the coffee pot.

"Does anyone want another cup?"

"Thanks, yes, I would," said Birgit.

"You would," said Kjell. "Home-brewed is a sight better than that gunk they had at the hospital. Do you remember how unhappy you were with their coffee?"

They were finished changing the bulb. Kjell turned on the lights and the round ceiling lamp gave off a harsh, almost blinding light. Birgit warded it off with her arms.

"Turn it off!"

Kjell cleared his throat.

"You're never happy, are you? But H.P.—sorry, Hans Peter— can you take a look at something else as long as you are here? I can't figure it out. As long as you're in the middle of fixing things anyway. Down in the basement. I think there's something loose. I see so damned badly nowadays."

The two men disappeared down the basement stairs. Justine remained sitting with Birgit. Hans Peter's mamma, she thought. She carried him inside her body, gave him food and warmth. I love him. I must like her.

"We once had a little girl," the old woman said slowly. "She was such a delightful little thing."

"Yes, you've told me about her. Margareta. That was a tragedy. I would have liked to meet Hans Peter's little sister. Very much.

"I was against the idea of her taking the car. I told Kjell we shouldn't let her drive that large car; she's just a little, little girl. But he wouldn't listen. Men are like that. Of course she could have the car, now that she had her driver's license. You know what? Young people believe they are invincible. I know young people. I saw them in school every day. I knew everything about them, how they thought, their way of looking at life and at challenges. Kjell knew nothing about these things. Nothing. Of course, she could have the car. Why else did she get her license?"

Justine had nothing to say to that.

Birgit took off her glasses. They remained hanging on a chain around her neck. She rubbed her eyes.

"Ending a life takes only a few seconds. But young people think that life and youth are forever."

"How old would Margareta have been today?"

"She would have been forty-four. She was such a darling little girl, always happy, I used to do her hair with tiny, damp braids so that they would have curls once her hair had dried. She used to sing when she was little. She would sing the whole day long and invent her own songs. I would write them down, I have them in the dresser drawer in the bedroom. Sometimes I take them out and remember."

"I see."

"It seems so wrong."

"I understand."

"She should have had a full life. Why wasn't she given that chance? Start a family. Have children and be happy with them. I was hoping for so much from her, but Fate took a different turn."

"Yes, no one can change Fate," Justine said lamely.

Birgit wrinkled her eyebrows.

"No," she said at last. Then she added: "Do you know what the most difficult thing in life is for a woman?"

Justine felt the roots of her hair prickling.

"I'm sure a number of things can be difficult."

"True enough. But the most difficult thing for a woman is to bury her own child. You know nothing about that, Justine; you've never had children. People who haven't had children have no idea how deep the emptiness in the soul can be once you've lost a son or a daughter."

Anger rose like a fever so that Justine leapt up and, without excusing herself, she went into the bathroom and locked the door. She stood there, hanging on to the sink, hanging on so hard that it hurt all the way to her fingernails. From a distance she heard how Hans Peter and his father were coming up the stairs, heard Hans Peter asking, "Where is Justine?"

Then she sank down on the toilet for the elderly and covered her eyes with her hands.

O F COURSE THERE'D BEEN WOMEN. Now and again there'd been women. Of course!

Micke sat in the gardening hut and a burning chill spread along his spine as he thought about what Nettan had said. Nettan and Katrin. He didn't realize until now that they would often talk about him. Dissect him and discuss him. *Do you think he might be one of those?* He could just imagine it, Nettan and Katrin behind the curtain where they sat and drank coffee when there were no customers in their shop. What the hell! Prattle on about things that were none of their business. What else did they say? About his body, his sexuality, his integrity? Dark spots appeared before his eyes and he had trouble concentrating. It felt as if they'd taken off his clothes and more or less raped him. Anger raged through him and he jumped up and grabbed the first thing that came to hand, a crossword puzzle dictionary, and he furiously threw it against the wall. The book fell onto the floor, open, spine broken, a number of pages fallen out. He would never be able to fix it. He picked up the book and poked the loose pages back inside. Put it back in its place.

Women, women, women. But no relationship, nothing which lasted. Just a few days at the most, then it would end. He hadn't introduced anyone to Nettan. They were more like one-night stands. He liked that English expression: one-night stand. The fact of the matter was that he didn't want a girlfriend. He really didn't need another person interfering with his life, trying to control him. Nettan was there, and she was enough.

That Katrin, Nettan's friend. Someone should give it to her! Give it to her so she'd shut up and stop sticking her nose into things that were none of her business! She always gave him such strange looks. Always making her stupid jokes, as if she couldn't decide whether to treat him like a kid or a grown-up.

"How are things going with you, Micke? How's life treating you?" As if his life was separate from him and he wasn't the one living it! Some kind of super life which steered him. And how could you answer a question like that? Was she even expecting an answer at all?

Not to mention Nettan. She was probably whining and complaining the whole time behind the curtain. *He doesn't do anyyyythiiiing! He doesn't have a job; he sponges off me, sucking me dry!*

He took a leak, and a picture of Katrin arose in his mind. She was lying in front of his eyes, fat and swelling on Henry and Märta's large table. She was naked. He'd told her to take off her clothes. She'd stared at him with wide-open eyes, complained, *You can't mean it, Micke; we know each other. I'm Nettan's friend,* but he stood there, straight, unmoved, pointing to the floor, *Put your stuff there.* She didn't want to, so he was forced to grab her, hard. That helped, and she did exactly as he asked: crept up on the table, clumsy and trembling; he forced her to lie on her back and draw up her knees and then he took out a rope.

His member swelled and grew as he thought of this, it became so hard that it was painful, dry and silky, and heating up. He leaned forward and grabbed a pillow from the sofa. It had red lines of embroidery: *East, West, Home is Best,* and he spurted his strong, wild seed right into the red lettering.

"LOOK IN THE BACK SEAT" was the first thing Tommy said when Ariadne opened the car door. She rubbed the rain from her cheeks and forehead. Christa was sitting behind him, her hair thick and curly from the rain. She looked morose. In her arms, she held two slightly soft cardboard boxes that had once held strawberries. Now they were filled with chanterelle mushrooms.

"Oh, you found some after all!" Ariadne exclaimed, and tried to sound surprised. "Great!" She sank down into the seat next to Tommy, and he started the motor right away.

"I have my secret spots." He chuckled contentedly and placed his hand on her leg. She felt her body stiffen;, she hoped he didn't notice.

"It was a misty rain," he continued, and turned on to Dalagatan. "But I knew where we should look. The same forest we were before, remember? You turn to the right after you get off the ferry."

"Oh, there."

"First I just found one. It stood there, shining wonderfully gold in the moss. And a little ways away, there was another one, and then some more . . . and more and more! What a feeling!" His hands left the wheel for a second, as he rubbed them together. He started to sing an old Swedish song about chanterelle mushrooms: *Har du sett herr Kantarell bort i enebaken, han kom dit i förrgår kväll med sin hatt på nacken.*

The traffic light at Fridhemsplan turned red as they approached. He turned his head toward her.

"But, really, it's almost the end of the chanterelle season. Or else folks had already gotten there and nabbed them. I'd hoped to find many more. Especially when you go out on a special trip to pick them."

"Weren't you freezing?"

"Freezing? What? You have to put up with some hardships! Or what do you say, Christa? Did you think it was cold in the forest?"

"Little bit," peeped a reply from the back seat.

"We'll warm up soon. We'll each take a long, warm shower, while Mamma fries the mushrooms in butter. You have to use real butter, Ariadne, remember that. And then we'll make a wonderful omelette with some mashed potatoes."

Then Ariadne put in her two cents: "This morning you were talking about mushroom sandwiches. Right? Remember? So I went and bought good Breakfast Bread. I know you like it. At the Konsum grocery store on Sveavägen."

"Oh, yum-yum! Bondgården's Breakfast Bread!" He imitated the TV ad. "That sounds a bit better than an omelette, of course. But considering the time of day, we ought to call it Bondgården's Evening Bread instead!"

They laughed. Tommy and Ariadne laughed. Christa's laugh came from the back seat.

Evening Bread. How funny it sounded.

He went right into the bathroom the moment they returned, pausing just long enough to hang up his jacket and the little black backpack he always kept with him. Pain shot down Ariadne's back. How long would he be in the shower? Ten minutes? Fifteen?

She clasped her hands, shut her eyes, almost as if she was praying, as if it would be absolutely necessary for her to have a God to Whom she prayed. Christa was sitting on the floor, working at untying her sneakers; there were some difficult knots in them.

"How's it going, Christa?" she said, trying to make her voice sound normal.

"They're stuck," came Christa's fretting voice.

"I'll untie them for you in just a minute. Mamma will untie them."

There was the sound of water pounding in the shower. He was singing, too, singing with his strong, thundering voice: "*Ack, som ett fjun så lätt är varje kvinna!*"

Some long shining pine needles shimmered on the floor. She thought they were alive, that they were crawling.

Please, dear Lord, be with me now!

"Come on, Mamma! Hurry up!"

She felt her lips moving.

"Right away, I just have to . . ."

She had to reach over Christa to get the backpack on the hook next to his jacket. She stretched over her daughter, didn't move her feet, felt the smooth, worn-out leather against her fingers. She unhooked the band. Right about that moment, the water stopped streaming down behind the bathroom door.

"I'll help you," he said, as he came into the kitchen. Ariande was already standing there with the plastic shopping bag, and had just put on her apron.

"No need," she said quickly.

"You've been working all day. Of course, I'll help you."

He took the shopping bag from her and pulled out the loaf of bread.

"It's been awhile since we've had this kind in the house."

"Yes. I not often don't shop in town; the shop at Brommaplan no sell it."

Tommy went over to the lamp over the counter and held up the bread package to the light. Looked through the list of ingredients, was content. Then he opened the package and took out a knife.

"How many slices should I cut? How many can you eat?"

"Maybe one," said Ariadne.

"Not more?"

"Two, then."

"And Christa, what about you?"

"Two."

"All right, I'll slice four for you two and four for me."

Ariadne rinsed the mushrooms and let them spatter in the frying pan for a while until the water had steamed off. Then she took some butter from the refrigerator and sliced some in. Tommy came up behind her, put his hands on her hips, kissed her. He had the pleasant aroma of bath gel.

"The plate isn't too hot, is it?" he asked. "So you don't burn the mushrooms."

"Oh, no."

"Chanterelles don't grow in Greece, do they?"

"No, don't think so."

"But there were many other beautiful things. Such as you."

She clucked out a laugh. Slowly turned, and kissed him. It was sharp and light inside her.

He was hungry. He'd already eaten two sandwiches before the first symptoms began to appear. He cleared his throat and stuck out his tongue, scratched it with his front teeth, as if he wanted to scrape away something unpleasant. At first, she pretended not to notice anything. She poured some milk for Christa and took some breadcrumbs off the table with her finger. She was reaching for the pepper; she hadn't used enough, and was just about to say so:

"Maybe you need to add pepper. I put on too little."

Instead, Tommy leapt up from his chair so quickly that it fell over.

"I don't understand," his gravelly voice said. "It feels like . . ."

She got up, too.

"What's going on, Tommy? What is the matter?"

"I must have eaten something wrong. Do you think . . . was there a poisonous mushroom among the chanterelles?"

"What?"

He grabbed her wrist and began to shake her. Had trouble articulating his words.

"Were all the mushrooms really chanterelles? All the same kind! Can you swear it?"

"Ye- . . . yes!"

"Not a red and white one among them?"

"You should know," she said with worry. "You picked them yourself."

"Yes . . . but Christa . . . she doesn't see, of course. Were all the mushrooms yellow, are you sure?"

There was an unpleasant raspy sound when he breathed. He let go of her and ran out into the hallway. Ariadne stayed by the table, heard how hangers and jackets were being thrown off the hooks.

"Fuuuuuck!" he howled. "My backpack . . . fuuuck, where the hell is my backpack!"

"It's got to be there . . . on the hook . . . you usually ha . . . hang it on the hook," she stammered.

"It's not on any damned hook!"

He was ripping and pulling at the jackets and coats. His jacket, her jacket, a winter coat which she rarely used but had no other place to hang—it was a nice coat, made of the softest egg-white wool. And then there was Christa's yellow down coat.

"Tommy!" she screamed. "What do you want me to do?"

"Search for it, damn it all! Search! You know what it looks like! Black, the same old one, with the needles and the medicine, the one I always, always have!"

Ariadne fluttered about, pretending to look. Tommy was in the living room now; it sounded as if he was ripping apart the entire house. She ran after him, tried to take hold of him, pleading: "Sweetheart, try to think clearly. You must have put it somewhere else. Maybe the bathroom. I go and look in the bathroom. Maybe under the towels, it is there."

Tommy was beginning to have difficulty speaking. Things were going more quickly, now. His windpipes were beginning to close, his face had changed color, his eyes were mere pricks; they almost disappeared in the grotesquely rearranged face.

He pulled at his T-shirt neck; he pulled down his pants, began to rip and scratch at his body as if possessed, stumbled into the kitchen, grabbed a fork and began to rip his entire body so that long bloody scratches appeared.

"No, sweetheart, no! Not do that!" She tried to calm him and plead with him, although she knew it served no purpose. A few times previously, when he'd had strong allergic reactions, he had become just as desperate and unable to listen. But then he also had his injections and was able to stave off the worst. Before it had gone so long that he suffocated. Or his heart stopped. Or what was going to happen now if he did not get help in time.

"The car," he hissed. "Car keys, I have to drive . . . hospital . . ."

"They are in the backpack," she was yelling now. "Maybe the backpack is in the car. Tommy, you have other keys? Two keys for the car? An extra key? Where is the extra key? Tell me, I get it!"

"I don't know," his voice rattled. "I don't remember."

"Ohhh, you can't drive! You too sick!"

He held her tightly and snot and slime was pouring from his nose.

"I call ambulance!" She screamed right into his burning hot ear. "Just let go. I call ambulance!"

He didn't hear, didn't understand, scratched off and on and otherwise held on to her like a drunken man. It was becoming more difficult for him to breathe; the cramps were coming. Soon it would be too late. He suddenly let go of her and fell to the floor, came to his knees, swaying back and forth with his head down as if he could get more air that way.

"Go . . . call!" he hissed.

She got up.

"Yes, I call."

He nodded desperately. The telephone was on a small table underneath the mirror. She looked at herself in the mirror, observed her eyes. There was a light in them, a strange, shimmering light.

She lifted the receiver and pretended to dial a number. A short number, three numbers. She imagined how a voice would sound on the other end. A female voice at the emergency service center somewhere in central Stockholm. Through the door to the kitchen, she watched her husband on his knees, throwing his body back and forth in compulsive movements.

"We need an ambulance," she said loudly, loud enough for him to hear, too. "It's my husband, he is having a severe allergic reaction. Please hurry! A matter of life and death!"

She listened to the usual sound of the dial tone.

Then she gave their address and waited as if they were writing it down.

"Yes, right," she said and then added, with tears in her voice, "You come quickly. Thank you, that is very good to hear."

She put down the receiver and went back to the kitchen. Leaned over Tommy, massaged his arms and shoulders. He rolled his head; there was fear in the small slits left of his eyes.

"They are on the way," she said formally. "Now we just wait."

She crept next to him, found his hand. It was slippery and sweaty and jerked in small spasms.

"It will be all right."

In one violent show of strength, he pulled her down onto the floor, grabbed her so hard so that she thought one of her ribs cracked. He rolled on top of her with a tortured, animal sound.

"Tommy, please," she flustered. "Not so, not like this."

He quieted down but still held her, did not loosen his bear-hold.

They remained in that position for a while. She was lying with one cheek against the cool floor, completely tired, exhausted.

She noticed someone moving in the hallway. It was Christa. She was creeping along the floor like an injured animal.

"Mamma," she whined.

"We are here. Go back in your room."

Christa did not react. Ariadne yelled again: "Go back to your room! Wait there!"

Still no reaction. With her cheek still pressed to the floor, Ariadne saw how her daughter mindfully found her way along the floorboard, how her fingers reached the telephone jack. Her round, still somewhat childlike hands followed the cord up to the receiver, grabbed it, and lifted it. It was a large, simple telephone, which they had purchased because of Christa, Tommy had taught her how to use it, taught her how to press the three important numbers for an emergency situation, and Ariadne lay there, chained by her husband's body, felt his heart's pounding heatbeat, and saw with clarity how her daughter dialed those very numbers.

A FEW DAYS LATER, Micke called Kevin again. His situation
was becoming desperate; he wouldn't even have gas money
soon. When Robin, Kevin's younger brother who'd been his classmate since first grade, answered the phone, he'd been surprised.
They hadn't been in contact since Micke dropped out of school.

"Hi, Micke, long time no hear. It's me, Robin."

"Huh? Why're you answering Kevin's phone?"

"Well, you see, Kevin . . . he lit out for foreign countries."

"Oh damn. Well, that sounds cool."

"You bet. Especially when you think of this fucking weather.
How're things with you?"

"All right."

"I heard a couple of your messages."

"So he didn't take his cell phone with him?"

"Uh . . . no."

"The thing is, I worked for him sometimes. Window
cleaning, that kind of thing."

"Yeah?"

"Just wanted to check and see if he had anything like that
now."

"Nah, you know what? His company is suspended until he
gets back."

"Okay. Just thought I'd check."

"Is it, *acute*, so to speak?"

"What do you mean?"

"You need cash?"

"Well . . ."

"I thought of something, you see. Maybe you want to do a gig with me?"

"What kind of gig?"

"Let's talk about it. Go out for beer together."

Robin didn't let the grass grow under his feet. They met later that same day. Robin decided on the place, the bar Klippet on Handverkargatan. Micke had taken out all of his savings, just a few hundred crowns. It felt bad to have no cash, but hopefully this would be an investment, something that would pay off in the long run.

Robin looked like he always had, with greasy bangs that hung over his forehead and hid his eyes. He was somewhat short and rather thin. He'd worn glasses in school, but not any more, and he had a thin, hardly visible, mustache as well as a goatee. Micke remembered that they'd had a dog in Robin's family, a dog which looked like the young owners, same blonde hair. Its name was Prilly, he remembered. Prilly was a happy, playful dog who loved to play fetch. Prilly must've kicked the bucket by now. Good Lord, how old would he have been now? He didn't feel comfortable enough to ask.

They each ordered a Guinness. Robin mentioned he'd worked at various construction jobs after he'd finished school. It was drudgery and it was trying, and you had to get up at a really unholy hour of the morning. But still, it had given him a steady income.

"And now I'm off work for a while. I just take on a few extra gigs now and again. Of a completely different kind, so to speak."

"I see."

"I wanted to talk to you about one of those jobs." Robin leaned forward over the burn marks on the table. He sank his voice. "I need a partner. Not just anybody, either. But I know you from school; we were pals, weren't we?"

Micke made a gesture with his head, difficult to interpret.

"So that's why I'm going to ask you."

"What's the deal with the gig?"

Robin shook his bangs back and aimed his small round eyes at Micke.

"I'll tell you right out: Transportation. We pick up stuff at one point and deliver the goods to another point for, so to speak, temporary storage."

"What kind of stuff?"

"Computers. That kind of stuff. When people renovate their houses. You can't have electronics sitting around at home when you're in the middle of a renovation, can you, right? Think of all the dust and vibrations and that crap. You following me?"

"Think so."

"So, during the renovation, the stuff has to be moved out of the house and stored somewhere else. That kind of service. It's heavy work, I have to have someone help me carry it all. I used to have another guy, but he . . . he got another line of work."

"Okay"

"You're going in on it?"

"Yeah, sure."

Robin pulled out his wallet. For a moment, Micke thought that he was going to get an advance on his pay. But that wasn't the case.

"I'm inviting you to another round. And you gotta keep this in mind: This is not the kind of thing you go bragging about, if you get my drift."

"I think so."

"Not to mention the taxes."

"All right."

"It's just the way it is. Not a word. To anyone. Any questions?"

"Nope."

"You get a percentage later. The next day. That fine by you?"

Micke nodded, but he had a prickly feeling in his stomach.

The first gig came the next day. Robin called and asked Micke to come and meet him at his apartment on Surbrunnsgatan, which he rented third-hand. Robin opened the door. He was wearing the usual blue work clothes people wore on construction projects, and a jacket with a company logo on it.

"Change into these!" Robin commanded, pointing to a heap of similar clothes which were on a chair in his minimal kitchen. Micke hesitated a minute, then took off his jeans. Robin looked restless; he kept glancing at the clock.

"They fit?"

Micke had put on the blue pants. They were a little bit tight, but they worked.

Robin looked him over.

"Damn, you put on muscles. You lift weights, or what?"

"Nah."

"It wasn't criticism. Muscles are a bonus, especially in this job."

Micke held up the jacket and read: "Cargo & Transportation Service. This the company you work for?"

"Yeah, yeah, but hurry up. We gotta be there right after four."

Robin had a VW bus which had seen better days. On the floor, paper, gravel, empty snoose cans and soda bottles. The passenger seat was so worn out that Micke felt a hard, metal spring prick his ass when he sat down. It hurt like hell.

Robin drove silently, south on E4, fast, but not taking risks.

"Where's the job?"

"Rönninge."

Micke tried to make conversation, but received monosyllable answers, so he stopped. After half an hour, they reached a nice neighborhood with well-kept mansions. It reminded Micke of Hässelby, and he felt a wave of anger wash through him. He took a deep breath, and found himself feeling stronger, strong and invincible. The car drove smoothly over the road, finally stopping in front of a two-story wooden mansion with construction materials. There were discarded wardrobes and drawers on the grounds. Right at the entrance, there was a light blue toilet with its lid up.

Robin turned off the motor.

"You need to take a dump?" he asked, and laughed shortly and artificially. He pushed his bangs aside.

"Come on, let's get going."

They got out. Robin carried a tool box and walked boldly into the yard and up to the front door. He rang the bell. A soft, melodic signal rang through the house and came back to them. They waited for a while, but no one opened the door.

"*Perkele!*" Robin swore in Finnish. "They were supposed to be here when we got here."

"Who's they?"

"The people from the construction company. What do we do now? I promised the old guy who lives here that I'd get his computer stuff."

A woman with a tiny schnauzer came walking by on the sidewalk. She stopped and looked at them quizzically. Robin sucked in his lower lip, his goatee stuck out. He looked stressed.

"Let's go around to the back," he decided.

Robin waved at the woman, who didn't wave back, but took a better hold on the leash and continued her walk. The house had a subterranean floor. Micke cupped his hands around his face and looked in the window. It looked like an office room with a desk and a great deal of electronic equipment, including two computers and a printer.

"Those are the ones we're supposed to get," Robin said.

Robin was quick. He probably had worked in construction. In just a few seconds, he'd gotten out the screwdriver and managed to unscrew the window and, with Micke's help, lifted it down to the ground.

"Is this really okay?" whispered Micke.

"No other way to get in. Shut up and help me out."

No way to get out of it at this stage of the game. Micke thought about it on the drive home, as they headed back to Stockholm. By that time he knew for sure what they'd been up to, even if he hadn't wanted to admit it at first. Breaking and entering. That was the job.

He had a sour, rotten taste in his mouth; he felt shaky. They had climbed into the open space where the window had been, and while Micke uncoupled the computers, the color printer, the brand new copier, Robin raided the rest of the house. He returned with an MP3 player, a digital camera, and a cell phone, which he'd placed in a plastic bag. They went out the front door and loaded all the things into the van. Calmly and in an orderly manner, they shut the front door, and then they drove away.

They took the old Stockholm highway back. Robin had relaxed; he was whistling a bit to himself, singing at times.

"You gotta understand," he said, elbowing Micke in the side. "This delicate machinery doesn't like construction dust."

"What about the license plates on the car?" Micke whispered. "That old lady saw us, the one with the dog. What if she went home and called the cops?"

Robin laughed. His teeth had black fillings.

"You damned idiot, don't think I'm keeping these plates. I'll change them, of course. We're going to take a rest stop here in the forest, and I'll fix it."

SOME IMAGES HAD ETCHED THEMSELVES directly into Justine's brain. One was a picture of Flora holding Justine's baby. Flora had been standing by the window in the narrow room, and she held him next to her dress, as if she wanted to offer him the breast, her empty, milkless breasts.

It was a baby boy, born much too early. A small, blue, and limp boy.

Another image was one of her pappa, how he came with the carton, a normal cardboard box which could have held shoes. His shoulders had shrunken and his face had changed to an animal's face, with snout and gray teeth. She screamed and tried to throw herself out of the bed, her voice thin and sharp, but mute.

The boy had stopped eating, stopped breathing.

During her entire pregnancy, Flora had pressed her, tried to find out who the father was. As if someone had raped her! Girls Justine's age were too young to play at the game of love. They were not of age.

Her eyelashes, looking like the legs of flies, fluttered.

We'll make sure he goes to jail! Such a terrible violent crime! He will be punished for what he has done to you! He'll pine away in jail!

Violent?

No it wasn't, but no one would be able to understand it.

He had lived on the old farm behind the oak trees near Lövsta. Since then, it had burned down or been torn down. Many years later, Justine had returned to the area, but only the ruins of the wall were left, as well as the apple tree with its hard apples. It was June, and the white blossoms fell from the branches like snow.

He'd been a secret from all of them. She called him the Hunter, and she didn't care to know any other name. At the time, she was fourteen and he was much, much older.

He used to keep the door locked to try and keep her out. He would hide, wander along the beach. Only his cat was there, sunning itself on the porch. She would stroke her electric fur while she figured out how to break in. She would creep into his bed and wait for him.

"What do you want from me?" he asked again and again, with sorrow in his eyes. "I told you not to come here any more. What we are doing is forbidden."

She would lie on his blanket and laugh. It was a new kind of laugh, a playful laugh which just built up inside her. It made her light in her entire body but at the same time astonished and confused.

"Who decides what is forbidden?"

"You know damned well what I mean."

His thin face turned ugly and helpless; he had tufts of hair in his ears. She opened her arms, made the cloth in her sweater slide across her breast buds; her nipples turned hard and smoldered.

"You look like a troll," she whispered. "You know that?"

He scratched his neck, his wrists.

"A big, bushy troll! But I like you so very much. Come lie down next to me for a while, warm me up. I'm freezing so much it feels like I'm going to die."

He would do it; finally, he would do it. Her hands were so strong. He was old and she was young. She made him laugh and cry.

"You must know one thing," she yelled right up to the ceiling, so loudly that the cat quickly left through the opening by the floor. She was naked, sitting astride his knees. He shut his eyes and bowed his head. "I need to tell you one thing."

"Stina, Stina, what do you need to tell me?"
"I need to tell you that I will never, never leave you!"

But still, she had to break her promise. In the beginning of summer, she moved to the island with her father and Flora. They were going to live in one of her paternal grandparents' houses. They were somewhere else. They were always somewhere else; they owned properties throughout the world.

Out on the island, she heard the first angry words between Flora and her father. Flora had set her hawkeyes right into Justine's body and seen how it had started to change. Not the way a young woman's body usually changes, no, but something more dangerous. Something had happened which was out of their control. Something that would damage the entire family if they didn't put a stop to it right away!

Justine had slid into a dreamy state, heard Flora's yelling and words about the narrow pelvic opening of a young woman. Flora's father, who was a quiet person, one who fled from conflict, suddenly had a backbone. For a while, Justine was aware that things were over, that Flora was going to leave them and never come back. She would pack up all her dresses and shoes and bottles of nail polish and be gone when she and her father returned to Hässelby.

Flora did leave, too. She got on the steamboat and went away. She went to her sister's in Stockholm, her sister Viola who sold cosmetics at the large NK Department Store.

It was a peaceful summer with warm days and rain appearing only in the early morning hours. For the most part, Justine lay in the hammock and dozed, she'd never felt such exhaustion before. Her father started to renovate things in the house, and although his hands weren't used to tools, he seemed content, and the sound of the hammer would put her to sleep. They rarely talked to each other. They never needed words. Once he came over to the hammock, pushed it slightly and set her swinging.

"Are you all right, my dearest girl?"
She smiled quietly and he nodded.

"We'll get through this, we will."
"Yes, Pappa, we'll get through this."

When summer was over, they moved back home again. Flora had returned by boat and her father had gone to the dock to meet her. Justine saw how their hands intertwined, but it no longer bothered her.

School started, but Justine did not go. She never went back to school after that.

Then just a fragment of an image here and there.

Flora's fingers as she washed Justine, the sound of scissors against her hair. And then the night the baby decided to be born. During all those long hours, her father sat beside her by the bed, and he did not leave her. His voice was calm; his look was frightened but also furious.

You'll get through this! I'll help you!

When dawn came, everything was over.

Her baby lived for four days. He was so little, born too early.

THE SIRENS, sawing and harsh, came closer and closer, more and more quickly. Tommy's arms had weakened. He was still lying on her, but no longer held her down. His lungs rattled and wheezed, a tortured, unpleasant sound. Ariadne worked herself loose, carefully at first, and then she gave a strong push so that he rolled away from her, his head hitting the stone floor. He didn't react.

Every part of her body was aching and sore. She got to her feet with difficulty, grabbed the table, heaved herself to her feet, stood swaying a minute, blood had left her brain, small black pricks circled, then the sirens, stronger and stronger.

Christa remained sitting on the floor with the telephone in her hand. Her eyes were shut. Her black eyelashes looked like wounds against her white, corpse-like skin. Christa's face glistened with sweat.

"Christa," she whispered. "My dearest, dearest child . . ."

At that moment, the ambulance swung into the yard, the brakes screeched, doors opened. A wild ringing on the doorbell.

Christa turned her face to Ariadne, still keeping her eyes closed.

"It will be all right, Christa. Everything is going to be okay."

She carefully climbed over her daughter and went to the door and opened it: "He's in the kitchen. Hurry!"

They asked her if she wanted to come with them. If she wanted to come, she'd have to jump into the ambulance immediately. They were so young. One of them went up very close to her, asked: "But what has happened to you, you look as if you need . . ."

"No, no," she replied, yelling. "Go now with him! Hurry!"

They were lifting Tommy on a stretcher and ran with it to the ambulance. They almost tripped over the mess in the hallway and one of the paramedics cursed.

She found herself standing barelegged on the wet gravel.

"We have to leave now. Coming or not?"

"No."

"All right."

"I can't leave my daughter. She has a handicap."

The man jumped behind the wheel.

"Okay. They'll call you."

She remained standing and watched the rotating blue lights disappear along the road by the field.

She went back into the house and began to straighten it up. She threw the leftovers from their meal into a garbage bag and went outside and threw it away. She washed the dishes, picked up the chairs from the floor, washed the table and placed a tablecloth on it, one that she'd received from her mother. It had been woven and embroidered by a woman from their village.

Christa had disappeared into her room. Ariadne was about to go to her when the telephone rang. She lifted the receiver.

"Yes?" she whispered, but they didn't hear her, so she had to repeat it, and her stomach hurt so hard she thought she would vomit.

A distant male voice. Ariadne wanted to sit down, but the chair, the one that was usually in the hallway, had disappeared. She now glimpsed it, one of the paramedics had shoved it aside into the living room so that they could get through.

"Hello!" the voice called. "Mrs. Jaglander, can you hear me?"

"Yes, yes, I hear."

"Ariadne Jaglander, am I right?"

"Yes, right."

"I'm Dick Skott, I'm a doctor at the emergency room. Your husband arrived a few minutes ago."

262 · THE SHADOW IN THE WATER

"Yes," she said, without breathing.

"I'm very sorry, Ariadne. It didn't go well."

She gasped.

"What?" she said, her voice empty.

"Ariadne, I am truly very sorry to have to inform you of this. But we . . . did not succeed in saving Tommy. We did everything we could, but it was too late."

She fell, then, slid down with her back against the wall, crept into a fetal position. She hugged the receiver in her hand.

"Hello!" the doctor called. He talked the same way as one of Tommy's fellow policemen, a guy who came from Skåne who'd been to their wedding.

"I am here," she said turbidly.

"Anaphilactic shock," the doctor continued. "That is what we call it when someone has a severe allergy, as your husband did. Was it nuts? Tommy had eaten something that he couldn't tolerate. Do you have any idea what it could have been?"

"I don't know," she said.

"It seems as if he'd just eaten. Is that right? Were you eating when it happened?"

"Mushrooms. He had picked chanterelles. We made mushroom sandwiches, he loves mushroom sandwiches, we sat and ate in the kitchen and then just . . ."

"Mushrooms. That's a possibility. I surmise that he's had this kind of reaction before, if not so severely. Is that correct?"

"Yes."

"Didn't he have any Epipen? You know, the adrenaline injections?"

"Injections and tablets . . . we didn't know where they were, we were looking everywhere . . . we couldn't find them."

"I am very, very sorry. Is there someone who can be with you? Shall I see if someone can come to your place?"

"That's all right. My daughter is here."

"How old is your daughter?"

"Sixteen."

"You may come to the hospital if you want to. It usually does some good to see a husband and father one more time, in spite of everything. I give this advice to all relatives. So if you have the chance . . ."

"Yes," she said. "I will, if I find a way."

She went to the pantry and pulled out the box with the Christmas ornaments. It was a large box, and when Christa was younger, Ariadne had glued wrapping paper with colorful *tomtar* on the outside. Why did I do that? she thought. It's totally meaningless. She took off the lid and lifted out the tree skirt; it was unraveling and had sticky patches of sap. It was from Tommy's home; they'd had it when he was a little boy.

Underneath the tree skirt was a layer of tree decorations. She lifted them out and placed them on the lid for the time being. She took both hands, and spread apart piles of glittery garlands to find Tommy's little black backpack. She quickly returned the Christmas things to their proper places, put the lid back on and shoved the box back into place.

The car keys were in the outer pocket. Ariadne put on her shoes and sneaked out to the carport. She clicked open the lock, opened the back door, and threw the backpack onto the back seat, right behind the driver's. Then she locked the car and went back into the house.

UNDERSTANDING CAME LIKE A SIGN on a totally normal Monday, and right away Micke knew that was the time. He'd hung with Robin on a few more "transportation" jobs, and things had gone well. He'd gotten over his initial, shaky fear. In the beginning, he thought that people would notice what they were really up to, but that was not the case. They had their sharp costumes, work uniforms with a company logo, and they made sure that any passers-by would be able to see the lettering on their backs: Cargo & Transportation Service. What an absolutely fantastic professional name!

Of course, it couldn't go on forever; they both knew that. Just a few more times, just a few, so they'd get a little more money.

By now, Robin owed him a few thousand crowns.

"Come tomorrow," Robin promised. "The delivery hasn't been made yet. But tomorrow . . ."

Robin had said this a few times, and once or twice, he didn't open the door when Micke rang.

"It didn't work out," Robin would say later on his cell phone. "This branch can be a little uncertain. But you'll get your money, don't worry. We're pals, you and me. Right? We trust each other."

Was Robin wriggling out of their agreement? Robin's eyes were looking wooly lately, strange and red-rimmed. His voice was high and giggly.

"I'm getting the flu," Robin said, his words hard to understand.

It was cold. Micke's ears were freezing. He'd forgotten his cap at home; things were so nasty at home when he took off. He had jumped the turnstile at the subway, and now he'd reached Robin's front door, pushed the entry code on the buttons.

"Come around lunch time. I swear, I'll have your money," Robin had told him on the telephone. There was a great deal of noise in the background, sounds as if some girl was bawling and howling in the background. Hard to say whether she was happy or sad.

"Where are you now?" Micke demanded.

"Not at home, but come by tomorrow."

Micke felt strangely emasculated.

The stairwell was shitty and full of garbage. That's not the way it was at their place, home in Bromma. Nettan would have raised hell if anyone so much as threw down a cigarette butt in front of their door. That morning had been a real nightmare. She'd stomped into his room and ripped off his blanket. She stood there in her jacket and waved her arms like a windmill. He should have locked his bedroom door, but he'd forgotten. He was resting nicely, so to speak, thinking of Karla Faye Tucker.

His mother was like a bucket of ice-cold water.

"What the hell, Micke, you are the most lazy fucking egotistical man I've ever met! Even worse than your father, much worse! You follow me? I'm not going to put up with this shit! You better damn well start fixing your life!"

"What the hell?" he pulled his blanket back over him.

"A travel agency! Ha! If *he* couldn't do it, you think *you* can! How did you even come up with such an idiotic idea? Jesus H. Christ, what an ego! You can sure boast all over the place, that you can manage; but actually do something? Not a single piss comes from it! When I was little, we had the saying *Big words, small deeds.* Mull over the meaning of *that*, Mr. Lazy Bones!"

"Shut up!" he said, dully.

"Saying shut up to your own mother! You don't *do* that!"

Nettan threw herself over the bed, grabbed his ears, and pulled him to a sitting position. She slapped him on the cheeks, first left, then right. It hurt like hell, and he lifted his hand to give back as good as he got. She pushed him back onto the bed with his pillow and left, banging the door after her so hard that a picture fell off the hallway wall, the glass splintering into a hundred pieces.

Robin didn't open the door. Micke rang the bell, but not a sound from inside.

"Fucking hell," he muttered.

He pressed down the door handle and discovered to his surprise that the door was not locked. He quickly slid inside and closed the door behind him.

"Robin?" he called. "You home? It's me, Micke."

A narrow stream of sunlight fell onto the hallway floor. He almost tripped over Robin's gym shoes. Next to the bathroom door, there were a few bags with advertising flyers held together with rubber bands. Low price diapers! he read. He called out again and thought he heard a sound from inside the apartment.

Robin was lying in bed. A dirty sheet covered one half of his body. He looked like he was dead. Lying in bed with his arms out as if he had been crucified, wearing his stinky underwear. He had a beard like Jesus, too. A few hairs grew on his chest, his mouth was open, his eyes sticky with pus.

"What's wrong with you?" Micke poked at Robin's sunken cheek, his skin felt like rubber.

A sound came from Robin's mouth, as well as the smell of rotting eggs.

"What's wrong with you?" Micke repeated. "Robin, what the hell! Answer me!"

Robin mumbled something incomprehensible. At least he was alive.

"You promised me my money! You told me I should come by today! I need my money. Don't you get it? I *need* my money!"

Robin smacked his lips and his tongue went in and out as if he was mentally incompetent. Micke sighed.

"Fuck it all. People really make me sick. What the fuck!"

Robin made a movement as if he wanted to turn over but wasn't able to. The sheet fell away from his left arm, which was covered with bruises and needle marks. And then Micke saw it. The needle! Its point was still in Robin's arm, hanging down toward the mattress.

What the fuck?

At that instant, he knew. It was a sign.

Using his thumb and forefinger, he worked the needle out of Robin's arm. It was empty, of course, but that didn't matter. Robin was still lying in the same position, didn't notice a thing.

Micke went to the kitchen nook and looked for something to wrap the needle in—paper towels, toilet paper—but he only found the typical green bag of the State Alcohol Monopoly, *Systembolaget.* He placed the needle inside and wrapped it into a flat package. He laughed inwardly while he did this, his mouth turned up with a large roar of laughter. Although the laugh did not actually come out of his mouth, it was triumphant.

Luck was with him. The sign.

For a while, he went through the apartment, looking for any money he could find. He opened drawers, looked inside the toilet. Not a single crown. He went back to the bed and had the urge to kick Robin. Robin had turned on his side; his leg had a bruise high up on his thigh.

"I'll be back!" Micke said, raising his voice while he straightened up. "I'm not a fucking idiot that you can just mess around with! You better get that straight!"

He left by subway, but instead of going home, he went to the gardening hut. He had a great deal to do. He cleared off the table and took out four ropes he'd found in the work shed. Henry had tied them around the shafts of the rakes and spades in order to keep them in one place during the winter. He was a man of order, old Henry.

Then the clothes. *One has to be properly dressed when Death approaches.* He liked the word *approach*; it was a dignified word: *approach,* to come nearer. Karla Faye Tucker slowly walking down the hall in her white dress, Death approaching, her punishment, tears running crookedly due to fear.

Back then when they sold Nathan's apartment, Nathan's belongings and everything belonging to his estate were divided. Nettan did not want anything. She didn't even bother to go. But the other women were there, the ex-wives, the twins, Micke's half-sisters: they'd all shaken hands and greeted each other, curious and hostile at the same time. He didn't know them, didn't have anything to do with them.

One of the women, Barbro, was the one who took care of everything, almost like an auctioneer. There was a fleshy man there, too, he wrote down everything, but there really wasn't all that much. Micke received just one thing: a box with a judo uniform. Nathan liked to try out different sports. There was an orange belt stuffed in a plastic bag.

Besides the twins, Jenny, Barbro's daughter, was the only person who talked to him. She was the youngest. She was already working as some kind of photo model, posing for clothing catalogues, like the one from *Ellos*.

"You look just like him, Micke," she exclaimed when she saw him. "God, how you resemble him, I almost start crying just looking at you."

She was good-looking. Too bad they were related, half-siblings. The question was forming on his tongue whether they should get together for a beer now and again, but he didn't know how to get out the words. He'd turned shy and wordless once she began to talk.

After their meeting in Nathan's apartment, he never saw her again. But whenever the *Ellos* catalogue arrived in the mail, he'd thumb through it looking for her. He didn't tell Nettan anything about it. She would just start finding fault. He could already hear her contemptuous voice: "How can she think she's a real photo model! Kiss my ass! It looks like they take anyone these days, regardless of their looks!"

The wind was blowing strongly. It shook the windowpanes and knocked and whined against the old walls. All he needed was the roof to blow off so that Henry and Märta would have to come out. He should give them a call later and calm them down. Everything was all right, he'd say to them. I just went to check. He had hidden the box with the judo clothes underneath one of the beds and behind the pot. Now he went to his knees and pulled it out. There were some rat droppings on it. Damn! Now he'd have to go get rat poison. Or put out traps with cheese bits in them.

Solemnly, he lifted the clothes out of the box. A pair of rough white pants and a white jacket without buttons. He burrowed his nose into the pants, but Nathan's smell had disappeared a long time ago. He held them out in front of him. Yes. They'd work.

One has to be dressed properly when Death approaches.

How tall was she? Maybe the same height as he was. Dressed white like a saint and contrite.

The time has come, Mrs. Tucker. The past always catches up. You betrayed him, not once but twice, two different ways, Mrs. Tucker. Now you will be punished.

ARIADNE PUSHED DOWN ON THE DOOR HANDLE to Christa's room. It was stuck. She couldn't open it.

"Christa!" she called. "What are you doing?"

No answer.

Ariadne tried again, used all her strength. The door handle moved slightly.

"Christa!" she called again. "What are you doing? We have to talk, you and me."

There was a despairing howl from inside the room. Then a series of hits and thuds. Ariadne stood there, her arms hanging uselessly. She felt as if her heart was cramping. She rattled the door handle and called out over and over again. Then she braced herself and threw her body against the door, pressed against it and pushed it and finally she was able to open it just wide enough to slip through. The room was dark. She turned on the ceiling lamp. Everything in the room was in total chaos. Furniture was thrown around, the bed pulled away from its place, the plastic bins in the closet pulled out with their contents dumped.

"Christa?" she said, and her voice cut her own heart, broken open from crying.

Her girl sat behind the bed. Her white, chubby hands were pressed against her forehead. She had the hiccoughs and she was shaking, but she didn't speak. Ariadne made her way over to Christa, crept up on the bed and bent over it. The same instant she got a push in the chest that made her fall over backwards into the bed clothes.

"Get out!" her girl screamed.

Ariadne got back up on her knees.

"Christa!"

"Get out!!!" Screaming. Shrieking.

Then Ariadne hit her. God forgive her, she hit her girl. Her palm, right against her child's round cheek, once, twice, three times. Christa opened her mouth. It gaped empty and ugly, but she made no sound.

"Forgive me, Christa. I had to, you were hysterical."

She managed to take hold of her daughter's arm and dragged her from the room. The girl succumbed, as if her will were gone, like a sleepwalker, like a sluggish and limp furry animal. Ariadne led her into the living room, pushed her onto the sofa, sat down close beside her. Outside, the sky had turned very dark. Raindrops shone on the windows.

Ariadne held her daughter, hugged her, whispered words against her temples, words in her own language, words and childhood songs which she'd sung for her when Christa was a baby, but in secret. Tommy didn't like it. *She is going to learn proper Swedish from the very first; she's not going to have some kind of ghetto Swedish as in Rinkeby. That'll put her right at the bottom rung of society.*

Slowly, slowly, her daughter began to relax.

"It is raining," Ariadne said. "Do you hear how hard it's raining?"

"Mmmm."

"It's nice to be inside where it is warm."

"Mmmm."

"You and Pappa . . ."

"Pappa is dead!" Christa screamed. "I know that Pappa is dead!"

"Yes, the doctor called. They couldn't save him."

"I know."

"So you do."

"We were in the forest and he was so happy. I liked it when Pappa was happy."

"Yes, my child," Ariadne answered tonelessly. "So did I."

Christa began to weep. Christa's weeping made Ariade cry, too. Ariadne took off Christa's clothes and put on her flannel pajamas. She put on her own nightgown, too, and the two of them lay down in the double bed. The rain pounded against the roof, heavy, melodic and sleep-inducing. Her daughter lay in her arms. She was not a child any longer; it felt as if Ariadne were holding a grown woman. Christa appeared calmer, their crying now only coming in small bursts, short jerks. Both of them, together.

"Where is Pappa now?" Christa asked suddenly, directly to the darkness.

"A room in the hospital."

"Do you think he's feeling cold?"

Ariadne shook her head.

"No, I don't think so. Pappa is fine now, where he is."

"Do you really believe that?"

"Yes, and you know . . . Pappa had his troubles in many ways. Now he no longer has to suffer."

"Was it my fault?"

"What do you mean?"

"The mushrooms!"

"Oh, no, sweetheart, it wasn't the mushrooms. How could you even think that? No, it wasn't the mushrooms."

"He showed me," Christa said, her voice thick and sluggish as if she had a mouth full of oatmeal. "I could feel with my fingers how they were supposed to be. I smelled them, too; they smelled like rain and moss. All mushrooms smell like that, rain and moss."

Ariadne pulled her daughter closer, put her face between her daughter's shoulder blades.

"It was not the mushrooms," she repeated.

Early Sunday morning, there was a crunching on the gravel driveway as a car drove up. Ariadne woke up at once. She hadn't slept for many hours; she'd been lying there listening for sounds, for footsteps, as if any minute Tommy would return. Once, she drifted into a hallucinatory dream: He was standing over her, his swollen face: *What have you done, you false whore? What have you done?* She woke up covered with sweat but didn't dare leave the bed, didn't dare change her position.

Now she leapt up and threw on her robe.

"What is it, Mamma?" Christa asked fearfully.

Ariadne looked out from behind the curtain. It was a black car; she didn't recognize it. A man got out. He was carrying a bouquet of flowers in his hands. It was Jonas Edgren, Tommy's old colleague from Skåne.

"It's someone who knew Pappa," Ariadne said. "You can stay in bed. I'll go out to see him."

"May I come in?" Jonas asked when she opened the door.

"Oh, I'm so sorry. I haven't gotten dressed yet."

"Don't worry. I just want to come in and talk for a moment."

Ariadne let the door swing wide open. Jonas took off his shoes in the hallway; they were identical to Tommy's, and Ariadne felt a twinge. He took her hand, squeezed it.

"I brought these flowers. I'm sorry I didn't find a better bouquet; only the gas stations are open at this hour, and they don't have the best selection."

"Thanks," she said lamely.

She led him to the living room.

"Sit down. I'll be right back."

Ariadne went to the bedroom again, pulled on long pants and a sweater. Christa lay still in bed.

"Who is it?" she asked.

"Just a friend of Pappa's. You can stay here, for now." She bent over and kissed her daughter on the cheek.

"I love you, Christa."

No answer.

Jonas Edgren was waiting in the living room. He was holding his hands behind his back, and studying the framed photographs in the bookcase. Christa as a child. Christa holding a cat in her arms. Tommy and Ariadne's wedding photo.

"Would you like coffee?" she asked.

"No, thanks. I don't need anything."

Ariadne poured water into a vase and brought the flowers to the table. Carnations and some dry blue ones which she didn't know the name of. One of the blossoms had broken during the trip. Jonas Edgren lifted up the wedding photo.

"This is a difficult morning," he said. "A very difficult morning."

She turned her head.

"How did you find out?"

He put the photo back and came over to her.

"Ariadne, I'm a policeman."

She wished she had had enough time to comb her hair and cover the marks on her face with make-up. But now things were what they were. He reached out and touched her face lightly, touched the skin under her left eye. Looked at her for a long time. She looked back without flinching.

"Tommy and I knew each other for years," he said. "Or at least, I thought I knew him."

She was silent.

"How are you doing?"

Then she began to cry. He took a few steps closer to her, as if he wanted to hug her, but she turned away. She searched in her pocket for a tissue.

"We'll sit down for a while," he said. She felt his hand under her elbow. "Come. Let's sit down."

She cried for a while, and then gradually the tears stopped. Jonas sat and watched her.

"Your daughter," he asked. "Where is she?"

"She's sleeping. Last night, we spent the night in the same bedroom."

"How do you think she'll deal with this?"

"She's sad."

"Ariadne. Now I want you to tell me what happened. Are you up to it?"

She started from the beginning. The mushroom hunting, the dinner.

"It was just so horrible," she said.

"I understand."

"He was suffering so terribly. And I couldn't . . . couldn't help him. I felt . . . how to put it . . . helpless."

"What about his injections? I know he always carried them in his backpack. His adrenaline injections and his medicine."

"We looked. We didn't find them."

He gave her a questioning look.

"We tore the house apart," she said. "Nowhere."

"That's strange."

"Imagine. Stand there, watch, can do nothing. How that feels."

"Yes."

"And then . . . then the ambulance came. I felt it took many hours."

"I wonder what could have set it off. I know he was allergic to millet. But he always managed to avoid it. Something else I ought to know? What about the bread? What kind of bread was it?"

"Bondgården's Breakfast Bread. He ate it many times."

"Nothing else?"

"No. Don't know. Don't think so."

"Do you still have the package that the bread came in?"

"I think so. In the kitchen."

"I'll take it with me when I leave. If that's all right."

"Certainly."

"Maybe he had a flare-up of a new allergy. I've heard that happens sometimes. One allergy leads to another."

"Maybe."

"Damned sad, all of this. Unbelievable. They'll do an autopsy later. They'll try to find out what triggered it. But it doesn't help much now after the fact. Neither him nor you."

"No," she said quietly. "It doesn't help."

Jonas Edgren drove them to the hospital in his car. He waited until both Ariadne and Christa were ready. He said the same thing the doctor had said. Saying a final farewell will help with the grief. When they came out into the yard, he went up to

Tommy's car and peeked through the window. Ariadne's mouth went dry. She heard him call her name.

"Yes?"

"Come here. I want to show you something."

She did as he said, went up to the BMW. Jonas' finger was pointing at the back seat.

"Do you see what's in there?"

"Oh! His backpack!"

"He must have forgotten to bring it inside last night."

"Yes."

"How could he have forgotten it?"

"Yes, it's strange," she whispered. "He usually always has his backpack with him."

Tommy's colleague went with them all the way into the hospital. She didn't know if she could have managed it otherwise.

The visitation room was down in the basement. They walked through long corridors, where dust mice rolled along the hallway floors; she thought they would never get there. Each step hammered into her brain. She had taken some painkillers, but they hadn't started to work yet. Christa walked between them; they each held one of her hands. She was pale and dogged, did not answer when Jonas Edgren tried to talk to her.

Two candles were burning in the room. Tommy was lying on a normal hospital bed with a light yellow pillow drawn up to his middle. He was wearing his everyday clothes, the ones he had on yesterday. The T-shirt had traces of vomit. His face was covered by a small cloth, and his hands, his strong, hard hands, were properly folded over his chest. Someone had stuck a rose into the space between the thumb and the forefinger. It was red and already starting to wilt.

"Tommy," she whispered. Next to her, she heard Christa sniffling and hiccoughing. Jonas Edgren was holding the girl, moving her hands toward the body.

"Here is your Pappa, little one, your Pappa Tommy. He is lying here so peacefully. Don't be afraid; there's nothing dangerous, nothing. We will just touch him a little and say goodbye to him. That's why we've come, in order to say goodbye, so that he somehow will know that we . . . that we are with him."

He gave Ariadne a questioning look.

"Do you have the strength to see his face?"

"Yes."

Jonas took a corner of the face cloth and pulled it to one side. Even though she felt she was ready, she gasped. Jonas Edgren couldn't help mumbling a swear word. Then he remembered that Christa was next to him. He cleared his throat and blew out some air.

"We're looking at your Pappa, now, Christa. You understand; you're a big girl now, a strong girl. Almost full grown. Your Pappa, he is . . . his face is all swollen. He doesn't look like he normally looks. Looked, I mean. That's why we . . . people's looks can change drastically with an allergy like that."

Christa's fingertips felt her father's body. They found the face, searched vigilantly over it.

"How hard he feels," she said astonished. She wasn't crying any longer. "He is as cold as a frozen chicken."

Ariadne began to sniffle.

"He is dead, my beloved daughter, that's why; he is dead. Your Pappa is dead."

BIRGIT WAS LEANING OVER THE DINING ROOM TABLE when Hans Peter and his father came up from the basement. Her face was ash-gray; her breath came in small gasps. Kjell ran over to her.

"Birgit . . . Biggan! What's wrong?"

"Nothing serious," she mumbled.

The two of them helped the old woman back into her chair. Hans Peter squatted down next to her. He took his mother's thin, shrunken hand between his. He felt how she was trembling.

"Mamma," he whispered. "Mamma, how are you feeling? Shall we call for help?"

"No!" she replied with unusual brusqueness.

Kjell had already lifted the receiver. She saw it and demanded he put it down.

"But the people at the hospital said . . ."

"I refuse to go back to that hospital!"

Hans Peter nodded toward his father, and he put down the receiver. Hans Peter got a glass of water and his mother's medicine. After a moment, she began to breathe normally again.

"The slightest little shake of my old woman's body doesn't mean I'm throwing in the towel that very minute," she chided, managing a grin.

"You rascal!" Kjell bent over her and kissed her on the forehead. His hair was standing straight up like a halo. "I think that you should go lie down a bit anyway. For my sake if nothing else."

"Maybe I should."

They supported her into the bedroom, laid her on the bed, and tucked the thick Gotland-plaid blanket over her, the one they'd gotten her for her 75th birthday. Her face on the pillow appeared so tiny.

"Are you sure we shouldn't call the doctor?" asked Kjell, and he looked tense, biting and chewing at his lower lip. Hans Peter patted him clumsily on the shoulder. How would his father manage if his mother died? It would be easier for his mother to outlive his father. Somehow, in spite of everything, she was the stronger one. Maybe, after all, it *was* time to look for a retirement home for them. They'd resist, of course. They wouldn't want to give up their normal lives and routines, their furniture, their memories. But they couldn't take all of it with them; they'd have to realize that. How would he be able to convince them? They became irritated every time he brought up the subject.

He looked around for Justine. She wasn't there.

"Mamma?" he asked.

"She's sneaked into the bathroom." His mother stared at her knotty fingers.

Hans Peter went to the bathroom door and knocked. Justine didn't answer. The door was locked. He called to her, called her name. Finally, after several minutes had passed, she came out and her gaze was unfocused and empty.

"Don't you think it's time for us to go home?" he asked.

She didn't answer.

Justine stood by the window. The wind was blowing hard, and the oak tree bent in the wind. The bird was sitting on her shoulder. She didn't seem to notice him.

"It's getting dark," Hans Peter said.

She was silent. It was as if she were no longer able to hear.

"What time is it? Shall we go to bed?"

He thought that she moved her head. What did that mean? Yes or no? He was free today; it was one of their rare evenings together. She usually longed for them, longed for the time where they would make dinner, something good; open a bottle of wine, maybe make love. Something had happened while they were visiting his parents. Something he didn't understand.

He reached out an arm, and the bird cawed and hopped over to him. It fluffed its feathers and poked its beak under them.

"Do you think he's hungry?"

She didn't move.

"He probably is. I'll make him some food." Hans Peter went into the kitchen and was just going to open the door to the refrigerator when the telephone rang. With a quick jerk, he made the bird fly off. It went up to the curtain rod, grabbed it with its talons, turned its neck and observed Hans Peter.

"I'm just getting the phone," Hans Peter muttered and realized he was talking to a bird, that he was getting more of a response from the bird than from the silent woman standing by the window in the other room.

At first he hardly recognized the voice. It was full and calm. Ariadne usually didn't sound like that; she always seemed nervous and pleading which made her voice sound childish.

"Am I disturbing you?" she asked.

"Not at all. We said you could call whenever you wanted."

"Yes, right. I know."

She became silent and he realized that something must have happened.

"Ariadne?" he asked, concerned.

He heard her pause, heard her prepare herself to say something.

"Has he started up again?" he asked. "Your husband? Tommy?"

She had a choking sound as if she were about to start crying and he hurried to continue.

"Can you tell me?"

"He . . ." Ariadne interrupted herself and he heard how she was using a tissue.

"Is he there? That son-of-a-bitch. I'll come and get you and Christa, I will. I'm going to jump right into the car and come get you."

"No," she said thickly. "You don't have to. Tommy is not alive any more. Tommy is dead."

"What?"

"Yes, it's true. He died last night. An allergic reaction."

It took her some time to describe what had happened. How it had tortured him, the wild fear in his eyes, the ambulance that came and took him away.

Hans Peter did not know what to say.

"I will never ever forget it," she said. "Not this. To see a human being die, a human being that I've known for such a long time and the one who is the father of my child. No matter what he did . . . just seeing him depart from his life."

Hans Peter let her talk. The words streamed out, mixed with crying spells. It took a while until she was calm again.

"How is Christa doing?" he asked.

"Sad, of course."

"Do you want to come here?"

"You're very kind, Hans Peter. You are really a kind person."

"I said that I could come and get you. It's not a problem, I'll gladly do it."

"You don't have to. Everything is peaceful and quiet at home now. My Christa and I, we have each other, just the two of us."

There was something different about her manner of speaking. He suddenly realized that her accent had disappeared.

A saying came to him. It was a saying that he had learned in school, a saying of Lao Tsu, the founder of Daoism, a sentence he had to learn in German class.

"Ariadne," he said. "Listen to this. There's an old saying, it sounds like this in German: *Ein Ende mit Schrecken ist besser als ein Schrecken ohne Ende.* This fits your situatation perfectly.

What does it mean?"

"A fearful end is better than fear without end. Your life can start over again, for real."

Justine was still standing in the same spot. He found an increasing sense of wrath bubbling up inside him.

"I'm not going to put up with this!" he said.

She kept silent.

"Something happened at my parents' place. I want you to tell me what it was."

Still no reaction.

"Was it my mother? I know that she can be clumsy sometimes. I know that. She doesn't mean any harm. She's a bitter, tired old woman. You must understand."

She slowly turned toward him.

"Tell me," he said, pleading. "We won't get anywhere, if we don't talk to each other."

She swallowed, closed her eyes.

"I know all about silence," he said. "I have endured silence for many years. I can't take it any longer. I can't stand living with silence."

"No . . ."

"Is there something you've been keeping from me?" He forced himself to keep talking, forced himself to ask her to open up even if their entire relationship would fall apart.

Justine took a step toward him. She looked completely different, as if she were someone he didn't know at all.

He turned a bit away from her, put his hands to his head.

"Justine, tell me what's bothering you, tormenting you. Does it have anything to do with death?"

"Perhaps," she whispered. "Yes. Yes, it does."

J ILL PULLED OUT HER CAR KEYS. When it came right down
to it, she really did not need to own a car. There were commuter
trains and buses if she wanted to go to Stockholm. And she could
take her bike to work, except during the winter when there was
snow. These days, there wasn't much snow, just for short periods
of time; then it would melt and the earth would be bare and icy.

Today was a Monday, and she was free from work. She had to
do it today. She couldn't put it off any longer; she had to do what
she had been dreading: drive out to Hässelby and see Justine. She
decided not to call first, not to give Justine any advance warning.
Just walk up to the front door and ring the bell.

Was that how Berit had done it?

Deep inside, she didn't believe that she would find out anything she didn't already know. Tor had already been there. And
the police. Justine had probably told them everything. Still, Jill
had to go. For Tor's sake. For her own sake. Maybe there still
would be a tiny thread to go on.

Her old car started after a few tries. She'd bought it when she
first moved to Södertälje. She thought she would get more use out
of it than she had. A Passat, 1991, and the rust had already begun
to eat through various spots.

"Watch the side bars," they warned her at the showroom. "If
rust takes hold there, the whole thing'll go; you might as well
drive it straight to the junkyard."

The side bars, she thought. Where are they?

She filled the tank at the station near Weda. Unbelievable how expensive gasoline had gotten lately. She realized that she hadn't needed to buy gas all summer, at least not in Sweden. She hadn't used the Passat since spring. She found it dusty and forlorn, and there were cat paw prints on the hood. It would be nice to have a garage to put it in, but there were no available spots in the vicinity and she certainly wasn't able to afford yet another expense. The car was expensive enough.

It was a sunny, cold day with a sharp wind. Waves streamed into the inlet where the family of swans usually swam around. She saw them that morning when she pulled up the blinds. Two grown ones and three gray youngsters, which would soon be turning color to white. She called the inlet *Svanviken*, Swan Inlet. During the summer she would go swimming there; if she was early enough, she could skinny dip.

But now it was fall. There was a melancholy feel of loss and desolation to this season. She was filled with sentimental thoughts. I'm alone: the thought went through her. Again, she thought that if she died, she didn't know who would take care of her funeral. Both of her parents had been dead for quite some time, and, like her friend Berit, she'd never had any brothers or sisters.

The guys at work, she thought. I guess they'd be the ones to plan the funeral. She wasn't even a member of the Swedish Lutheran Church. Did they even know that?

And Tor, of course. Tor.

The smell of his body remained on her skin. She hadn't bothered to take a shower. Right after midnight, they'd gotten undressed and lain right next to each other in her bed. Their hands had begun to wander; his member was so yielding in her palm, soft but strong and growing. When he came inside her, it hurt. It had been such a long time since she last made love. He noticed and slowed the pace. This did not change their astonished, shameful happiness, his mouth on her eyelashes, the cooling traces of his tongue's tip. Visions flew before her eyes when she closed them, her wide red dress that she'd owned when she was very young, how she twirled around and whirled so that the cloth made a circle like a sun. She held tightly to his hips, sucked, bit: *I want you. I want to be your heat and your juice; come inside me, be in me, grow!* He swelled like a root, a line up her vagina and she was filled by his thrusting warmth.

Afterwards, he lay with his head turned to the wall.

"What is it, Tor?" she whispered. "Dear, dear Tor, what's the matter?"

All at once she realized that this might have been the first time that he'd made love to someone after Berit.

"No," she said, and she lay over him with her sweaty, soaked body. "Don't think like that, Tor. Don't think like that." As if exhorting a child.

"Berit," he said, his voice gravelly.

"If you're thinking that you've betrayed her, stop right now! Tor, it's not true. You haven't betrayed her!"

She searched for his cheeks, found tears on her fingertips. She was filled with anger and despair.

"Do you really think that Berit would want you to live in celibacy for the rest of your life?" she exclaimed. "Do you really believe that? Does that seem realistic?"

He swallowed heavily.

"Or is it because you were sleeping with me, her best friend, because you had sex with me?"

"Forgive me," he said, reaching for his cigarette pack. "Forgive me. That's not what I meant."

He got up and stayed in the bathroom for a long time. The smell of tobacco came filtering through the darkness. She heard him turning on the shower. She thought that it was almost two o'clock in the morning; her neighbors would complain, especially the old lady one floor up.

Then she fell asleep. When she woke up, Tor was gone.

For a few minutes, she searched through her apartment to see if he left a note, a few written words? She didn't find anything. He had washed up their mugs and cleaned the kitchen table.

She hadn't even heard his car start.

It was just after one in the afternoon when she arrived in Hässelby. She parked up on the hill and walked slowly toward the house, that tall, stone house which Justine had lived in her whole life. At first, she couldn't find it and thought for a few confusing seconds that she was in the wrong place. She was no longer at home in these small roads. Then, through the bushes, she caught sight of it: A narrow white house, the plaster starting to flake off.

She didn't remember the trees so tall. But still, it had been a long time since she was here last—six years since Berit disappeared. She had searched the area, but she hadn't been able to go up to Justine Dalvik's house.

To think that she'd lived there all these years! That she hadn't bothered to move! It was strange. But Justine had always been an unusual person.

Jill came to stand in front of the gate, the rusty, open gate, obviously no longer in use. Tendrils of withered morning glory wound around the bars. Old labels, empty capsules on the ground had blown into it. Worry churned in her stomach. There was no car in sight. Could Justine even drive? That little sharp entity, could she ever have managed to get a driver's license?

They'd used the gate a lot, when they were small. Flora Dalvik had minced through it in her high-heeled shoes, out to the taxi which waited with the motor running. Jill and Berit had spied on her, had seen her shiny hose slide into the back seat.

And Justine had hung on the gate, got it to swing: *Come and play with me! Come and play!* Her short, pleated skirt and her blouse with the sailor's collar. Her stepmother tried to dress her in fine, store-bought clothes, but they didn't sit well on her; they twisted, got dirty. They teased her about it: *dirty rags, dirty rags.* As if they'd been much better.

Everything was quiet, just the wind rustling in the leaves, the leaves whirling around, whirling until they sailed away behind the corner of the house and disappeared. Jill had taken a few steps onto the gravel path, her lips suddenly so dry, her throat hurting, as if she were coming down with a cold. I should turn around, she thought. What right do I have to be here after all these years? She's probably not at home either; everything looks totally deserted.

But was there a movement in the window? Something black flapping past? She went closer, now on her guard. No, nothing. Taut, straight curtains, no plants, nothing green. Was there someone inside watching her? Someone who hid within the darkness of the rooms and observed her slightest move?

"Now you'll have to yield!" she muttered and walked quickly right up to the door. Lifted her finger, rang the bell. She heard the sound burrow into the house. Jill remembered the stairway, and the large sunny room where Justine's mother had died. Her palms started to sweat. No footsteps, no voices. Total silence. She rang the bell again, now with a feeling of relief. No, Justine wasn't home. Jill could turn around and leave this place.

When Jill turned around, there was a figure on the steps. A woman. Jill hadn't heard her come, and she jumped straight in the air from fright. The woman also appeared frightened. She was pressing her hands to her chest, her eyes wide open.

"I'm sorry," Jill mumbled. "I was just looking for someone. Someone I thought lived here."

The woman was unnaturally pale. She was wearing rubber boots, jeans and a black, fraying corduroy jacket. Over that was a half-removed life jacket. Her hair was hidden behind a roughly knitted hat. She stared at Jill, did not lower her gaze.

"Excuse me. I'll leave right away . . . I didn't want to disturb you."

The woman in the life jacket shook herself. She grimaced, then smoothed the expression away. She pulled off her hat and ran her fingers through her curly, unwashed hair.

"I know you," she said in a monotone. "You're Jill."

"Ye . . . yes. Are you . . . Justine?"

"Yes."

"I can't believe you remembered my name! You . . . you're actually the person I've come to see. I just didn't realize it was you. Sorry, it was so long ago; I didn't recognize you."

Justine was silent as if she hadn't heard.

"Sooo, you were out on the water?" Jill asked.

"Yes." A short answer.

"The wind's blowing hard, isn't it?"

"It is."

"I thought no one was at home."

"You thought."

"Maybe you think it's strange that I'm just showing up like this. But I was thinking . . ."

"What?"

"Maybe you know what I came here for?"

"No."

"Many years have gone by. It's been so long. But I'm here mostly for Tor's sake. You know, Tor Assarsson, who was married to Berit? Is married . . . I mean. Her husband. You remember Berit? Her last name was Blomgren in those days. Our classmate, the one who disappeared. He came to see you, right after she disappeared. He's not doing well, Justine. He's like a zombie. His whole life is going to hell in a handbasket; he's not working, he's lost touch with his boys, everything is falling apart all around him. You see what I mean? Everything."

Justine took out a handkerchief and blew her nose.

"Well," she said, acidly, "what do you want me to do about it?"

"I don't know. Maybe nothing. But it seems that you were the last one to see her. At least, that's what people say. Could you tell me just a little bit about it? Just for a moment? That is, if you want to. If you have time."

"She was here. I told him that."

"I know."

"I told the police, too."

"Yes, I know."

"She came out here twice. We sat and talked, I've forgotten what we talked about. What do you want me to tell you?"

"Why do you think she came here? What did she want?"

"No idea. She was probably at the cemetery."

"I see."

"We sat and talked about things for an hour or two. Then she left. The last time she was here, she was really drunk. I can tell you that much. She drank a great deal of *glögg* and wine. To say the least, she was wobbly."

"She was drunk, you're saying."

"Yes."

"Do you think she might have gone and fallen into the lake?"

"The lake was covered with ice. And I don't think she went in that direction. I watched her go. I stood inside and watched her go. I was afraid she was going to fall down. She was wearing some kind of plaid cap, I believe. I saw her make her way up the hill."

"A taxi, then. Do you think she took a taxi?"

"I asked her, don't you think you should take a taxi. I can pay for it if you want. I thought she might not have enough money for one."

"What did she say then?"

"She didn't want to. She wanted to walk, to walk off the alcohol, I think. Get sober. 'Nah, I'll just walk,' she said. She was stubborn."

"I see."

"That was it." Justine shook her arm out of her life jacket and finished taking it off.

"I have to ask you one more time, why did she even come out to see you? Why do *you* think?"

The woman, Justine, wrinkled her forehead.

"No idea."

"I've been in contact with her husband. He said that Berit had been thinking a great deal about what happened in school in the past. You know, what happened when we were small. You know . . . we weren't all that nice. If I may put it like that."

"Children are children."

"Right. But I was told it began to torture her, what she and the rest of us had done. That we . . . teased you sometimes and all that. I, too, have thought about it at times. I have to admit that."

"I see."

Jill shrugged her shoulders.

"We were, well, like . . ."

"Children are children." Justine repeated.

"But . . . do you remember if you talked about it with her? Did she raise the subject?"

"No, absolutely not. She was mostly upset that she and that Tor guy weren't getting along. If I remember rightly." She laughed—it was a fake laugh. "I'm not getting any younger. Alzheimer's runs in my family."

"But that she would come to you, that she would talk to you about all that? Such a personal thing, and she didn't really know you, I mean, people usually don't . . ."

"Pure chance," Justine interrupted. She was placing the life jacket against the wall of the house. The arms of her coat were wet. "She happened to be going by and then she caught sight of me."

"That's what you believe?"

"Yes."

"And you really have no idea where she might have gone? You have to admit, it is a mystery. People don't usually vanish in a puff of smoke like that."

"Sure, it's strange. But strange things happen."

"You don't have any theories?"

"No, I've told you. And now, if you will excuse me, I'd like to go inside."

"All right. I understand. Thanks, anyway."

Jill felt disappointment like a lump in her throat. She suddenly felt a real urge to pee. The mere thought of getting in the car and driving away was unendurable.

"Excuse me, I don't mean to keep you," she exclaimed. "I'll leave now, but before I go, . . . may I use your bathroom?"

SHE WAS STANDING IN HER GARDEN when Micke arrived. She was nervous, as if she were waiting. This time, he parked right at the front gate; there was no reason to keep on sneaking around. He walked over the gravel and it crunched and sang. A memory from his childhood, his disappointment that his feet, the feet of a child, could not make as loud a crunch as Nathan's grown feet wearing his hard shoes. His father had laughed, didn't understand what he meant.

"Soon enough, you'll have big boats for feet. Yes, you, too, if that's something you really long for."

Micke had thrown himself on the stones and begun to howl. A memory picture, as if a light turned on and then off again.

She stiffened when she saw him. Her face was white as paper.

He walked right up to her, took her hand.

"Do you know who I am?" he asked.

She nodded. Wisps of hair went in all directions from her head.

"Micke Gendser," he said. "We've met before. But it has been a long time. I was just sixteen years old then."

She was wearing an ugly corduroy coat with frayed cuffs. A black one. She was standing there, pulling at it, trying to hide her chapped hands. She looked out from underneath her hair. Her hair was beginning to turn gray; she was old. Much older than he had imagined.

"God, how you frightened me!" she said.

"Why would I frighten you?"

"At first . . . ," she was stammering. "At f . . . first, I thought, it was him."

"Nathan?"

She looked at the ground, didn't answer.

"You believed it was Nathan come back from the jungle?"

"No . . . but . . . you're so alike."

"That's what they say."

"It's almost scary, how alike you are. But you're much younger, of course."

The wind was blowing hard. Leaves swirled around their legs. He looked past her, down to the dock, where a rowboat was tied up, bobbing. Next to the tree was a big chicken-wire cage. It was empty.

"What do you want?" she asked.

"I want to show you something," he said.

"What?"

"You'll see."

She pressed her hands against her thighs, brought her knees closer together.

"We're not going inside?" she said, stiffly.

"What are you talking about?"

"Not going inside my house?"

"Oh no, we're not going there."

"You were afraid of the bird."

"Maybe I was. But that was then."

"You were sitting on the stairs and you were so afraid."

"It just swooped down. I was surprised."

"I remember I played for you. I played my horn."

"That's right."

"You were sitting on the stairs and you were sad."

"Because of him. Nathan."

"When I was little, I used to go to the beach and play that old horn. My father had given it to me. It's one of my memories of him."

"I also have memories of my father."

"Nathan."

"That's right. Nathan. And that's what I want to show you."

"Right now?"

"Yes, right now. It would mean a great deal to me if you would come with me for a little while. It'll be good for both of us."

"But we're not going into my house?"

"Not your house. A different house. You'll see."

She was sitting next to him in his car. It had been a long time since anyone had sat there, except Nettan when they went shopping. No one else. No important person. Justine was an important person. And now she was sitting next to him. Her jacket was wet. She was shivering.

"You're freezing. I'll turn up the heat."

Micke surprised himself, that he could sound so thoughtful. That was good. It was part of the plan.

She gave him a quick smile. She seemed calmer now, no longer so tense.

"Nice and thoughtful of you. He was like that, too. Your pappa."

"Right."

"You're so much like him. I can hardly believe it."

"People keep telling me that."

It was slightly after four o'clock in the afternoon. The evening rush hour had started, not in their direction, more on the side heading to Hässelby.

"Where do you live?" she asked.

"In Abrahamsberg."

"Are you studying at the university?"

"No. I'm busy with a travel agency. Cheap Trips. I took it over from my dad."

"I see," she said quietly.

"But admit it's a great concept. Cheap and exciting. Lots of people want that. I mean, those who can't afford those package tours to the usual vacation destinations. They want a little something extra at a good price. That's exactly what Nathan thought. Agree that it's a fantastic niche."

"Cheap Trips," she echoed.

"I thought of the name myself."

"Good name."

"I haven't gotten it off the ground yet. I'm waiting for some cash. But soon, soon."

"He would have liked that. That his idea is being brought to life."

"Yep, that's what he would have liked."

"What do you want to show me?" she asked. "Does it have anything to do with your travel agency?"

He smiled at her.

"You'll see."

It was starting to heat up in the car. She was still freezing, however. Even her pants were wet. He decided to comment on that.

"Were you out fishing?"

"Sometimes I take out the rowboat."

"Nathan liked to fish, remember?"

"Maybe."

"You don't remember? Didn't he talk about it?"

"I don't know if he did."

Micke thought about her other man. The one living with her now. That man was taking over all her memories. A surge of anger, *keep it cool, keep it cool.* He couldn't scare her now, destroy the plan.

"We went out a couple of times," he said, swallowing. "Like fathers and sons. Once we went to Lambar Island."

That wasn't true. Nathan had never taken him fishing. Nathan hadn't even owned a boat. With a quick jerk, he switched into third gear and passed a lousy Toyota with a Sunday driver behind the wheel. His Chevy motor thundered. Just as long as it didn't start to fall to pieces.

"Did you catch anything?"

"Oh yeah, we caught stuff. A pike. Some perch."

"You must have been proud."

"Yep."

"Do you have any children?"

"Me? Hell, no!"

"Of course not. You're too young for that. How old are you?"

"Turning twenty-three."

"That's not much."

"Old enough."

"Can you tell me where we're going?"

"Not far. We're almost there. Just a little farther."

"How . . . how am I supposed to get home again? You're going to drive me home, right?"

"It'll work out. Don't worry."

When he turned into Hemslöjdvägen, he was struck by the fear of running into Nettan. What if she got off work early today? What if she came home in order to throw him out of the house? He thought he saw a woman who looked at them; his hands clutched the steering wheel. He felt Justine's eyes on him; he stared straight ahead. Right in front of the kiosk, the motor died. That bothered him, it did. It took away some of the ceremonial feel. Finally he got the motor to turn over, and drove to Lillsjövägen. He parked right in front of the entrance. The sun had disappeared; it was raining hard all over the villages.

"Please, step outside," he said. "We've arrived."

A S SOON AS THEY APPROACHED THE TINY HOUSE, he changed. The minute they entered the door, he pushed her inside. At first, she thought he didn't mean it. Then she saw the rifle. The blood fled from her face.

"What are you doing?"

He had pointy teeth, not like Nathan's teeth at all.

"An experiment."

They stood and stared at each other. Her heart beat strongly; it thumped. She'd been walking through the day as if in sleep. Now she was ice-cold, awake, and frightened.

"What do you want from me?"

He waved the barrels.

"You'll see soon enough."

The room was cramped. There was a rough, solid pine table right in the middle of the floor. It didn't fit. It made the rest of the room appear smaller.

This house was part of a gardening colony. She'd driven past many times before; you could see it from Drottningholmsvägen, small, picturesque cabins with tiny garden patches.

She forced herself to sound calm.

"What am I supposed to see?"

"Soon."

"Does it have anything to do with Nathan?"

He put the butt of the rifle on his shoulder and aimed it right at her.

"Yes."

"Cut that out!" She could hear the weakness in her voice; that was not good.

He laughed and let the weapon sink. Maybe he was just joking.

"You're freezing."

"Yes, I am."

"Your clothes are all wet. You can catch a cold."

"Right."

"Take them off!"

"Micke, let me go now. I have to go home."

He shook his head.

"Yes, I have to go home!"

"Don't get hysterical."

Then she saw Nathan in his eyes and she fell silent.

She would have to do as he said; she realized that. He was dangerous. She turned her back to him and took off her boots, her pants, her jacket, her sweater. Her skin was covered in goose bumps. Her heart beat wildly, throbbed.

She remained standing there, her arms crossed around her breasts as if to protect them. She heard him moving behind her, felt something ice-cold against her shoulder blades. The rifle. She whimpered. It seemed to egg him on. She would have to force herself to stay silent.

"Think about what you are doing," she whispered.

"I'm thinking."

"You could get in trouble."

"You think."

"It can be seen as kidnapping."

"And?"

"You still have a chance to let me go. I won't tell. I promise."

The blow made her dizzy. Right on the side of her head, at her temple.

Why?

There was a pile of clothes on a chair. The kind that people wore when they practiced Japanese martial arts. When he was young, Nathan was involved with judo. Once he brought his judo uniform to her place and demonstrated some moves. He said he'd forgotten most of it.

Now his son was standing there and pointing at those very clothes.

"See that uniform?"

She touched her ear; there was no blood.

"Yes."

"Judo uniform. Used to be Nathan's."

"I see."

"Put it on!"

"What?"

"Do what I tell you!"

"You want me to wear his judo clothes?"

"Yes!"

The clothes were stiff and cold. She held onto the table as she put on the pants. Tied them around her middle. Then took on the jacket. It fit. She and Nathan had been the same height. No buttons. She wrapped it around herself and waited.

He was standing there, hugging the weapon.

"Is this your house?" she asked.

"Yep."

"Has he ever been here?"

"Who?"

"Nathan."

"No. Not at all." Micke began to laugh. "And he never will come here!"

She kept quiet.

"You deserted him! You left him!" he yelled.

"What are you saying?"

"You heard me."

"I did not leave him."

"Don't lie!"

"But there . . . w . . . wasn't anything else we could do!"

Micke raised his weapon and aimed it right at her. Right at her right hand clutched the judo jacket. Her right hand over her heart, and he aimed at that. She started to breathe heavily. She moved her hand; the jacket fell open, revealing her bra underneath. She was standing on the floor with naked feet.

"You betrayed him! You abandoned him! Admit it!" He was yelling, his voice broke into falsetto.

"No, we searched for him!" she screamed back. "We searched for days. He was gone!"

"Shut up!"

"It's true. You have to believe me!"

"Lie down on the table!"

"Micke . . ."

"Do what I say before I lose my patience! Lie down on the table, on your back!"

"You're out of your mind! What are you planning to do?"

Then he was holding some ropes in his hands. She felt like vomiting. Her stomach turned over, then she felt warmth and wetness on her feet. The room whirled. She saw him like a shadow. His long rifle stood straight up. He was going to kill her; he was out of his mind. She rubbed her mouth with her sleeve. Remnants of slime and vomit on the cloth. As long as he didn't see it and it set him off.

She did as he said. Crept up onto the table, lay down. He forced her arms up, tied them to the table legs. A thought went through her brain like lightning:If she pulled loose, attacked him. He had set the weapon to the side; maybe she could subdue him. No. She didn't dare. The risk was too great. He was young and muscular. It would be safer to try talking to him. Maybe make him change his mind.

Now he was tying her legs to the table. They were hanging over the edge of the table. He squatted with the ropes. She could not move her legs or her arms. She threw her head back and forth; she was shaking. The judo jacket gaped open.

A sudden slamming noise! Was there someone at the door? They both listened intently. She saw his eyes as narrow, crooked slits. She opened her mouth to scream, but he covered it with his hand. The taste of salt and blood on her tongue. He stood still. She listened.

No, no one was there. The wind was picking up, thumping the hut.

Micke was standing over her. She observed his child-like chin. Nathan's son.

She moved her head so that her hair crackled against the table. Her lips felt numb.

"You betrayed him," he said.

"That's not true," she said; her mouth couldn't form the words properly. "I couldn't do anything else."

"Don't lie to me."

"I'm not lying."

"You left him in the jungle. Therefore, you betrayed him."

"That's not true. Micke, I told you: we looked for him."

"Not enough."

"We couldn't stay there forever. We were running out of food. It was so hot. There were so many mosquitoes."

"Poor you. All those mosquitoes biting you."

"They did."

"Poor pitiful you."

"It was suffocating; it was hot . . . we started to hallucinate."

"But he didn't? He didn't have hallucinations? Of course, he had food and drink and mosquito lotion! He was feeling just fine!"

"We looked for him! I'm telling you the truth! We were a large group. Ben was the one who decided we had to leave. He was the one who said it was time to stop the search."

"Don't put the blame on someone else!"

"I'm not!"

"You're telling me it was that Ben guy's fault."

"It was no one's fault. You can't talk about fault and guilt in that situation!"

"You're blaming Ben for everything!"

"I wasn't the one leading the group! I was the one who most wanted to stay and keep looking! I was sick with worry and anxiety."

Micke hit the table hard with his fist right next to her ear. It made her scream.

"Don't do that! You're frightening me!"

"Sick with worry," he imitated her. "Still, you got out in a hurry."

"I couldn't stay there all by myself. You have to understand that! The jungle was too much for me. I would have died!"

"You would not have been alone."

"Sure I would have been alone!"

"He would have been there. Maybe he was hurt somewhere."

"That's what we thought. That's why we kept looking for him!"

"Be quiet!" he shouted. "Shut your damn mouth!"

She stared up at the ceiling. It was getting dark. Twilight came earlier every day now; winter was approaching.

"Micke," she whispered. "Please, Micke, please, what should I have done? If you had been with him in the jungle, what would you have done if he had just disappeared like that?"

"I would have kept searching."

"But we did that!"

"I would have stayed until we found him."

"What if you never found him?"

"Then I would have stayed in that country and mourned him the rest of my life!"

Her mouth was dry; she was thirsty. She asked him for some water, but he said there wasn't any.

"The water's turned off at this time of year."

"No," she wept.

"No one is here. Just the two of us. The whole area is closed for the season. They won't open again until spring. We have time to talk, undisturbed, as long as we need to talk. You and me."

"We have been talking."

"We're not done."

"What are we supposed to talk about?"

Now he was sitting in the old arm chair. He'd lit some candles. The shadows fluttered near the ceiling.

"For example, his photographs."

"What photographs?"

"From when he was a child."

"I've never seen anything like that."

He jumped up and bent over her.

"Don't lie! You have them!"

She turned her face away. Tears were streaming into her hair.

"I only had one photo of him. He was on a motorcycle. I swear, it was the only one I had!"

He sank back into the armchair.

"When I went to your place for the first time," he said. "When you'd just come back from that trip of betrayal."

"I did not betray him!"

"When you had just come back from that trip of betrayal!" She nodded.

"Do you remember what you said?"

"What did I say?"

"You said you had never loved anyone as much as Nathan."

"I know."

"You found another guy."

"Wha . . . what are you talking about?"

"I've seen the two of you. He lives in your house."

Fear hammered her.

"You betrayed Nathan in more ways than one, you horny bitch! You've forgotten him and found yourself someone else."

"I didn't forget him! But life goes on!"

He was now standing in the middle of the room. He threw his head back and laughed loudly.

"That's what you think, Mrs. Tucker!"

THE WIND INCREASED. It knocked trees to the ground, blew over their gaping roots. In the cities, it ripped tiles from the roofs; it tore at construction projects, blowing them to the ground. It shook loose the last leaves from the crowns of trees and hurled them to the ground. It crashed branches onto electrical lines, cutting off power to households. It hurled a linden tree onto the roof of a car, crushing its roof. The driver died on the spot.

Along the coast, warnings went out to the vessels; many were already in trouble. Waves were driven high in the inner lakes, which were now brown from bottom slime and mud. Twenty or so small boats not yet brought in for the winter were loosened from their moorings and beaten to pieces on the shore. Even docks were broken in half, dashed to pieces on the waves. The wind dug so deeply that the bottoms of the lakes were moved, hard stones shifted; the pattern of the sand changed.

It was a wild, grim storm, as hard as the icy wind with its bitter taste of mountain ash, and it raged night and day, for days.

At dawn on the last day of the storm, she floated to the surface. Not at all at the same place where she had been sunk. No, she had been driven by the currents to another beach. At least, all that remained of her.

It was impossible to tell that she had once been a woman.

TOR WAS THE FIRST PERSON THEY CONTACTED with the information. Tor was sitting in bed when the phone rang. He had pulled his legs underneath his body as he used to do when he was young, the days when he was still in school, tussling with homework: history and preparing for math tests. For his future.

He was tired, but not like he'd felt in a long time. It was more a tiredness as after hard, physical labor. He thought he needed to sleep. He had to find some kind of rhythm in his life and return to the land of the living.

The person on the other end of the line was from the police.

"We have found the remains of a body in Lake Mälar. It was blown onto land because of the storm and there are signs that this could be your missing wife."

It was a policewoman; her name was Mary. He managed to hear her name: Mary Jonsén. Women are better at this job, informing the relatives. Those difficult, heavy conversations. The final piece of information that must be given.

The remains of a body. What a strange, macabre word: *remains*. Nothing having to do with life at all. That which is left afterwards.

"What kind of signs?" he heard himself ask, and felt the taste of metal against his gums.

"Well, for instance . . . her teeth. She had a gap in her upper front teeth. But we still have to check her dental records for positive identification."

"Where did you find her?"

"In Hässelby villastad. Near the Lövsta Bathhouse. If you know where that is."

"I do."

"We have to wait for the final confirmation from forensics and a dentist. But indications are that this is, in fact, your wife. I just want you to know."

"Who found her?" He had to know everything, details, the time, the people involved.

"There was a man taking a walk with his dog. The dog noticed something and refused to move. The man had his cell phone and called us. We sent people out right away."

"What else can you tell me?"

"There is a tree growing next to the water, an alder, I believe it was, and it had long roots. She had been washed into the roots, and it looked as if she were being embraced."

Did she say *embraced* or did he imagine it?

"Where is she now? Where did you take her?"

"To the forensic department in Solna."

He felt as if the room was spinning.

"May I see her?"

A few seconds of silence. Then he heard Mary Jonsén's sympathetic voice: "I would advise you against it, actually."

He had to get hold of Jill, his first thought after he hung up the phone. He had to tell her. He called both her home number and her cell phone. She didn't answer, and neither did her answering machine.

She's asleep, he thought. Can she really be sleeping at this hour?

Then he called the boys. He started with Jörgen, his eldest. A girl answered, well, maybe she was a woman. She had a Danish accent.

He told her who he was, and her voice changed immediately.

"Well, hello there, Tor! Sorry, Jörgen isn't at home."

"Where is he?"

"He's at work. But he'll be home soon."

At work? When did Jörgen get a job? He felt he shouldn't ask. "Is that you, Helle?" he asked.

"Of course it's me, good old Helle, the same one as before. Has something happened?"

"Do you think the two of you can come over here?"

"Something happened?"

"Please, just come over here as soon as you can."

"Is it your heart, Tor?"

"My heart? God, no."

He called Jens. At first he couldn't find Jens' number. He didn't know it by heart. As a father, shouldn't he know these things? His boy lived in an apartment on Essingestråket. Tor had been there one summer evening. They'd sat on the balcony. His girlfriend had set the table with wine and snacks. Marika was her name. Jens and Marika. She was a thin, boyish girl, quiet and reserved. She was studying psychology, which Tor could not understand. She didn't seem to be the type.

Jens was not as direct as his older brother. He had a way of coming at things sideways, never directly criticizing. He had always been a mamma's boy.

Jens picked up the phone.

"Hi. It's your pappa."

"Hi, Pappa."

"It's been awhile."

"Yes, it has. I've tried to call you a few times, but you weren't home."

"You have?"

"Yep."

"What are you up to right now?"

"Nothing much."

"Can you come here right away?"

"Has something happened?"

"I want to tell you in person."

"It's Mamma, isn't it?" he said. "They've found her, haven't they?"

"That's what they believe."

"Is she dead?"

"Yes, she is."

He heard how his boy tried to stifle sobs in his throat. His own throat felt thick and rough.

"Jens, please come here. I didn't want to tell you on the phone, but you asked."

"I knew it. I've known it all the time."

"Jens!"

"I knew she had to be dead."

"Well, get yourself into a taxi and get over here. We'll all talk about it together."

He made some tea and found a roll of cookies. Although the Best-By date had passed six months ago, he still arranged them on a plate, laid them out in a ring along the edge. He didn't have to wait long until the boys arrived. They had both brought their girlfriends. Tor didn't know whether that was a good idea or not. Outside, the wind was still blowing and the rain made long streaks on the windows.

"Please sit down," he said, and showed them into the living room. As if they didn't know where it was. As if they hadn't grown up with him in this very house. He had set out a portrait of Berit in the blue dress. She watched them with lowered lids.

"Jens told us," Jörgen said. His appearance had changed. He had shaved off all his hair. His oldest son was now a grown man with a bald head.

His youngest hadn't changed as much. He fiddled with his glasses; his face was streaked with tears. This made Tor lose control himself. He began to cry.

"So, if it is her, then . . . it seems like some kind of ending," mumbled Helle. Her cheeks were shining and round; she must have put on some weight. "And I think it's good for us. Although it is sad, it is a definite end."

Marika nodded. "We've all thought that it had to be something like that. It was not like Mamma to stay away from the family for such a long time. She was not like that."

What do you know about her, Tor thought.

"So she drowned?" asked Jörgen, direct and in control, as if this was news about a stranger.

"They think so."

"But wasn't Lake Mälar covered with ice the day she disappeared?"

"She must have gone out on the ice. And it must have broken."

He imagined the scene, the deep, cold hole, how she tried to grasp the icy edges, how she screamed in panic, how she called for help. She was alone out on the ice. What the hell was she doing out there?

Jens sat biting his nails.

"So stupid," he said, gruffly. "To go out on the ice all by herself like that. Even a young child knows better than that."

"Reason doesn't always win out," said Marika. Her hair had grown longer; she had put it into a bun. It made her appear more mature. She paused, as if she were thinking of saying something more, but she fell silent.

Jens looked at Tor, shy and helpless.

"May I ask you something, Pappa? Did the two of you have a fight that day?"

He shook his head.

"I'd gone out to the cabin on Vätö. No real reason, I just wanted to go there. I'd had a lot of work. I asked her to come with me quite a few times. But she didn't want to. She told me that she absolutely had to go to Hässelby.

"Would you like some more tea?" he asked.

Marika lifted the teapot and poured some. It was a stupid teapot, not practical at all, in the shape of a house. Berit had gotten it as a birthday present. No one was eating the cookies. Tor took one and broke it in half.

"We still have to wait for the final determination," he said. "It might take a few months. They'll do DNA tests and things like that."

"Well, it must be her," Jörgen said. "Think of what they said about her teeth."

"Yes, well, they must be one hundred percent sure."

"Are we going to have a funeral then?" asked Jens. He was much calmer; he sat holding Marika's hand.

"Yes, I believe we should have one," Tor said evasively.

"Where should she be buried?" asked Jörgen. Jörgen was wearing a ring on his finger, a ring of white gold. Helle had an identical ring. Did they get engaged without letting him know? Maybe they even got married!

"I really don't know," he answered.

"Shall we bury her in Grandma's and Grandpa's grave in Hässelby?"

"Let's wait and see."

"Not that godforsaken goddamned Hässelby!" Jens exclaimed. "I refuse! That place is cursed! It should be erased from all the maps!"

Tor went into the kitchen to make some more tea. He heard their voices from the living room. It seemed so unusual; it was usually so quiet. Someone came quietly up behind him. Marika. One of her hair pins had fallen out, and she stood there trying to tie her hair back up.

"Jens is so sad. He has so many deep feelings, but it's good that he now can let them go. It's been quite a few rough years. It hasn't been easy for him."

"Not for any of us." Tor drew in a breath.

"How are you feeling now?"

"It's as if everything is spinning around."

"I understand."

"We still don't know for sure."

"Of course not."

"But if it is her . . . if it really is her as we believe . . ."

"Yes, that's right."

He began to cry. He ripped off a sheet of paper towel and put it to his eyes.

"Tor," she said, "we've been thinking about you so much. All of us."

When it was time for them to go, he hugged them. First the girls, then Jörgen and Jens.

"I'm so glad that you could come back home," he said, trying to keep his voice clear. It sounded pathetic.

"By the way," said Jörgen as he was putting on his jacket, "there's something we thought you ought to know." He went over to Helle and patted her on the stomach.

"Yes?"

"Well, you're going to be a grandfather sometime after New Year's. We're having a baby."

He wept as he saw them all get into Jörgen's car. He washed up the mugs and threw the cookies into the garbage. He cried so much it seemed his head would split open.

Berit. If she were only here now. She would have been laughing, her head back, laughing heartily. He heard her voice, so real it almost seemed to come from the kitchen: "Oh, I can't wait to be a grandmother! I'm looking forward to it! But to be married to a grandfather . . . well, that's something else entirely!"

He picked up her photograph and looked at it.

"My little girl," he said. "My little friend."

MICKE HAD LEFT THE LITTLE HOUSE for a minute. He said he wouldn't be long, that he would be back. She didn't know what was worse, having him in the room, crafty and dangerous, or to lie there alone not knowing if she would ever be able to free herself. Her arms and legs throbbed. The ropes were tight. She tried to move her fingers, move her toes, get her blood circulation going. Her entire body ached.

She heard rustling sounds from the storage room behind the curtain. Like small feet running, small claws and paws. He'd blown out the candle when he left. The room was musty; she froze and felt ill. This was hell. She was in hell, now. In hell with all the old ghosts.

First there was that woman Jill. Justine's first thought: Berit! Their faces flowed together for an instant. It seemed as if snakes were battling in her stomach. Then she realized that history was repeating itself.

She had come asking questions. Pulling up all that old stuff from their childhood. All that was over! Why couldn't they understand that?

She started to ask about Berit. What Berit said and did.

She didn't want to have Jill in her house. Not have her sully it. Berit had sullied it. She'd come into her most private sphere, stomping all over it, tearing it apart. It had taken many years to repair the damage.

"May I please use the bathroom?" Jill's pleading eyes. Facial features are so big on grown people. Lumpy noses and ears, skin full of pores and rough. Still, Justine had recognized her immediately, just like she had recognized Berit.

There had been a whole gang there on the mountainside. Berit and Evy and Gerd, and then Jill, somewhere in the background. They had wrestled her down to the rough rocks and sat on her. *Now let's see what she looks like!* Justine had fought them, violently, torn at them with her fingernails until they were bloody and broken. It didn't help. They were pulling off her clothes.

"Please," Jill repeated, and it was the grown Jill with her big nose. "May I just use the bathroom?"

"No, sorry," she'd replied. "That's not possible."

Jill turned and practically fled to the gate.

And then Micke showed up moments later.

She should have gone inside, gone inside and locked the door. Her clothes were wet; she should have gone inside and changed them. Instead, she was still standing there in the wind.

Hans Peter, she thought now. He must be very worried. Did he try to call her from the hotel? Or would he not notice that she was gone until tomorrow morning when he came home from work? Or what did he say? Was he working tonight or not? Something had happened to Ariadne. Her husband had died suddenly. Hans Peter had gone to help Ariadne.

What if she, herself, were now to die at the hands of a maniac?

He had been talking so strangely, calling her Mrs. Tucker. Who the hell was that?

"Some people deserve to die," he said. In the light from the candle, his face seemed skewed. He had acne on his forehead. He had a sore right over his nose. He was going to kill her! She realized this at last. He was not right in the head. She pulled desperately at the ropes. They didn't give an inch.

A young man, barely over twenty. He was still like a child. An abandoned child. A wounded, abandoned child with sick fantasies.

Just like her.

When the door opened, she screamed in terror. That made him furious. She heard how he tore off his jacket and shook it to get rid of the water. Then he rushed over to her.

"Keep quiet!" he growled. "A murderer has no right to speak." His fingers were wet and cold. Water dropped from his hair.

"Murderer?" she whispered, despairing.

He walked through the room, lighting the kinds of candles you put on gravestones.

"Please, Micke, let me go. Please, just let me go."

"Nope," he said, imitating the Texan, Bush.

"I'm begging you; you can have anything. I have money. I can pay. I'll give you anything you want. Just let me go."

He lifted a candle and held it over her head. Hot wax ran down and fell onto her chin. It burned, but she didn't feel it.

"Even the Pope pled for mercy," he said. "But I say: Nope!"

She began to scream and throw her body from side to side; panic gripped her like red flames. He hit her again, on the head. And everything went silent.

It wasn't a dream; it was reality. An evil, evil reality. She was conscious again. He was standing next to the table; he was holding her arm. Pain shot through behind her eyes. She was lying in the flickering light, but she wasn't freezing any longer; she was burning up.

He was standing there, pulling the sleeve of the judo jacket, trying to roll it up. The cloth was stiff and filled with seams. Finally, he loosened the rope on her left arm, pulled it out of the sleeve and then tied it down again. She had lost all feeling in her limbs. Sweat broke out over her body, while at the same time she was shivering from the cold.

She tried to catch his eye, but he was busy. He rustled around with a bag. Something shined in the light, a needle. Her teeth banged each other so loudly that he heard it.

"Are you afraid of death, Mrs. Tucker?" he said, and he

stroked her over her cheek.

She tried to answer, tried to sit up, tried to say something; her tongue was stiff, paralyzed.

It was a needle for injections, she realized. She felt how she began to hyperventilate. He held up the needle to the light. He was humming. Took hold of her exposed arm.

"Are you ready now, Mrs. Tucker? Now it is time."

ARIADNE HAD ASKED HANS PETER TO COME AND MEET HER at the hotel. Neutral ground, she called it. Hans Peter did not understand what she meant by that. But she had probably been thrown off balance by what had happened.

She was waiting in the breakfast nook. Christa was with her, tall and hefty, wearing a yellow down coat. Even though they were inside, Christa still wore it, with the zipper all the way up to her chin. Her hand was flabby and large.

"Hi, Christa. I'm Hans Peter, if you remember me. You used to come here often when you were little."

She didn't answer.

Ariadne had made coffee. She'd bought coffeecake, too, the kind shaped like a ring. She was standing and cutting some sticky slices. She gave him an uncertain smile. The bruises on her face were still there, but starting to turn yellow and fade.

"Thanks for coming," she said.

They heard the vacuum cleaner on the upper floor. It was the alternate team: the other cleaning lady, and the person who had Hans Peter's job when he wasn't at work. They didn't know each other, had hardly even seen each other.

He did not know what to say.

"So, it's just the two of us now!" she exclaimed, and her cheeks reddened, her whole face, all the way to her neck. She was wearing a knitted rose sweater with embroidered flowers on it. She had wide golden earrings, something new for her; she almost never wore jewelry.

"You and Christa," he said.

"That's right!"

"How are the two of you doing?"

She smiled nervously.

"It's strange, but it's like I don't feel a thing."

Hans Peter took a bite of coffee bread, and his fingers got sticky.

"Well, from what I understand, sometimes it takes awhile to react. Maybe you're in shock now, you and Christa."

"Maybe so."

"Have you been able to talk to someone about the funeral?"

"Jonas Edgren is helping us. One of Tommy's colleagues. But it won't be a large funeral. Just the family, we decided."

"I see."

"And then we'll let him rest in a *minneslund*, a meadow for spreading cremated remains. We talked about how nice *minneslundar* can be. Anonymous, but still close. I'm convinced that Tommy would like that."

Hans Peter poured himself another cup of coffee.

"What do you intend to do? Are you going to keep on living out in Ekerö after all of this? Have you thought about it at all?"

"We're going to move," she said quickly.

"It's not easy finding a cheap apartment."

"I'll sell the house. Out where we live, I'm sure we'll get a lot of money."

"And then? How will you manage? I mean, how will you provide for yourself and Christa?"

She brushed some crumbs into her palm and emptied them into her coffee mug.

"He had life insurance," she said. "I didn't even know it."

A key turned in the door lock, and Britta Svantesson came in. She had been to the market square to buy three potted plants with mini-roses, which she began to place on the windowsills.

"I thought we could brighten the place up," she said. "And this place is called *Tre Rosor*, The Three Roses, isn't it? Correct me if I'm wrong!"

She laid her coat on the back of a chair and came over.

"A cup of coffee is just what I need right now."

Hans Peter glanced toward Christa. She'd pulled on some earphones; she didn't appear aware of anything but the music. He turned back to Britta.

"Do you know what happened?"

"Oh yes, I know."

"I called Britta yesterday evening," said Ariadne. "I had to talk to someone."

Ulf's mother sighed.

"Well, what can you say? You'll have a difficult time ahead of you, you and the girl. But to tell the truth, you haven't had an easy time of it before, either."

Ariadne's eyes filled with tears.

"You're right," she said.

"And we talked about something else, too, didn't we? Right, Ariadne?"

Ariadne nodded, and the two of them looked at Hans Peter.

"What?" he asked.

"It's about Ulf."

"I hope that nothing's happened?" he asked tensely.

"Oh, he's in a relatively good mood. He's going to have an operation next week and he seems to have confidence in his American doctors."

"Well, that's positive news."

"And there's one doctor who fills him with more than mere confidence," Britta continued. "A female brain surgeon named Joyce. I talked to him yesterday evening and it has been a long time since he was filled with that kind of *confidence*."

"I see."

"It appears to be love at first sight."

"But he's seriously ill!" Hans Peter felt dumb the minute he said it.

"Love can work miracles," Britta smiled. "By the way, he asked me to ask you a question. He's decided to sell this hotel. Just in case one of you wants to buy it. First dibs."

IT WAS ALL WRONG! It was all fucked up. She was just some flabby old woman; it wasn't *her!* Nathan would have never chosen a woman like this. Everything was all wrong, all messed up. Micke put down the needle and stood there. His arms hung heavy, toward the ground, ape arms, a large misshaped baboon. A curse snarled out of his mouth; it sounded like a yowl, like that of a dog someone was trying to suffocate.

"Get out of here!" he yelled. "Go on, get out!"

She didn't move.

He stumbled over to the wall, turned on the lights. A weak shine, bleak, hardly illuminating the room. He would have to remember to change the light bulbs later, screw in new ones. Henry and Märta wouldn't be able to manage it. Or maybe they wanted to save on electricity costs, preferring to stumble around in the dark than spend money on stronger wattage.

A woman lying on the table wearing Nathan's judo clothes. What a farce! What a fucking farce!

"Hey!" he yelled.

She didn't answer. What if she were dead? Think if he'd scared the shit out of her, that he now had a corpse to deal with. What a fucking mess! God daaaaamn!

He was seriously scared now. What if she really was dead?

He hadn't managed to get the needle into her. And even if he had, there was nothing in it. He'd tried to force the needle into her skin. He'd pushed hard, but it'd just dimpled the skin, didn't break

318

it. It didn't go in. Her chest had pumped up and down as if she were running a marathon. Her red bra like a bloody wound. What if her heart had stopped? People can die of shock, of terror; he remembered the rabbit one of his classmates had, a male with hanging ears. One day Robin came by with his dog. The dog was happy and wanted to play. Full of curiosity it ran to the rabbit huddled on the floor of its cage. After one peeping, sniffing sound, the rabbit was dead. It lay there with spasmodic, fading paw movements.

"Hey you," he said. "Sorry, look, I changed my mind. Get out of here."

She was all tied up. Of course! That's why she was not moving. He had to untie her so that she could get up and go. He hoped that was why she didn't respond. That *was* why, right? He was standing at the door, ready to flee. If she was cold and stiff and didn't wake up, what should he do then? What the hell should he do?

No, he had to check. He shook himself, crept up to the table. Touched her cheek, not cold. Not warm either. It took a while for *rigor mortis* to set in. He felt the skin on his back crawl.

Get hold of yourself!

He found the knots and undid them. Her body stirred, and he raised his knuckles to his teeth. Yes, she was alive. She was breathing. In fact, she was starting to cough.

He put his arm behind her back, lifted her up.

"You can go now," he said. "I told you to get going."

She slowly opened her eyes. Looked past him.

He picked up her clothes and threw them on the table next to her.

"Here. Get dressed and get out of here."

Carefully, she got down onto the floor. Rubbed her wrists, massaged them. He walked over to the window. It was not possible to see outside. The window shades. He picked up a small object from the windowsill, a little ceramic cat. It felt like ice in his palm.

He leaned with his forehead on the window. He heard her get dressed. She was hesitant, defensive, as if she believed he would change his mind at any moment. He knew what she would do: go to the police, of course! The police would come here and arrest him, thunder up in their vehicles, pull their weapons on him. Wrestle him to the floor, put on handcuffs.

All right, go to the police then, God damn you!

He would stay here and wait for them.

It's true. I'm sick in the head. Put me in jail; lock me in for good, damn it!

He heard the door open, and felt the chill rush inside. A faded leaf blew in, whirled around a few seconds, fell to the carpet, stayed. Then he heard her voice, hoarse as if she had been sick with a bad cold.

"Micke," she said. His name. He gave her a look but didn't answer.

"Are we . . . can we say that we're even, now?"

"What the hell are you talking about?"

She was sniffling.

"Nothing . . . but, good luck."

He held his breath.

"With what?"

"Your travel agency. Good luck. I mean it."

"Get the fuck out of here!" he yelled. "Before I change my mind!"

JUSTINE RAN ALONG THE GRAVEL ROAD and along the entire grassy lane. She continued on the sidewalk, quickly, quickly, don't stop for a second. The rain pounded on the asphalt. She had no money, no keys. When he'd picked her up, she didn't have the chance to get them. What was she supposed to do now? Her brain was fuzzy, as if she were running in a nightmare, or in water.

She began to cross Drottninggatan and saw how a subway train had just left the station at Abrahamsberg. She didn't have even enough for the subway. What time was it? How long had she been held prisoner in that hut? All sense of time had been erased from her mind. Was it already night?

If she only had her cell phone with her. Then she could call Hans Peter. He would come and get her, no matter where he was. She took refuge under the bridge and tried to pull herself together. Her lungs burned as if on fire.

What if he were following her? She shouldn't have said anything; maybe it made him angry. What if he were after her, to bring her back? She looked around nervously, but there weren't any people about, just herself and a few lone cars.

A taxi. That was the only way. A taxi would drive her home and wait while she ran in to get some money to pay.

But what if Hans Peter was not at home and the door was locked? Then she couldn't get in.

After a while, she walked down to the main road and held out her hand. A taxi came gliding in; she waved at it. The driver looked her over suspiciously.

"I need to get to Hässelby," she said. "Can you drive me there?"

The driver had stubble and a small, pointed mouth. He gave her an expressionless look.

"Can you drive me there?" she repeated.

"Sometimes I demand payment in advance," he said slowly. She sniffed loudly.

"But I've been robbed!"

"What?"

"I can't pay you until we get there!"

"What the hell are you saying, you've been robbed?"

"Yes!" she screamed.

"All right, then." He gestured to the back seat, and she crept in.

The car smelled new. It was a good smell. It was warm. The radio was playing pop music. Her clothes made a wet blot on the seat. She saw his eyes in the rearview mirror. He turned down the volume, but didn't turn it off.

"You say you've been robbed?"

"Yeah."

"Now? Just now?"

"A few minutes ago."

"You're not lying, are you?"

"No, no." She ground her teeth together so hard it hurt.

"How'd it happen?"

"I don't know."

"What do you mean by that?"

"He pushed me in the back so I fell down. Then my purse was gone."

"You didn't see him?"

"No."

"You have to go to the police. Shall I drive you there?"

"No, no. I want to go home first. Home to my husband."

"So you have no idea who it was?"

"Kind of young. Don't know for sure."

"Are you hurt?"

"I'm in shock, I think. But I'll be all right."

"You sure about that?"

"Yes, yes, I'm sure."

"Sweden is changing into a lawless country," he said angrily. "People have no honor any longer. No morals."

"No," she said slowly. "You're right about that."

There were lights on at the house when they drove up. Relief filled her. Hans Peter stood on the front porch, his mouth in a firm line.

"Justine, you shouldn't scare me like this! I can't stand to be scared like that!"

"Sorry," she whispered. "Can you pay the taxi?"

The driver stuck his head out the window.

"She says she's been robbed," he said. "I offered to drive her to the police, but she refused."

Tor stayed to talk with the driver as Justine entered the house. The minute she stepped into the hallway, she saw that they had guests. She walked up the stairs and saw Ariadne and an almost full-grown teenager, who resembled Ariadne. The girl leaned back, holding one of her wrists with her other hand. The bird had landed on her outstretched knuckles.

The girl turned her face to the door. Her eyes wandered and fluttered.

"Hi," she said, uncertainly.

"Hi, Christa," Justine replied.

"Is he your bird?"

"Yes, he is."

"He likes me; he flew right toward me."

"I can see that."

"Justine has been out in the rain," Ariadne said. "Let her go change her clothes and then the two of you can talk some more." Ariadne went up to Justine and gave her a quick, embarrassed hug.

"We've imposed ourselves on you," she said.

"Ah, don't worry about it. We don't mind having you as our guests."

"I'll never forget what you told me at the hotel. It's been good to think about."

Justine nodded. Ariadne looked right into her eyes.

"That other thing, you know . . . ," she said. "It's over now, all over."

"I know."

"Thank you for standing up for me."

The bird flapped his wings and hissed. Then he flew onto Christa's head. Christa laughed, delighted.

"Eeee! He tickles!"

"He likes to sit on peoples' hair," Justine said. "I think it feels good on his feet."

"Why doesn't he have a name?" the girl asked.

"It just never happened."

"Couldn't you think of a good name?"

"Actually, no."

"I . . . I've thought of two names. But Mamma says one of the names is not so good; it's also the name of a vacuum cleaner brand."

"Well, which names did you think of? Let me hear them."

"Hugin. Or Munin. Most likely Munin. But maybe you don't like the name Munin?"

Justine walked up to her Swedish tiled stove. The doors were open and Hans Peter had lit a fire in the fireplace. She opened her arms and held her body against the warm tiles. Her mind became calm and still.

"Munin? The raven of Memory?" she said thoughtfully. "Well, why not?"

THE WIND HAD FINALLY LET UP, the air was clear and clean. Out at the Lövsta Baths, all the changing rooms had been closed for the season with heavy locks hung from the doors. The kiosk was also closed, a wooden panel nailed over the window. The swimming docks had been brought up on land. A flock of Canada geese were sitting on them, and they waddled around, furiously honking. A broken ball, heavy with sand and water, was between the rocks. Tor kicked it. In the gap where it had been, small insects scurried away.

He stood there waiting for Jill to catch up to him. He had been impatient to come here, but now he was feeling shy.

They looked around for a while; then they found the tree. It was a tall old alder with a huge root mound. The roots ran down into the water and curled about in the vague shape of a heart. The remains of a body could very well have nestled there.

Yes, it did look like it could embrace her, he thought, although he couldn't quite remember if it was Mary, the police-woman, who had said it or whether it came from his own mind. He fell to his knees in the wet sand and looked for any traces. But if there had been any marks, the water had already washed them away, rinsed everything clean, removed everything. He formed his hand into a cup, lifted some water which immediately glided through his fingers and went back to the sea.

When they'd gotten out of the car earlier, they found some blue asters with long rangy stems on the slope. They were the kind that kept blooming long into fall, well into late October. Jill picked a few and then broke off a branch of a *nypon* rose that held numerous shining red hips. It was a simple bouquet. She tied them all together with a rubber band that she found in her pocket.

"When Berit and I were little," she said, "we used to go out on the ice to play. It was forbidden, of course, but we did it anyway."

"Children know nothing of the risks."

"That's right. Once a piece of ice broke off while I was standing on it. It just loosened and started to drift away. I wanted to jump, but I felt how the edge sank down and I was about to fall. Then when I saw the distance growing between me and the fast ice, only then was I frightened."

Tor turned to her. She had swept a scarf over her hair and she was cold.

"How did you get to land?"

"Funnily enough, I've forgotten."

"How could you forget?"

"What I want to say is that people are not always afraid of dangerous things," she continued. "People are afraid of things which are not dangerous. Things that they can master, in fact."

He lit a cigarette.

"Why did she go out on the ice?" he cried out. "Can you give me an answer for that?"

"Maybe to feel a bit of eternity," she answered slowly. "Maybe to hear that magical crack of frozen water that you can't hear in the city."

He stared out over the water. Small, soft, barely noticeable waves.

"I've wondered about her fear of dying," he said. "How long it took."

"We'll never know," she replied. "But I've heard tell that death by drowning is one of the milder forms death can take."

She squatted down and carefully let the bouquet float in the water. It bobbed about for a moment, and then floated between the roots of the alder and came to rest.

They stood there for a while and watched it, before they turned back to the car.

part III

FIVE MONTHS LATER

The short notice in the newspaper appeared on the same day that Ariadne was going to celebrate the grand opening of her hotel. It was on the left-hand side, fairly far down, and it was just by chance that Justine saw it.

SEVEN-YEAR DISAPPEARANCE EXPLAINED
DNA-tests have shown that the female body found last October near the Lövsta Baths belonged to Berit Assarsson, Bromma. Assarsson disappeared mysteriously seven years ago after visiting a friend in Hässelby. The body was found by a private citizen walking his dog. The body washed to shore after a strong storm. According to the police, no crime can be connected to the remains. The most possible explanation is a drowning accident.

Justine walked over to the window, holding the newspaper in her hand. About five inches of snow was covering the ground and made the trees appear like frosted silhouettes. On Lake Mälar, there were blocks of half-frozen ice, but the water was not going to freeze over completely this winter. It was already the beginning of March.

She read through the text again, more slowly, as if she were memorizing each and every word.

"Seven years," she whispered. "Can it really have been seven years?"

In this very room, an eternity ago, two people had lost their lives: first, her mother when her brain blood vessel broke, the sound of a thud as her head hit the floor. Justine turned and imagined her four-year-old self, seemed to see her; the room arched above her, arched like a church, with echoing screams.

After that: Berit.

She heard the sharp sounds of anger, of violence.

"Forgive me," she whispered. "I went too far, and I've learned to regret it."

At that very moment, lightning flashed right in front of the window. A bolt of bright light against the blue-gray sky.

She heard Hans Peter's voice in the stairwell: "Did you see that? What the heck?"

"I don't know," she replied.

"How can there be a thunderstorm at this time of year? But so much of the weather has gotten strange lately. You can't depend on anything any more."

"No, you can't."

"By the way, we're going to have to hurry to make it in time."

Justine looked at her watch. It was twenty minutes to noon. The re-opening of The Three Roses was set to start at three o'clock and she and Hans Peter had promised to help with the arrangements.

"Yes," she called down to him. "I'm coming!"

Author's Thanks

Many thanks go to the following people who have given me practical and theoretical insights into their workplaces and taken the time to read, answer questions and give practical advice: Åke Carlsson, Mikael Karlsson, and Mirjam Rior, all VTS operators at the VTS center in Södertälje, as well as their boss Anders Brödje; Stefan Petersson, sea captain; and pilot Patrick Widell; the police chief of Östermalm, Berit Astridsdotter Svensson; the specialist in forensic and general medicine, Vasilios Varfis; Nina Karmelitow at Nordstedts as well as the publishing director Peter Karlsson, who with great care have gone over and edited this manuscript.

Many thanks also to my husband Jan and my daughter Hanna.

Södertälje, January 2005
Inger Frimansson

Translator's Thanks: to Joy Wideburg (also known as my mom), for all her expertise in editing.

Seattle, August 2007
Laura A. Wideburg

Books from *Pleasure Boat Studio: A Literary Press*

(Note: Caravel Books is a new imprint of Pleasure Boat Studio: A Literary Press. Caravel Books is the imprint for mysteries only. Aequitas Books is another imprint which includes non-fiction with philosophical and sociological themes. Empty Bowl Press is a Division of Pleasure Boat Studio.)

UPCOMING: *Working the Woods, Working the Sea* • **an empty bowl book**
UPCOMING: *Listening to the Rhino* • **Dr. Janet Dallett** • **an aequitas book**

Weinstock Among the Dying • Michael Blumenthal • $18
The War Journal of Lila Ann Smith • Irving Warner • $18
The Woman Who Wrote King Lear, and Other Stories • Louis Phillips • $16
Dream of the Dragon Pool: A Daoist Quest • Albert A. Dalia • $18
Good Night, My Darling • Inger Frimansson, Trans by Laura Wideburg • $18 •
    a caravel book
Falling Awake: An American Woman Gets a Grip on the Whole Changing World—
    One Essay at a Time • Mary Lou Sanelli • $15 • **an aequitas book**
Way Out There: Lyrical Essays • Michael Daley • $16 • **an aequitas book**
The Case of Emily V. • Keith Oatley • mystery • $18 • **a caravel book**
Monique • Luisa Coehlo, Trans fm Portuguese by Maria de Vasconcelos and
    Dolores DeLuise • $14
The Blossoms Are Ghosts at the Wedding • Tom Jay • $15 • **an empty bowl book**
Against Romance • Michael Blumenthal • $14
Speak to the Mountain: The Tommie Waites Story • Dr. Bessie Blake • $18 / $26 •
    an aequitas book
Artrage • Everett Aison • $15
Days We Would Rather Know • Michael Blumenthal • $14
Puget Sound: 15 Stories • C. C. Long • $14
Homicide My Own • Anne Argula • $16
Craving Water • Mary Lou Sanelli • $15
When the Tiger Weeps • Mike O'Connor • 15
Wagner, Descending: The Wrath of the Salmon Queen • Irving Warner • $16
Concentricity • Sheila E. Murphy • $14
Schilling, from a study in lost time • Terrell Guillory • $16
Rumours: A Memoir of a British POW in WWII • Chas Mayhead • $16
The Immigrant's Table • Mary Lou Sanelli • $14
The Enduring Vision of Norman Mailer • Dr. Barry H. Leeds • $18
Women in the Garden • Mary Lou Sanelli • $13.95
Pronoun Music • Richard Cohen • $16
If You Were With Me Everything Would Be All Right • Ken Harvey • $16
The 8th Day of the Week • Al Kessler • $16
Another Life, and Other Stories • Edwin Weihe • $16
Saying the Necessary • Edward Harkness • $14
Nature Lovers • Charles Potts • $10
In Memory of Hawks, & Other Stories from Alaska • Irving Warner • $15
The Politics of My Heart • William Slaughter • $13
The Rape Poems • Frances Driscoll • $13
When History Enters the House: Essays from Central Europe • Michael Blumenthal • $15

Setting Out: The Education of Lili • Tung Nien • Trans fm Chinese by Mike O'Connor • $15

Our Chapbook Series:
No. 1: *The Handful of Seeds: Three and a Half Essays* • Andrew Schelling • $7
No. 2: *Original Sin* • Michael Daley • $8
No. 3: *Too Small to Hold You* • Kate Reavey • $8
No. 4: *The Light on Our Faces: A Therapy Dialogue* • Lee Miriam WhitmanRaymond $8
No. 5: *Eye* • William Bridges • $8
No. 6: *Selected* **New Poems** *of Rainer Maria Rilke* • Trans fm German by Alice Derry • $10
No. 7: *Through High Still Air: A Season at Sourdough Mountain* • Tim McNulty • $9
No. 8: *Sight Progress* • Zhang Er, Trans fm Chinese by Rachel Levitsky • $9
No. 9: *The Perfect Hour* • Blas Falconer • $9
No. 10: Fervor • Zaedryn Meade • $10

From other publishers (in limited editions):
Desire • Jody Aliesan • $14 • an empty bowl book
Deams of the Hand • Susan Goldwitz • $14 • an empty bowl book
Lineage • Mary Lou Sanelli • $14 • an empty bowl book
The Basin: Poems from a Chinese Province • Mike O'Connor • $10 • an empty bowl book
The Straits • Michael • $10 • an empty bowl book
In Our Hearts and Minds: The Northwest and Central America • Ed. Michael Daley • $12 • an empty bowl book
The Rainshadow • Mike O'Connor • $16 • an empty bowl book
Untold Stories • William Slaughter • $10 • an empty bowl book
In Blue Mountain Dusk • Tim McNulty • $12.95 • an empty bowl book
China Basin • Clemens Starck • $14 • a Story Line Press book
Journeyman's Wages • Clemens Starck • $11 • a Story Line Press book

Orders: Pleasure Boat Studio books are available by order from your bookstore, directly from PBS, or through the following:
SPD (Small Press Distribution) Tel. 800-869-7553, Fax 510-524-0852
Partners/West Tel. 425-227-8486, Fax 425-204-2448
Baker & Taylor 800-775-1100, Fax 800-775-7480
Ingram Tel. 615-793-5000, Fax 615-287-5429
Amazon.com or **Barnesandnoble.com**

Pleasure Boat Studio: A Literary Press
201 West 89th Street
New York, NY 10024
Tel: 2123628563 / Fax: 8888105308
www.pleasureboatstudio.com / *pleasboat@nyc.rr.com*